SO-AHH-357

Readers everywhere
love the novels of
Patricia Veryan!

Also by Patricia Veryan:

LOGIC OF THE HEART*
THE DEDICATED VILLAIN*
CHERISHED ENEMY*
LOVE ALTERS NOT*
GIVE ALL TO LOVE*
THE TYRANT*
JOURNEY TO ENCHANTMENT
PRACTICE TO DECEIVE
SANGUINET'S CROWN*
THE WAGERED WIDOW*
THE NOBLEST FRAILTY*
MARRIED PAST REDEMPTION*
FEATHER CASTLES*
SOME BRIEF FOLLY*
NANETTE*
MISTRESS OF WILLOWVALE*
LOVE'S DUET*
THE LORD AND THE GYPSY*

Published by Fawcett Books

TIME'S FOOL

Patricia Veryan

FAWCETT CREST • NEW YORK

A Fawcett Crest Book
Published by Ballantine Books
Copyright © 1991 by Patricia Veryan

Library of Congress Catalog Card Number: 90-27673

ISBN 0-449-22077-X

This edition published by arrangement with St. Martin's Press, Inc.

Manufactured in the United States of America

First Ballantine Books Edition: August 1992

For Phyllis and Bill Bultmann

"Words are easy, like the wind
Faithful friends are hard to find . . ."
—Richard Barnfield

Love's not Time's fool,
though rosy lips and cheeks
Within his bending sickle's compass come.

—William Shakespeare
Sonnet 116

❧ *Chapter 1* ❧

England
Early Spring, 1748

Was it, d'you suppose, absolutely essential that it be raining?''
Lieutenant James Morris wiped a handkerchief across his cherubic face and blinked indignantly through the drizzle. "My first sight of home for two years, and be damned if I can see the cliffs!'' He turned to the thin young officer who leaned on the rail beside him, his intent gaze on the distant loom that was England. "Whereas I suppose *you* can make out the castle with those eagle orbs of yours!''

Swaying to the motion of the frigate as it ploughed through the blackish green waves, Captain Gideon Rossiter took off his three-cornered hat and shook water from the brim. Strands of his thick brown hair had escaped the riband that attempted to hold it in severe restraint, and wet curls had crept to cling about his gaunt features. "Of course," he drawled, a twinkle replacing the rather sombre look in his grey eyes. "And I'm glad to see that fine white cat sitting on the walls. 'Tis likely a good omen.''

"Cat, you say?" Morris jerked around and peered uneasily through the misted curtain of the rain. "Where?"

"You're looking the wrong way, you clod. More to the right. If you bring your eyes down from the flagpole, you can't miss him.''

"*Flagpole?* Devil take me if I can see the castle, much less—'' Morris' guileless features suddenly became suspicious. "Now blast your eyes, Ross! You're bamming me again! I'll go bail you can't see the castle no more than I can!'' Rossiter laughed at his mortification, and he added with a fine show of resentment, "Most amusing! I may not be able to see the castle, but I can see you, my Buck! A fine figure you cut, with pretty

1

curls glued all about your brow! Not content with leaving our gentle Holland nurses wallowing in tears, you mean to captivate the crowd of beauties who wait to welcome you home from the wars, eh?''

A faint flush warmed Rossiter's cheeks. He thrust a hand through his wet hair, creating considerable havoc, then slammed his tricorne over it. "Birdwit! The nurses wept for every fellow who left their care. And there will be no beauties to welcome a battered old soldier!''

The shadowy outlines of Dover's chalk cliffs were materializing now. The ship's officers began to bellow orders, and there was a sudden frenzy of activity as sailors scurried about, shouting to one another as they hauled on ropes or scrambled nimbly up the rigging to lighten the sails.

The two army men were briefly silent, each straining his eyes for a clear glimpse of the beloved land.

Rossiter thought, 'Home!' and emotion misted his eyes and brought a lump to his throat.

Morris murmured, "Jove!" Then, fearing such eloquence had betrayed his feelings, he said argumentatively, "Battered old soldier, indeed! You're a wisp of hair and a hunk of bone perhaps, but you look not a day over thirty, and—''

"*Merci bien!* I was eight and twenty last month!''

"—and did you but condescend to at least powder your hair—''

" 'Twould by now resemble glue, as does yours!''

"—your so admired Naomi might possibly view you without measuring her length at your feet!''

Rossiter stiffened and a steely light came into his eyes. "I think I have never spoken to you of Lady Lutonville.''

Undaunted by that sudden glacial hauteur, Morris' puckish grin dawned. "Oho, but you have, my Tulip! You forget that when I was dragged into our miserable hole of a hospital you'd just suffered that relapse. For four horrid days I was obliged to lie and listen to you raving about the Lady Naomi, and how you are contracted, and how much you yearn to wed and settle down with her, and how many chil—'' He gave a whoop, and ducked the flying fist of his wrathful and very red-faced companion. The tall heavyset major who had come up behind them unheard in the general uproar gave a shout and leapt back to avoid receiving the blow.

"Oh—egad!'' gasped Rossiter, grabbing the rail as the ship gave a violent lurch. "My apologies, sir!''

2

"So I should think!" Major Sturtevant clutched at him instinctively, then exclaimed in a great boom of a voice, "Damn, but I'm a clumsy ass! Sorry, old fellow. That shoulder still gives you pepper, does it?"

Rossiter, who had lost all his colour, managed a rather twitching grin and declared that he was "very fit."

"My fault, sir," admitted Morris. "I was quizzing Ross about his lady."

"Aha! And is the Lady Naomi to meet you at Dover?" roared the major, a glint coming into his pale and rather protuberant brown eyes.

Stunned, Rossiter wondered if every patient in the overcrowded military hospital had been entertained by his delirium.

"Heard she's a proper Fair," Sturtevant continued. "M'wife writ she has all London at her feet. Lady Lutonville has, I mean. Not m'wife. Which is as well, or she'd never put up with me!"

They both laughed obediently, and, pleased by their appreciation of his wit, Sturtevant said, "Sink me, but you're a lucky dog, Rossiter! I mean to demand an introduction when we dock. Is her hair really flaming red?"

Rossiter said feebly that he rather doubted it. The other two men were staring at him, and he added with a wry smile, "I've not met the lady since she was sixteen, and barely out of the schoolroom."

"Arranged, was it?" Watching him narrowly, Sturtevant asked, "Shall you recognize her? I'd quite counted on bragging to m'wife that I've met the—ah, famous beauty."

His grasp on the rail very tight, Rossiter answered, "I really don't expect her, sir. Don't expect anyone, matter of fact." They both looked shocked. He thought, 'Blast!' and went on, "I doubt they know I was hit."

Morris blinked and blurted out, "But—that was at Lauffeld, wasn't it, Ross?"

"Damn near a year ago," said the major, patently appalled. "Haven't you even writ?"

"I—er, I seldom write letters, sir."

"Dashed under-statement! You ought to be ashamed, you heartless young cub! Don't it concern you that Sir Mark is likely beside himself with worry?"

"You are acquainted with my father, sir?"

"No!" Sturtevant flushed at his own vehemence, and added hurriedly, "Well, ah—that is to say, he was—is a member of White's, as is my own sire. And—er, one hears ah, this'n that,

3

y'know. Now, you're looking decidedly wrung out, m'dear fellow. Best get below. We'll be entering the Tidal Basin very soon, and you'd do well to rest a bit before we dock.''

Thanking him for his kindness, Rossiter saluted, and with an inward sigh of relief made his escape. He walked swiftly, adjusting his stride to the pitch of the wet decks, breathing deep of the clean fresh scent of the sea. The wind sent his cloak billowing, and he drew it closer. The sails flapped, the waves crashed against the bow, the shouts of the sailors rang cheerily through the chilly air. Despite the rain, gulls were wheeling about the vessel now, uttering their piercing cries, their presence a sure sign that the great ship was nearing land.

Rossiter could all but feel the stares that followed him, and knew they both very likely judged him a cold fish with not one whit of filial responsibility. He was glad to reach the companionway, and escape down the steps.

The men he had left watched his retreat in a silence that continued for a minute or two after he was out of sight. Then, Sturtevant asked in a less jovial voice, ''How long have you known him?''

''Only in the hospital, sir. He'd been there about six months before I was admitted. He was quite the nurses' darling. They'd none of them expected him to survive all those operations. The surgeons used to come and apologize because they'd found another sliver of steel or hunk of lead they must dig out.'' Morris hesitated. ''I used to wonder how he stood it, but I never once heard him whine.''

Sturtevant smiled faintly. ''Value him high, don't you? You'd likely heard of him before you met, eh?''

''I'd heard of his family, naturally,'' said Morris, looking annoyed. ''Lord, who hasn't? Rossiter Bank, Rossiter Shipping and Trading, Rossiter Court, Promontory Point. But I'd no idea who he was when I finally met him, for I don't move in those circles, you know. There was not a bit of height in his manner, though he can be damned frosty when he's vexed. I took him for just another well-born young fellow. When I realized who he was—'' He paused, then said defiantly, ''My colonel told me he was a splendid officer.''

''So he was. You should've seen him on the battlefield. Knew those damned great cannon like no man I ever met. Knew how to handle his men, too. I saw him put new spirit into 'em, Lord knows how many times!'' Sturtevant pursed up his lips. ''Did you—er, ever know him to receive a letter?''

4

"Never, sir."

"Not even from his sister? I understand he is devoted to her."

"I believe he is. But I never knew him to get a letter from the lady."

Sturtevant took off his tricorne, then made a grab for his wig as the capricious wind tugged at it. Shaking rainwater from the oilcloth that protected the tricorne, he swore, then said, "Is it possible, Morris, that, er—that he don't know?"

Lieutenant Morris' youthful face was troubled. He answered slowly, "I fear it is, sir. You may be sure none of us have breathed a word. But—I suppose he'll soon find out."

"Good God!"

"I've been wondering, sir." Morris stared fixedly at the now visible might of Dover Castle. "Do you think . . . I mean, 'twould be kinder perhaps, to—ah, warn him?"

"Oh, yes. Definitely kinder."

Their eyes met. Sturtevant squared his jaw. "How d'you mean to word it?"

Blanching, Morris gasped, "Me? Now, God forbid!"

"You are a coward, Lieutenant," accused the major sternly.

"You've the right of that, sir! A downright poltroon! Never will win any medals! M'father said so. M'brother said so. Everyone who—who knows me . . ." The panicked declaration from this young man who had faced massed enemy bayonets with not the blink of an eye, faded into an awkward silence.

They looked at each other.

Major Sturtevant sighed. "Alas, I am a coward too."

"Oh, Maggie! Did you ever in your life see such an awe-inspiring sight?"

A tall, powerfully built gentleman, moving softly down the nave of Canterbury Cathedral, overheard the quiet words and paused to smile admiringly at the young lady who had uttered them. She was, he thought, an awe-inspiring sight herself. Her figure was dainty, her complexion fair, the features delicate and lit by wide green eyes. Thick, powdered ringlets clustered charmingly beside her left ear and flirted with the shoulder of her light cloak. Altogether an adorable little creature, from the lacy ruffles that edged her pink cap, to the hem of her wide hooped skirts.

"But 'tis so hugeous big, milady," murmured the neatly clad girl who accompanied this delicious vision. "And though I look and look at this map, I haven't found it yet."

5

The young beauty leaned to knit her brows over the map, and the gentleman moved nearer.

"Your pardon, ma'am," he said with a graceful bow. "I could not but overhear. An I may be of some small assistance, 'twould be my pleasure."

How swift the upward sweep of the firm little chin; how haughty the flash of the green eyes. The gentleman was enchanted. He was a good-looking man of early middle-age, with an exceptionally fine pair of dark eyes deep-set under bushy black brows. His smooth skin was bronzed by the sun, his wig was neat, his attire of the finest style and cut. Both voice and manners were cultured, and he had a very kind and winning smile. "I mean no disrespect," he murmured. "But I am fairly well acquaint with the present plan of the cathedral. It has been rebuilt several times since the days of St. Augustine, you know. Might I direct you to some particular spot . . . ?" His eyes glinted, and he said whimsically, "The shrine of St. Thomas á Becket, perchance?"

The hauteur in the lady's eyes gave way to a sparkle of amusement. "La, but we are sadly inept pilgrims," she said in a rich, musical voice. "Yes, sir. Your assistance would be most appreciated."

"My *lady*!" exclaimed the abigail, eyeing the stranger askance.

Despite the many visitors wandering about the enormous cathedral, voices were kept low, and a reverent hush prevailed. Two older ladies looked censoriously at the small group.

The gentleman grinned, and acknowledged in a whisper, "Your woman is quite right, ma'am. May I present myself properly? My name is Bracksby. Rudolph Bracksby. My estate lies about two miles east of here, and I promise you my reputation is not too sadly tarnished. St. Thomas' shrine is in the Trinity Chapel. This way."

He led them along the north aisle, pointing out the choir with its splendid screen, and the tombs of St. Alphege and St. Dunstan, and guiding them at last via the lovely curve of the arcades into the Trinity Chapel.

As they approached the saint's tomb, Lady Naomi halted, and with pretty politeness thanked Mr. Bracksby for his aid. It was very apparent that he desired to know the name of the lady he guided, but her demeanour, though pleasant, was not encouraging, and he was much too well bred to press her. He accepted his dismissal, therefore, bowed again, and took himself off.

6

In the south aisle he was pleased to recognize a friend, and prevailed upon that clerical individual to accompany him back to the Trinity Chapel.

"There," he murmured, nodding his head toward the shrine. "The enchanting creature in pink. I know she is Lady Somebody, but for the life of me I cannot recollect her name."

"Then you're a regular chawbacon, Rudi," said his friend with a grin. "That little beauty is the Lady Naomi Lutonville. The reigning Toast. You surely must have heard of some of her escapades." He winked. "Rather a minx, they say."

Mr. Rudolph Bracksby's dark eyes grew troubled. "Oh, is she, by Jupiter!"

"I'm amazed you are not acquainted. Did you but spend more time in England, Rudi, you might keep abreast of such vital matters. Well, I must be off. Looks as if we're in for a storm, and I'd as lief get home before it starts."

That his decision was wise was soon apparent. The mist became drizzle, and the drizzle turned to rain. By half-past two o'clock my Lady Lutonville's luxurious carriage was caught in a downpour, and having already suffered a damaged wheel, turned off the highway and proceeded gingerly along a lane that was soon little better than a mass of puddled ruts. The wheel was bumping ominously, and Maggie Osgood's scared brown eyes became even more apprehensive when Roger Coachman opened the trap and shouted his opinion that they'd do better to let him leave them under a tree while he rode in search of aid. "This wheel's going to split any minute, marm," he howled, raindrops coursing down his weathered and forbidding countenance. "And there ain't any lodge gates as far as I can see."

"Yes, but you cannot see very far," pointed out Naomi, ignoring Maggie's wail. "And I do not propose to sit in this plaguey wet for an hour while you ride about looking for a smithy. If the wheel splits we shall have to stop, but 'til then, keep on, Roger. I'm sure this is the right lane and it cannot be very much farther."

"Was Promontory Point half a inch round the next raindrop I dunno what the earl would say bout me taking you there, marm," he grumbled.

"Roger Coachman is right, milady," put in Maggie tearfully. "An the coach turns over—"

"Do not be such a goose," scolded Naomi. "He will not allow the coach to turn over, will you, Roger? Hasten, now. I chance to know that Sir Mark is in London at Rossiter Court,

7

but I am very sure his people will have something to warm us all."

The vision of a mug of hot rum, the better for some lemon and cloves, did much to lighten the coachman's mood, and they were soon limping along once more. My lady gave a little crow of triumph when iron lodge gates loomed through the deluge. There was another delay while the guard shouted in vain for the gatekeeper, resorting at length to the yard of tin. The stentorian blast he awoke from that instrument brought a drowsy-looking man hurrying to open the gates and stare from the crest on the door panel to the beauteous face of the lady who leaned from the window to enquire if there was anyone up at the house.

"Sometimes," he said, stifling a yawn.

Adjured by the coachman to keep a civil tongue in his head, the gatekeeper offered belligerently to darken his daylights for him.

"You are insolent," said Naomi, frowning at him. "Drive on at once, Roger."

The coachman, who had started to climb down from his perch, obeyed with reluctance, hissing some sizzling epithets at the gatekeeper, who responded in kind but with a wary eye on her ladyship's now closed window.

The carriage jerked into motion once more and proceeded unevenly along the drivepath, which seemed to wind for miles through a wilderness area that at length became a spacious park.

Lady Naomi peered about, curious to see if she recollected anything of this great estate of which she had for so many years expected to become mistress. Lined by dripping yews, the drive swung in a wide easterly curve. A grey mist hovered, limiting the view, but at last the gables of the three-storeyed Elizabethan house loomed up. It looked only vaguely familiar to Naomi, although she did remember the gardens in what had once been the moat, which surrounded the original pile. Noting the impressive entrance front, its forecourt sheltered by projecting wings, the countless latticed casements, the tall works of art that were the chimneys, she thought it a truly beautiful old place, so much more inviting than Collington Manor. The ancient mill and the now shallow millstream near the west side of the house evoked the shadowy image of a youth with brown curls and laughing grey eyes, playing with a liver and white spaniel . . .

The coach rumbled over the narrow wooden bridge spanning the sunken gardens, and creaked to a stop. No stableboy or groom came running. No footman appeared at the deeply re-

8

cessed front door. The house slumbered quietly under the steady beat of the rain.

The guard swung down from the box and opened the carriage door. Naomi gave him her card and sent him off to request assistance.

"There bean't no one at home," said Maggie, watching him nervously. "We'll have to send Roger Coachman for help and goodness only knows when—"

"No, but somebody *is* there," Naomi interrupted. The front door had swung wide, and after a hurried colloquy the footman ran back to the coach, followed by a manservant with a far from pleased expression, and a large umbrella.

"An my lady's coachman 'e will drive to ze stables," said this fussy little individual, his French accent pronounced, "zere should be ze wheel you can 'ave. Meantimes, you will be kind to come in ze 'ouse."

Naomi was more than willing to avail herself of this offer. She and Maggie were handed from the vehicle and ushered into a great hall with a fine, though coldly empty, fireplace at one end. The only furnishings were several bishop's chairs and some ancient-looking chests. The air was chill and there were no maids bustling to greet them, no candles or lamps sending out a welcoming glow. The withdrawing room, however, was a wainscoted delight, richly furnished, and lit by the flames of a dying fire. The manservant left them, muttering something about tea, and after a few minutes an elegant gentleman hurried into the room.

" 'Tis my very great pleasure to welcome you, Lady Lutonville," he said with a sweeping and magnificent bow.

She had believed that Gideon Rossiter was safely in Europe with his regiment, and that she might suddenly come face-to-face with him had not occurred to her. For a panicked moment she was speechless, staring blankly at the tall young man who advanced to bow over her hand, and taking in the meticulously curled and tied wig, the lean, proud face with its finely cut features, the splendid physique, the peerlessly tailored riding coat of dull gold, the moleskin breeches and gleaming topboots. She drew a breath of relief when she realized that the eyes watching her with such patent admiration were hazel. 'Newby!' she thought, and said, "Your pardon. La, but I must seem a proper wool gatherer! I had not expected to—"

"To find anyone here?" He smiled faintly. "To say truth, we were on the point of leaving. Is my good fortune that I am tardy as ever, and thus win the privilege of being of some service to so lovely a lady.''

'Hmm,' thought Naomi, and gently detached the hand he still held. "I am truly grateful for your hospitality, Mr. Rossiter. Especially in—in view of the circumstances. I would not have dreamed of intruding, save that one of the wheels of my carriage split, and I recollected that your—that Promontory Point was nearby.''

Although his eyes laughed at her, he said solemnly, "Thank heaven for your excellent memory, my lady. But your hand is like ice. Allow me to draw a chair closer to the fire. There. Your woman will want to go to the kitchens, I fancy.''

Maggie gave a gasp and turned shocked eyes on her ladyship.

Before Naomi could dispute this naughty suggestion, however, Mr. Rossiter went on apologetically, "I fear most of our servants have already gone to the Town house, and my man will appreciate her assistance.''

He turned a winning smile on Maggie, and led her to the door. " 'Tis this way, m'dear. All the way to the end there, then turn to the right and you'll find it.''

Maggie darted another scandalised glance at her mistress, but Naomi jerked her head and the girl went out.

Rossiter sauntered back to the hearth. "I think you did not at first recognize me, my lady. I protest, I am desolate. I should know *you* anywhere.''

The glint in the eyes, the provocative half-smile, were all too familiar. A handsome rascal, and very sure of his charm was Newby Rossiter, thought Naomi. Still, he was a gentleman and would doubtless behave himself did she show no inclination to flirt with him.

She said with cool hauteur, "Faith, but you have a most excellent memory, sir. It must be at least seven years since last we met.''

"Ah, but I travel also, Lady Naomi. You were pointed out to me in Rome four years ago, and the year before that I saw you in Vienna. What a tragedy that your sire's duties for so long denied London the very fairest of her flowers.''

He stepped closer, smiling down at her with a glow in his eyes she did not at all care for. Her manner became frigid. "Fie, sir! Such blatant flattery! I vow the Ambassador could benefit from your services. There are doubtless occasions when a silver tongue is an asset.''

Refusing to accept the set-down, he put one hand on the arm

of her chair and bent to her, saying lightly, "Ah, but then 'twould be a case of being obliged to flatter the vast spouse of some foreign dignitary, or waste my talents on elderly harridans and dowagers. Whereas, in this case, I have no need to flatter—only to speak purest truth."

He expected his words to evoke a blush, or shyly downcast eyes. Naomi gave him a cold stare, and asked, "Did you travel in Europe so as to visit Captain Rossiter, sir?"

"No, I did not." Amused, he said, "So we turn the conversation to my graceless twin, at last." He noted her slight frown and laughed. "But of course, for *that* is why you are here! That is why you looked so startled when first I came into the room! You hoped to find Gideon come home! Why, you little minx!" He touched her cheek gently. "But such a very lovely minx."

Naomi came to her feet. "You forget yourself, sir! My maid accompanied me to the cathedral and—"

"And you just *chanced* to break down upon my doorstep? Come now, fairest. Be honest and admit you came to discover is my brother as black as he's painted. I'll wager you believed all the rumours, poor child. Do you not yet know that you can trust to very little of what you hear? Only look at what is said of—you, m'dear . . . Were Gideon to believe all the tales—"

"Your brother is at liberty to believe whatsoever he wishes, sir!" She started for the door, but Rossiter moved very fast to block her way.

"Do you beat a hasty retreat because you dare not face the facts, dear lady?"

Allowing rage to overcome her reluctance to bandy words with this man, she said, "To what facts do you refer, Mr. Rossiter? The fact that I committed some silly indiscretions which have been exaggerated out of all proportion to the actual events? Or—"

"But my poor brother might well say the same, sweet soul. Likely, people exaggerate his—er, liaison with the beautiful lady of the gardens. Only think how discreetly he conducted this *affaire de coeur*, for even now nobody knows who she was, nor where they met—save that it was very frequently . . ." Watching her slyly, he went on: "And as for the little Belgian lovely he took for his mistress, that is not so dreadful, surely? I'll admit 'twas unfortunate there was a by-blow, but you may be sure he's left 'em by this time. Troth, but when a man is at war, one cannot expect him to be a saint."

Her chin very high, her eyelids drooping with disdain, she

11

said icily, "Nor would I expect any *gentleman* to discuss such things with an unwed lady. But since you have been so crude as to put the matter into words, Mr. Rossiter, I will tell you that I believe any gentleman who gives a lady a child and then leaves both to starve is 'neath contempt! Indeed, I wonder he was not asked to resign his commission! Good day to you."

With a swift pounce he had caught her by the arms. "Little prudery," he said, amused.

His hands were bruisingly hard, and knowing she could not escape she stood very still, looking up into his laughing face, seething with rage. "I see you have forgot what few manners you possessed. I've a mind to be released, sir. At once!"

"But 'tis not *my* mind to release you, Lady Lovely.'Twould be perfectly horrid. Now, if you will only be at ease, I shall dismiss Gideon from your thoughts, and we can be—"

"Your twin occupies none of my thoughts," she declared hotly, now struggling to free herself. "Which is as well, an he has grown to be anything like you."

He chuckled and pulled her closer. "But he has neither my looks nor my address, poor fellow. As you should recollect if—" The words were cut off by a pained yowl as Naomi ground her heel into his toe, then ran back several paces.

Newby sank into the nearest chair and clutched his foot. "You damnable little shrew!"

"For shame, Mr. Rossiter! I am a guest in your house. Your behaviour is insupportable. When my father learns—"

"You'd best not tell him, my lady Prim! He'd likely spank you for setting foot on this estate. And if he feels obliged to call me out—well, I would really dislike to take advantage of an old man!"

"The earl is far from old, and an excellent shot. Furthermore, sir, do not judge yourself safe because I have no brothers. I have cousins a'plenty, and good friends to whom I may turn for protection."

Knowing this to be true, he suffered a momentary qualm, then laughed sneeringly. "Such as your good friend the Mandarin?"

With her hand on the door Naomi checked and said with regal hauteur, "There are far more despicable things than to have mixed blood, Mr. Rossiter. I give you joy of your tea. Good day."

She slammed the door before she was obliged to listen to his rageful response, and hurried down the chilly hall. In the kitchens she found Maggie, flushed and angry, and tea still not made. Naomi issued commands. In short order they were in the stables, where Roger Coachman and the guard had replaced the damaged wheel and were preparing to adjourn to the house for the promised refreshments. They looked disappointed when Naomi said curtly that there would be no further delays.

"Anything wrong, ma'am?" asked the sturdy coachman, eyeing his beautiful charge narrowly.

"Only that you were perfectly right," said Naomi, the slightest tremor in her voice. "We should never have come here."

His rugged features even more formidable, he scowled at the house. "I thought as you were flying your colours! Do but say the word, milady, and—"

Grateful for his loyalty, she put a hand on his sleeve and said fondly, "No, Roger, you dare not touch the wretch! Let us leave at once, and pray do not mention this episode to my father, for 'twould certainly lead to trouble!"

In the coach, she leaned back, still flushed with wrath. She had not cared for Newby as a boy, but what a despicable creature he had become! Her hands were so cold. She gripped them tightly, furious with herself because she had been so stupid as to come here, and unable to shut out the silly thought that would not seem to leave her mind: 'So there was a child . . .'

❧ *Chapter 2* ❧

It was raining again by the time the coach rolled up the Collington drivepath. Gideon had never admired the long sprawl of the two-storeyed mansion, which could boast of neither bays, conservatory, nor the shallowest of projecting wings to alleviate its plain front. The unrelieved grey of stone and trim he found depressing, and the balustrades above the cornices too heavy, adding to an overall impression of frowning gloom. The chilly veil of the rain did nothing to improve his memory of this birthplace of his betrothed, and as the postboys drew the horses to a halt, he was beginning to regret the impulse that had led him to travel west toward Tonbridge, instead of north to Promontory Point.

Collington offered no porte-cochère or porch to shelter its visitors, but the large front door was flung open as the carriage approached, and a lackey under an open umbrella came to usher the caller inside.

The entrance hall was vastly ostentatious with its painted ceilings, thick carpets, and a great quantity of red velvet and gilt furniture. Rossiter presented his card to the tall and stately butler and desired that it be conveyed to the earl.

The butler's gaze lingered on the calling card, then lifted to scan the gaunt-faced young officer. "His lordship," he said, in a voice as dreary as the persistent rain, "is not at home."

"In which case," said Rossiter, "you may tell the Lady Naomi that I am here."

"Lady Lutonville is not at home either, sir. Nor," added the butler loftily, "is she expected."

There came a burst of laughter from somewhere in the house. The butler exchanged a sly grin with the footman who waited nearby. "In point of fact," said the butler, "there is—ah, no one at home. At all. Sir."

Rossiter smiled and moved a step closer. "Do you know," he said, "I really believe you have made a mistake. Take my card to Lady Lutonville. Without delay."

The captain had not raised his voice, but for an instant the butler had the distinct impression that he had been transfixed by a steel lance. Shocked, he looked away from the icy glare in what he was later to describe as the nastiest pair of eyes he ever had beheld. In a far more respectful tone, he bowed, desired the captain to wait, and trod with rare speed across the hall.

He returned in a few minutes, rather pale, and followed by a sturdy lackey. "My regrets, Captain Rossiter," he said uneasily. "But—'tis as I told you. There is—er, no one—er, at home."

Rossiter heard soft footsteps behind him. 'The reserves,' he thought, 'have been called in.' Rage blazed through him, but there was nothing to be gained by losing his temper. The servants were merely obeying orders. And however incomprehensible this treatment of a prospective family member, Collington had a perfect right to refuse to see anyone.

He nodded, said a brusque "I see," and turned on his heel.

Two footmen and the lackey with the umbrella moved hurriedly from his path as he strode to the door.

Someone murmured, "You reckon as he really does?"

"Does—what?"

"See."

A smothered laugh.

Rossiter checked and turned about.

The servants looked wooden but wary.

"You!" snapped Rossiter, jabbing his finger at the sturdiest of them.

The lackey jumped. "Not me, sir! Straight, Captain sir. 'Tweren't me!"

"The umbrella," said Rossiter. "If you're man enough to pick it up instead of giggling like a girl."

The lackey flushed scarlet and fairly flew to snatch the umbrella and whip the door open.

Not a drop of rain fell upon the unwanted caller as he was escorted to his carriage.

The rosy cheeks of the proprietor of the Red Pheasant Inn glowed, and his shrewd brown eyes beamed with gratification as he ushered his fair charges out of the rain. Bowing as deeply as his well-padded middle would allow, he led the way across a parlour that made up in warmth and fragrance what it lacked in elegance. Little more than a hedge tavern, the old inn was too isolated to do a brisk trade and usually had to rely on the custom of occasional travellers unable to find accommodation at the fashionable posting houses, or who perhaps found such establishments beyond their means. In bad weather, however, when the condition of the roads took heavy toll of such vital necessities as horseshoes, wheels, and (with luck) axles, the Red Pheasant did a roaring trade.

It was roaring today. The yard was crammed with vehicles, some of whose owners had stopped here only for a tankard of ale, but a few coaches being in need of repairs, which would necessitate a longer stay. Such was the case with the vehicle owned by this lovely young female. Her wine velvet cloak, the rich laces that embellished her pink silken gown, and the prideful tilt to her pretty head, all spoke of the Quality. She paused on the threshold of the crowded dining room with a tiny frown in her eyes. Used to having the place to herself, guessed mine host, and didn't much like having to mingle with the common herd. He stifled a sigh. She looked as if she'd have paid for her privacy, and it was a great pity he couldn't lighten her purse, but his last bedchamber had been hired an hour since, and there was no—

"Naomi!"

The beauty's green eyes widened, her face lit up, and she reached out to embrace the young lady who hurried with a shushing of silks to greet her. Heads turned, and for a moment the noisy room quieted as people watched the pair. That they should attract admiration was inevitable. The Lady Naomi was a fair beauty, and her friend was dark but just as lovely. She stood a little above the average height but she was fine boned and her creamy beige travelling gown clung to a tiny waist. Her ivory-hued skin was clear, her mouth sweetly bowed, her cheekbones rather broad but beautifully molded. Her black brows arched over a pair of velvety eyes of so dark a blue that at first sight they appeared to be black also. Despite their size and rich colour, however, it was her eyes alone which prevented her beauty from being termed perfection. Gentlemen found their slightly almond shape fascinating, but that her grandmama had been born to a lady of the Orient was well known. Her eyes were a reminder of that fact, and her mixed blood provided many less well-favoured ladies with an opportunity to sneer.

16

There was no sign of a sneer on Lady Naomi's face, however. "Katrina!" she exclaimed, still clasping her friend's hands. "Oh, but this is splendid! How come you to be here? Have you been at Ashleigh? Is August with you? Do you stay here? Surely not, when you are so close to the Manor?"

Katrina Falcon laughed softly and admitted she did stay here. "Come dearest, we have a table. You must take your tea with us." She threaded her way across the warm room, apparently oblivious of the variously admiring and curious stares that followed them. Her table was advantageously located in a less-crowded corner, shielded from draughts, and close enough to the fire to benefit from the warmth without being roasted. The host seated them with a flourish, Maggie was sent to join Miss Falcon's servants, and the host went in search of a serving maid.

Naomi chuckled. "I see August *is* with you."

"Now you cannot be sure of that, madam all wise. How if I am escorted by one of my cousins?"

"Fiddlesticks! I know your cousins and not one of them could have secured this table in such a crush! Now, wicked girl, answer my questions!"

Amused, Miss Falcon admitted that her brother did escort her. "As for the rest of your questions, yes, we were at Ashleigh. Papa is there and you know how lonely he gets in Sussex, so we joined him for a space. We had intended to visit you on our way back to Town, but one of the leaders came up lame, so August directed our coachman to this funny old place."

A serving maid brought more china and a tray of warm scones, jam, and seed cake. Miss Falcon poured tea for her friend, and asked eagerly, "Now tell me how you go on, and why you travel the roads in such atrocious weather."

" 'Twas not atrocious when we left home. And I have never properly visited Canterbury, so I wandered about the cathedral for an hour, and stared and was overawed along with the rest of the world."

The dark girl put down the teapot and leaned back, staring. "Do you say you went alone? Unescorted? I wonder your papa permitted it."

"Pish!" A roguish dimple peeped beside Naomi's mouth. "I do as I choose. I have my own fortune, and you will recall that I came of age last year. Besides, the main reason I went out was to execute a small commission for my father."

"Ah. Then he wished you to bring him something from the Cathedral?"

"No, you prying miss! He asked that I collect a package from the jeweller in Canterbury. And so long as I was playing messenger for him, why should I not use a little time for my own pleasure and proceed to the Cathedral?"

"Because you know very well he would not approve, you saucy creature."

Naomi's rich chuckle sounded. "Oh, he would have made a fuss and forbade me, I do not doubt. Now, he cannot, can he?"

Her friend shook her head. "Faith, but you never cease to astound me. You are so fearless. I should be quite terrified of his anger."

"Perhaps because you are so gentle. August guards you like any fierce gladiator, and your papa adores you and I doubt has ever spoken to you in anger. My life has been . . . different."

Miss Falcon saw the wistfulness that came into her friend's eyes, and her kind heart was touched.

Twenty years earlier, when Simon Lutonville was an impoverished younger son, living at the Manor on his brother's charity but with no expectations of ever becoming the Earl of Collington, two friends had stood by him. One of these had been Mr. Neville Falcon, and it was through his good offices that Lutonville had been appointed secretary to Count Leonardo Paviani, then one of the wealthiest and most influential men in the world of finance. Lutonville's gratitude to Falcon had kept the two families close for some years. Throughout her early childhood, Naomi had played with and adored Katrina, and had been teased by, and quarrelled with her domineering older brother. When Count Paviani returned to Italy, and Mr. Lutonville began to spend more time out of England than in it, he sent for his wife and two daughters, and the childhood friendship might have been forgotten had not Naomi and Katrina been faithful correspondents.

Remembering those letters and what she had thought to read between the lines, Katrina had seldom referred to the period of separation, and when she'd done so Naomi had been reticent and quickly changed the subject. Intuition whispered that her friend was troubled today, and reaching out to clasp her hand, Katrina asked, "Was it very bad, dearest? You never speak of those years in Rome."

"Of course it was not bad." Naomi's head tossed upward, but then she met Katrina's concerned gaze and her defences crumbled. She looked down at her plate and muttered, "It was horrid. I had lost you and—and all my friends."

"Thank goodness that you had your sister, at least. Oh, la! I did not mean—"

"I know just what you meant, Trina," said Naomi with a rueful smile. "And 'tis true that Joan and I were not close friends. Faith, but she gave me five years, and found me dull. Mama talked to me, but she never heard whatever I had to say. And Papa—well, you have seen how much he is changed."

"Yes. But I had thought it was only since he became a peer and returned to England. Or that perhaps it was because— Well, August and I are not good *ton*." She cut off Naomi's immediate and angry denial by remarking quickly, "How very lonely you must have been. I suspected that was so at first, but later your letters made it sound as though you had such a jolly time."

"After dear Count Paviani died and made me one of his principal beneficiaries, I had a—" Naomi shrugged. "Oh, I suppose 'twas a jolly time. Certainly, it was better than the first year." She gave a faint, defiant smile. "Even if it did win me a reputation for wildness."

Katrina said hesitantly, "Your parents seem to have kept you so very close at first. Did they not put a check on you when you—er—"

"Flouted parental authority at last and began to make some friends of my own? When I sang with the crowds going to the opera? Or danced with Prince diFaggioli in the Colosseum in my ball gown? Oh, no. Papa laughed and said that when one is rich one can do anything. Besides, he was by then much too busy with success—and his Roman birds of paradise. And Mama—" She paused and was silent.

Katrina had long judged Mrs. Lutonville a beautiful but selfish lady, who was proud of her handsome husband but had not the slightest interest in her children. After a moment she said carefully, "She must surely have enjoyed the sunshine."

"That alone, I think. She was miserable because of Papa's neglect of her, and very bored. When Joan married there was much to be planned, for it was a very large wedding, as you know. It gave Mama something to brighten her days, but—she soon lost interest. I sometimes thought she did not much care for being a mother. I wish she had . . ."

Katrina soothed, "Never mind, dearest. From what you wrote, Joan is quite settled in Rome. And although you have lost your dear mama, here you are safe back in England again, and only look, in less than a year you have become the Toast of London, and—"

"But I do not *want* to be a Toast! All I ever wanted was to—" She checked again, then, gripping her friend's hand very tightly said in a sort of desperation, "Oh, Trina, I do so envy you!"

With a gasp of astonishment, Katrina echoed, "Envy—*me*? Good gracious! Why? You are beautiful, admired, sought-after, and most comfortably circumstanced! How many offers have you received this year? A dozen? A score more like! I am ogled by the fortune hunters but few well-born gentlemen would offer more than a slip on the shoulder to a half-caste; the ladies tolerate me only for the sake of dear Papa; and I am—"

"You are *loved*, you silly goose! Do you not see? You are loved! For a while I thought—But *never* have I known . . . that wonder!"

Suddenly, there was such grief in the green eyes, such a note of pathos in the halting voice that Katrina was struck to the heart, and said tenderly, "We love you, dearest. August and I, and my father also."

Naomi blinked rapidly, and recovering her poise, reached for the jam and said with a rather shaken chuckle, "August thinks I am a scamp, as well you know. And why you or your dear papa should care for me, I cannot think, after the way my father has served you."

"*You* have never been unkind to us. And as for your papa, 'tis true he has become perhaps too grand for us, but he is very proud of *you*, I feel sure."

"As one might be proud of a possession. But I am not his possession, do you see?"

"No, no! I did not mean that kind of pride! He loves you, of course."

Naomi sank her white teeth into the warm scone, then said a rather muffled, "Stuff!"

"Naomi!"

"Well, it is, and you know it. No, be honest, Trina. Were I to expire this afternoon and August carried the word to my sire, he would interrupt his card game long enough to say," she lowered her voice and growled, "What's that, Falcon? Begad, but 'tis a pity! Well, make your move, Abel! Don't take all night, man!"

Katrina looked, and was, scandalised. Glancing up, Naomi brightened. "Aha! Your grimly guardian makes his entrance, I see."

"In time to hear you behaving like any hoyden, as usual,"

came a deep voice from behind her, and August Falcon lowered his long length into the third chair.

"August, dearest," she cried gaily, reaching out to him in her impulsive way. "Faith, 'tis lovely to see you!"

With unfailing grace he touched her fingers to his lips, but said, "Rubbish! I think you cannot find it 'lovely' to see a 'grimly guardian.' "

She did find it lovely, although at times she would have been hard pressed to explain why, for Falcon was not an easy man to like. Many women found him irresistible, but an early tendency towards sarcasm had deepened over the years, his caustic tongue alienating those few gentlemen in Society willing to befriend him despite his unfortunate birth. His unpopularity was increased by his immutable refusal to approve applicants for the hand of his sister. The contempt and finality with which he dismissed all comers, even gentlemen of breeding and fortune, had driven three stricken and insulted admirers to call him out. They had all recovered, but the speed and ease with which they were vanquished had discouraged others. And although he was by this time as disliked as he was despised, men trod softly around Mr. August Falcon.

"An I am truly glad to see you," said Naomi, twinkling at him, " 'tis because I am as gracious as you are odious. And you must not make a repulsive response, dear August, for Katrina has but now been vowing how much you love me."

He raised one eyebrow and said dryly, "My sister has a soft area of the brain that tends to interfere with her occasional common sense." He took the cup an amused Katrina handed him, and went on: "I believe in Ovid one may read that 'love is a kind of warfare.' Since I have no more use for the one than for the other, you may draw your own conclusions, Lady Lutonville. I trust you will not fall into a decline."

"Alas," moaned Naomi, throwing one hand to her brow despairingly. "All is lost! I must put a period to my wretched existence. Woe is me! Though, I guessed how t'would be."

"Did you. I should like to know how you also guessed that I was coming up behind you just now. Am I allowed a scone?"

Katrina scolded that he did not deserve one. But Naomi chuckled and passed the plate, telling him that guessing had played no part in her remark. "I *knew* you were coming because the eyes of every woman in the room turned this way."

"Do you mean to talk nonsense," he said with disgust, "I shall leave you."

21

She laughed. "You have only to look about you for confirmation of my 'nonsense.' "

He had no need to do so. His riding habit of dark grey broadcloth might have been plain on another man but served only to accent the commanding height and perfect physique that were allied to features as handsome as his sister's were beautiful. He had the same high and broad cheekbones and thin chiselled nose. Unlike Katrina's, his complexion was inclined to be sallow, but the dark blue eyes were as brilliant and thickly lashed and had the same faintly alien slant. The resemblance ended there, however, for his lips were thinner, his flaring black brows and stubborn chin betrayed a tempestuous nature, and his expression was cold and forbidding. He had been on the Town since he was nineteen, and the ensuing ten years had made him quite aware of his power over the fair sex. He selected his paramours with care, often from the dancers of the Opera, and none lasted longer than six months. But for the more cultured ladies, whose flirtatious and admiring glances invariably followed him, he had only scorn.

"Do not tease him, dearest," pleaded Katrina, passing her brother the jam pot. "You will put him out of humour."

"Goodness me! Are you *in* humour, August? You might have told me so."

"You have the disposition of a shrew, my lady," he riposted. "Do but continue along the same lines and you may yet win me."

Both ladies laughed merrily. Naomi said, "No, Trina is right. I must not tease you, for truly I am very glad to see you both. So glad in fact, that I mean to kidnap you away to Collington and will hear no arguments, sirrah, so you had as lief say yes at once!"

"No. And do not be giving yourself airs. You may be the most talked-about heiress in London Town, but you're still a grubby little brat to me! And your conversation when I came up just now, was improper in the extreme. Such a way to speak of your father!"

She sipped her tea, watching him over the brim of her cup, then said lightly, "Since you so admire him, you will want to come and see the great man."

"Nothing of the kind," he contradicted rudely, spreading strawberry jam with a lavish hand. "And I think the earl will thank us for not desecrating his doorstep."

Naomi saw Katrina flinch at this, and said frowningly, "I think you have never been turned away from Collington."

"So long as your father was profitably engaged with mine, no." He glanced at her from under his lashes. "The great god Mammon can render anyone acceptable."

"Now you are being horrid, August!"

"Aha! Then you believe he would approve an I asked for your hand?" His lip curled. "I wish I may see it! He would prefer even poor Rossiter, be damned if he wouldn't! And much as you profess to adore me, my poppet, I find it unlikely you would be willing to be known as Mrs. Mandarin."

Katrina gave a gasp and turned her face away.

Flushed with anger, Naomi flared, "I do not adore you, August Falcon! And heaven help the lady who loves you enough to spend the rest of her life enduring your nasty cynicism! But one might think that after all these years you would know me better than to think me guilty of such—such—"

"Such typical British aristocratic prejudices? Why not? You're an Englishwoman and an aristocrat, and fairly brimming with hoity-toityness."

Between her teeth she hissed, "An I *did* love you, wretched creature, nothing or no one would stop me from accepting your offer!"

"You may be grateful my girl," he waved his scone at her, "that nothing would induce me to put your resolution to the test."

"Beast!" exclaimed Naomi.

"No, but that is prodigious unkind, August," said Katrina, troubled.

He smiled, and sketched a careless bow.

Naomi glared at him. "You are too provoking, August. You have made me cross, and I vowed I would not be so again today!"

"So much for resolution. Personally, I never make vows, then I am spared the anguish of breaking them. One always does, you know."

Ignoring this confidence, she asked after a moment, "Why do you name him 'poor' Rossiter? Are you acquaint?"

"Not—I thank heaven—since he was a quarrelsome and pushing brat at Eton. I had nothing to do with him. He cut no great swath in academia as I recollect."

"Whereas your achievements will live on forever, I collect."

"An you doubt it, m'dear, ask him." He smiled at her with

23

lazy mockery. "The next time you are—er, *tête-à-tête*, as it were . . . Rossiter detests me, but being a jolly good sportsman, I feel sure he will with true nobility verify the brilliance of my record. How do you go on, Roger?"

Roger Coachman approached the table, touched his hat respectfully to the Falcons, said he was very well thank you, and advised my lady that the horses were rested and it would soon grow dark.

"There is no need for your horses," said Falcon with a glance at the window and the lowering skies. "You will rack up here for the night. You may share Trina's room, Naomi."

Quite out of patience with him, Naomi said dryly, "Your generosity is beyond peer, but I shall do no such thing. I had far rather be comfortable in my own bed than risk fleas and damp sheets in this shabby little hovel!"

Falcon put up his quizzing glass and regarded her through it. "Ruffled your feathers, did I?" he drawled.

"Yes. Precisely as you intended." She took his arm then, and levelled her enchanting smile at him. "Now, you have had a lovely time teasing me, so you may be done with being such a great grump, dear August. Come back to Collington. Or at least permit Katrina to visit me for a little time. We've not had a proper cose in an age, and have so much to talk about."

Her cajolery did not prevail. He had, he said, not the least doubt that the two ladies "could gossip for a month if given the opportunity," but he would neither visit Collington, nor allow his sister to go there. He agreed with her ladyship when she argued that it had been his intention to take Katrina to Collington, but said blandly that there was not now the need to do so since they had met here.

"Further," he went on, "although I make no doubt I am as unamiable as you have declared (with a sad want of manners, I might add), had you the wit of a wardrobe you would overnight here rather than travel through a countryside swarming with rank riders, and plaguely damp. Especially since these clouds will bring an early dusk, and 'twill likely be full dark before you reach home. Always supposing," he appended as a final touch, "another wheel does not drop off en route."

Katrina gave a little cry of dismay.

Her inner apprehension deepened by the concurring nod of Roger Coachman, Naomi tossed her curls and said defiantly, "La, sir! But how charming you are not! I vow you make me shake in my slippers. I doubt there is a single highwayman from here to—to Tooting!''

Falcon reached for another scone. ''Should you object to a married one? What an odd requirement. Their marital state interests me not at all.''

Naomi's dimples flickered in appreciation of this sally, but Katrina cried, ''August, pray do not jest! Do you really suppose they might be held up? Lud, Naomi, you *must* stay here!''

''I shall stay long enough to chat with you, after your disobliging brother has been so good as to take himself off,'' said Naomi. ''Then I shall wend my lonely and forsaken way back to my despised home.''

Falcon shrugged. ''Upon your own head be it, wilful chit.''

Genuinely worried, Katrina said, ''I had not so much as thought of highwaymen, but if you persist in travelling on, Naomi, you must leave at once! Is there a guard on your coach? August, belike you should ride escort, dearest?''

''The devil I will!'' exclaimed Mr. Falcon.

❧ *Chapter 3* ❧

If the earl and his sire had quarrelled, thought Rossiter, staring unseeingly at his own face reflected in the window of the carriage, it was unlikely to have been a really grim dispute. Had the two men fought a duel, that would throw an entirely different light on the situation, of course. But such a turn of events was out of the question. When the Earl of Collington had been merely Mr. Simon Lutonville, of large debts, small fortune, and no prospects, Sir Mark Rossiter had never refused to extend a helping hand to his old school friend, however the debts mounted, however remote the chance of repayment. Lutonville had been deeply grateful, and it was because the two men were such bosom bows that the marriage of their children had been arranged. So deep a friendship was not likely to have been irreparably damaged because of some silly difference of opinion, or whatever it was that had set their backs up.

At all events, whatever had caused the wrangling between their parents, Rossiter was very sure that Naomi would not have changed. She had been devoted to him throughout their early years. She would not forget. Shy and sweetly loyal was his beloved. He sighed, smiling at the rain-splashed window the fond smile of lovers. Only . . . His smile went a little awry. Only he'd been away for so long. Six years. Was it asking too much to expect that any girl would remain constant for such a length of time? Forever, was what they had vowed when they'd plighted their troth that lovely summer morning. "I will wait for you forever, if I must," she'd whispered, her eyes adoring him.

But . . . she had been only sixteen years old. And while that exploding shell had not scarred his face, it had changed him. Sometimes, when he looked into the mirror while shaving, he scarce recognized the gaunt features staring back at him: the sunken eyes and hollow cheeks, and the lines pain had carved beside his nostrils. He'd heard Naomi had become so beautiful— so courted. The rage of London. Doubtless, the most eligible bachelors in the kingdom were vying for her hand. What would she think when they met again? She had said once in her loving way that he was the most handsome and dashing young man she ever had seen. Would she be horrified because her dashing young beau had vanished, and in his place was this worn and far from dashing stranger?

His fist clenched suddenly, and he thought a vexed, 'Damn you for a fool, Gideon! Why could you not have done as Papa wished and joined him at the bank? Why must you enrage him by rushing off and buying a commission? All you got for it was six years of fighting and hardship!' But that wasn't true either; there had been good times along with the bad. He'd seen loyalty and heroism, and learned to the full what real comradeship meant. So many fine young men he had fought beside; so many shared grumbles, triumphs, and disasters. So much laughter. And all too frequent the times when he had wept for gallant lives cut short. Still, he wouldn't change those years. If only that confounded blast hadn't put him into the hospital only a month before the end of his fifth year away, when he had promised faithfully to sell out and come home.

Memory of the hospital brought with it a glimpse of Tranquillity Terrace. 'Which was utter nonsense,' he thought. At the time, however, it had been a Godsend. His companions in the crowded hospital had been the best of men and unfailingly cheerful, but there had been dreary periods when he'd been in too much pain to want to talk, and out of misery and desperation he had built his refuge.

Tranquillity Terrace was a garden. There was the shadowy outline of a nearby house; not a great house like Collington Manor or Promontory Point, but a rambling country house after the style of Emerald Farm, with whitewashed and half-timbered walls and a thatched roof shielded by venerable oaks. He had never entered the house. His dreams all took place in the garden. A garden fragrant with blossoms, with benches here and there, and a big weeping willow tree trailing its branches over a stream. It was by the stream that he'd met the girl to whom he was promised. At first, he'd pictured her as last he had seen her—a kind, pretty creature, already showing the promise of womanhood.

27

In Tranquillity Terrace he had allowed her to grow up, and he had made her small and petite, with a rather breathless soft voice, and a gentle manner. She had begun to go into Society, and he'd costumed her in the latest fashions: great-skirted gowns of softly swirling and delicately hued silks, satins, and velvets, trimmed with laces or embroidery. By the time she was nineteen, she was bewitchingly lovely, her every movement a study in grace, her laugh like the trill of a nightingale. Her fame spread so that other young men began to come and call to her from the wall he'd hurriedly thrown up about the garden. But his lovely Naomi saw only him. Never once did he arrive to find the garden empty. Always, she was there, her arms reaching out yearningly to embrace him; her kisses for him alone. She was the one person who would never change, the unfailing refuge, the ever-faithful heart. He unburdened himself to her, sharing his joys and sorrows, while she listened with ready sympathy, or helped him plan their future; a golden plan that even encompassed the three fine sons and two gentle daughters who would come to share the garden with them.

Smiling faintly, he set memory aside. His lady of Tranquillity Terrace had served him well in those dark days, but there was not the need for dreams now. If Naomi had been at the Manor she would have come to him. Since she had not come it was very likely that she was at the earl's residence in Town. Lord, but he longed to see her! And with luck he would be able to seek her out tomorrow, or the next day. He must first mend his fences with his father, but hopefully he would be forgiven and would soon discover the quarrel with Lord Collington to have been a trifling matter that could easily be set to rights.

The carriage lurched and he saw that the postilions had turned the team into the yard of a small inn. They would rest the horses here before completing the journey. He opened the door and climbed out, his boots splashing onto the puddled cobblestones. In his preoccupation he hadn't noticed how the weather had deteriorated. The postilions were soaked, and he tossed them a florin and told them to dry out and buy themselves a meal. To cross the yard was a hazardous business, and he had to dodge muddied vehicles and stamping horses; ostlers who darted about, poling up one team, unharnessing another, all the while heartily damning the stableboys; and impatient grooms and coachmen in hot pursuit of and just as heartily damning the ostlers.

Escaping the cold bedlam of the yard, Rossiter entered the warm bedlam of the parlour. Over the din, mine host bellowed redundantly that the Red Pheasant Inn was full to capacity, and there was not a table to be had in the dining room. Rossiter's uniform won him a place with a group of military men, and although their table was in a chilly corner far from the fire, he spent a pleasantly uproarious half-hour with them. The roast beef he ordered was tough as leather, but the apple pie that followed was succulent, the coffee hot and strong, and he felt renewed and more optimistic as he left his new friends and made his way from the noisy room.

Near the door, a hand on his arm arrested him. A familiar voice cried an exuberant, "Blister me, but here's good luck!" Rising from a table littered with used crockery Lieutenant James Morris grinned engagingly. "Do you stay here, old lad? If you've snabbled a room, I'll share it with you."

Rossiter said with an answering smile, "You're too kind, Jamie, but my stay has been only for an hour, and is now done. I'd supposed you to have reached Sevenoaks by this time. Trouble?"

"No. Just dawdling about." Morris walked to the door with him. "Riding in this weather is a bore, so thought I'd rack up here. Hah! I say, did you rest your orbs on those two beauties who just left? Be dashed if ever I saw such a pair. I'd have wangled an introduction, but the fellow with them was a curst cold-looking old duck, so I daren't try my hand."

Rossiter expressed his regrets at having missed the "two beauties" and enquired what Morris meant to do. "If you'd care to come to the Point with me, you can overnight there, then continue to your home tomorrow. Out of your way, I know, but you've no chance of hiring a coach tonight. We can tie your hack on behind, and at least you'll have a dry ride and a decent bed."

Morris hesitated. He had no wish to become involved in what he suspected would be a sticky homecoming. On the other hand, his wound was a little troublesome and he was rather tired, and the prospect of a night spent on two chairs did not appeal. His was not a quick mind, and his silence had caused his friend's eyebrows to lift enquiringly. He reddened and said hurriedly, "Jove! Yes! Thank you, Ross. Dashed good of you. Wouldn't want to intrude, mind. Family gathering, what?"

Rossiter assured him it would be no intrusion and they started out to pay their reckoning. Morris said, "Did I tell you about those two beauties? One was the small, vivacious type. A real Fair. But the other! Curse me if ever I saw such loveliness. Graceful as a—a young—er, gazelle. And—"

"And went leaping out of your life, eh?" interposed Rossiter, laughing at him.

Morris said aggrievedly that some insensitive clods had no understanding of matters of the heart, and debating this, the two men paid the host's cheerful wife, and repaired to the stableyard. The rain had stopped, the horses were rested, and the postilions, having eaten well and enjoyed some good Kentish ale, were ready to leave. They were just as eager as their customers to complete the journey before nightfall, and in no time Morris' heavy saddlebags had been loaded into the boot, his horse tied on behind, and the light coach was off, rattling along the muddy roads at a respectable pace.

It very soon became obvious that Rossiter would have little chance to dwell on his problems. Morris, in a garrulous mood, continued to rave about the dark-eyed goddess who, with one fatal smile, had apparently won his heart. She was sublime, exquisite, and as kind as she was beautiful, he dare swear. He discoursed upon her dainty nose, the sweet curves of her red lips, the pale purity of her skin, until Rossiter cried for mercy.

"Enough, Jamie! I beg of you! I acknowledge her to be incomparable. I apprehend you are *aux anges* and have met your Fate. If ever you see the lady again, you must at once drop to your knees before her and beg her hand in marriage. Either that or shoot yourself, old boy!"

He had no sooner spoken than both men tensed to a distant sound. Through the deepening gloom of this very gloomy dusk their eyes met.

Morris said, "A shot. No?"

Rossiter opened the window. "What's to do?" he shouted.

"Looks to be trouble ahead, sir," called a postilion. "You want as we should take another road?"

"Devil I do! Spring 'em!"

The horses leaned into their collars and were off at the gallop. The coach fairly flew.

Soon, another coach loomed up with several men about it. A dark shape lay motionless on the ground. A woman was struggling with a big, roughly dressed individual.

"A hold-up, by Jupiter!" exclaimed Rossiter, and was out of the vehicle and running before the coach stopped. Morris charged along behind, trying to extricate a pistol from his pocket.

The woman had fallen and was sprawled in the mud. With the arrival of reinforcements the big man fled, one of his cronies hobbling along after him.

"Stop! In the King's name!" thundered Rossiter, sword in hand.

A fourth man had ridden up and flung himself from the saddle. At Rossiter's shout, he swung around, a long-barrelled pistol levelled.

"No you don't, you murdering hound!" roared Morris, and fired.

The rider dropped his weapon, staggered back, and went down.

Dragging herself to her feet, the woman let out a piercing scream. "You *monster*!" she cried wildly.

"Eh?" said Morris, surprised.

She ran to drop to her knees beside the fallen man. "Oh! My heavens! Are you much hurt?" She reached out imperatively. "One of you, give me something I can use for a bandage."

"Women!" said Morris in admiration. "They're saints, curse me if they ain't. Here's the lady willing to bind the wound of the very scoundrel who robbed her and—"

"You triple-damned . . . clodpole . . . ," groaned August Falcon, blood trickling between the fingers that gripped his left arm.

Peering at his victim, Morris exclaimed, "If it ain't the cold old duck! Be dashed if I'd have taken him for a rank rider."

"Fool!" hissed Lady Naomi Lutonville, glaring at him furiously. "He was my escort!"

"Whoops!" muttered the lieutenant and drew back.

Rossiter passed his large handkerchief to the distraught lady, and looking down at the injured man said ruefully, "I suspect we erred, Jamie. Falcon—isn't it, sir?"

"Yes. Curse you! Confound it but—but you and your idiot friend . . . will answer . . . to me."

Naomi had fashioned the handkerchief into a pad which she now pressed against the wound in Falcon's upper arm, and he lapsed into tight-lipped silence.

Lieutenant Morris started to apologize, but checked as he stepped on an extremely sharp pebble. He glanced down instinctively. Beside some wet and crushed papers something gleamed faintly in the dim light from the carriage lamps. Curious, he bent and took up a tiny figure crafted from pink stone and set with red beads. A child's toy, probably, dropped here by some youngster. He started to throw it aside, but it was rather quaint and his little niece might like to have it. He dropped it into his

31

pocket, then joined Rossiter as a liveried coachman ran up, wheezingly out of breath.

"They had hacks . . . waiting, and they got clean away. . . . Leastways, they didn't get your . . . jewels, milady."

"And they didn't all get away," observed Morris. "Unless that fella lying over there is one of your people, ma'am?"

Naomi jerked her head around. "Oh, the poor creature! Well, do not stand there like stones! Cannot one of you help him?"

"He's dead," muttered Falcon rather faintly.

"Shot to kill, did you?" said Morris. "Better check, coachman. Just in case. Can't always trust your aim in this kind of light, sir. I've known—"

"Check and be damned t'you," snarled Falcon. "I never miss—as you'll discover when . . . when . . ." His voice trailed off.

Distressed, Naomi said, "Oh, he is faint, poor soul!"

"A good time to get him into the coach," said Rossiter with calm common sense. "Give a hand here, coachman. We'd better take him back to the inn. Would you wish that he journey in my carriage, ma'am?"

Morris and the coachman lifted Falcon, and ignoring his protestations that he could walk, started towards Rossiter's carriage.

"No," said my lady autocratically. "Nor shall we take him back to that horrid inn! You will come home with me, August, where you can receive proper care. This person can take a message to—"

"The devil!" Falcon's drooping head jerked up again. "I'll not be maudled over in that pretentious pile, thank you! We'll go back to the inn. My sister's the best nurse I know."

Naomi said with considerable indignation, "If you are not the most perverse and ungrateful of men! That inn is dirty and stuffy, and you will have much better treatment with us! We will take my coach, if you please, gentlemen!"

Obediently, they turned to her coach.

"*Stop!*" roared Falcon. His bearers halted, and he said heatedly, "Had it not been for you, Milady Wilful, we might all be cozily in . . . in feather beds by now. Instead of . . . me having this stupid hole in my arm, and you being dragged through the mud till you look a—proper fright! Now do as I say, you dolts, and put me in the carriage of the block who shot me."

Back turned the bearers with their burden.

"Do not listen to him," said Naomi angrily. "Can you not see that—"

"Enough!" Rossiter's voice cracked like a whip. "Be dashed if ever I heard such tomfoolery!"

"Your opinion carries no weight here," she flared.

"And yours is rubbishing," he said unequivocally. "The gentleman needs medical help, and the closest place for him to get it is the inn. If you persist in journeying on, so be it. I shall escort you. Jamie, put Mr. Falcon in my coach, and—"

"No such thing," raged Falcon, struggling in the arms of his much tried bearers. "I'll not trust myself to the man who tried to murder me!"

"Good God," groaned Rossiter, exasperated. "Must we spend the night here while you two ridiculous people argue? Do *you* escort the lady then, James. I'll take Falcon in charge."

"Had it not been for you, he would not be shot," exclaimed Naomi, who was trembling now and too close to hysteria to be sensible. "Do you fancy I mean to abandon him to your bloodthirsty—"

Her words were cut off by an enraged squeal as Rossiter swept her up in his arms, carried her to the carriage and tossed her inside. "Be quiet, and do as you're told," he said curtly. His stern gaze turned to Maggie who huddled weeping in the far corner. "As for you, my good girl—stop snivelling and tend to your mistress! She's soaked through by the feel of it. Have you far to go, coachman?"

"Better'n twelve miles, sir."

"Oh, egad! 'Tis almost dark and I fancy there will be little sight of the moon tonight. Shall you be able to find your way?"

"Know this country like the back o' me hand, sir, never fear."

"Very good. Then, off you go, coachman! God speed, Jamie."

Swinging into the saddle, Morris said, "I may continue on to Sevenoaks. An I do, I shall call on you when I come to Town. Have a care, dear boy!"

Naomi, however, had no intention of leaving Falcon until she knew he was in good hands. Managing to open the window, she leaned out, and called peremptorily, "Roger, pay no heed to this person. We will follow them and make sure that Mr. Falcon is carried safely to the inn."

Rossiter's shoulder was aching wretchedly, he felt beyond words tired, and his impatience with this bedraggled and argumentative female boiled over. He said irritably, "Good God! Are you still nittering, woman? I vow you're as witless as you are wet! Unless you crave the attentions of another rank rider, spare a thought for your servants and your horses and refrain from frippering about all night.'' He slapped his gloved hand on the rump of the near leader and the carriage jerked forward.

A squeal of rage rang from the carriage as Naomi was flung back against the squabs.

The grinning coachman saluted Rossiter with a wave of his whip, then cracked it over his horses' heads, and the cumbersome vehicle lurched and creaked away.

Rossiter stared after it for a moment. It occurred to him belatedly that he had no idea of the identity of the infuriating woman, and in the dimness had only been able to ascertain that, as Falcon had said, she'd looked a proper fright with her hair all tangled and askew and herself soaked and muddy. To judge from the way she'd spoken to Falcon, she was probably his latest paramour.

'His taste is not what it was,' thought Rossiter dryly.

Leaning back against the heavy oak sideboard in the tiny parlour, Rossiter watched the girl seated on the lumpy sofa and thought that in all his life he had only seen one lady who was lovelier. ''I wish you will not be so worried,'' he said gently. ''It did not appear to me that the bone was broke, and your brother seems in excellent health.''

Half an hour had passed since they'd pulled into the yard of the Red Pheasant Inn, with the excited postboys shouting the news of the murderous hold-up. A great stir had resulted; an awed crowd rushing out to hear the grisly details and watch as the wounded gentleman was assisted inside. This had exasperated Falcon, who'd growled a suggestion that the host charge admission to ''all the yokels having nothing better to do than gawk'' at him. Miss Falcon's appearance had brought an expectant hush, but although the beauty had turned pale, she had disappointed many by neither screaming nor succumbing to a fit of the vapours. Far from disappointed, Rossiter had ordered that a groom be sent off to summon the constable and the apothecary from the neighbouring village, and the injured man had been borne upstairs.

The constable was small, sour, and annoyed to have been summoned from his fireplace. He had made a few notes, declared importantly that the malefactors would be ''dealt with,'' and gone away to send the saddler, who was also the undertaker, after the corpse. Now, Falcon lay in the bed he had bespoken for his sister, while the apothecary did what he might to aid him.

Katrina Falcon turned her fascinating and anxious eyes to Rossiter. "I suppose, as a soldier, you have experience of bullet wounds, Captain. I only know that my father deplores pistols, for he says they are so very deadly. Indeed, whenever August fights a duel Papa begs that he will choose swords."

He smiled. "One might suppose your brother to be very often called out."

"I have lost count," she said simply. "Has he challenged you? From what he told me when he was carried in here, I gained the impression he means to do so."

"He probably does, though it will be some time before he can fight anyone, I suspect. The poor fellow will have to contain his impatience."

His attempt at lightness failed. She said, "One could scarce blame him for being vexed, sir. To have fired a pistol at another man without taking the time to discover his identity was quite insupportable. In truth, I think your friend must be prodigious hot headed."

"I wish you will believe 'twas an accident," he said earnestly. "When a man comes upon a hold-up in the darkness and a fellow rides up with a pistol aimed straight at him—well, he'd be a fool to take chances. Especially when there are already corpses lying about, and—"

At this point, with an irked flush on his pock-marked face, the apothecary joined them, sped upon his way by a blast of profanity.

Miss Falcon stood at once. "Is my brother very badly injured?"

"No, ma'am." For an instant Rossiter thought the apothecary would add "unfortunately," but he restrained himself and reported, "I believe the bone was grazed, but if he keeps to his bed and takes the elixir I'll send round, he should be up and about in a week or so. If not—" He shrugged.

Anxious, she hurried into the bedchamber.

The apothecary glowered at Rossiter. "He says you're responsible, Captain, and will pay me." His hard eyes fastened to the fat purse Rossiter pulled from his pocket, and he grumbled, "I work long enough hours in the daylight, and don't usually come out at night, as I told the man they sent for me. I hope he let you know 'twould be double fee. Five guineas."

"Nonsense! Do you take me for a flat?"

" 'Tis clear you been away at the wars, sir," wailed the apothecary, watching anxiously as Rossiter's long fingers paused on the clasp of the purse. "Prices has gone up since you—"

"They have not quadrupled! I shall pay you two guineas, only because of your disturbed slumbers." He saw the man's small mouth opening for a protest, and added, "But I do not care to be milked, so if this doesn't suit we shall have in the host and I'll enquire of him as to your regular fee, which is likely a crown. Make up your mind."

The apothecary bemoaned the fact that soldiers were hard-hearted men, but he snatched the two guineas as Rossiter made to draw them away, and then looked so smug it was apparent he'd not expected as much.

Rossiter asked, "What was Mr. Falcon ranting about?"

"My hands was too cold and too clumsy, and the bandage was too tight, and he wouldn't swallow the medicine I tried to get down his stubborn throat. An he's a friend of yours, sir, I'm sorry. But he's a difficult gent. Most cantankerous."

Miss Falcon came out looking worried. "He desires a glass of brandy. Is it allowed, sir?"

"By all means, if you want him in a high fever. He may have a tisane, rather."

Picturing the volatile Falcon sipping medicinal tea, Rossiter smothered a grin.

"I sent my woman to fetch some tea half an hour ago," said Miss Falcon. "I suppose they are very busy in the kitchen. I shall have to go down and see if I cannot make it myself. Could you please stay with my brother, sir, until I return?"

The apothecary made a dart for the door. He most certainly could not stay. He had to take a man's foot off in the morning, and must be up early. The door slammed behind him and they could hear him grumbling his way along the hall with many references to the cantankerous Quality.

"Good Lord," muttered Rossiter. "I pity his patient! Well, I'll get on my way, ma'am."

She begged him to remain "just a few minutes" longer. He wanted nothing more than to get to his home, but he could not resist those pleading eyes, and agreed. "Though I doubt you'll get Falcon to drink a tisane."

An unexpectedly militant light came into her eyes. "He will drink it," she declared, and hurried away.

Rossiter glanced at the closed bedroom door, then sat down and stretched out his long legs. Gad, but he was tired! He gripped

36

his left shoulder and flexed it carefully, wondering if the confounded wound would ever stop aching. Of all the beastly luck, to be involved in this nonsensical farce instead of tending to his own—

A crash resounded, followed by Falcon's irate howl. "Has everybody died? I require assistance! This year! *Katrina!*"

From the next room came a pounding on the wall, and an irritated guest roared something about being allowed to get some sleep. His answer was a crash indicative of glass shattering against the wall, followed by shouted insults expressing Falcon's decided lack of interest in his neighbour's wishes.

Rossiter stuck his head around the bedroom door. "You'll have the Watch here if you do not cease your caterwauling. What assistance do you require?"

"Some brandy—and your blood," snarled Falcon, sinking back against the pillows.

Despite his hostile manner, he was very pale and looked exhausted. Rossiter knew all too well what a visit from an apothecary could be like, especially if a bone was chipped, and he checked the scornful remark he'd been about to utter. Walking into the room, he said instead, "Try to behave with a *soupçon* of sense, else you'll never kill anyone again."

"Do not refine on that!"

"Dash it all, man! You certainly know 'twas an accident!"

"Easy to say, when *you're* standing there, and *I'm* lying here." Falcon's jaw set. After a brief pause through which he appeared to be holding his breath, he said in a less sure voice, "I fancy you think this poetic justice."

Rossiter leaned against the bedpost and watched him thoughtfully. "An you refer to our brawl at Eton, you must attach a deal more importance to it than I did."

"Importance—hell! I thought it damned ridiculous. I did not plead for your so gallant intervention."

"Charming as ever, I see," drawled Rossiter. "You must not fail to write to me if ever you should plan on saying anything pleasant. I'd not miss it for the world."

A faint glint of amusement came into Falcon's eyes, but the single word he uttered was not conciliating.

"I entered your little fray," explained Rossiter, "only because the odds were four to one. I'd have done the same for any fellow."

"And won yourself precisely the same reward. A black eye and broken nose as I remember—no?"

"Your memory is reliable, at least. Most gentlemen would surely have offered a word or two of thanks. Still, I soon realized that the withholding of such courtesies was not remarkable in your case."

"Then I taught you something," sneered Falcon.

"Just so." Rossiter straightened up. "Good day to you, sir."

"No—don't just walk off, dammitall! If you must abandon me, at least have the decency to fetch me some brandy before you go. There's a decanter in that revolting parlour."

"Yes, and your sister would have my ears did I give you some. She has gone to brew you a tisane." He chuckled at the response, and when Falcon ran out of expletives, he said, "The lady has my sympathy. Is there anything you would like me to do for *her* before I leave?"

"No, fiend seize you! Wait! Be sure she has enough blankets. She'll likely insist on me remaining in this accursed bed."

"Yes. She seems a most unselfish creature."

"Does she indeed! Keep your eyes from her, I warn you!"

"Oh, Lord! Must you be such a fool? No man could keep his eyes from her. She's one of the most beautiful women I ever saw."

His eyes blazing, Falcon struggled to one elbow. He was panting, two spots of colour high on his cheekbones. "An you dare pester her whilst I'm laid here by—by the heels . . . !"

"Be at ease, you silly clod. I admired the lady merely. A fine villain you take me for!"

"Be assured of it!"

"If you weren't in that bed, by God—" Rossiter broke off. "No! For God's sake—get back—" He sprang to catch the injured man as he managed to clamber out of bed, only to sag dizzily. Guiding him back onto the pillows, Rossiter wrenched his shoulder and said with considerable irritation, "If ever I saw such a fire-eater! I've barely set foot in England, and have no slightest designs upon your sister."

"You had best not have! My . . . prejudices are few, but 'fore heaven I draw the line at . . . at having Katrina plagued by a man whose name is a by-word for . . . treachery and dishonour!"

For an instant Rossiter was so astounded he could do no more than stare at Falcon's pale and sweating face. Then, he said very softly, "I think you must explain that, sir."

"Faith, but your astonishment is well done!" Falcon's lip curled. "Much I need to explain! Why are you come home save

38

to support your sire? Though 'tis little he'll gain from your presence after the unlovely record you've built in the Low Countries, and—"

Rossiter threw up one hand peremptorily. "We do not discuss my record. Why should my father need my support?"

"Oh, stop your gammoning, man! Am I to believe you did not know that three months ago Rossiter Bank failed; Rossiter Investment Company failed; that your sire was proved a thief and embezzler, and has sunk your name in deep dis—"

Rossiter had turned very white, but now his face became livid. His hand whipped out to fasten on Falcon's nightshirt. Hauling him up, he said between his teeth, "Curse you for a liar! My father never did a dishonest thing in his life!"

"Go and ask him!" Falcon beat feebly at Rossiter's arm. "And—and then you may come back and go down on your . . . knees and—and beg me not to run you through!"

"Let him go! Oh! What are you doing to him?"

The shrieked words cut through the red haze of wrath that had enveloped Rossiter. He released his grip abruptly, derived a savage satisfaction from hearing Falcon swear as he fell back on the pillows, and stalked to the door.

Two women stood on the threshold. One was a thin and stern-faced abigail who carried a laden tray; the other was Katrina Falcon. Her horror-filled eyes accused him. She pulled her skirts closer as he passed. "For shame, to attack a helpless man," she said in disgust.

"Your brother will never be helpless, madam," he riposted, "until someone amputates his vicious tongue!"

Running down the stairs, his conscience acknowledged that he had behaved like a cad in handling Falcon roughly. It was a small and barely heard voice. Most of his concern was with his father. He must get home at once and learn exactly what had happened.

He frowned grimly. He had thought his fighting days were done. Now, it appeared, they might be just beginning!

❄ *Chapter 4* ❧

but I am very sure his pockets contained nothing to warrant

Naomi coaxed a tendril of her damp hair into place and inspected herself in the dressing table mirror. Wet and witless, he had called her. The horrid boor! She had, perhaps, been a trifle upset. Who would not be after such a terrifying experience? But he'd shown her not the slightest compassion. Wet and witless, indeed! She had been soaked and dirty, true, but her face was free of mud now, and Maggie had brushed her hair into a richly shining mantle about her shoulders. She was a little pale from shock and weariness, but this served to emphasize the clear green of her eyes. If the tall soldier could see her now . . . She tossed her head impatiently, and drew the lacy collar of her white satin dressing gown higher. Much she cared what he would think. Only, although it had been almost dark and she'd not really seen him clearly, there was something about the captain that troubled her. Something that hovered at the back of her mind, refusing to be drawn to full recollection.

"I know as you're worrying for poor Mr. Falcon," said Maggie, hurrying from the door and a whispered conversation with the first footman. "But—"

"Mr. Falcon!" exclaimed Naomi with a guilty start. "Yes, of course I am. I think his wound was not serious, but poor Miss Katrina is likely in need of me. I should be with her now but for that horrid soldier!"

"Wicked, I calls it," agreed Maggie with gratifying indignation. "To pick you up like a sack of oats and toss you—"

The memory of that unheard-of indignity brought rage smouldering into Naomi's eyes once more. "He was an arrogant brute!"

"What had no right to seize your sweet self in his great strong fists and throw you in the coach like any—"

"If I'd but had my little silver pistol to hand he would not have touched me so, I promise you!"

"Touched you, milady! Mauled you, more like! And heaved you about as if you was any bale of hay, with no least—"

My lady's eyes narrowed dangerously. "Refer to me as a sack or a bale once more, wretched minx," she warned between her teeth, "and I shall pinch you! Hard!"

Maggie lowered her big brown eyes demurely, and murmured her apologies, but her lips twitched suspiciously. Long before Mr. Simon Lutonville had gone out to Italy, or entertained any hope of acceding to the earldom, little Maggie Osgood, the head gardener's daughter, and Miss Naomi had played with their dolls together. They had been mistress and maid since Naomi had returned to England, but the affection between them remained. The pert village lass knew just how far she could go before she was in danger, and that however heinous her offence she would never collect a hard box on the ear, or have to endure the endless succession of slaps or scratches that many of her friends received from their employers.

" 'Tis because I so loves you that I am put about to think of him daring to treat you so rough," she declared earnestly. "And after his evil friend shooting down that dear handsome Mr. Falcon like he was a common thief! Whatever the earl will have to say, I dassen't think. Best hasten, milady. His lor'ship be waiting for you like a proper thundercloud."

Naomi stood, stifling a yawn. "I wish my father would let me explain in the morning."

"Aye, you're proper wore out, poor lamb. Just tell his lor'ship as quick as you can, and don't loiter about down there."

Naomi's smile was rueful. Maggie followed her into the hall and said, "I be going to put a hot brick 'twixt the sheets, so by the time you come back upstairs your bed will be all toasty warm waiting for you."

Naomi thanked her and walked along the hall.

Watching that rather slow progress to the stairs, it seemed to Maggie that her lady's glowing head was not held quite as proudly as usual. She thought, 'I hope she doesn't tell his lor'ship where we was today.' She had seen the earl's scowl, and picturing his reaction to that piece of news, murmured, "Lawks a mussy! The fox would be in with the hens and no mistake!"

41

She gave a little squeak as the first footman came up silent-footed to bestow a pinch upon her plump derrière.

"That won't be nothing new and strange," he said with a grin. "Not in this here household it won't. Why're you droopin' like last week's dirty wash, Maggie?"

"No such thing, Mister Audacious," denied Maggie huffily, then added with a worried frown, "only . . . sometimes I feel that sorry for her. She's so alone, poor little thing."

"Go on, woman! What is it? You got windmills aloft, or something? Ain't she surrounded by friends, and all the fine gents admiring and flattering her day and night? Ain't she got a great fortune to keep her company, and everything she could want for?"

"You're a wicked young man, Robert Hinton," said Maggie without equivocation. "With naughty roving hands. And like most men you don't see what's under your nose 'til you get bit by it! My lady's got everything, all right—'cepting the thing she most wants. *Kindness*, Mr. H. A look with a bit o'love in it now and then." She scowled. "Precious little affection she got from her mama. And *he* don't know the meaning of the word, with his high-in-the-instep pride, and his glooms and rages!"

"Ar, well you should've heard his peership ranting and raving when you was so late coming home. Cor! And the look on his face just now'll have her shaking in her shoes, I shouldn't wonder!"

Maggie looked troubled, but said staunchly, "She ain't afeared of him, never think it! Not of him nor of nothing! A right plucked 'un she be."

When Naomi entered the withdrawing room, however, for a brief moment she did feel a surge of fear. Simon Ordway Lutonville, seventh Earl of Collington, was standing by the glowing hearth, one hand on the mantel, the other holding a half-full wineglass. He was not a tall man and enjoyed his table, but he had refused to allow himself to run to fat, and at three and fifty wore his clothes well. He stood very still, his immaculately bewigged head slightly downbent as he gazed into the flames, but anger radiated from every line of him, and when he swung around as the lackey closed the doors, the expression on his handsome face was the one his wife had so dreaded.

Nerving herself, Naomi walked across the luxuriously appointed room, affecting not to notice the heavy scowling brows, the spark in the light green eyes, the tight set of the jaw of this man who had sired her, and whom she so little understood.

"Why, Papa," she said, with faint irony, "how upset you are, and have left your card party early! I had not dreamed you would be anxious for my sake."

His lips thinned, and the scowl deepened. He said coldly, "So you take me for an unnatural parent. Be comforted. I already ascertained that you were not hurt. When the rogues are caught, they'll pay for daring to lay hands on you. That, I promise! Was your fool of a coachman foxed? How came he to squat there like a curst block while a lady of Quality was assaulted by crude animals?"

Politely stifling a yawn, Naomi sank into a chair. "I am very tired, sir. Might this not wait until morning?"

The earl watched her. The rich satin dressing gown clung to her shapely figure, and her hair, brushed free of powder, glowed in a rich chestnut-brown cloud about her lovely face. She was a vexatious and defiant chit, not yet broken to bridle, but in a way he was proud of her spirit, and certainly she was a credit to him. Controlling his burning impatience, he crossed to the sideboard, poured a glass of wine and carried it to her. "No, it might not wait 'til morning. Here. This will restore you. And let me hear no missish airs about its being the first you've ever tasted."

Naomi sipped the wine, then said demurely, "As you say, Papa."

He gave a faintly amused grunt, and returned to prop his broad shoulders against the mantel. "Well?"

"I think you have already questioned Roger Coach—"

"The man's a dolt. I'll have it from you, if you please. And firstly, I'll know what the devil you were doing frippering around Canterbury Cathedral."

"Improving my mind, sir. I was so long out of England there is much I've not seen of my own land."

"You shall see it when you've my permission, and are properly chaperoned."

"With all due respect, Papa, I am of age and—"

"And are a lady of Quality, and will behave like one."

"La, but you are become very prim of a sudden."

"Perhaps. But I have told you before that what I countenanced in Italy will not do in England. Never flash your eyes at me like that, my girl! You're not too grown up to be spanked, I'll remind you, and so long as you dwell under my roof, you'll obey me!"

Pale with anger, she said, "On the day you raise your hand to me, sir, I shall leave your roof. I am not cut of the same cloth as poor Mama."

43

The earl's lips set tightly and he took a pace towards her. She saw the fine eyes narrow with wrath, and her heart beat faster. "Besides," she went on, struggling to keep her voice steady, "had I been accompanied by three chaperones and Falcon's hound, they would have availed me nothing. The thieves were waiting for us and we were surrounded before Roger had a chance to so much as think of his blunderbuss."

"Waiting for you? What the deuce d'you mean by that?"

"I mean that they were evidently hiding in the shrubs, waiting for some likely looking coach to come along." Puzzled by such a silly question, she added, "Whatever did you think?"

He shrugged. "I suppose I must admit 'twas a fortunate circumstance that you met the Falcons. I've no love for the half-breed, but at least he was able to prevent your being robbed. He knows one end of a pistol from t'other, certainly." He had seen her irked frown and said slyly, "Alas, and I have offended Madame Tolerance. I should have used his proper title, I collect. 'The Mandarin' then, is that acceptable?"

She said with cold emphasis, "August Falcon's grandmama on his mother's side was the daughter of a Chinese princess and a Russian nobleman. His grandfather was English, as were his father's parents. I believe that would result in his having less than one-fourth mixed blood. Furthermore, if her portrait is even a remotely close likeness, Mrs. Natasha Falcon must have been the most beautiful lady in London, half-breed or no, and I—"

"She was ravishing, and if you fancy that makes her grandson one jot more acceptable, disabuse your mind of the notion. What is it, m'dear? Have you a fondness for his fortune? An inducement, and he's a handsome young devil, I admit, but I'll not give my consent to an alliance in *that* direction, and so I warn you."

"I believe I have not asked it of you, sir. But it is thanks to August that my valuables were not taken. He was shot, were you aware?"

"So your fool of a coachman said." The earl paced closer, watching her narrowly. "What he did not say, but that I discovered by merest chance, was that you called at Promontory Point today. You will be so good as to explain why."

Naomi's nerves jumped, but she managed to answer with an assumption of nonchalance. "The weather was dreadful and our wheel about to fall off. I knew we were near the Point, so I instructed Roger to try for help there."

44

"Very plausible." He smiled thinly. "And now pray let me hear the truth. You went hoping to see young Rossiter again. Still pant for him, do you? Have you no pride?"

Her cheeks hot, she said, "I would think I have made it abundantly clear that I do *not* pant for him, as you rather inelegantly put it, sir! And my pride is intact, I promise you!"

"I hope the same may be said for mine! Old Rossiter must have properly sniggered to see you go crawling—"

"Sir Mark was in Town, as I knew, else I'd never have set foot on the property!"

"Well, that's something, at least. Place closed up, eh? Then you got no help after all?"

"We did, in point of fact. Mr. Newby Rossiter was there."

"Indeed? You must have found much to talk about."

"I had—a few words with the gentleman."

"Since Newby Rossiter bears no resemblance to a gentleman, one can but hope they were very few." Fully expecting a heated contradiction, the earl heard none. Intrigued, he sat on the arm of a great wing chair and said shrewdly, "Stole a kiss, did he? I'm not surprised. You invited it by calling on him unchaperoned."

"I did *not* call on him," she declared, goaded. "At least, not knowingly! And as for a kiss, all the creature got was a broken toe."

He gave a shout of laughter. "Bravo! The young rake will know better than to maul a ginger tabby next time! Well, then. Are you ready to honour your wager?"

"Wager?" Puzzled, she said, "I do not follow you, sir."

"Oh yes you do, Madam Trickery! Did I not tell you that despite the fascinations of the Low Countries, your gallant captain would now find it expedient to return home and try to mend his fences? Come now, never pretend you have forgot. You wagered me fifty guineas that he would not be so gauche. You must pay up, m'dear."

She stared at him. "Do you say . . . Gideon is—is back in England?"

"What, didn't Newby tell you? I'd have thought—" He checked, and said musingly, "Unless . . . Did the rogue come here before ever he showed his face to his sire, I wonder?" And with a scornful snort, "There's desperation for you!"

"Here?" she gasped. "Gideon was here? At Collington?"

"You may believe he was! The young varmint had the bare-faced gall to present himself on my doorstep. And soon got thrown off it, you may be sure!''

"But—but whatever did he say? Did you ask him—''

"I asked him nothing. I refused to receive him!''

"Papa! Whatever else, Gideon is well born and the son of your good friend. I cannot—''

"My former friend," put in the earl dulcetly.

"Even so, I cannot credit that you did not at least have the courtesy to explain matters.''

"*Courtesy*, is it? Much courtesy he has shown *you*, flaunting his wantons about, with not a scruple for the fact he was betrothed to you!''

She said rather wearily, "I think he is not the first man to take a mistress, Papa.''

"I collect you refer to my own reputation,'' he snapped, bristling.

Naomi looked at him steadily, for his numerous successes with London's ladies were no secret.

"The situation is entirely different," he said, taking a turn about the room and waving his wineglass to emphasize his statements. "I am a widower, my children grown." He avoided her eyes here, since his amorous adventures had distressed his wife long before her demise. "A gentleman may take one mistress, or a dozen—can he afford the pretty creatures. But he is required to exercise discretion. Young Rossiter pays small heed to the conventions, and evidently ain't learned yet that the man who is so callous as to leave his mistress and her brat to starve, has put himself beyond the pale! For that alone, he'd be blackballed.''

"So you knew there was a child," she said quietly.

"Of course I knew! All England knows, I shouldn't wonder. Men enjoy a juicy piece of gossip just as much as you ladies, m'dear. If I heard it once, I heard it a score of times, to say nothing of his frequent assignations with a lightskirt in some garden or other. But''—he gave a gesture of impatience—''you knew all this, and were no less disgusted than I, as I recall.''

"I had not known about the—the child.''

"Humph. And Master Newby was pleased to put you in possession of that detail, was he? Famous! And typical that he should repeat such tales to a lady. Well, if nothing else, it should convince you that explanations from me are neither required nor necessary. Captain Rossiter would have to be a proper fool not to know damned well where he stands with us. When he had the gall to demand that Pawson carry up his card, I could scarce believe it. I was so sure 'twas a ruse in fact, I stole a look at him from the landing. Blessed if I'd have recognized him, for he's thin as any rail and bears little resemblance to the arrogant young Buck who went riding off to—''

''My God!'' Her father's words had struck a chord, and Naomi paled, the wine splashing onto her dressing gown as she cried out a shocked, ''Then—'twas him!''

''Eh? What the deuce are you flying into a pucker about now?''

''The men who rid up to help us during the hold-up were both officers. I had never met the one who shot August, but I kept thinking there was something familiar about his friend. I realize now that it must—Oh, Lud! 'Tis incredible! But—it must have been—''

''*Gideon . . . Rossiter?*'' he interrupted, almost equally astonished. ''The deuce!'' They stared at each other for a stunned instant. Then the earl said with a slow grin, ''In that event, I'd not be surprised to discover 'twas all a hoax! The young devil likely arranged the hold-up only to try and restore himself to your good graces.''

Shocked, she said, ''No, how can you think so awful a thing? Two men were killed, and—''

''Yokels! Pah! England has an over-abundance of such!''

''—and Gideon—if 'twas Gideon—did not even recognize me.''

Her caveat was disregarded. Vastly amused, he said, ''I've come at the heart of it, stap me if I ain't! Why, the slippery rascal! No, never look so starched up. Give him credit for a good try, at least!''

She shook her head stubbornly. ''I know he has behaved very badly, but I'll not believe this of him. Besides, an his motives are as you say, he played his cards poorly. His manner towards me was far from conciliating, to say the least of it. I feel *sure* that he did not recognize me. 'Twas almost dark, and I had fallen and was soaking wet, with my hair all down and over my face. I doubt *you* would have known me at that moment.'' More shaken than she wished to reveal, she set her unfinished wine aside and came to her feet. ''Now, sir, with your permission, I shall bid you good night.''

My lord stood as his daughter swept him a curtsy. ''Very well, get to your bed, child, and we shall be charitable and accept your version of the affair. In which case, I should offer up thanks for your—er, knights in shining armour.'' He chuckled to him-

47

self. "Falcon and Rossiter! A half-breed, and a rascally and disgraced opportunist! The devil anoint me if ever a lady won herself two more dubious champions!"

Naomi paused and observed coldly, "You were the one chose him for my husband, Papa."

"True enough. But that was long ago, and now you are the one refuses all others. You've rejected some damned fine offers. 'Tis past time you allied yourself with a worthy gentleman."

"Is there such a creature, sir?" Her lip curled. " 'Pon rep, but I begin to doubt it."

He chuckled. "Not such a green girl, are you, my pet? Then settle for a rich one, worthy or not. You're two and twenty, and I am being hinted that you're on the shelf—though damn 'em, that's nine parts jealousy on the part of the women, at least. Still, it does not suit me to have a spinster daughter, so make up your mind, or I'll make it up for you! There's a fine gentleman fairly slavering to lay his riches at your feet, and—Well, I shall say no more tonight. You look hagged. Get to your bed, and pleasant dreams."

Pleasant dreams! If she had any dreams tonight he had ensured that they would be nightmares . . .

Lord Simon strolled to the door with her, then said casually, "Oh, by the bye, send down the package before you retire."

Naomi tried to gather her badly scattered wits. "Package . . . ?"

"The package you collected from the jeweller in Canterbury." His smile a little tight, he added, "Your head is really full of windmills tonight."

"Oh, my goodness! What with all the excitement, I had quite forgot."

The earl's fingers tightened about the door handle. "You *did* get it?"

"Yes, sir. 'Tis—in my reticule, I think."

He said very softly, "One trusts it is! We'll have your woman down here with it. Now." He crossed to the bell pull.

Five minutes later, his howl of rage set knees to knocking all over the great house.

The postilions had become minor celebrities and the patrons of the Red Pheasant Inn had been quite willing to gratify their thirst in exchange for ever more lurid descriptions of the highwaymen. By the time Rossiter found them in the stables they were so inebriated that they were quite unable to ride. He was unable to find a light carriage, so hired a hack to carry him home, and packing only his basic necessities in the saddlebags, desired the proprietor to hold the rest of his belongings at the inn until he sent a servant for them the following day.

It was a long and unpleasant journey. Like Roger Coachman, he knew the road well, and now that the rain had stopped, a quarter moon occasionally crept from behind shredding clouds to light his way. The air was still damp, however, and a strong wind had come up, chilling him to the bone and whipping occasional sprays of water from the drenched trees. He scarcely noticed his discomfort. Mile after mile, August Falcon's harsh words haunted him: "Your sire was proved a thief and embezzler . . ." It was a mistake, of course. Or a deliberate lie.

His thoughts drifted back to Eton. Falcon had been a year ahead of him and although his birth brought him mockery and derision, his fists had won him a measure of respect. Gideon, hiding his own loneliness behind an air of cool self-possession, had rather admired the older boy and would have liked to make a friend of him. His one attempt along those lines had been made when Falcon was attacked and outnumbered, and his intervention had won him only blazing resentment, and a snarled, "In future, keep your pure English nose out of my affairs!" Rossiter had taken Falcon at his word and had avoided him like the plague, but although they were not, nor ever could be friends, he had never heard of Falcon being less than square and aboveboard in his dealings, and could not credit that the man was a liar.

Impatient to be at home and get to the bottom of it all, Rossiter knew better than to risk a gallop on bad roads made worse by heavy rains. There were few travellers abroad on such a dismal night. An occasional solitary horseman or a labouring carriage would loom up and quickly disappear again. Rossiter swung his mount around a laden wain bound for London's early market, oilcloth tied over the cargo, and a cheery hail issuing from what appeared to be a pile of sacking but was presumably the driver. Half an hour later, a stagecoach rushed past at reckless speed with a great blaring of the horn and a thunder of hooves. The heavy wheels sent up another spray of mud, but Rossiter was glad to see the coach, since it bore testimony to the fact that the roads were passable, at least as far as Canterbury.

He turned east three miles before reaching that city, and at once conditions worsened. The moonlight filtered between wind-whipped glistening black branches to show a lane that was a river of mud and ruts. Rossiter guided the horse along the hedgerows, but there were places where the ditch was steep and treacherous and he had to go cautiously. He had dreamed so often of returning to his home, but had pictured doing so on a bright, sunny morning, through grounds brilliant with flowers, the great house waiting in serene dignity to welcome him, and the mill lifting its ancient roof against the trees. This was a far cry from such a pleasant homecoming. There was something ominous about the stormy night. The wind seemed to howl a warning; the sudden gusts might almost have been striving to push him back the way he had come. Foolish fancies, he thought. Born of weariness and a nagging worry.

His unease intensified when he reached the lodge gates. There was no sign of life, nor did anyone respond to his hail. The rain began to pound down again. He dismounted, muttering curses, tethered the hack to a shrub and struggled with the heavy gate. Riding on again, it occurred to him that either everyone at the Point must have gone early to bed, or the trees had become very dense, for he should by now have been able to see some light from the windows of the main house.

He guided the horse along the drivepath, his eyes straining up the hill for some sign of life. By the time he reached the moat he had accepted the fact that his family must be in Town. Some servants had certainly been left, but they had evidently retired. He crossed the bridge and rode around to the stableyard. Not a glimmer showed from the long building that housed the outside staff. His shout echoed eerily but brought no response. He threw one leg over the pommel and slid from the saddle, then staggered. Lord, but he was so tired he ached with it. Angry and frustrated, he shouted again. "Dammit! Where *is* everybody?"

He had as well have questioned the puddle his boot splashed into, and not wasting more time he led the hack into the barn and his cold fingers groped for tinder box and flint. The feeble flame revealed a row of stalls with only one occupant, a sway-backed old grey that blinked at him sleepily. The animal must belong to a servant, but where the deuce were all the other horses? His mind was too numbed to grapple with the problem now. He must get to his bed before he fell asleep on his feet. First, however, the hack must be tended. Wearily, he lighted a lantern. Ten minutes later, having rubbed down the animal and provided it with oats and water, he took up the saddlebags, tossed them over his shoulder, and stumbled across the yard, making his way through the kitchen garden and up the back steps.

Unprecendentedly, the door was locked.

It was the last straw. With a cry of wrath he drove his boot at the handle. The wood splintered and a second kick sent the door slamming open.

The house was black as pitch and utterly silent. He groped his way across the kitchen and along the service corridor. In the Great Hall he tugged on the bell pull to no avail, then shouted again, his "Is anyone at home?" causing the prisms on the chandeliers to chime gently, but winning no other response. Disappointed, and reeling with exhaustion, he dragged himself up the stairs. His own bed would not be made up, of course, but there might be blankets in Sir Mark's bedchamber. Coming to the door, he opened it and made his way to the great tester bed. His outstretched hand encountered an eiderdown. With a groan of relief he let the saddlebags slide to the floor, and stopping only to shed his cloak and boots and unbuckle his sword-belt, he crawled between the blankets.

He had scarcely closed his eyes than the sounds awoke him. Violent sounds. Thumps, crashes, voices raised in wrath and anguish. For a few seconds he thought himself back with his regiment, then he remembered and, groaning a curse, pulled the covers over his head. The sounds grew louder and the floor vibrated. A full-throated howl propelled him from the bed. Seething with rage, he took a step, then paused, taken aback to see sunlight streaming through the windows of his father's vast bedchamber. He must have slept the night away. His swift scan of the room revealed only the furnishings—no trace of clothing or personal effects. They were away, all right. Nothing in that to cause alarm. If they were not in Town at Rossiter Court, Papa could have gone into the shires, or taken Gwen to Bath for the waters. Still, 'twas odd that not one servant had come to wait on him, for the grooms must surely have seen his hack in the stable and realized someone of the family was home. Besides, even when Sir Mark departed for a lengthy journey, most of the staff remained at Promontory Point, and never had this room been so stripped of all personal belongings . . .

Another crash recalled him to his purpose. Not waiting to pull on his boots, he wrenched the door open and strode along the corridor.

From the head of the stairs he had a full view of the altercation. "What the *devil*? Have done!" he shouted.

51

The larger of the combatants hurtled across the Great Hall, slammed against a medieval oak chair, and slithered to the floor. The survivor ran one hand through his considerably dishevelled hair and looked up.

"As you . . . wish, dear boy," panted Lieutenant James Morris. "Sorry to throw your . . . your people about, but the silly fella wouldn't listen to a . . . word I said."

Rossiter ran down the stairs and clasped his hand strongly. "Jamie! Welcome! Did you just arrive?"

"Got here last night, my pippin. Couldn't raise a soul at the front, but found a back door open. Wouldn't have intruded y'know, but you have all my gear, and my spare lettuce is in my razor case."

"Gad! I should have thought of that! My apologies, but I couldn't hire a coach, so left most of our things at the Red Pheasant, meaning to—"

"*What?* D'you say I've to ride all the way back to that blasted inn again? Well, if that ain't the shabbiest thing I ever heard! Pox on you, Ross!"

"I'll send one of my father's servants down there and have your things delivered, I promise you. Meanwhile, you can use my razor. How the deuce did you find your way here?"

"With considerable difficulty! Luckily I was given quite understandable directions by a most obliging midwife making a late call. Thought I might not find you here, to say truth. Had I not seen *my* lady for six years, I'd likely head first in her direction." The smile faded from Rossiter's eyes, noting which Morris added warily, "Ah! You did, I see. No—er, difficulties, I trust?"

"None I cannot come to the root of speedily enough. Why have you such a glum face? Are you thinking my lady has forgot me? Well, do not. She's not the type to vow and forget."

"Still . . . six years . . . ," said Morris, watching him from the corner of his eye. "A frightful lapse, old lad. Not that I wish to blow out your candles, but—anything might have happened, y'know."

"What a dismals dispenser! Come now, cheer up. You're in need of sustenance is what it is. Where did you sleep?"

"Took the liberty of racking up in your withdrawing room. Too tired to climb the stairs." Taking in his host's rumpled appearance and shoeless feet, Morris asked, "Your man—ah, away, old lad?"

"Don't have one at present, but there must be someone keeping an eye on the place. With luck there'll be food in the—"

"Ho, no you don't!" interrupted a grim and husky voice. The lieutenant's antagonist had risen and was aiming a large horse pistol at them. "The imperdence of it," he said, his scratch wig tilted over one eyebrow, but his square features flushed and belligerent. "A fine state of affairs we've come to in this 'ere country when military coves break into the 'ouses of the gentry, make theirselves at 'ome, and then—wiv not so much as a twinge of conscience fer their sins—plan to raid the larder! Shocking is what I calls it! Proper shocking! I'm taking you two soldier boys in charge."

"Who the devil are you?" demanded Rossiter.

"If it was any of your bread and butter, which it ain't, I'd tell you as me name's Enoch Tummet. Now you and yer friend is going to take a little trot to the cellar where you can stay while I fetch the constable. The idea! Trying to mill a ken while Tummet's guarding it! The very idea!"

"You are a fool," said Morris. "I stole nothing. Furthermore, this gentleman is Captain Gideon Rossiter and he lives here."

"My eye and Uncle 'Arry," scoffed the large Mr. Tummet, stepping forward and waving his pistol suggestively towards the kitchen hall.

"I cannot vouch for your relations," said Rossiter. "And why the deuce my father would hire you to guard his house I cannot guess. But I assure you that I am Gideon Rossiter."

"Ar, but even if you is, which you ain't, number one: I'm a *proper* guard executing of me duty, and number two: this 'ere 'ouse don't belong to the Rossiters no more, it don't. Now you two fancy talking scroungers best get along 'fore me finger gets tired of 'olding back this 'ere trigger."

The colour drained from Rossiter's face and a blaze came into his eyes. He said grittily, "I will move not a step 'til I know what the devil you're talking about."

"Here we go gathering nuts in May," sang Morris, starting to skip about holding out his coattails. "Nuts in May, nuts in May. Here we go gathering nuts in May, all of a Sunday morning."

Mr. Tummet's jaw sagged, and watching this performance glassy eyed, he whispered, "Cor lumme! The poor cove's gone orf 'is tibby!"

Rossiter blurred across the space between them. Before Tummet could recover, the pistol was smashed from his hand. A brick seemed to explode under his chin, and for a while he quite lost touch with the performance of his duty.

Massaging bruised knuckles and looking down at the sprawled guard, Rossiter muttered, "Jolly well done, Jamie."

Morris looked at him with compassion. The poor fellow was white as any sheet. "That was a hell of a way to learn of it, Gideon," he said. "My apologies. I should have warned you."

"Bin in all the newspapers," said Mr. Tummet, spreading butter thickly on a slice of toast. " 'Course, you two gents couldn't be 'spected to know that, seein's you bin orf fighting." Apparently holding no grudge for having been knocked down, he winked at Rossiter across the laden kitchen table, and once again expressed his admiration for "any gent what 'as such a beautiful right. Furthermore," he went on, "bein' as I'm yer prisoner o'war, sir, might I be allowed another slice o' that there 'am? Partial to 'am, I is. Not as I'd 'ave took it uninvited, like. Agin the law. But since yer forcing me into crime, as y'might say, I can't be blamed. Right, sir?"

They had placed the guard under what Morris called a "flag of truce," to which bending of the law he had agreed when presented with a gold sovereign and the promise of a hearty breakfast. In no time he had started the kitchen fire and set a pan of water to heat. Their raid on the larder had shown it well stocked, which, Tummet explained, was because the family had been in residence only yesterday. While the two officers washed and shaved, their "prisoner of war" had cheerfully fried ham and eggs, found a keg of ale, and a slab of cheese, and toasted several slices of bread.

By the time they had come down to the fragrant kitchen, Rossiter was somewhat recovered from the initial shock, and now, sliding another slice of ham onto Tummet's plate, he said, "I find it all so inexplicable, Jamie. My father is a very rich man."

"So 'e was, sir," said Tummet around a mouthful of ham. " 'Til 'e tried to pay orf them as 'e owed." He waved his knife at the stunned soldier, and added lugubriously, "Ruinated 'isself is what he done. Don't do no good, mate. They got 'im anyway, and now the Courts is trying to force 'im to sell this 'ere loverly mansion fer debt. Cor! 'E'd 'ave done better to grab what 'e could lay 'is 'ands on and clear orf outta the country."

"'Twill break his heart,' thought Rossiter.

"Sir Mark Rossiter is an honourable gentleman," declared Morris, then spoiled this impressive reproof by adding, "but there's something in what Tummet says, Gideon. If your papa had—"

"Don't talk such fustian," interrupted Rossiter, his voice harsh. "Do you fancy my father would let his stockholders and investors down?"

"They didn't waste no time in letting 'im dahn, guv'nor." Tummet reached for another piece of toast. "I dunno the whole lot, mind, but from what I 'eard, some o' the richest gents as 'ad funds in Rossiter Bank, drawed out every last groat, the night 'fore the scandal got known. Dirty, I calls it. Proper dirty."

"My . . . God . . . ," breathed Rossiter, leaning back in his chair and staring blindly at the bowl of mustard.

"If you don't mind my asking, Ross," said Morris. "Who—er, were they?"

Rossiter drew a hand across his eyes. "I don't know all of them. My father and I disagreed on business matters and my interests were more with the shipyards. I wish to heaven I'd—" He caught himself up and added, "Norberly was one. And Derrydene. And some others, to a lesser extent, I think."

The lieutenant's honest hazel eyes grew round with astonishment. "What, Lord Norberly and Sir Louis Derrydene? Damn! I can scarce credit it! They're *very* fine gentlemen."

Rossiter jerked upright in his chair and glared fiercely at him. "My father is a fine gentlemen too, I'll have you know!"

"Oh, I've not—not the least doubt of it," stammered Morris, dismayed. "I meant no—That is, I only mean—well, one would think they were not the type one would find mixed up in—"

"Mixed up in—*what*, pray?" snarled Rossiter, a flush of anger on his thin face. "Embezzlement, perchance?"

Tummet said soothingly, "Now, now. Be easy, gents. Don't go getting all warm round the perishing ear 'oles."

Rossiter stood, fists clenched and eyes blazing. "I would like an explanation, if you please, Lieutenant."

"Hello . . . ? Is anyone about . . . ?"

The three men stared speechlessly at one another as the gruff male voice rang from the direction of the front hall.

" 'Ere," said Tummet, heaving himself from his chair with a scared look. "I'd best go and find out who's come to pay me a morning call." He ran out, then stuck his head around the door and hissed, "You gents better get ready to 'op 'orf. Quick-like!" He vanished from sight.

Morris said urgently, "I'll go and collect my things."

"Afraid to be seen with me?" sneered Rossiter.

"Don't be such a gudgeon." Considerably irritated, Morris stamped along the hall to the rear servants' stairs.

Tummet ran back into the kitchen, his brown eyes very round. "A lady's come calling, Cap'n," he wheezed. "But not fer me, more's the pity! 'Er groom says it's you as she's looking fer. A Lady Naomi Lutonville! Cor! Whatta piece of toast!"

❧ *Chapter 5* ❧

So she had come! Rossiter's heavy heart gave a leap. "Glory, glory!" he whispered, and ran for the door.

Lady Lutonville was sitting in the Great Hall, a riding crop in her hand. She came to her feet as Rossiter entered, and faced him in silence. He paused for a moment, staring, trying to equate this poised and bewitchingly lovely creature with the shy girl he had left behind so long ago.

She watched him unsmilingly, her head very high, her firm chin tilted upward. Her riding habit was of a dark green that made her fair skin look almost translucent, and white lace gleamed at her throat and wrists. A broad-brimmed green hat, one side turned up and decorated with a sweeping white feather, was set upon her powdered hair, and thick ringlets had been pulled into a cluster below her left ear. Her beauty was not as exotic as that of Miss Falcon, but he found her delicate little nose adorable, the moulding of her face superb, her mouth sweetly curved and very kissable, the slim but well-rounded shape of her exactly as he had dreamed. The top of her proud head reached to his ear, just as it should. She was the personification of his gentle lady from Tranquillity Terrace, only inestimably more perfect.

"Naomi!" Hands outstretched, he started eagerly towards her.

She sank into a deep curtsy. "How kind in you to recognize me today, Captain Rossiter."

There was a mocking edge to her voice, a hauteur to her manner, and after one disdainful glance at his hands, she ignored them.

She had as well have thrown a jug of cold water in his face, and Rossiter halted, and stood motionless.

"Faith," she said with a brittle laugh, "I cannot wonder at your surprise. 'Tis most improper for a single lady to call at the home of a bachelor. Particularly"—a spark came into those great green eyes—"after he has brutalised her."

Brutalised . . . ? Bewildered, he said, "What—on earth—?"

"So you did not recognize me after all. Yesterday evening, sir. The hold-up."

"Good God! *You* were the silly chit who—?" He cut the words off quickly, but not quickly enough.

Naomi's lips tightened, and anger deepened the colour in her cheeks. "A true gentleman, sir, might have found it in his heart to show some compassion to a lady in distress, rather than reviling her."

How coldly she spoke, with no least vestige of affection. And what an ironic twist of fate, that of all the women in the world, it had to be his dream wife he had handled so shabbily! Forgetting her infuriating obstinacy, he could think only of how impatiently he had tossed her into the carriage, and, dismayed, he stammered, "I did not mean—That is, I would not for the world—Oh, Lord, Naomi! I wish you will believe—"

"La, what vehemence," she interpolated with a bored shrug. "And it is, after all, of *peu d'importance*." From the corner of her eye she saw him stiffen. Concentrating on straightening the cuff of her glove, she added, "Nor did I come here for an apology, sir."

"I had thought perhaps you came to offer one," he said quietly.

"I!" Outraged, she frowned at him.

He stepped closer. "The reception I was accorded at the Manor was not what a man might expect when calling on his betrothed. I realize we have been long apart, but we *are* betrothed—or so I believed."

How sincere and earnest he managed to appear! She yearned to scratch him, but there were more deadly things than scratches. And so she laughed, soft and liltingly, and had the satisfaction of seeing him flinch. "Are we? Lud, I must have forgot! But never think you were quite out of our thoughts. Rumours *do* manage to drift back to England. Sooner or later."

She "must have forgot . . ." Gideon took a steadying breath. "And you began to forget—when, my lady? Five minutes after you left London? Or was it only after you became a Toast? Rumours reach Holland also, you see, and your reputation has

58

provided many a rank joke over slopping tankards in verminous alehouses.''

Quivering with wrath, she half-whispered, "How *dare* you?"

He gripped her wrist, and jerking her close, said through his teeth, "I dare because I fought the man who said you had been seen leaving Lord Wellby's house unchaperoned at two in the morning! I knocked down the newspaper writer who named you hoyden for galloping your horse along St. James' and scattering a herd of cows, causing a fine uproar. Like a fool I believed none of the gossip from Italy, but dreamed only of coming home; of finding you at last, and starting the life we had planned together." Sadness came into his grey eyes. He added slowly, "I had such hopes . . . such wonderful plans to share with my little meadow sprite . . ."

It was the name he had called her when she was a worshipful sixteen and he a magnificent twenty-two. Naomi had to look away.

So intent were they upon their quarrel that they had failed to hear Lieutenant Morris, who came down the main stairs pulling on his gauntlets and humming to himself. He saw them, heard Rossiter's last few words, and froze, then started to turn about. The stair creaked under his foot. In an agony of embarrassment he checked again, dreading lest he be discovered and judged to have been listening.

Rossiter's entire attention was on Naomi. Perhaps she was simply overwrought . . . In years past he had always been able to win her from anger or sadness. He said gently, "My dear, I am very sorry. I know I've handled this badly. An you will but listen . . ."

Although she said nothing, it seemed to him that she swayed to him a little. Releasing her wrist, he tried to see her face, but it was concealed by the brim of her hat. Carefully, he removed the offending article. She raised no objection, and he drew her closer and touched her averted cheek. "I should not have said such things. Forgive me, I beg you. Rumour is such a vicious thing, Naomi. We must not let it come between us and destroy all our dreams."

She said in a voice that trembled, "It—has been so long, Gideon."

"Yes, beloved. But a whole glorious future stretches before us. I will try very hard to make you happy always. I swear it."

Her head was bowed still, but one hand crept up to rest on

his cravat. "When I had no word from you, I thought perhaps . . . you had found—another love."

"What rubbish! You are the only lady I ever have, or ever will love. I thought you knew that!"

Burying her face against his chest she said a muffled, "Then you always meant to—to come back to me?"

"Be assured of it! These six years I have counted the moments 'til I can call you Mrs. Gideon Rossiter." It was going to be all right, after all! Blissfully enveloped in a glow of happiness, he pressed his cheek against her fragrant hair. "My Naomi," he murmured. "Did you but know how I have longed to hold you like this! How very much I worship—"

And he stopped, because she was laughing.

Lifting her head she revealed a merry countenance. "Oh," she gasped. "How very well you do it, Captain! My apologies. I should not laugh, I know. But did you think word of your liaison with your little Dutch—er, lady would not reach our ears?"

Stunned, he corrected, "Belgian. I fancy I deserved that. But—"

"Lud, dear sir, you must not fancy I mean to chastise you. Ladies only pretend to be blind to these little *affaires*, you know. And one cannot expect gentlemen—especially military gentlemen—to be saints." she waved her whip under his nose reprovingly, "it *was* rather naughty in you to abandon the poor lady with—'tis a little girl . . . no?"

His hands clenched. He said tautly, "No. A boy and two girls. A set of twins this year, you see."

For a moment her eyes were very wide, but she made a fast recover, and, pouting, said rather breathlessly, "Out upon you, sirrah! You spoil Papa's scenario. He wagered you would have a thousand excuses, and swear to me that the talk was all lies, and you loved only me." Again, her rippling laugh rang out. She turned away, and said, "You will think me a perfect quiz, but I told him that since you had not come nor sent any word, you must surely have been wounded." From under the dark screen of her lashes, she watched him intently. "I even sent a friend to enquire of Sir Mark if your Commanding Officer had been in touch with him."

Rossiter took a slow breath. His pride again! His damnable pride that had rushed him into the army in the first place, then forbidden that his father be notified of the likelihood of his death!

He said, "No doubt the earl told you what the answer would be; that my father had heard nothing."

"Oh, yes, and he thought me such a great silly, and said I must be prepared lest you should claim you *had* been brought down, and use it as an excuse for having stayed with your *chère*—or is it *chères*? *amies*."

Rossiter looked at her innocent face steadily, and she trilled, "La, la! But I have angered the gentleman once more! Did I perchance spoil some carefully planned little speech? I shall make amends." She dimpled, and fluttered her eyelashes at him, then said with exaggerated naïveté, "You are so much changed, Captain Rossiter. Did army life not agree with you?"

Gideon flushed, and his nails dug into the palms of his hands. How contemptuous she was; how willing to believe the worst of him. His Achilles heel mastered him yet again, and all prideful hauteur he drawled, " 'Tis a life of many facets, ma'am. But, alas, I have no palliative speeches for you."

"Palliative," she echoed musingly, patting her firm little chin with her riding crop. "Such a big word, and I but a simple girl. Could it perchance mean . . . begging forgiveness?" On the last word her lovely eyes, hard and scornful now, met his squarely.

He suggested, "Perhaps you should discover the meaning from your papa, ma'am, since you rely so heavily on his wisdom."

She nodded. "In truth, he is exceeding shrewd, my dear Papa. You will scarce believe, but only last month he predicted that due to recent—er, events, you would now come racing home. That you would assure me your sudden return had nothing, but *nothing* to do with the fact that your father has been so silly as to ruin himself, so that 'tis vital you secure a rich wife!"

At this, a gasp escaped him. For an instant the hurt was so intense as to be a physical pain. Then, something inside him seemed to turn to ice.

With infinite care, Morris had been tiptoeing back up the stairs. At this point, having reached the landing, he gave a muffled groan of relief, and crept from earshot, still unobserved by the two people in the hall.

Naomi's eyes were glittering—with malice, no doubt, thought Rossiter. Yet even now she was so heart-rendingly beautiful. And so very far removed from her counterpart in Tranquillity Terrace. Determined not to let her see how deeply she had wounded him, he managed somehow to say coldly, "You are

61

vulgar. But then, as you said—no respectable single lady would call at the home of a bachelor.''

She started a furious rejoinder, then closed her lips and walked a few paces away. With a little giggle, she spun around and said brightly, "*Touché*. And I must not forget the reason for my call. It is that I have lost quite a valuable antique chess piece. 'Twas accidentally broken, and my father had sent it away to be repaired. I collected it from the jeweller in Stour Street yesterday."

"Indeed? And the highwaymen stole it from you, ma'am?"

"No. They got nothing. Only, it is gone from my reticule, and—"

Rossiter's head tossed an inch higher. "But of course. You thought I had stolen it." His eyes narrowed with rage. "A logical assumption when dealing with so dastardly a villain."

"No, no. We do not believe you would stoop to—*small* knaveries, Captain Rossiter."

A muscle twitched in his jaw, and for an instant his stare became a blazing glare that frightened her. Then he bowed mockingly, and she went on, "I merely hoped you might have seen it. My father's men found the wrappings near the spot where your friend shot Mr. Falcon."

"So that is why James shot him." His smile contemptuous, he drawled, "I'd no idea he was so ardent a player as to kill for a chess piece. Though most men—"

Angered by his sarcasm, she flared, "Most men are despicable!"

He bowed again. "Before—or after they suffer a reversal of fortunes, madam?"

Naomi's riding whip swung up but her wrist was caught in a grip of iron.

"Temper, temper," chided Rossiter. "With all his vaunted shrewdness, 'tis remarkable that your papa has failed to teach you that a lady of Quality should not behave like a guttersnipe."

She was shaking with anger, but when she wrenched free, he was not treated to the blistering denunciation he anticipated. Instead, she demanded loftily, "Am I to understand you did not see the piece? It is quite small, and fashioned of pink jade and rubies."

"But—dear lady, surely you must apprehend there is no point in asking me. An I had seen it, I certainly would never tell the truth of the matter. And since one is judged by the company one keeps, you will appreciate that to question my friend would be as pointless.''

He strode past her, swung the front door wide, and proffered her hat. ''Speaking as an accomplished cheat, lecher, and—liar, I have no hesitation in saying—to have met you again, my lady, has been . . . a pleasure.''

She should be able to find an answer to that barb, surely? But there was something about the haggard face and sardonic smile that made her feel cheapened and oddly disturbed. Words eluded her, and taking up the train of her habit, she snatched her hat, and swept past him regally, but in silence.

Hearing the door close, Lieutenant Morris paced to the stairs and started down once more, only to hesitate yet again. Rossiter stood facing the door, his head bowed against it. He had heard Morris' steps and turned quickly. The lieutenant caught a glimpse of a despair that appalled him. Then, a flush stained the gaunt cheeks, and Rossiter asked quietly, ''How long have you been there, Jamie?''

''Longer than I liked, blister it! Stumbled on your—ah, conversation before I realized you were there, and then your blasted creaking stairs trapped me. Took me the deuce of a time to escape. Damned embarrassing, I don't mind telling you.''

Rossiter sighed as if he was very weary. ''Yes. I'm sorry.''

''So am I.''

There was sympathy in the freckled face. Rossiter shrank from it. ''Thank you. But—'tis as well to know where I stand, I suppose.''

''Do you?'' Morris came down the rest of the stairs. ''Not my bread and butter, of course, but—Bless it, Gideon! Why in Hades didn't you tell the poor girl the truth? If her ladyship knew you'd come damned near to cocking up your toes this past year and more—''

Crossing the hall to join him, Rossiter said bleakly, ''Do you really fancy I would work on a woman's sympathy to win her? Even did I still wish to do so? Thank you—no!''

They started to walk towards the kitchen hall, and Morris said, ''Of all the high-in-the-instep—''

Rossiter cut him off impatiently. ''I cannot be too surprised, Jamie. She was little more than a child when we plighted our troth. She likely found quite soon that she had mistaken her heart. Certainly, I mistook mine, and I am free now to do what I may to help my family. You will be eager to get on your way, no? Never worry about our belongings. As soon as I reach Town

I'll send one of my father's people down to the Red Pheasant to collect 'em.''

Morris checked his stride, and said sternly, "You are indulging your perishing pride again, and I tell you, Ross, that pride is worth—"

"Very little, I know," interrupted Rossiter coolly. "Whereas time is of the essence, and the sooner we're away the better."

Their departure was not as prompt as he had hoped, but at last Tummet, the richer by two guineas, had wished his captors a blithe farewell, the horses were saddled, and the two men rode from the stableyard and started across the wide expanse of the park. With a great effort of will Rossiter did not once look back at his birthplace. Morris could all too well imagine his state of mind, however, and remained discreetly silent.

They were passing through the lodge gates before Rossiter said, "May I ask when you learned of my father's troubles?"

"My mama writ to me. I collect there was quite a—I mean, it caused somewhat of a stir."

Rossiter asked expressionlessly, "Did everybody else know? At the hospital, I mean."

"Really couldn't say, old lad."

Rossiter turned his head and looked at him levelly, and Morris added a hurried, "My mama writes dashed *enormous* letters. Shouldn't think any other fella's parent would scribble so much. Always crossed and both sides of the page covered. Makes it hard as the deuce to decipher."

"I scarce remember my mother," said Rossiter absently. "She died when Gwendolyn was born . . ." His mind felt bruised, but he wrenched it from a cruel and lovely face to deal with the here and now. "So your mama told you that my father's bank had failed, and that there were charges of"—he had to force himself to utter that awful word—"of embezzlement?"

"No, no, dear boy! Merely that 'twas a—er, nasty sort of business and there was bad feeling 'gainst your papa. Because so many were ruined, y'see. Never used the term 'embezzlement.' " He grinned. "Probably couldn't spell it." Then, realizing he had blundered again, his comely face reddened.

"Falcon used the term."

"Falcon! Who pays heed to anything that frizzle brain says? He's so curst hot at hand I'm surprised he didn't catch fire, only because I made a little mistake."

Rossiter managed a fairly creditable laugh. "I hope you never make a large one!"

When they turned onto the Maidstone Road they at once began to encounter traffic. Guiding his mount past a lumbering hay wain, Rossiter was caught up in the sounds and sights and smells of the Down country. England was so beautiful, and for a while he'd thought he might never see her again. He could not but experience a surge of gratitude that he was safely back in his own land, and although still mentally reeling from the hammer blows Fate had dealt him, he began instinctively to try and pull the pieces back together again. The great estate where so much of his youth had been spent was gone, and if his father's disaster had been as extensive as Tummet said, they were likely pockets to let. As for Naomi . . . He realized that Morris was chattering on about something. It had been blasted good of the man to come, in view of what he'd heard of the Rossiter family. He said, "My apologies, Jamie. I fear my mind was woolgathering."

"Better than gathering nuts in May—what?"

Rossiter grinned. "That was a jolly good ploy. Your capering saved the day."

"*And* my fine baritone, do not forget."

"Truly, you were superb. And Tummet turned out to be a good fellow after all. I hope he'll not find himself in a bobbery over this."

They rode on in silence for a while, then Morris said, "It rather worries me, now that I come to think on it."

"Tummet does?"

"Eh? Oh, he'll land on his feet, never fear. Finagle his way out of anything, that fellow. *Booberkin!*" This last was directed with great indignation at a carter whose wheels had come uncomfortably close. "No, I was thinking 'twas probably a Saturday. More likely, don't you agree?"

"More likely for what?"

"Good Gad, man! Where are your wits? It wouldn't be proper to go gathering nuts on a *Sunday*. I'd think you'd have realized that!"

"Gudgeon," said Rossiter, laughing at him. "Are you still puzzling over that old nursery song?"

"I like to keep things tidy," said Morris primly. "Speaking of which"—he waited while Rossiter's mount took violent exception to a flock of geese, then finished—"Falcon has a neatish country seat, I hear."

Resettling his tricorne, Rossiter panted. "Ashleigh. Does it occur to you, Jamie, that the roads have become a deal worse since we left England?''

"Most decidedly. In—ah, Middlesex, ain't it?''

"What? Oh—Ashleigh. No, Sussex.'' Rossiter glanced at him. "Why?''

"Why would you think, my lad?'' Morris winked mischievously. "Falcon may be a cod's head, but his sister—horse of a different colour entirely.''

"You not only mix your metaphors, my good fool, but you are properly addlebrained. Falcon warns off every man who dares come near the lady, even the more eligible bachelors. And you committed what you refer to as a 'little mistake,' but what he doubtless considers an excuse for bloody murder! He's an extreme dangerous man with all the instincts of a scorpion. Stay clear, and enjoy a good long life.''

Morris sighed. "But—she is so very glorious, do you see?''

"The lovelier they are,'' said Rossiter bitterly, "the more spoiled and flighty.''

"Aye. You've the right of it, I fancy.''

This meek capitulation brought a suspicious glint to Rossiter's eyes, but he was diverted by a stentorian blast as a stagecoach driver demanded and seized the right of way.

"Curst mountebank,'' grumbled Morris, urging his hack onto the road once more. "The riffraff they allow to tool the coaches nowadays are little better than rank riders! I shall talk to my guv'nor about it. A good old boy is my guv'nor.'' He went on at some length enumerating the virtues of his worthy sire, while contriving to avoid Rossiter's thoughtful gaze until they came to a bustling crossroad where they drew clear of the stream of traffic, and reined to a halt.

Morris stretched out his hand. "Here we part company. Good hunting, Ross, and—er, all that kind of fustian. I shall expect you to come down and meet my guv'nor. Soon, dear boy.''

Their handshake was firm, their smiles holding the warmth of true friendship.

"I would like that very much,'' said Rossiter. "When do you fancy you'll get back from Sussex?''

"Oh, I likely won't leave till—'' Morris broke off, flushing, then said a rueful, "Devil!''

Rossiter reached over to seize his bridle. "For once in your life, Jamie, use some of the wits God gave you! Falcon's a shark!''

Morris laughed heartily, and breaking away from Rossiter's

hold, exclaimed, "And you accused *me* of mixing my metaphors! Is the fellow a shark, or a scorpion?"

"Both, you idiot! I fancy he'll demand satisfaction of each of us sooner or later, but—"

"But in the meantime," said Morris, "I may contrive to at least rest these old orbs upon the incomparable Miss Katrina! Farewell, dear boy. And God speed!" With a wave and a grin, he drove home his spurs and galloped off on the road that led westward to Maidstone and Sevenoaks.

Frowning after his rapidly diminishing figure, Rossiter shook his head worriedly. Jamie was a fair shot at best, and as for swords—he shuddered. Still, Falcon would be unable to fight anyone until that arm healed, which would require at least two weeks. He would call on the fellow and arrange a meeting. If he could disable Falcon, it might be a considerable time before Morris would have to face him. At the moment, however, his first duty must be to his father.

He reined around and joined the ever-increasing traffic following the London Road. He missed Jamie's cheerful presence. Naomi's lovely face came into his mind's eye, bringing with it that terrible ache of grief for something that had been very beautiful and was now destroyed. All these years—all this wasted time! He had been a proper fool . . . Shakespeare had said something about time and a fool . . . How did it go? "Love's not Time's fool . . . ?" something of the kind. Perhaps it was not love, but the lover who was time's fool. Certainly he must be a classic example of such folly.

Well, the time for foolishness was done, and he must start again. First, he would make a push to set things to rights insofar as Papa's difficulties were concerned. If worst came to worst, they could all live at the country house his grandmama had bequeathed to him. Emerald Farm was a lovely and peaceful old place, and although Newby could be counted upon to despise it, little Gwendolyn would likely be happy there.

Dear little Gwen . . . He found himself very eager to see his sister again, and spurred his horse to a faster gait.

Naomi walked into Collington Manor with eyes that saw nothing of the arched entrance hall, the grand sweep of the central staircase in the second hall, or the fine ceiling paintings. She felt crushed and dispirited and dreaded facing her father. Pawson admitted her, his dark eyes blank as usual. Relieved when her enquiry elicited the information that his lordship was closeted with "a gentleman," her spirits picked up even more when Pawson added mournfully, "Miss Falcon has called, and is waiting in your ladyship's private parlour."

Miss Falcon, a picture in pink and white, was sitting in the window seat engrossed in the *London Gazette*. She looked up, smiling in response to her friend's delighted welcome, and said absently, "Hello, love. They say there will be a treaty signed to end this ridiculous Austrian war. I have never understood it, have you?"

"No," said Naomi, stripping off her gloves. "And I fancy most of the soldiers have no least idea of what they're fighting for—or against. However, I would not refine upon there being a speedy end to the war, dearest. There will always be wars, simply because men delight in them."

It was unlike Naomi to be cynical, and Katrina set aside the newspaper and looked at her in surprise. "Rich men perhaps, for the sake of trade. But do you think the poor men who have to fight, really enjoy it? Surely they cannot, when they see how many are killed and wounded."

"Much they care," said Naomi ferociously. "At all events, 'tis the officers who are first to be slain in every battle. Most of them are rich men's sons and do not *have* to follow the drum. But they go anyway. Is in keeping with the male nature. Only l-look how . . . how little boys are always . . . fighting." She dashed her gloves and whip onto the bed, and tearing off her hat, suddenly burst into tears.

"Good heavens!" Katrina flew up to hug her friend and lead her to the window seat, then sink down beside her, murmuring soothing endearments. When the storm eased a little, she said in her gentle way, "Men are hopeless, I own, my love. Never waste your tears upon them."

"W-well, they are!" wailed Naomi, groping for her handkerchief. "And—and they do enjoy to—to fight! Oh, how—*stupid*! Why am I crying like this?"

Katrina dabbed with care at the tearful eyes. "Because you are overwrought, my dear. And quite rightly so after what you have gone through. I doubt your grief had anything to do with the fact that gentlemen are prone to fight. Though I must admit," she added with a sigh, "my brother fits that description."

Naomi blew her nose daintily, summoned a tremulous smile, and crossed to tug on the bell pull. "What a ninny I am, to behave like a watering pot. I should instead be telling you how sorry I am that poor August was shot! And only for trying to protect me!''

Secretly disturbed by such an unusual display of emotion, Katrina said kindly, '' 'Twas not your fault. Certainly August does not hold you responsible. And, Lud! What a frightful experience! Were you quite distracted? I should have fallen down in a swoon, I know it.''

"No, you would not." Naomi sat beside her again. "You appear so gently delicate, yet you have an inner strength and fortitude that awes me. Indeed I often marvel at how well you bear up under"—she broke off with a mental groan, wishing she had not spoken so impulsively—"under life's buffets," she finished lamely. Katrina's grave little smile told her that what she had started to say had been guessed at, and she was grateful for the interruption when Maggie came in, bobbed a curtsy, and went scurrying off again when asked to fetch tea.

"Now," said Naomi, "do pray tell me how poor August goes on, and why you are here. Never say you have abandoned him in that horrid little inn?"

"Of course I have not, you goose. The wound is painful, but the apothecary said 'twas not serious. But when Captain Rossiter came back last evening they immediately came to cuffs and—''

Shocked, Naomi interrupted, "Your pardon, but how can one come to cuffs with a wounded man?"

"The captain appeared to find no difficulty in doing so. Nor in wrenching my poor brother about in a most savage fashion!"

"Good God! Is the man *quite* without honour?"

"You may be sure I was furious and cried shame on him. As for August, he was practically berserk, and raged and ranted half the night, and this morning swore at the poor apothecary until he washed his hands of the entire case and went off in a huff.''

"I think the apothecary has my sympathy. Was he dreadfully inept?"

"I rather think he was not of the first stare, but 'twas because he refused to allow us to return to Town, that my brother became so angry. He soon repented, and suffered such pangs of contrition that nothing would do but I must go into the village and beg the apothecary to call again in the afternoon. Whilst I was gone, my sly brother bullied the landlord into finding him a coach and postilions, and off he went at the gallop for London!"

"A true feather wit!" said Naomi indignantly. "Leaving you to worry yourself into a proper pucker. A country apothecary

69

would have been better endured than a long and bumpy ride to Town. Men!''

"Well, I did worry, because even if 'tis not serious, the wound is quite nasty and he will likely run himself into a fever." She murmured thoughtfully, "Which may not be a very bad thing, now that I think of it . . . But I found myself quite out of charity with him, and was of no mind to follow him straight away to Falcon House as he no doubt expects me to do."

"So you came instead to visit me." Naomi swooped to embrace her. "Then 'tis my good fortune. But what did you mean by saying it will not be a bad thing if August frets his way into a fever?"

Katrina folded her hands in her lap and said demurely, "Simply that he cannot fight a duel if he is ill."

"Ah. Lieutenant Morris?"

"And Gideon Rossiter."

"Oh." Naomi began to curl the lace at her cuff, then asked in a subdued voice, "Did you know who he was, Katrina? When he brought August back to you at that dirty little inn, I mean?"

"Not at first. He told me his name when he arrived, but I was so shocked and upset, it did not occur to me it was your—" She broke off, watching the downbent head curiously. "I mean— that it was Captain *Gideon* Rossiter. From what you'd told me, love, I had expected quite another type of man."

"So had I," said Naomi, stifling a sigh. "He is so changed, which, of course, I should have anticipated after six years. If all that is said of him is truth, you know, he *must* be far different from the gentle boy I knew. He was horrid at the hold-up, and *threw* me into the coach most brutally!"

"Monstrous!" gasped Katrina. "And you so terrified, besides being distraught for August's sake! How could a gentleman be so unfeeling?"

Naomi lifted a rather guilty face. "Well, I may have been— just a trifle—er, tiresome. But, I'd never had judged Gideon Rossiter the type to strike a wounded man."

"Here comes your tea, milady," announced Maggie cheerfully, carrying a laden tray through the door a lackey held open for her. She dared a keen look at her mistress. "Are ye feeling well, ma'am?"

"Her ladyship is disturbed," said Katrina.

"Little wonder." The abigail set the tray on the table by the windows. "Why, the earl hisself was saying—"

70

"The earl!" gasped Naomi, one hand pressed to her temple. "Oh, heavens! His chess piece!"

Arranging teacups, Maggie asked anxiously, "Had the captain found it, milady?"

"No," wailed Naomi. "We quarrelled, and Captain Rossiter was rude, and—and I became so angry . . . Oh, dear! Oh, dear! Papa will be furious!"

An infuriated Lord Collington was the last thing Naomi needed, thought Katrina. His lordship's tongue was almost as acid as her brother's. She said, "You plan to attend the Glendenning Ball next week, Naomi. Why not come to Town with me? Now. Maggie can follow with your portmanteau, we can shop and have a lovely cose. By the time the ball is over, your papa will have come out of the hips, I daresay."

Naomi considered for only a moment. " 'Tis a splendid notion! I shall be a wretched coward and leave him a note. Maggie—do you go and tell Miss Falcon's coachman to get the team ready. An we hurry, Katrina, I can leave before Papa ever knows I had returned!"

Acquainted with his lordship's rages, Miss Falcon thought that would be as well.

❧ *Chapter 6* ❧

London had grown to an astonishing extent during Rossiter's absence, and the traffic seemed to have doubled. Great wains and waggons, luxurious coaches, carts, sedan chairs, and horsemen vied for space on the busy streets. The flagways were crowded with people from all walks of life and in every imaginable mode of dress; the rags of link boys, the laces and velvets of aristocrats, the magnificence of stern Life Guardsmen in their scarlet, blue and gold, the smocks and gaiters of country folk, housewives with their baskets, immaculate and haughty servants, darting, whooping children, gentlemen of the Halbardiers in their long red coats. It seemed to Rossiter that the noise had increased tenfold. A Portsmouth Machine rumbled past, the coachman bellowing warnings to the outside passengers and bullying surrounding drivers. Vendors hawked their wares at the tops of lungs apparently strengthened by their trade, and chairmen sang lustily as they bore their passengers through the throng.

A great new house was being built on Conduit Street, the sound of hammers adding to the din. Unnerved when he was all but run down by a coach and four, Rossiter dismounted and led his horse along the kennel. His attention was caught by a scrawny fellow who carried what must have been a heavy hod of bricks, but who scampered up the scaffolding as nimbly as if he carried feathers.

"Pies! Getcher pies! Hot pies! Chickenpizenporkenfineol-Englishbeef!" A vendor took the tray of steaming wares from his head and swung it enticingly under Rossiter's nose.

The pies smelled delicious, but he was close to home now and although he was ravenous he smilingly declined.

72

"Poor fellow," came a sneering voice. "I fancy he cannot afford one. Should we take up a collection, do you think?"

Rossiter stiffened and jerked around.

Two elegant gentlemen watched him from the windows of a dark red carriage. Raising a jewelled quizzing glass for a closer look, the younger of the two said indignantly, "His sire took up a collection, Smythe. From half the demned population of the demned south country! Let the beastly fellow starve, I say. Drive on, coachman. Blasted stench hereabouts!"

Taut with anger, Rossiter sprang for the door of the coach, only to leap for his life as a troop of horses, breastplates and helms glittering in the sunlight, clattered past.

" 'Ere," said the pieman. "Where you orf to, soldier?"

Rossiter had recognized those two cowards. One had been Reginald Smythe, and the other Sir Gilbert Fowles. Simpering dandies who'd made themselves thoroughly obnoxious at school and had since become pests who spent their time in gormandizing, gaming, and gossip. Both would probably faint if faced with a closed fist, but they were not above throwing insults from carriage windows.

He answered the pieman's question mechanically. "My home lies just along the street."

"Ar. Yer name wouldn't be Rossiter, by any chance?"

There was unconcealed impudence in the tone. Gideon threw a quick glance at him, saw the smirk on the dirty face and said icily, "How is that your concern?"

It appeared to the pieman that the thin soldier had grown in both height and menace. He replaced the tray on his head and retreated a few paces. " 'Cause I'm grateful as it ain't mine," he jeered. "And if you'd like ter know, yer home ain't just along the street. Not no more it ain't. The high an' mighty Rossiters don't live there no more. Come dahn in the world, they has! A long way dahn!"

His anger supplanted by anxiety for his family, Rossiter sprang to the saddle and turned the hack. Fearing reprisals, the pieman took to his heels, his shrill voice echoing after him, "Rossiter! Yah! Boo! Fer shame!"

Several people had paused to listen to this exchange, and a man said sharply, "What did he say? Is that fellow a Rossiter?"

Another man shouted, "I'll lay odds he is! One of 'em was in the army I heard!"

"Seize the thieving bastard!"

"Pull him off that there nag! Quick! 'Fore the Watch comes!"

They surged towards him. Someone snatched up a brick and threw it. Rossiter ducked and a passing horse squealed and bolted. Another brick flew. Surrounded by rageful faces, he decided that this was no time to take a stand. He touched home his spurs. The hack bounded forward. The crowd scattered, shouting in alarm. A third brick caught Rossiter across the back of the head, the impact sending his tricorne flying and half stunning him. Dimly, he heard a triumphant howl. The pain was blinding. He had lost the reins somehow. Bowing forward, he clung to the hack's mane, determined not to fall . . . The morning was growing strangely dark . . .

"There, I think he's coming around now."

"Poor fellow. Badly wounded you say, sir?"

"Yes, sad to tell. I believe he's just now returned home. Must have hit his head when he tumbled out of the saddle."

The words echoed at first, gradually becoming clearer. The final voice was familiar. Rossiter tried to smile and said rather feebly, "Hello, Tio. That you?"

A hand gripped his shoulder. " 'Tis myself in all my glory."

Rossiter blinked up into a pair of green eyes with laugh lines at the corners. The aristocratic features were uncharacteristically grave at the moment, and Horatio Clement Laindon, Viscount Glendenning, son and heir of the powerful and formidable Earl of Bowers-Malden, went on in a very gentle voice, "What a slowtop you are, to be riding when you ain't fit to go. Came down from your hack right under the hoofs of my team. My poor coachman nigh suffered a seizure."

The mists surrounding his lordship faded away, and Rossiter found that he lay on a settle in a low-ceilinged room. Several men stood watching him with sympathetic curiosity. One of these individuals, wearing a grubby white apron, was holding a rag that dripped water, but the rest were either customers of this ordinary (for such he guessed it to be), or pedestrians who had come in from the street. "Oh—egad," he muttered, and horribly embarrassed started up.

His head seemed to split in two. An arm was about his shoulders, supporting him.

Glendenning said sharply, "If one of you gentleman would be so kind as to lend a hand, I'll take him to my rooms."

"I . . . can walk . . . ," declared Rossiter thickly, and managed somehow to stumble where they led him.

He was being half-lifted into a carriage. The door slammed.

A flask was at his lips. He drank, choked, and swore. But after a few minutes he was able to gather his thoughts.

The carriage was moving smoothly, and the noise seemed to lessen. He opened his eyes and saw trees and the green of well-kept lawns.

"Feeling better?" asked his lordship.

"Much." He peered out of the window. "Where are we going?"

"My flat, off the Strand. Shall that suit?"

"No." Gingerly investigating the back of his head Rossiter muttered, "Hold up a minute, will you please, Tio?"

Glendenning pulled the checkstring, and called to the coachman to turn onto a quieter side street. "Not going to cast up your accounts, are you, Gideon?" he asked uneasily.

"No, I promise you," said Rossiter, with more conviction than was altogether warranted. "It was jolly good of you to—to help. Did I really . . . fall under your team?"

"You came very close, dear boy." The viscount turned his neatly wigged head, scanned his companion's pale face and asked, "What happened?"

"A brick. Deedily tossed."

"Curious." His lordship tapped a handsome amber cane against his chin. "I think I know you well, but after all this time I'd not have recognized you at first glance. I wonder anybody else did. You're—something changed, dear lad. Bayonet?"

Rossiter grinned faintly. "Shell." And then, in sudden hideous comprehension, "Jove! My apologies, sir! You'd best let me out at once. I think my presence must be an humiliation, and—"

"Do you know," interposed his lordship mildly, "if you didn't look as if you'd been spat out by a warthog, I should punch your head for you." He passed the flask again. "Have another pull at this. I've no desire to be arrested for corpse stealing. I have enough trouble."

Grateful, Rossiter complied, and asked, blinking, "Trouble?"

"I suppose you'd not be aware, but I am suspected of having been—er, embroiled in the late Rebellion. On the wrong side," he added with a wry grin.

"I see." Rossiter looked at him steadily. "Kindred spirits, is that what you mean?"

It was the viscount's turn to be discomfitted. "I do not scruple to remark that you've dashed unpleasant eyes. Are you saying

75

there is more to your father's unhappy predicament than is generally believed?''

"I don't know. I don't even know what is my father's 'unhappy predicament.' ''

"Good God!" Glendenning looked aghast. "I thought that was why you had come home."

"So do others, I gather. No, do not tell me of it, Tio. I had prefer to hear the whole story from Sir Mark. An I can find him."

His lordship pulled on the checkstring again, and when the coachman peered down from the trap, "Snow Hill," he said. The coachman uttered an audible and shocked exclamation. With a sly grin Lord Horatio added, "It really don't seem fair to you, Gideon. But since you have more or less survived shells and bricks, you might live through the ride."

Half an hour later, white and shaken, Rossiter descended the steps and clung to the open door. "Damn you, Tio," he croaked. "How can you be so heartless as to sit there and—and laugh?''

His insensate friend's mirth rising to a howl, Rossiter started towards the back of the coach, clinging to the wheel as he went.

Glendenning leapt from the carriage and offered his arm. "Just—just do not look down, my heroic friend," he chortled.

Rossiter, who was petrified by heights, took one glance at the sheer hill they had climbed, and moaned. "Why in the name of Beelzebub must my father elect to remove to the side of a mountain? No, really, Tio. However will your poor cattle get down?''

"The same way they got up, I fear." They came around to the back of the vehicle, and Glendenning went on, "Here is your hack, safe and sound."

"Aye. And only look—he has turned white, poor fellow!''

Laughing, Glendenning said, "What—had he not a blaze when you hired him?''

"I cannot—" Rossiter interrupted himself wrathfully, "I'll tell you something he *did* have. My saddlebags! Where the devil are they? Did your coachman throw them in the boot?''

Sobering, Glendenning questioned his servants, but neither coachman nor footman had removed the saddlebags. The footman searched about, but it was soon determined that the missing articles were neither on, in, nor under the coach, and he was sent back down the hill to see if they had fallen en route. Watching his mincing and reluctant progress, Glendenning said, "I'd think we could see them from here, wouldn't you, Ross?''

"I would. But I do not."

"Small doubt then. They must have been stolen. Gad! Whatever is old London Town coming to? Nothing of great value, I hope?"

"My dressing case. Some small gifts for my family. Nothing to warrant taking such a risk, and in broad daylight."

The footman waved from the bottom of the hill, his gestures clearly indicating failure.

Rossiter swore, and turned back to the tall and rather shabby house that stood silent and unwelcoming among its more prosperous-looking neighbours.

Of a somewhat superstitious nature, Glendenning caught his arm. "If ever I heard of so wretched a homecoming! Your stars must harbour a grudge against you today. Indeed, I shudder to think what tidbit Fate prepares to hurl at you next! You will do much better to come home with me and hide in bed. In the morning you can start afresh."

Rossiter clapped him on the back. "You really are a good fellow, and I thank you, Tio. But I'd not wish to be held responsible should your rooms catch fire!"

They shook hands, Rossiter promised to attend the Glendenning Ball on the seventeenth, which was invariably one of the first highlights of the Season, and they parted.

Rossiter mounted the two front steps and gave the door knocker a vigorous exercise. He heard measured footsteps, then the door swung open and a haughty countenance was scanning him. He was hatless, and undoubtedly looked dishevelled, and that he was judged and found wanting was immediately apparent. He said curtly, "I am Captain Gideon Rossiter. Conduct me to Sir Mark, if you please."

The butler stared, admitted him with obvious trepidation, and sketched a bow. "If you will wait here, sir, I will apprise Sir Mark of your arrival." He started for the stairs. In two swift strides Gideon reached the flight. The butler checked and drew back. "Sir Mark does not care to be disturbed without—" he began.

"Idiot," said Rossiter pithily, and passed him.

The upper hall was long and narrow and rather gloomy. He heard voices from a room on the right. Pausing, he nerved himself, and entered a formal withdrawing room.

Sir Mark Rossiter stood with one hand on the mantel, and turned, frowning at this intrusion. His bag wig was elaborate; an inspired tailor had fashioned his velvet habit of dark gold;

77

and the quizzing glass he raised to a pale blue eye was richly jewelled. "The devil, sir," he began, indignantly.

Gideon was momentarily struck to silence. His father was still as tall and well-built; still carried himself with prideful arrogance. But he had aged more than might have been expected in six years, and the lines in the distinguished face, the pallor of the skin, came as a shock.

Elegant in shades of rose, his wig of the very latest style, Newby Rossiter rose from a wing chair. Briefly, baffled fury glinted in his eyes. Then, "Well, well, well . . . " he murmured, strolling closer to his brother and scanning him mockingly. "Damme if our Prodigal ain't come home, after all! We thought you was dead, twin."

"I wonder you are not in black gloves." Gideon walked over to his father who had let the quizzing glass fall and stared at him in stunned disbelief. They had parted bitterly and there was still a constraint between them. "Hello, sir," he said awkwardly.

"Gideon . . . ?" The word was almost indistinguishable. Sir Mark put out a trembling hand.

Gideon bowed over it and touched the cold fingers to his lips. "I'm aware I have not pleased you, Father, but I came as soon as I was able."

Sir Mark gripped his shoulder emotionally, felt his son shrink away, and pulled himself together. "I was prepared to give you a proper raking down for not coming home as arranged. I collect I cannot do that. Sit down, boy. Hit, were you? When?"

Sinking gratefully into the chair, Gideon said, "Lauffeld, sir."

"Lauffeld?" Sir Mark frowned. "But—that was nigh a year since! Why was I not notified?"

Gideon took a swallow of the wine Newby handed him. "I had caused you exceeding vexation when I purchased a commission against your wishes. I'd a mind to worry you no further."

Pulling another chair closer, Sir Mark sat down, and stared at this son who had always seemed such an enigma. "Be so good as to overcome your scruples."

"There's not much to tell," said Gideon uncomfortably. "I was too close to an exploding shell. It—er, took the doctors a confounded age to put me back together again."

"Good . . . God!" breathed Sir Mark. "And how fit are you now?"

"Not sufficiently so to attend to his toilette, evidently," purred Newby. "You look like an unmade bed, twin."

Gideon flushed, ran a tidying hand through his hair, then

winced. "Some rabble rouser hove a brick at me. Not a mark-edly warm welcome home."

"A far cry from the parade and hero's welcome you no doubt expected," said Newby with his neighing laugh.

Gideon gritted his teeth, but Sir Mark ignored the remark. He insisted upon inspecting his heir's damaged head, pronounced it a very nasty bump, and told Newby to ring for the butler. "We'll get you to bed, Gideon, and my physician must have a look at you. We can talk later."

The thought of bed in a quiet room was enticing, but Gideon resisted temptation. "If you do not object, I'd as lief talk for a while, sir. I collect we are in some kind of trouble."

"Oh, come now," said Newby in disgust. "Do not pretend you don't know. We are ruined, brother mine. Your arrival is well timed, for you've contrived to miss most of the ugly busi-ness. You may be able to escape back to your regiment before we have to face the final act. Arrest. Trial. Conviction, impris-onment or deportation!"

"Good God!" exclaimed Gideon. "Is it really that bad, sir?"

Sir Mark paced over to the window. "You must have heard some of it, surely?"

"No, Father. On my honour, the first I knew of it was—was from a remark someone made after I'd landed."

"How very convenient." Newby sniggered. "Perchance that is part of the lure of army life. In addition to the pretty uniform that so impresses gullible ladies, you are shielded from the mun-dane affairs that bedevil ordinary mortals!"

Gideon leapt up and said with flashing anger, "Come with me to the Low Countries, twin. I'll conduct you through the bones of those shielded from 'mundane affairs'!"

Sir Mark jerked around. " 'Twas your own decision to join the military, and desert me for six years!"

Fighting anger, Gideon met his father's eyes across the sud-denly quiet room, and it was as if the clock rolled backward; as if they again confronted each other on that icy November after-noon. Almost he could hear the angry voices . . .

"I sent you up to Merseyside to meet my superintendent and familiarize yourself with the shipyard and its operation. 'Twas my hope you might learn something of the business. Instead, in one month you set my staff in a turmoil, damn near caused a riot, and brought work to a grinding halt! It will take weeks to undo the mischief you've done with your damnable revolution-ary notions!"

"It was because I *did* learn something of the business, that I intervened when—"

"Intervened! What right had you to intervene in *anything*? You are two and twenty and know *nothing*, yet you dared to challenge the ability and authority of a man who has spent his life building ships!"

"Murchison is a callous bungler, who cares less for his people than—"

"Be silent, sir! Your opinion is neither valued nor asked! You are a pest, sir! An unfailing source of dissension in this household and out of it. You quarrel with your brother, affront my friends, and now you have upset my shipyard! Well, I'll not have a hostile, ill-mannered, dog in the manger rabble rouser succeed me as head of this family! Mend your ways, or—"

"Mayhap I would offend you less by my absence, sir. In which event, I'll ride to Whitehall this afternoon. I've no doubt my quarrelsome nature will be more welcome in the Low Countries than in Mayfair . . ."

Returning with an effort to the here and now, Gideon said, "I fear that even had I known you were in trouble, sir, I was in the hospital, and—"

"And who is to blame for that unhappy circumstance? No one but yourself! I suppose you will say you did not receive my letters apprising you of my situation and requiring that you return home at once. Well, you *should* have received them, sir! I wouldn't even entrust 'em to the servants for fear some dullard might drop one along the way. I sent Newby off to the post office to deliver every one with his own hands. Right, boy?"

Newby said smoothly, "We certainly did our possible, father."

Gideon viewed his twin's bland smile and knew that battle was not worth the fighting. "The post was unreliable, to say the least. But at all events, that's water under the bridge now and—"

As always, the trace of impatience in his son's voice goaded Sir Mark. "Aye, it is," he said angrily. "Over and done with, so forget it quickly—that's your philosophy, eh, Gideon? Still the same hot-headed young here-and-thereian!"

Frowning, Gideon attempted to speak, but with an autocratic wave of one hand his father swept on. "Perchance you are well satisfied with what you've accomplished these six years. 'Fore God, you're a fool if that's the case, and so I tell you! You were a splendid-looking young Buck when you stamped out of here sooner than submit to my authority, and now look at you! What did independence win you, eh? You'd to submit to authority in the army, I am very sure, and your sole reward was to be put out of action for months, at a time when you were sorely needed here!''

"Yes," admitted Gideon, tight-lipped. "My apologies for that. But I'm here now, sir. Anything I can do to help—"

Sir Mark gave an exasperated snort. "Help, is it? Faith, but you are in no condition to help anyone! 'Tis very obvious you've brought yourself home properly knocked up!''

'Nothing has changed,' thought Gideon. His head was pounding brutally now, his shoulder throbbed persistently, and he could not fail to resent being combed out when he felt so wretched. But he did not propose to be again defeated by his temper, and to an extent his father was justified. He stifled his irritation, and said quietly, "Sir, I think you know in your heart that had it been possible, I would have come at once, but the sincerest declarations cannot change the past. Pray tell me what has happened.''

Newby said with a scowl, "My father don't want to rake it all up again! Had you been here, as you should—''

"I think it has been thoroughly established that I was not here," snapped Gideon, his patience deserting him. Newby's glare scorched at him, and well aware that his survival must have thwarted his brother's ambitions, Gideon added ironically, "Overjoyed to see me, eh, twin?''

"I give you joy of your inheritance," riposted Newby, "if nothing—''

Sir Mark's voice was harsh. "Have done, both of you! Have done! Newby, you may leave us. No need to hear all this.''

Newby said sulkily, "I do not want you to be upset, sir.''

"I know, I know. You're a good boy. But go now. Gideon is my heir, and has a right to be told.''

Newby hesitated, then shrugged, bowed to his father, and sauntered from the room.

"I hear most twins are regular bosom bows," muttered Sir Mark, as the door closed.

Gideon choked back an involuntary rejoinder and said instead, "Sir, I am not come home to cut up your peace. If 'tis unpleasant for you, Gwendolyn can tell me the details.''

"Your sister don't know the details. We've shielded her insofar as we were able. Sit yourself down, boy." Sir Mark went to the sideboard, refilled his glass, and stood staring down at

81

the rich amber wine. "It began simply enough," he said with slow reluctance. "Loans, mostly. To men I'd known all my life. Fine fellows, to whom I was under some obligation or other. Large loans, but certainly they were good for it. Then—there was a fire at the shipyard. You likely did not hear of it, but 'twas a most ghastly thing. The night watchmen were drunk—as we then thought! People came to help, but by the time the bell was rung there was no stopping it. They no sooner quenched it in one place than 'twould flare up in another. When dawn came . . ." He sighed heavily. "The buildings were gutted. Four men burned to death—dozens badly injured, three nigh completed frigates destroyed. The newspapers blamed me and the directors. They held we'd not taken proper precautions, and that flammable supplies were stored too close to the stoves. There was an official investigation. That weasel Murchison testified he had warned me that we stood in dire need of pumps and hoses, and that many buckets were rusted through. He claimed I said they'd cost more than they were worth!" He drove one fist into his palm, his face flushed with wrath. "Lies! All lies! He never breathed a word to me about the need for new fire equipment!"

Gideon kept his thoughts to himself, and watched in silence as his father paced agitatedly about the room.

"I did what I could for the bereaved." Sir Mark gave a snort of bitter frustration. "What can one supply that will replace a life? I diverted a large sum from my private account, and we began to get the shipyard set to rights. Then—everything happened at once. We had invested heavily—damned heavily!—in a most promising company trading with China. Norberly insisted on extensive investigation, and it still looked to be a regular mine of gold, so we bought controlling shares. It turned out that the stock had been sold many times over, but by the time we discovered that accursed fact, it was too late. We lost an enormous sum. Three days later, Samuel Davies, one of my most trusted officers at the bank, absconded with bonds and cash to the value of . . . of over a hundred thousand. We understood the fellow was ill, and by the time his accounts were checked . . ." He shrugged. "He was away clear, and I began to see ruin creeping up on me. But—damn! we still could have recouped, had not the rumour mills started! Before we knew it, we were faced with panic. A run on the bank—demands for funds we could not cover. Within one day we were . . . wiped out."

Appalled by this litany of mismanagement, Gideon contrived to keep his voice calm. "You said you'd authorized large loans to some old friends. Could they not have helped, sir?"

"Oh, they could! Undeniably! But"—his mouth twisting into a sneer, Sir Mark said—" 'twould seem they'd been called out of the country. Suddenly. On urgent business."

"I see. And my lord Norberly? Sir Louis Derrydene? Your other investors and stockholders?"

"Many of 'em managed by one means or another to quietly withdraw their funds."

"Good God! At the time of the run on the bank?"

"The day before." Avoiding his son's eyes, the baronet muttered, "I was down at the Point with—" He broke off, and looked down, reddening. "And unaware of it 'til 'twas much too late."

"Of all the damnable tricks!"

Sir Mark's abased head swung upward again. "Tricks, you say? *Tricks? No!* That ain't the word, deuce take me if it is! *Conspiracy*, rather!"

Gideon's jaw dropped. Staring at his father's convulsed face, he echoed, "*Conspiracy?* Sir—what in heaven's name . . . ?"

"Aye, you may stare! Think me mad, do you? You're not alone, burn it! But conspiracy I say, and conspiracy I mean! To the fullest extent of the word!" Sir Mark dragged a chair to face Gideon and sat down, leaning forward and speaking with passionate intensity. "I could accept it as coincidence that some major investments failed; that some large loans were in default. But that Davies should embezzle so gigantic a sum—and vanish from the face of the earth? That my shipyard should have *chanced* to catch fire; my principal stockholders should withdraw their funds; and all within *two weeks*? No, by God!"

Stunned, Gideon stared at his father in silence. Then, he said slowly, "You mentioned that the guards at the shipyard were drunk. You said, 'As we then thought.' What did you mean?"

"That I now believe them to have been drugged! Do you see? Do you *see*? 'Twas a conspiracy, I tell you! A deliberate and merciless plan to ruin me! That is why I need you, Gideon! To prove me innocent. To restore my good name, even if my fortune, my estates, are lost!"

It was very clear that the poor old boy had cracked under the strain. Small wonder. Gideon said carefully, "Er—have you any suspicions, sir? Do you guess who is behind it?"

"Would that I did!" Sir Mark sprang to his feet again and set his glass on a table. "I've appealed to my friends, argued with Bow Street, hired investigators—in vain. Behind my back they all laugh at me and—damn their ears!—they think I will not accept the responsibility for my failure. That I seek to cloud the truth!"

"I see . . . Well, 'tis said that if murder is done, find first the man who has most to gain."

"They all gained! The promoters of that damnable trading company. The men who took out loans, and then left the country! The treacherous bastard who embezzled." Sir Mark muttered broodingly, "All in league against me, fiend seize 'em!"

"But—sir, they were your friends! Besides, they all are independently wealthy. I'd think *their* reputations are lost also. Surely such an involved plot as you envision must be extreme costly, as well as a very great risk. Besides, who gained from burning your shipyard? I cannot—"

"You are saying you do not believe me, I think?"

Shocked by the savage fury in his father's face, Gideon said hurriedly, "I certainly do not rule out the possibility of such a conspiracy, sir. You'll recollect that I never had any use for Norberly and Derrydene! And as for that slimy wart Murchison—"

His cheeks flushing, Sir Mark snarled, "You warned me, is that what you say? By heaven, if you've come home to gloat over me—to say 'I told you so'—I'll not have it! You may take yourself back to your confounded regiment and—"

Gideon sprang up and went to throw his arm about his father's shoulders. "No, sir. How can you think it of me? We'll come at the root of this somehow. We must, if we're to keep Promontory Point and—"

"So you know about that, do you, twin?" Newby wandered into the room, his eyes narrowing when he saw Gideon's arm about Sir Mark. "How did you learn that item of gossip, pray? From your ex–light o'love, perhaps? I heard you'd called on her."

Sir Mark stiffened and stepped back. "You've never been to Collington, Gideon?"

"I have, sir."

"Do not—*ever*—do so again! That ungrateful swine was in the forefront of those naming me . . . embezzler—thief. *Me!* He could scarce wait to cry off from your betrothal to his daughter. As though that young woman had not won her share of notoriety with her disgraceful behaviour both here and on the Continent!"

His face dark with anger, he went on, "Why the *devil* did you have to go crawling there? You should have come to me first! Not to that little jade!"

Gideon's jaw tightened. He said, "I was not aware the betrothal was terminated, sir. And when I went to the Point—"

"Gad, *did* you?" Amused, Newby asked, "Yesterday? You must have just missed her. That would have been a jolly meeting, I declare!"

Gideon demanded sharply, "What d'you mean? Was Naomi at the Point?"

"Yes, indeed. She came driving in, all airy-fairy innocence, pretending she'd supposed us all away. I fancy she came to have a look at you, twin."

"Confounded gall!" raged Sir Mark.

"One must be objective, Papa." Newby swung his quizzing glass and smiled at his brother's expressionless face. "My lady is a tasty morsel—even if she has been . . . ah, tasted—by numerous gentlemen of—"

Gideon was on him in a pantherish leap. The quizzing glass was seized and jerked up to be twisted about Newby's throat. An impassioned voice growled, "Your lying mouth is as full of the gutter as ever! You'd best control it whilst I'm within hearing, brother, for a very little time spent in your company inspires me with the desire to throw you through the nearest window!"

Sir Mark ran to tear Gideon's grip from the riband that was choking Newby, and thrust him away. "Let him be, you young savage!"

Gideon reeled back. With every breath now, his head seemed to split apart then clap back together. He began to feel sick, and grasped a chair for support.

"Damn . . . you . . . ," uttered Newby hoarsely, clutching his throat. "If it ain't typical you'd . . . cuddle up to—m'father's enemies!"

Sir Mark stamped to the bell pull and gave it a series of tugs which galvanized those in the lower regions of the house. "You are very obviously ill, so I shall excuse you—this time," he said, his voice quivering with anger. "But know this, Gideon. Your betrothal to the Lady Naomi Lutonville is at an end. If you *ever* have anything to say to that wanton, or her ungrateful wretch of a father—you may remove yourself from my house! I cannot disinherit you. I *can* make sure that for the duration of my life you cease to be a son of mine!"

Gideon's attempt to respond was foiled. His bones felt like

water, and the scene was becoming blurred and indistinct. He was vaguely aware that someone had come into the room, that his father was giving orders, and that he was being gently led out and half-carried up the stairs. As from a great distance he heard Newby's bray of a laugh and heard him say, "Quite like old times, eh, Papa?"

Another voice was echoing in his ears—Tio Glendenning's easy drawl. ". . . If ever I heard of so wretched a homecoming!"

The footman supporting Captain Rossiter's wavering figure glanced up. "What'd he say?"

Sir Mark's valet answered, "Something about 'tea' being very right."

The footman grunted. "Well, we all knows that, don't we!"

❧ *Chapter 7* ❧

" 'Tis very kind of Miss Falcon," agreed Naomi, making her way along the crowded aisle of the Bloomsbury Bazaar. "But I've a notion she intended to wear that particular shawl herself. Besides, I really would like one trimmed with swansdown to match my gown."

Maggie, following in the wake of her employer, said repentantly, "I be that sorry, milady. How I come to not pack it I cannot think."

"Oh, pish. We left in such a scramble 'twas no more your fault than mine own. Ah! See—on that table over there; the zephyr gauze! It looks to be just the pale pink of the embroidery on the underskirt, and can we but find an ell or two of white swansdown 'twill look divinely."

Maggie, slightly nearsighted, peered uncertainly. "Oh, does you mean by the crippled lady?"

"Hush! She'll hear you!" Naomi slipped through the throng in the popular bazaar. The young lady Maggie had referred to was inspecting an ell of fine lace, and Naomi waited politely for a chance to reach the gauze.

Leaning on a walking cane, the crippled girl moved awkwardly, collided with Naomi, and glanced up, smiling in shy apology. She was not a beauty, but the fine-boned face with its high forehead and generous mouth had a rare sweetness of expression, and her short powdered ringlets were charmingly arranged under the dainty laced cap. She gave a gasp and her blue eyes lit up. "Naomi!"

One mittened hand went out instinctively, then was withdrawn. Blushing, she stammered in confusion, "Oh! Your pardon. I should not—"

"Gwen . . . ? Is it—*Gwendolyn*?"

"Yes. But I should not have spoken. Pray—"

Her attempt to escape was hampered by her necessarily slow movements, and she was swept into a warm embrace and a kiss pressed on her cheek before she could evade it.

"My dear little Gwen!" exclaimed Naomi, the years that had separated them quite forgotten. "I've not seen you in an age! How are—"

"*If* you please, madam," said an irate female voice, and a middle-aged lady very sharp of eyes and elbows pushed her way between them.

"Oh, dear," murmured Naomi. "We block the way, I fear. Gwen, do come next door with me. The lending library has a charming little teashop, and we can have a nice cose."

"B-but . . ." protested Gwendolyn Rossiter in dismay. "Under the—the circumstances—"

A sharp elbow and an indignant glare came her way, and she recoiled. Naomi giggled, gripped her free hand, and they made their way into the sunny street where more bustling crowds forbade conversation until they were seated at a table in the relative peace of the lending library.

"Now tell me about yourself," urged Naomi. "Oh, heavens! I have mislaid my maid!"

Gwendolyn smiled. "Maggie and my footman have taken a table over there."

Naomi glanced at the pair. The footman was a well set up young man with a fine pair of bold brown eyes. "That saucy minx," she said, amused, then ordered tea and currant cakes for two, and told the serving maid to provide similar fare to her abigail's table and the bill to her own. Turning back to her companion, she was forestalled.

"Naomi, you should not be speaking to me. Your papa—"

"My father is still in Kent. Besides, our friendship has nothing to do with our families. Or"—she added hurriedly, seeing Gwendolyn's lips part for a comment—"let us pretend it does not. Tell me how you go on. I had thought you were to have an operation on your"—she glanced around and whispered—"on your knee. Did you not?"

"I did. But," Gwendolyn sighed a little, "it was unsuccessful. I'm afraid nothing can be done. I shall always limp."

"My dear, I am so sorry."

The expressive little face clouded very briefly. "The worst

of it was the disappointment for poor Papa. He was so hopeful . . .''

"Nonsense! The worst part was your suffering, which you are so brave as to disregard. But you know, Gwen, I think most of your friends do not even notice your small affliction. You have such a warm and sunny nature it renders so trite a thing quite unimportant.''

Gwendolyn leaned to press Naomi's hand gratefully. "How kind you are. Oh, I do so wish—'' She broke off in embarrassment, and drew back. "Indeed, I wonder you dare to be seen with me.''

Naomi said with a twinkle, "I give not a button for public opinion, as you should know.''

"Yet you terminated your betrothal to my brother.''

Startled, Naomi met the candid blue eyes, then gave a rueful smile. "That gave me back my own! Lud, but I had forgot how outspoken you are.''

" 'Tis a great fault, I know,'' admitted Gwendolyn, with a sigh. "Most ladies have always to say just the right thing, for fear of offending the gentlemen. But since I shall never marry, there is not the need for me to guard my words.''

The serving maid brought their tea and cake, and Naomi busied herself with cups and saucers. "What a blessing, to be so at ease,'' she said merrily. "But I would not refine too much upon your remaining a spinster, Gwen. You are very pretty and will make some lucky gentleman a delightful wife.''

Accepting a piece of cake, Gwendolyn said thoughtfully. "Thank you. But it must be a rare gentleman, I think, who would be willing to overlook my many faults. Despite your kindness, I am really not very pretty. Gideon used to say I was, bless him. But Newby is more honest. He says I have countenance . . .'' She made a face. "And worse than that—I am a bluestocking. Furthermore, did my husband deny me the right to read, or to entertain opinions on books, or politics, I should very likely murder him. So you see it is much better I remain a spinster than wind up hanged on Tyburn Tree.''

This ingenuous little speech, so gravely rendered, sent Naomi into whoops of laughter. "Oh, Gwen!'' she gasped. "How delightful you are! I wish I could spend more time with you so that we could talk about old times, but friends are waiting and I cannot stay. We *must* meet again. Can you come and see me? I stay with the Falcons at the moment. Katrina and August are there, and Mrs. Dudley Falcon—do you recall their aunt? Such a quaint lady. You know where Falcon House is, on Great Ormond Street? Or perhaps I shall see you at the Glendenning Ball?''

"Er—no, I fear not," said Gwendolyn, concentrating upon stirring her tea, and looking miserable.

"Oh!" exclaimed Naomi, staring at her in belated comprehension. "What a ninny I am!" She paused, then said rather sadly, "There is a wall between us now. Because of Gideon we can no longer be friends."

Irked by any criticism of her favourite brother, Gwendolyn's little chin came up. "An we cannot be friends 'tis because you chose to believe all the rumours about—about the lady he is said to er, call upon."

"And his children." Naomi jabbed her fork rather savagely into the cake.

"What?" Gwendolyn flushed and her eyes sparked with anger. "Now that is the outside of enough! If ever I heard such vicious gossip!"

"So I thought," said Naomi. "And like a fool, closed my ears to it—for months! But now I have had it straight from the horse's mouth, as they say."

Frowning, Gwendolyn asked with cold hauteur, "You have been to Holland, ma'am?"

"Holland? Why—no. Gwen? Have you not seen your brother?"

The ice between them was banished. With breathless eagerness Gwendolyn asked, "Do you mean—*Gideon*? He is home? You—you have spoken with him?"

"Yes. I thought you would know by this time."

"Oh! Thank God! I was sure—" For an instant it seemed she would burst into tears, then she asked in a voice that shook, "He is well? Is he much changed? Oh, heavens! He will not know where to find us!" Taking up her cane, she said, "I must go home at once. Pray forgive me! Lud, but I am forgetting! Thank you so much for the tea." She stood. "Good—good day to you, my lady."

Her footman came hurrying to usher her out, and Naomi was left staring after her.

"If ever I saw such a start!" Reining down his rambunctious grey stallion, August Falcon had to ride out two whirligigs before he could continue with his tirade, but he did so, in spite of the irrepressible dance of mischief in Naomi's eyes. "Not content," he said, avoiding a heavily laden baker's cart with an inch to spare, "with drawing half the gentlemen in London to your side—"

"Come now, August. Few of London's gentlemen have left their beds by seven o'clock in the morning. I may have met one or two acquaintances, perhaps, but—"

"One or two score! 'Twas like a blasted parade! And then you've to go off at the gallop with Tio Glendenning and that starched-up Chandler!"

" 'Twas a fast trot, merely," she protested demurely. "And Gordie Chandler is *not* starched up, August. A little reserved, perhaps."

The great city was relatively quiet at this early hour, the air clean and brisk, the work-bound throngs not yet crowding the flagways, and as they turned into Great Ormond Street, Naomi said cajolingly, " 'Tis such a glorious morning. Only see how the sun shines on those pretty geraniums. How can you be so grumpy? Smile, my dear friend, before that handsome face of yours forgets how!"

He directed an irked glance at her, but she was a sight to banish vexation, dimples peeping as she easily controlled the spirited bay mare, the sunlight gleaming on her powdered curls, the wine-coloured riding habit accentuating the shapely curves of her figure. With a reluctant grin, Falcon prepared to be less stern with this lively creature, but his forbearance fled when another irritant met his eye. "Smile, is it!" he exclaimed. "I'm more like to laugh aloud. Only look what you've attracted now, you siren!"

Startled, Naomi turned her head.

A man was running along behind them. A most disreputable figure, his clothing old and shabby, his scratch wig dishevelled, a battered hat flourished in his hand, and one eye decidedly blackened. "Poor thing," she said with ready sympathy. " 'Tis just a beggar. Have you a florin, August?"

"A florin my eye! He'll take a sixpence and like it!" He spun the coin at their pursuer. "Now be off with you!"

To their mutual surprise, the man ignored the coin and continued to stagger after them, waving his hat and calling gaspingly, "My . . . lady! Wait! Please . . . wait a bit!"

"Good gracious," said Naomi, reining to a halt. "He must have a message for me."

Falcon swung his mount between Naomi and their pursuer, and demanded, "What is your business with this lady?"

91

The runner, however, was so breathless he could not at once reply, but stood clinging to the railing outside a great house, and wheezing distressfully.

Watching him, Naomi said, "Why, I do believe I know you! Were you not at Promontory Point the other day?"

Falcon looked at her sharply. "*He* may have been, but what the deuce were you doing there?"

"I will tell you later. Oh, he is exhausted. Follow us to Falcon House, poor soul, and you shall have something to eat and then tell me why you have come."

"Now, see here," grumbled Falcon. "I'll not have any of Rossiter's people hanging about my father's—"

"I know what it is, dear August," said Naomi. "Your arm troubles you, that is why you are so out of sorts. I am scarce surprised. You had no business riding today. Truly, you are a most difficult patient. Come along now, do not sit there mumbling or you'll be taken up for a drunkard!" And with a furtive twinkle, and a flourish of her whip, she was off, Falcon following her perforce, and Mr. Tummet bringing up the rear.

Despite his exasperated protests that he was *not* tired, and that he would take his breakfast with the ladies, Falcon's arm was indeed paining him, and he was secretly repenting his earlier decision to accompany Naomi on her morning ride. With a great show of indignation, he eventually obeyed his sister and stamped upstairs. Once inside his bedchamber, he submitted meekly to the strictures of his man, was divested of riding boots and coat, and went grumbling but grateful to rest on his bed. He had dropped off to sleep by the time a tray was brought to him. His valet rested his fingers lightly on the pale forehead, noted the slightly flushed cheeks, and shook his head worriedly.

Mrs. Dudley Falcon was a plump and amiable widow who might have inspired the term "creature comforts," for she was a creature who had dedicated her life to comfort. No matter what the circumstances, she was always to be found in the coziest corners, in the softest chair, or commanding the prettiest view. She was never disappointed in achieving her aims, for if an occasion carried even a whiff of discomfort, she avoided it. It pleased her erratic brother, Mr. Neville Falcon, to suppose that his sister-in-law made an exemplary chaperone to his beautiful daughter. Actually, Mrs. Dudley, as she was known, paid small heed to the activities of her charge, beaming on her fondly from a comfortable distance while comfortably convinced that the gentle Katrina could never behave improperly. She never arose before noon, and at this early hour she was, as usual, comfortably in bed, a tray across her lap, while she enjoyed the scandalous gossip conveyed in the several letters which lay about the eiderdown.

Downstairs, Katrina and Naomi chattered merrily over breakfast, deciding which of many invitations to accept for tomorrow, and what to wear to the musicale they were to attend on Monday afternoon. These were lengthy discussions and half an hour had passed before Naomi rang the handbell and told the footman he might bring "that poor man" to her if he had finished his breakfast.

"I hope you will not object, dearest," she added, turning to her friend. "He was following us along the street, and looked half starved, so I sent him to the kitchen for a meal."

"But—who on earth is he?" asked Katrina.

"I believe he is one of Gid—the Rossiters' servants. He admitted me to Promontory Point when I called there yesterday morning.

"You *called* there? Again? Good heavens!"

"Well, never look so sanctimonious. I told you that my papa was enraged because I lost his silly chess piece."

"Yes. But—what has that to do with—"

"Only that he thought Captain Rossiter might have found it. So he asked me to enquire."

Knitting her brows Katrina said a mystified, "But—surely, your papa should better have sent one of his menservants on such an errand?"

"Perhaps, but"—Naomi shrugged airily—"I was curious to see what my notorious ex-fiancé looked like after all these years, and I thought 'twould be fun to watch him implore my forgiveness for his disgraceful behaviour in Europe. To say nothing," she added, with a sudden scowl, "of how he tossed me into the carriage, the wretch! And then I could trample him! In the mire!"

"La, Naomi," exclaimed Katrina, admiringly. "How daring you are. You told me none of this. They have lost the estate, you know."

Naomi blanched. "Oh, no! That lovely old place? Gideon must be—" She caught herself up. " 'Tis passing tragic!"

"Well, so I think, but August says Sir Mark brought it on himself by placing his faith in idiots. And that he has dragged many innocents down with him. Which is truth, I suppose. But pray tell what you said to Captain Rossiter? What did *he* say? Was he repentant? *Did* you trample him in the mire?''

Naomi gazed down at the pearl ring she wore, and did not at once reply. Then she said in a low voice, ''He bragged to me of his children . . . Three! All born out of wedlock, poor little things.''

''My *heavens*!''

''Yet he dared to name *me*—guttersnipe!'' That recollection brought a blaze into Naomi's eyes. She said through her teeth, ''And dared to imply I had jilted him because his father is disgraced and the fortune lost.''

''Oh, my dear!'' Katrina reached across the table to clasp her friend's hand fondly. ''*What* a narrow escape you have had! The man is beneath contempt!''

For another moment Naomi was very still and silent. Looking up then, she said lightly, ''And I am inconsolable, for I was unable to trample him in the mire. We did our quarrelling inside the house, you see, and alas, there was none. At least, not in evidence.''

They were both laughing merrily at this when the footman announced in a most disapproving tone that Mr. Enoch Tummet awaited my lady's convenience.

''Very well.'' Naomi stood. ''With your permission, Trina, I will see him in the red parlour.''

''Yes, of course. But you cannot see him alone. I'll come with you.''

''Now you must not be Gothic, dear. Johnson will wait in the hall, and I am very sure one of Rossiter's people will not attack me. You know you are anxious about August. Do you run along, and I shall be up directly to change my dress.''

Katrina hesitated, looking dubiously at the shabby individual who waited in the hall behind Johnson. It was very clear that Naomi wished to talk to the man alone, however, and she really was rather worried about her brother, so she nodded and hurried off.

Hat in hand, Mr. Tummet followed Naomi along the hall, his one functioning eye taking in the luxury all about him, and his lips registering a silent ''Cor!'' as he was shown into the elegant red and gold parlour.

''Remember your manners, my good man,'' adjured the footman in a lofty aside.

''I'll try, me good cove,'' said Tummet, dropping him a clumsy and exaggerated curtsy.

Naomi stifled a laugh. The footman gave Tummet a frigid glare, and took up a position outside the door.

"Well now," said Naomi, seating herself on a gold brocade sofa. "Were you given a satisfactory meal, Mr.—er, Tummet?"

"Thankee, yus, milady. Fork and gaiters." Noting her puzzled look, he grinned broadly. "Pork and taters, to you, ma'am. Most ample to me innards they was, and more'n welcome arter being on the road all night. E. Tummet thanks you kindly for the 'orspitality."

Amusement danced into Naomi's eyes. 'A proper rascal,' she thought. 'But an engaging one.' She indicated a straightbacked chair. "Pray be seated. You must be tired."

He sat down gingerly. "Orl right, ma'am, though I ain't dressed fer it. I'll get on me way, if you'll be so very kind as to tell me where 'e is."

"Me? I am confused. Do you not work for Captain Rossiter?"

"No, melady. I'm a guard. Or was. I was 'ired to guard Promontory Point 'til the Courts make up their minds what to do wiv it."

"I see." She was vaguely disappointed. "I had thought you came with a message for me."

"Well, that's right, in a manner o'speaking, ma'am. The message is from E. Tummet. And it says, 'Please to 'elp 'im find Cap'n Rossiter,' on account of which gent I lost me sovereign nation—er, sittyation, that is, melady. And got one 'o me daylights darkened."

Mystified, and groping, Naomi said, "Captain Rossiter caused you to lose your situation? And er . . . ?"

Tummet jerked a thumb at his face and explained patiently, "Me daylight, ma'am. Me orb—or ogle."

"Oh! Your eye! So that's what 'a darkened daylight' means! The captain gave you a black eye!"

"Not 'im, melady. Them other coves what come arter 'im and the lieutenant 'ad sloped orf. Knocked me abaht something awful they done, then searched the premises fer something Cap'n Rossiter 'ad, what 'e shouldn't oughter."

Naomi frowned. "I will own Captain Rossiter's character leaves much to be desired. But—I cannot think him a thief."

"And 'ow right you are, melady," said Tummet, beaming at her. "A fine gent, if ever I see one. But them coves, they kept carrying on about 'the Squire.' The Squire said as it musta bin Rossiter, they says. And they better find it, or it would go 'ard

95

with 'em. And 'cause I didn't know what they was a talking of, they went 'ard with *me*, they did! And then they started searching about, and by the time they was done searching, you'd'a thought fifty-nine bulls 'ad been chasing one o' they Spanish matty-doors through the 'ouse!''

"Good gracious! Do you say they ransacked Promontory Point?"

He eyed her doubtfully. "As to that, I couldn't say, ma'am. But they fair tore it to shreds, and I knowed if they still didn't find what they was looking fer, they'd come arter me again. So I managed to creep orf and I 'id, ma'am. 'Til they sloped. But not long arterwards, 'oo should come riding in but the gent what 'ired me. Cor! Was 'e in a me-and-you—er, that means—"

"Let me guess," said Naomi, fascinated by her first exposure to rhyming cant. "Me-and-you . . . hmm. Stew?"

"That's it, melady. We'll 'ave you talking the King's English yet! But the thing is, y'see, my gent blames *me* fer all the mess. And so I loses me—"

"Sovereign nation—situation," she interpolated, gaining confidence.

He nodded. "Yus'm."

"And you feel that since all this took place in Captain Rossiter's home, because of some mischief he'd been about, he is responsible."

"Well—I asks you," said Tummet, giving her a pontifical look. "Put yerself in my shoes. Proper case of nobly siege, I calls it."

Here, Naomi was out of her depth, and it took a moment for her to translate. "*Noblesse oblige!* Yes, of course. You are quite justified, and you may tell Captain Rossiter that in my opinion he should hire you himself, to make amends for having placed you in so unenviable a position." She scanned her disreputable-looking caller, and added with exquisite enjoyment, "As—his valet, perhaps."

Mr. Tummet gave her a rather startled look, received an encouraging smile, and pursing his lips declared that he "might consider" such a post.

Restraining her mirth with difficulty, she asked, "However did you know I was in London?"

"I didn't, ma'am. Knowed the Cap'n was coming to London, so I cadged a ride with a carter yesterday and a 'edge and sta-ble—er, vegetable—merchant let me kip on 'is waggon last night.

'S morning I was lucky enough to see you out riding, so I 'oped as you could find it in yer beeootiful and kind 'eart to 'elp me."

Naomi said staunchly that she would do so, and calling in the footman asked if he knew Sir Mark Rossiter's new direction. The footman was able to oblige, and shortly thereafter Mr. Tummet departed, bowing, and expressing the depth of his gratitude—a gratitude that deepened when Naomi made him the richer of a gold crown. "Out of sympathy," she said rather fallaciously, "with your tragic tale."

She stood at the window, smiling, as she watched him hurry along the flagway. "Let that be a lesson to you, Captain Gideon Rossiter," she murmured. "And never say this guttersnipe has not done her very best for you!"

Gideon slept late and awoke feeling much refreshed and cheered by the bright sunshine that flooded his room. His tug on the bell pull brought his brother's servant, Henri Delatouche, with a breakfast tray. Gideon had never cared for the unctuous little valet and had decided long since that the man's humility was as suspect as his accent. The breakfast was excellent, however, and as soon as he had done justice to it he turned his attention to his wardrobe.

Six years had not effected a great change in fashions, and although there was now some talk of making waistcoats sleeveless, the style had not as yet been widely adopted. He had feared that his long illness had left him so thin that his civilian clothes would be useless, and was rather pleased to find that, if anything, the coats were a trifle snug across the shoulders. He selected a coat of dark grey velvet, the great cuffs and pockets rich with scarlet embroidery. His waistcoat was silver brocade patterned with red, and his breeches grey silk. Delatouche groaned over so sober a habit for a young man, and when he learned the captain did not intend to have his hair cut short to accommodate a wig, he threw up his hands in despair.

"I did not wear a wig in the Low Countries," growled Gideon.

"But, monsieur, consider, I implore. 'Ere in London, ze gentleman of fashion 'e would as soon go naked about ze streets as to appear in 'is natural 'air! If no wig, *Monsieur le Capitaine must* but 'e must *certainement* 'ave ze powder and ze patches!"

The patches Gideon refused in so stern a voice that Delatouche tearfully surrendered, but an appeal to consider the feelings of his noble papa overcame his resistance to powder and he was ushered to the powder closet, enfolded in a wrapper, and subjected to pomatum and pounce pot. Whatever his vices, Delatouche was skilled in his craft. By the time Gideon was dressed, a great ruby ring slipped onto his hand, and a tricorne tucked under his arm, his mirror showed him an elegant stranger. Even Delatouche was mollified, and said that *Monsieur le Capitaine* would "drive ze mademoiselles distracted!"

Seconds later, the much tried valet was clutching his brow in despair once more, for no sooner did the Captain step into the hall than Miss Rossiter rose from a chair and with a cry of joy flung herself into his arms.

"Gwendolyn!" Gideon swept her off her feet. "My cheerful sparrow," he said between kisses. "How lovely you are grown! Why a'God's name did you perch here in the hall as if I've not been yearning to see you? You should have come in at once!"

"I am only thankful you are home safe!" Gwendolyn wiped away happy tears. "I knew you had been wounded, and was fairly beside myself with anxiety. Oh, Gideon, can we talk before you go downstairs?"

"Of course." Of all his family, this frail, crippled girl was closest to his heart, and with his arm tight around her, he led her back into his room. They sat in the window seat together and scanned each other hungrily; he with prideful approval, she with such obvious anxiety that he tugged a glistening ringlet and asked laughingly, "Am I such a shock, Gwen? You said you knew I'd been brought down. How, by the way?"

"Papa and Newby said I was silly, but I just . . . knew."

Naomi had also said she'd thought he'd been hit. He frowned a little. Was it possible that she really had sensed—He dismissed such nonsense impatiently. Such prescience must also argue affection, and if Lady Naomi Lutonville gave affection to anyone it was to her innumerable flirts.

Deeply moved by her brother's sombre expression, Gwendolyn seized his hand and nursed it to her cheek. "You are alive and will be your old self again in no time. But *mon pauvre*, I see that it must have been very bad."

His eyes became blank, and she said at once, "No, please, Gideon, do not shut me out. I have worried for such a long while."

Repentant, he murmured, "My poor little one. What a fellow I am not to have written. But in truth at first there was small opportunity, and when the opportunity was there," he gave a wry grin, "the ability was not. Besides, I had no wish to send

98

you bad news. Which was as well, I am persuaded. You had enough already! Gwen, what can you tell me of this disaster?''

"Very little, I fear. I only know there was a run on the bank and that all the other investors backed away and left poor Papa to take full blame. And he did, Gideon. He made no attempt to save what he could for himself, but was concerned only in trying to repay as many as possible of those who had lost their money. You'd scarce believe the nightmare of it. The people who would shout curses after our carriage in the streets . . . the stones they threw at the windows of the house . . . the dreadful things that were written in the newspapers!''

He groaned. "Had I been here I might have been able to avert this. At least I could have stood by my father. Small wonder he is disgusted with me!''

"No, no! Just a little put out, perhaps, when you did not sell out as he asked, but I am very sure that now he is only relieved that you are safe home. At all events, it has not been quite so horrid since we moved here. Only . . . Papa is so proud, you know, and I think it broke his heart when we had to leave Promontory Point.'' Her voice became a little scratchy. "I don't know how long we will be able to stay here. Or . . . what will become of us.''

She looked very small and wan suddenly, and he pulled her close and gave her a buss. "Silly chit. Had you forgot Emerald Farm? If we are obliged to leave Town, we all can go and live there. You would like that—no?''

Her woebegone face lit up. "Oh, Gideon! I should love it! I had indeed forgot. But—'tis *yours*, you will be wanting to marry and—'' She broke off, her eyes opening very wide. "Or—are you already wed, perchance?''

"Not wed, love. But I fancy you will have heard I am a father.''

She gave a gasp, searching his face but finding it unreadable. "Then it really is truth? I could scarce believe it! Oh, then I am an *aunt*! How marvellous! Tell me about them, Gideon. What are their names? When can I see them? Shall your lady of the garden come here? Or—oh dear! Was it the—other one?''

The frown which had crept into his eyes was banished by a reluctant laugh. "Good God! Has all London Town wallowed in mine iniquities?''

"There has been rather an astonishing amount of gossip, but I did not know of the children until yesterday when Naomi mentioned—''

"Naomi?" His voice harsh, he demanded, "Did she call here?"

"No. I chanced to meet her in Bloomsbury and nothing would do but that I take tea with her. I've not seen her in an age. She is more beautiful than I had recollected, though I thought her rather sad, but—Oh!" Horrified, she exclaimed, "My heavens! You *did* know? About the betrothal?"

He said grimly, "I do now. I went to Collington and was sent off with a flea in my ear. Later, I met my betrothed, and she handed me a proper set-down."

"I am so sorry. But, do you know, I think she was not so wild 'til—"

She was interrupted by a knock at the door, and the footman advised that Sir Mark sent his compliments, and was waiting for Captain Rossiter in the study. Promising that they would have a long chat later in the day, Gideon ushered his sister into the hall, then watched rather sadly as she made her way towards her own room, leaning on her cane. One of the few letters he'd received had advised that the hopefully anticipated surgery to correct her knee, damaged at birth, had failed. Her limp seemed, if anything, more pronounced. She could have been such a little beauty, if only—He cut off such disloyalty. Gwen *was* a little beauty, limp or no. The people to be pitied were the stupid idiots who did not see what a darling she was.

On the stairs he encountered Newby, resplendent in shades of puce and wearing a bag wig with three curls that Gideon thought appalling. Newby leaned back against the banister scanning his brother through a jewelled quizzing glass. "Unimaginative," he said in his supercilious way. "But at least you begin to resemble something human."

Gideon closed his lips over an instinctive retort and went past without a word.

"I fancy you know that my father awaits your valiant presence," called Newby. "Be careful what you say, twin." Gideon turned and looked at him, and after a swift glance around, Newby went on softly, "I believe the old fool cherishes the hope that you have come riding home on your trusty charger to slay his ridiculous dragon called Conspiracy. One trusts your armour is polished and your lance sharpened."

Ignoring the sarcasm in voice and look, Gideon said, "You do judge it ridiculous, then?"

Newby shrugged. "I judge his wits are properly addled. The fault is his own, and needed no embroidering by fiendish conspirators. I wonder you doubt it. As I recall, the main cause of your so frequent disagreements was that you felt he relied too heavily on ill-chosen subordinates—no?''

"I do not recollect your backing me on those issues at the time.''

With a deprecatory wave of his quizzing glass, Newby said, "But my dear twin, you beat me into this world by five and twenty minutes. *You* are the heir apparent to this sorry kingdom.'' He smiled sweetly. "And its indebtedness.''

"Yet I fancy you mean to enlighten me as to the best way to proceed.''

"There is but one way.'' Newby straightened, his voice losing its sneering drawl to become sharp with urgency. "The old man must gather whatever assets still are left to us, and emigrate. In the New World we can start again. I hear there are quite charming estates to be had in some of the colonies, and—''

"I might have known,'' interrupted Gideon in disgust. "You advocate a full retreat. To run away and leave our name sunk in dishonour. Brave advice, 'pon my word!''

Flushing darkly, Newby leaned nearer. "Don't look down your haughty nose at me! Will our name be any less dishonoured does he stay to face trial, conviction, and deportation? Rather, we will come out of it pauperized *and* dishonoured!''

"Not an we prove him innocent of wrongdoing. Perhaps—''

"Gammon! Do you fancy we have not tried? Whilst you were cavorting with your plump little paramours, Papa and I have wrestled with irate creditors and solicitors. We've fended off the set of ghouls who write for the newspapers. We've battled Bow Street and government enquiries and were able to prove only that he made mice feet of the whole and deserved exactly what he got!''

Gideon shook his head and with a curl of the lip trod to the next stair.

Seizing his arm, Newby wrenched him around and said through his teeth, "For once will you try to be less of a fool? Do we both prevail upon him to act now, we may come out of this with *some* funds and the hope for a comfortable way of life!''

"I may be a fool, brother—indeed, I suspect I am a very great fool—but I do not know the whole of this as yet. When I do, and if there is the smallest chance of restoring our good name, that is the course I shall—''

Newby's attention had been arrested by a movement in the

101

lower hall and he now demanded wrathfully, "You there! Who the devil are you?"

Mr. Enoch Tummet stepped back to leer up at them. "Now that there's a right coincidence," he said. "Them's the first words what yer brother spoke to me, Guv'nor."

"How did you know this gentleman is my brother?" demanded Newby. "Damn you, I think you were listening! Be off with you before—"

"No, no. I think Mr. Tummet came to see me," said Gideon, and hurrying down the remaining stairs, ignored Newby's predictably sarcastic response and drew the caller into a small book room.

Closing the doors, he asked, "How the deuce did you find me? And why?"

"Proper posh you look," said Tummet, his one visible eye scanning Gideon's tall figure admiringly. "But yer brother's right, y'know. 'Op orf. Quick. Grab yer valleybles, an' run. While you can. Them's me advice, give free and wiv all goodwill fer yer honour."

Amused by his impudence, Gideon motioned to a chair and occupying one himself said, "That's what you would do in my circumstances, is it?"

" 'Ere!" Tummet's bright brown eye became very round and he raised one hand in a delaying gesture. "I never said *that*, mate. There's the rub—like Mr. Shakespeare says—ain't it? It's easy to tell a cove what 'e oughtta do—when it's *'im* what's gotta do it. But to know what to do when it's *you* what's gotta do it—well now, that's another tale."

Intrigued, Gideon said curiously, "You can read, can you?"

"Yussir. Learned 'ow when I was a lackey. Not much to do 'cept stand around and look like a stuffed owl." He drew himself up and assumed a frozen expression, then sat down with a mischievous wink. "There was a framed pome on the wall where I useter stand, and I stared at it by the hour, I did. One day I asked the 'ousekeeper what it was all about. A nice little old woman she were, and she taught me 'ow to read. Very slow, mind you. But once you can read—well! Opens a 'ole new world, don't it, mate?"

"I'm not your mate, you rogue. And my father is waiting, so we'd best get to your reason for coming here. Start by answering my first question, an you please."

" 'Ow did I find yer, right? Cor! Ain't no one can 'ide in this 'ere village from the likes o' me, Cap'n. And I come so's you

102

could do right by me. Like a 'onourable gent oughter. You being one, like you told yer brother.''

"You rascally opportunist! Are you asking compensation because Lieutenant Morris blacked your eye?''

"Ar, but he didn't, mate—er, Cap'n, sir. It was them other coves.'' He launched into the tale he had told earlier at a certain house on Great Ormond Street.

Gideon listened in frowning silence. At the end, he swore angrily. "Has all this been relayed to the authorities?''

"Such as they is. Yus, Guv.''

"And you don't know who these men were? No names spoken, or anything to reveal what they were after, or who they might work for?''

"All they done was talk about 'the Squire.' Whoever their squire might be, 'e's a ugly customer, I can tell you. Same as them. I'd know 'em if I ever seed 'em, you may be sure! 'Specially the cove what give me this.'' He touched his swollen eye tenderly. "A big 'un. Taller'n you, and twice as wide as me, with a face like a mangle-wurzel, and only four fingers and a bit on 'is left 'and.''

Gideon stood, wandered to the window and stared at the weedy garden, thinking in mixed rage and sadness of the great estate and the pleasant life they had enjoyed there. Why the devil would anyone want to wreck it? What were they looking for? Most of the family's personal effects had been removed. The furnishings were valuable but had evidently not been stolen. He had brought home nothing of great worth and, in fact, some of his possessions were still at the Red Pheasant Inn. Most of the articles stolen with his saddlebags had been gifts he'd hoped to present to his family. Jewelry, fans, and laces for Gwen and his female relations; snuff boxes, a filigreed quizzing glass, assorted war souvenirs for the men. Certainly nothing to justify all this violence.

"So, I come 'ere,'' said Tummet, growing tired of the long silence, " 'oping and *trusting* as you'd make it up to me, seein's it's on account o' you I bin robbed o' me 'ole fortune, everything in the wide world as I owned.''

"Gad! They robbed you, too?''

"Manner o'speaking, they did. Me sovereign nation—me sittyation, that is—was lost to me. And seein's it was all I got, I lost everything.''

Gideon could not repress a smile, but it occurred to him that what this crafty fellow said was very likely true. The loss of his

103

position might constitute as great a disaster to him as the loss now facing the Rossiters. "Very well," he said, reaching for his purse. "I'll pay you—"

Tummet sprang to his feet and declared with a theatrical gesture which would have made the great Garrick envious that he did not want money. "I come 'ere in good faith, 'oping you'd do like the lady said, and take me into yer service."

"Take you into my *service*?" echoed Gideon, dumbfounded. "What bird-wit—I mean, who is the lady who said such a thing?"

"Lady Lutonville," said Tummet, looking aggrieved. "She says I was to say as in 'er 'pinion, you oughta take me on, to make up fer the grief and woe you caused me." He looked at the ceiling and added innocently, "As yer valet."

"As my—*what*?" Torn between hilarity and disbelief, Gideon started to say that he did not believe Lady Lutonville would say so bacon-brained a thing, but then he paused. My lady had likely had a fine time picturing his indignation when this eminently unsuitable man arrived with her ridiculous recommendation. Tummet seemed a good enough fellow, and the question now became how to get out of this bumble-broth without hurting his feelings. Yearning to give her obliging ladyship a hard shake, he smiled at Tummet and said, man-to-man fashion, "You are probably aware of my family's—er, temporarily difficult circumstances."

"Yus. Well, I'd be willing to overlook that."

"You'd be—" With an outraged gasp, Gideon said, "Why, you insolent hedgebird! I doubt you know the difference 'twixt a cravat and a stock! And as for being willing to overlook—Be damned if I shouldn't have you thrown out for—" He checked. Tummet was watching him, so hopeful a leer on his unlovely features that it was hard to hold anger.

"I know I ain't much to look at," admitted Tummet. "But I'd be a good servant, Cap'n. I'm honest and loyal, and I knows more about cravats and stocks *and* other things than what you might think. Matter o'fact," he added with a knowing wink, "you might just find I'm a sight more use t'you than 'alf a dozen starched-up Town valets with poached eggs fer eyes and their noses stuck up so 'igh you'd 'ardly dare ask 'em to kiss yer 'and."

"I am not in the habit of asking my servants to kiss my hand! And furthermore, you may tell Lady Lutonville—"

Without the courtesy of a knock, Newby opened the door and

strolled in. "My father is in a proper taking, dear brother. You will recollect I told you he was waiting?"

"So you did." Gideon stood, with an inward sigh of relief. "I'll come at once."

"I should think so." Lifting his quizzing glass and lazily surveying Tummet, who had respectfully come to his feet, Newby grinned. "What in the deuce could you find to discuss with *this*?"

"I was—er, interviewing applicants," said Gideon, as always chafed by his brother's arrogance.

"Applicants for what? Resident chimney sweep?"

Gideon frowned, and threw an apologetic look at the applicant.

Tummet maintained his one-eyed gaze at the ceiling and drew himself up to assume his "stuffed owl" stance.

"For the position of my—er, valet," explained Gideon.

Newby's jaw dropped, his astounded gaze taking in Mr. Tummet's down-at-heel boots, ragged clothes, and lurid black eye. Then he gave a whoop. "Zounds! If you ain't a complete hand, twin! No really, what is it?"

Gideon smiled. "Matter of fact," he drawled, "I've just decided to take him on."

Tummet blinked rather rapidly.

Gideon experienced the sinking feeling that once again he'd allowed temper to push him into a proper bog.

"Good . . . God!" gasped Mr. Newby Rossiter.

❈ *Chapter 8* ❈

The Musicale was a great success. When it ended and the guests adjourned to the refreshment room, little eddies of eager gentlemen formed around the reigning Toasts. In one corner, Katrina Falcon's admirers jostled one another so as to see her sweet smile and hear the soft voice. Nearby, a vivacious and amply endowed young widow held court, while across the room Lady Naomi Lutonville was surrounded by as ardent beaux, who vied with one another to bring her refreshments, exclaim over the enchantments of her light blue gown, its creamy underdress patterned with dainty blue flowers, or to wax poetical over her glorious eyes, her petal soft skin, her vivid mouth, the allure of her dimples, the perfection of her shapeliness.

Mr. Gordon Chandler, quietly attractive in a dark red velvet coat, the cuffs and pocket flaps rich with silver thread, brought my lady a plate of delicacies and implored that she allow him to escort her to the Glendenning Ball, since Falcon was indisposed. Mr. Alfred Harrier, a plump and fashionably pale youth of great fortune and a slight lisp, held a cup of iced punch ready should the beauty desire it, and pronounced Chandler a pirate, villainously attempting to steal the lady away from him.

"Alas, I am unmasked!" Chandler's rare smile lit his rather grave features. "Only see how you unnerve me, Lady Naomi! I am so distracted by your beauty as to commit social solecisms, and I dare not guess how my sire will react does he hear of it! Simple kindness demands that you restore my shattered nerves by accompanying me to Tio's hop."

"Hop!" Naomi chided him with the familiarity of lifelong friendship. "Fie, Gordie! I think Bowers-Malden would not smile to hear his ball referred to in such a way."

"You do right to refuse Chandler," exclaimed Mr. Harrier. "He was so dull as to not exert himself to discover which gown you meant to wear today! I, on the other hand, made discreet enquiries, and thus was able to match my colours to your own, fair goddess! Such devotion surely must be rewarded!"

He was indeed clad in shades of blue, and although jeering cries arose from the gentlemen, Naomi agreed that he must be rewarded, and carefully detaching a tiny white rose from her corsage, passed it to him.

Mr. Harrier received the dainty flower ecstatically, kissed it, and placed it amid the curls of the very high French wig, which did little to conceal his lack of stature.

At once, Naomi was beset by anxious enquiries as to whether this meant she was promised to attend the ball with Harrier.

"No, really, gentlemen," she protested, laughing. "I am promised to Mr. Falcon, who vows he means to come."

Lord Sommers, large, ruddy-complected, and unfailingly good-natured, grumbled, "Blister the fellow! I'd heard he would be laid down upon his bed for a month at least."

"Did you, begad?" A very tall young man whose quizzing glass was a vital necessity, peered at Naomi through it, and asked, "Is't that bad, ma'am? The highwayman—what?"

"Indirectly, Duke," answered Naomi. "Falcon was mistaken for one when Captain Rossiter and his friend came to our aid."

Sommers pursed his lips. "Rossiter has enough to answer for without he must frighten one of London's fairest flowers and shoot down—"

"No, no, my lord!" interrupted Naomi. "In all fairness I must own that Rossiter was not the culprit."

"Only see how generous is the dear soul," lisped Mr. Harrier. "To defend him in spite of—" He received a strong nudge in the ribs, and floundering, turned a bright pink.

Naomi took refuge behind her fan, eyelashes demurely lowered.

Known for his stubborn nature, and loyal to an old friend, Chandler argued, "I fancy Rossiter needs no defence. He'd have no hand in such a fiasco."

"Then 'tis one of few things that cannot be laid at the Rossiters' door," growled Sommers.

"Gideon Rossiter denies 'em," argued Mr. Harrier. "Faith, but he denies 'em all over Town. Long and loud. Making a regular cake of himself with his questions and investigations. M'father says gentlemen are bolting their doors 'gainst him!"

"Good gracious," said Naomi. "He has been in England barely a week. What is it he questions?"

The duke waved his quizzing glass. "Everything, dear lady. Seems to be trying to prove his ignoble papa was innocent of all wrongdoing."

The scornful laughter that greeted this remark was interrupted by a new voice.

"And all England united in a gigantic plot 'gainst Sir Mark, eh?"

The younger gentlemen laughed, and fell back respectfully.

Surprised, Naomi turned to face the newcomer. The great panniers of her skirts were as cumbersome as they were fashionable, but she handled them expertly, and dropped a graceful curtsy. "Papa! I had thought you meant to remain in Kent."

Resplendent in purple and gold, the earl smiled and bent to kiss her forehead. "I don't tell you all my secrets, child. Do you enjoy a pleasant stay with your friends?"

He looked amiable enough, but Naomi watched him warily. "Thank you, yes. And you, sir?"

"I was obliged to come into Town, and guessed I might find you here. Come—I'll have a word with you."

"No, really, Collington," protested the short-sighted duke. "Your lovely daughter has not yet chosen her escort for the Glendenning Ball. Come now, my lady. You know Falcon is too ill to attend. Spare our torment."

"Really, I cannot," Naomi answered with a smile. "But—an I find Mr. Falcon unimproved when I return this evening, I will choose my escort—tomorrow."

Another concerted groan. Chandler called, "When, Lady Naomi? Where?"

The earl was leading her away. Over her shoulder she called, "At the Dowling Soiree. I shall throw my flowers, and the gentleman who catches them may escort me to the ball."

This pleased them with its suggestion of sport, and a babble of comment arose.

Amused, the earl guided her through the crowded room. "You are quite the Toast, child. I dare swear you may take your pick among 'em."

"Oh, they are silly boys," she said lightly. They turned into the wide corridor, and she added, "I am surprised to find you here, sir."

"Truth to tell, *I* was surprised when you left Collington so— ah, precipitately." He smiled down at her and opened the door

108

to an ante room. "Did I frighten you away with my bad humours?"

Naomi made her way to a loveseat and sat amid billows of taffeta, wondering why he was really here, and dreading lest he demand that she return to Collington Manor and meet the "fine gentleman" who was "slavering" to lay his riches at her feet. "I do not frighten easily, Papa," she declared bravely. "But I'll own you seemed somewhat overset."

He wandered to the hearth and inspected the Grecian urn placed before the empty grate. "If I was, m'dear, 'twas not by reason of a lost chess piece." He turned to face her, his eyes grave. "That was vexing, I'll own, but 'tis not every day one's child is attacked by rascally rank riders. I have writ to Captain Rossiter expressing my gratitude for his intervention—however clumsily achieved. I—er, trust this was appropriate . . . ?"

"I do not follow you, sir. How could it be inappropriate? Because of the injury to August Falcon?"

"Not at all. However, your footman believed you to have been upset when you left Promontory Point on Tuesday. If young Rossiter dared annoy you . . ."

Her colour rising, Naomi said, "He did not annoy me, sir. He infuriated me!"

"Did he now," murmured the earl. "You will favour me by having nothing more to do with him. As to his friend, besides shooting down Falcon, for which I really cannot fault him, would you say he was of some assistance to you?"

"Besides shooting down Falcon, for which I shall not forgive him," she said, her angry eyes challenging his mocking ones, "I suppose he helped—yes."

"Escorted you home, I understand. Which was likely quite out of his path. Any soldier returning to England desires to reach home as soon as may be."

She shrugged. "I did not ask such a sacrifice of him."

"Even so, I collect I must send him a note also. You said his name was—Moore?"

"Morris, Papa. Lieutenant James Morris."

"Alas, memory fails me. Morris . . . I believe there is a prominent Cornwall family of that name. I wonder . . . ?"

"I seem to recall Rossiter mentioned something about the lieutenant going on to Sevenoaks."

"Is that so? Then I shall have no difficulty in learning his direction. Now tell me of young Falcon. He will recover?"

Naomi looked at him steadily. "His death would grieve you, sir?"

"Not in the least. Save that I'd prefer not to be involved in the way of it."

"Then you may be at ease. August took a ball in his arm. A flesh wound merely. He would be recovered by now, save that he stubbornly persisted in returning to London before he was able to withstand the journey, and the following day must ride with me, whereby he took a fever."

"Typical. And since the fair Katrina is devoted to her firebrand brother, you mean to stay by her through this—ordeal, eh?"

"For the time being, sir."

Collington smiled. "You do not ask if I approve. You know what my answer would be. They are indeed fortunate that a lady of your position recognizes them in public."

"'Pon rep, sir! Did you not remark the number of highly born gentlemen who appear to have no difficulty recognizing Miss Falcon?"

"Ah, yes. But with entirely different motives, I suspect. And much as I enjoy sparring with you, I must take my leave. Farewell, child. Pray embrace no further disasters."

Naomi's taut nerves relaxed. Thank heaven! He meant to go without taxing her about marriage. Walking with him to the door, she said, "Truly, I am sorry about your loss, Papa. 'Twas vastly careless in me."

He looked at her with upraised brows. "Loss?"

"Your chess piece."

"Ah, yes. I think that is best forgot. Is provoking to think that some uncouth rank rider, or a yokel with no appreciation of its antiquity, likely found it. But there. What use to cry over spilt milk? Adieu. Do not stay too long from Kent. We miss you."

He patted her cheek, smiled with rare warmth, and was gone.

There was a haze in the air on this Tuesday morning, and the sunlight was diffused so that her beams fell softly upon London's countless chimney pots, towers, and domes. Gideon stood at the window of the book room, contemplating the scene thoughtfully. A warm little hand crept into his own. He turned, smiling down at Gwendolyn's bright face.

"Are you thinking how different is the prospect?" she asked. "From that of Rossiter Court, I mean? The hill gives us a fine view, Gideon."

He bent to press a kiss on her forehead. "Which is one thing to be said for it, eh little one? No, I was thinking of my father's—er—"

"Obsession?" Newby closed the door behind him and sauntered across the room. "I wonder you waste your time with such balderdash." He embraced his sister and said smilingly, "Do not encourage him, my poppet."

Gideon pulled out a chair for her, and Gwendolyn sat down and said with a sigh, "I wish I *might* offer some encouragement. 'Twould be passing wonderful to find we were not really responsible for so much grief and tragedy."

"*We* are not, love." Newby disposed himself languidly against the edge of the reference table. "Our inept old gentleman is. And my heroic brother would do well to employ his mind to the avoidance of prosecution rather than try to sniff out a non-existent band of dastardly conspirators. No—use your wits do, Gideon! Why in the devil would anyone go to so much trouble and expense? 'Tis not as if there were vast fortunes to be made from this catastrophe."

"I would call one hundred thousand pounds a vast fortune," interposed Gwendolyn indignantly.

"Yes, dear," said Gideon. "But that was stolen by one rascal. Most expertly. Where was the need for all the rest of it? I think that's what Newby means."

"Your brilliance, dear twin, is dazzling," sneered Newby.

"And your filial loyalty non-existent. My father is not a blockhead—"

"Just an exceeding maladroit Chairman of the Board? Oh, never give me your pious looks or pretend a devotion you do not feel. Six years ago you could scarce wait to buy yourself a pair of colours so as to get away from him."

"From his policies, rather."

"Time proved you right in that, at least."

"Even so, I never held him to be a fool, and there is a deal too much of coincidence in all this for us to laugh at his suspicions."

Newby said contemptuously, "As I do? Is that what you say? Then pray tell, dear twin, what you with your *superior* understanding have discovered whilst you puttered about asking questions. You must have succeeded in stirring up somebody. Papa tells me his solicitor is already imploring him to keep you from his door!"

"I called on him, certainly, and learned how much a man

111

may say while saying nothing. I also called on many others. Hiat, for instance—''

"Ah, yes. Our worthy ex-bank manager. Who is ill, or so one is told, and can see nobody."

"He must have improved, for he saw me. He's a nervous wreck, poor fellow, but said he'd advised against making such large loans when there were rumours the trading company investment was shaky.''

"Upon which our revered sire undoubtedly behaved as though Hiat had spat in a cathedral, since the largest loans were made to his school mates—fine gentlemen of title *et sans reproche*. Unhappily, my father judges men by lineage and schooling instead of by their knowledge and ability. Did you ask the worthy Hiat what the vanishing stockholders had to say?''

"Both Lord Norberly and Sir Louis Derrydene concurred in the loans. I also asked him if he had any suspicion that the failure of the bank and the investment company, the embezzlement, the trading company swindle, and the fire at the shipyards were in some way connected.''

Newby laughed softly. "But how fascinating. We await Hiat's answer with bated breath, do we not, my Gwen?''

"Do not be horrid, Newby,'' she said, gently tapping his hand. "Gideon has been trying so hard.''

"I believe he thought I was raving mad,'' said Gideon slowly.

"Sensible man. And are you now convinced, twin?''

Frowning, Gideon hesitated. "I'll own that at first I thought Papa's nerves were overset and he was at the brink of a breakdown. But now . . .'' He wandered to the window again, and muttered, "Jupiter, but there's *something*, I think.''

Newby covered his eyes and groaned.

Gideon turned back. "I was able to discover the direction of two of the men who had worked up at Merseyside. They both— *both*, Newby!—said they were convinced the fire was arson, and that the foreman was of the same mind.''

"Which the official investigators say is nonsensical and cannot be proved.''

"It could be proven were we to find the men who set the fire!''

"Dearest,'' put in Gwendolyn. "Do you really *believe* a conspiracy?''

"Not exactly, love. Yet—I cannot but wonder why so many people I have tried to talk with are so frightened.''

"Heaven protect us all,'' moaned Newby. "My dear clod,

112

they are not *frightened* of you! They *despise* you! They do not wish to be seen conversing with you! Can you not understand yet? We are—*untouchables*! All of us!"

"I did not say they were frightened of *me*. I said they were frightened. Lady Norberly, for instance."

"Good Gad! You called on that dragon? She did not receive you, I'll warrant!"

"I think she would not have done, save that I chanced to arrive just as she was leaving the house. She vowed she has no least notion where his lordship may be, only that he travels in Scotland. Or perhaps Wales. She was trembling. And when I tried to speak again, she became loudly abusive. Her servants all but knocked me down."

With an exclamation of impatience Newby sprang to his feet. "Which has nothing to say to the purpose! Plague take it, where's the use in raking over old coals now? Shall we be any less ruined an you do track down that embezzling rogue, Davies? Are we any less to blame because we had overextended ourselves on what proved fraudulent foreign investments? 'Twas my father's *responsibility*, no matter how you seek to wrap it in clean linen! Since the enquiries, I have done all in my power to quiet things down! Now, *you* must come home and start stirring coals and throwing everyone into an uproar again! The last thing we need is for the whole beastly mess to flare up once more. Let be! 'Tis done and over with and nothing can undo it. Let it *alone*, I say, else there is no telling where it may end!"

Gideon looked into that flushed and angry face and persisted, "You were here, twin, and I was not. Is there *nothing* you judge to have been peculiar? Nothing that struck you as contrived or that might be worth looking into?"

Breathing hard, Newby answered, "Yes, there is something worth looking into! The conserving of what resources we have left. My father is, even now, not without some friends. We could ship our belongings quietly and be out of the country ere anyone could detain us. He and his men of the law have been able to stave off the Courts for the time, but how long can we hope to delay the inevitable? If you have any influence at all, my valiant captain, you had best exert it to convince him to emigrate. Do you *yearn* to see my sister living in Newgate? Well, I do not! Nor do I mean to stand idly by while you compound his blunders! Conspiracy, indeed! My God—what folly!"

He strode rapidly to the door, then turned about. "I forgot.

113

You've a caller, I believe. Best see him. Such events are rare in this house.''

Viscount Horatio Glendenning was seated in Gideon's small parlour, in close converse with Tummet. A very different Tummet this, his wig sleek, his person immaculate in a neat black habit that lent him a dignity somewhat at variance with his craggy face and discoloured eye.

"How good of you to come, Tio," said Gideon, walking into the room and shaking hands with his friend. "What has this rogue been telling you?"

"Incidents from his extreme checkered career," said the viscount with a grin. "If all else fails, Ross, you can write 'em down, put your sheets between marble covers, and make a fortune!"

"Oh, yes. I could entitle it, 'Diary of a Skinner of Whales.' " And as his lordship stared uncertainly, Rossiter smiled and translated, "That's 'Spinner of Tales' to you, old lad. What, has he not favoured you with his rhyming cant yet? Sometimes, 'tis the only way I can be sure he's my man, and not some bishop who has chanced to wander into my rooms."

The fledgling valet said an amused, "Garn! You staying 'ere fer a bit, Cap'n?"

"Yes. Bring cognac to the balcony if you please. One thing this house offers is a view, Tio. And 'tis a pretty day."

"Pretty rare," said Glendenning. "You'll not need an umbrella do you plan to accompany me to the Dowling Soiree this evening."

Rossiter glanced at him in surprise. "My thanks, but I've no least wish to do so. You cannot have thought I had been invited?"

"No, but I have, my Tulip. And you've been complaining that you're unable to come up with Bracksby. I chance to know he'll be there."

Lowering himself into one of the wooden chairs on the small balcony, Rossiter said quizzically, "My presence would not help your standing with the *ton*, you know. Any more than will my attendance at your ball."

"Very true. You're a dirty dish if ever there was one. But I shall contrive to bear it. Yea, or nay, Ross?"

"Yea! And most gratefully. I've been trying to see Rudi since I came home. He and Derrydene were friends and he may be able to tell me where to find the man. But he's elusive as a shadow in November!''

"Very fast on 'is stampers," agreed Tummet, brashly entering the conversation as he set down the tray and unstoppered a decanter of cognac. "And a real top o'the trees. A quality gent to 'is toenails. Which is more'n I can say fer some.''

Fascinated by Rossiter's unorthodox servant, Glendenning accepted a glass and asked, "Such as?''

"You ever bin to Falcon 'Ouse, me lord?" enquired Tummet, wiping a glass on his sleeve and eyeing it suspiciously before measuring cognac into it.

"Yes, I have. What has that to say to the matter?''

"Mr. August Falcon's got a 'ound o' the devil in that there 'ouse. Black as pitch, big as a bear, and twice as ugly. Come at me like 'e 'ad 'ider—ranger, or whatever it's called.''

"Hydrophobia," supplied Rossiter with a quirk of the lips.

"Ar. Tore the knee clean outta me new unmentionables, 'e done! And that there rosy-and-rare—''

For his lordship's benefit, Rossiter interjected, "Nose in the air.''

"—of a butler, 'e says as Apollo is a very fine dawg! Very fine dawg me eye and Cleo-Patria!" Tummet thrust the glass at his employer. " 'Ere, Guv. Sluice that over yer ivories.''

Glendenning could not hold back a laugh.

Rossiter groaned, then asked, "Do you, with all this round-aboutation, say that Mr. August Falcon is *not* a fine gentleman?''

" 'Oo—*me*?" Tummet blinked and said piously, "Why, I'd never presoom to criticize me betters. All I'm a'saying of is, 'e's better looking than 'is dawg. But twice as nasty." Ignoring his lordship's renewed hilarity, he fixed Rossiter with a minatory stare. "And not no one fer a gent t'be coming to cuffs with when said gent just come 'ome fulla 'oles!''

"Thank you," said Rossiter, trying to be stern. "That will be all.''

"It'll be all, all right," said Tummet grimly.

"Damn your impudence! Go!''

Tummet looked aggrieved, and took himself off.

Still chuckling, Glendenning asked, "Where *ever* did you find him, Ross? Whitechapel? Westminster? Covent Garden?''

"Impertinent ruffian, isn't he?''

"As the deuce! He was taking me to task when you arrived. In no uncertain terms.''

"Gad! What had you done to incur my fine valet's displeasure?"

"Your fine valet! Your fine fishmonger more like! No, really, you cannot keep the fellow!"

"Why? D'you fancy he will lower my consequence? I have none. And to say truth, he amuses me. Now tell me how you have displeased him."

"Simple. For all his—ah, peculiarities, he appears devoted to you, and he guessed why I came here."

"Aha! You've word?"

"Falcon named Kadenworthy and Perry Cranford. They all are agreed that the choice of weapons is yours." Rossiter raised his brows, and his lordship shrugged. "You struck him, after all."

"*Au contraire*. I throttled him. And I believe I challenged him also."

"Can't do both, my pippin. Ain't done. You attack. He challenges. You've choice of weapons, being the challenged. Pistols? You're a damned good shot."

Rossiter pursed his lips. "D'you think he's up to swords? I don't want to kill the silly fellow."

Glendenning pointed out, "You ain't terribly good with a sword, Ross."

"Is he?"

"Good with everything. Had lots of practice."

"He'll likely be somewhat slowed if we set an early date, which may even the odds. Swords, Tio. Preferably in the next day or so." His lordship was clearly preparing to enter a caveat, and Rossiter forestalled him by calling, "Tummet!"

The valet appeared, as innocent as though he'd not listened to every word. "Yus, Cap'n?"

"Lay out my new burgundy coat, and the white satin waistcoat with the pink clocks. I attend a soiree this evening. And tell Wilson to put out another cover. You will join us for dinner, Tio?"

"No, no, dear boy. My thanks but—that beast of a hill! To negotiate it after dining would ruin my digestion for the rest of the evening. You shall dine with me, rather."

"Capital notion! In that event, I'll change now. Oh, and Tummet—I shall wear the dress sword with the ruby in the hilt."

"Right, Guv. But we won't be 'aving no ship-yer-oars—that's to say 'little wars,' melord—will we now, Cap'n? You ain't proper recovered o' all them 'oles in—"

116

"No wars, you hedgebird," promised Rossiter, touched but exasperated. "Go and put out my clothes, as I told you!"

Mr. Enoch Tummet was not reassured, and made his way into the bedchamber grumbling audibly about high-in-the-instep young fire-eaters.

"But I assure you 'twas so." Mr. Rudolph Bracksby bowed as the stately dance ended. "Certainly you must know that any gentleman once having met you counts the moments 'til he does so again?"

The great skirts of Naomi's white satin gown swirled as she sank into the curtsy. Her green eyes laughed at Bracksby as he raised her, but his admiration was plain, and she was pleased by the awareness that she looked well tonight. The swansdown-trimmed stomacher emphasized her tiny waist; the overskirts of her gown looped back to reveal the pink embroidered under-dress. Her hair was swept up from her face and arranged into loose curls at the sides with a pink silk flower pinned above her left ear. About her white throat was a golden chain from which hung a pendant of pearls and rubies, and jewelled slippers glittered on her little feet.

She had been surprised to find this charming but rather quiet gentleman at the Dowling Soiree, and more surprised when he had prevailed upon Lady Dowling to "properly introduce" him. Naomi was not inclined to simper or pretend she did not at once recognize him from their encounter in the cathedral. She had assumed, however, that he would soon leave her to go upstairs where many gentlemen sat at card tables, or to the large saloon where guests were gathering to hear Signor Guido Lambini read from and discuss his new book of poems. Instead, almost before Naomi knew what he was about, Mr. Bracksby had deftly appropriated her dance card, scrawled his name, and swept her from under the outraged noses of the eager group of young gallants surrounding her and into the quadrille.

Now, as he led her from the floor, she murmured, "You've a silver tongue, sir."

"Then I shall hope it wags to your pleasure and my benefit. For example, may I call for you in the morning? An early ride, perhaps?"

She laughed a little. "La, but it's a determined gentleman."

"Be assured of that, ma'am. Shall we say—seven o'clock?"

"I should be pleased to say seven o'clock. But—my regrets. I am engaged tomorrow."

"Then in the after—"

But her admirers had regrouped and now crowded in about her. Mr. Bracksby, a decade older than most of them, was smiled on politely, stepped past gently, and gradually closed out by ardent youth. He took it in good part, wandered from the crowded room and made his way up the graceful curve of the main staircase. In the first-floor hall he was hailed by a familiar voice. Horatio Glendenning was bearing down on him, accompanied by a tall young man whose grey eyes sparked anger, and whose gaunt cheeks were slightly flushed. For just an instant Bracksby stood very still. Then, he said, "Good evening, Tio," and extended his hand. "Hello, Gideon. How glad I am to see you safely home."

Rossiter said sardonically, "Then you are in the minority, Rudi. I am very much *persona non grata*, you know. I doubt Lady Dowling will ever speak to Tio again, for having brought me."

"Oh, Tio can bring all the ladies round his thumb," said Bracksby, smiling as they exchanged a firm grip.

Heads were turning in that crowded hallway, and several quizzing glasses were brought to bear to further emphasize the affronted stares of their owners. Apparently oblivious of this byplay, Bracksby went on, "What a beast of a homecoming you have had, poor fellow. I wish—"

"I do not want sympathy," interrupted Rossiter savagely. "What I need is help."

"And some privacy," said Glendenning, noting that several gentlemen had halted and were muttering together. He swept open a nearby door, peeped into an unoccupied ante room, and ushered his friends inside. Lady Dowling's breeding had not failed her when he'd greeted her with Rossiter at his side, but the look of stricken horror she had directed at him as he walked away could not be ignored. He left the two men alone, therefore, and with the determination to make his peace with their hostess, went in search of her.

" 'Twas all so blasted sudden." Bracksby leaned back in his chair, looking very much the affluent country gentleman despite his well-cut grey brocade coat and the quilted violet satin waistcoat. "One day your father's bank was prospering; the next, frantic investors were beating the doors down. How the word spread so swiftly, is beyond me. Would to heaven I'd reacted as fast. But I was still sitting waiting for things to right 'emselves,

118

whilst men like Collington had seen the inevitable and recouped what they might.''

Rossiter shrank a little. "Oh, Lord! Rudi, I knew you banked with my father, but—''

"Of course I did, dear boy,'' interpolated Bracksby. "I'm not a scion of one of Kent's old-time families, as are you. But since I bought my little place I've always found your papa a dashed good neighbour, and with never a whisper of height in his manner. The least I could do was take my business to him.''

A distant part of Rossiter's mind was amused by Bracksby's designation of Overlake Lodge as a "little place,'' for it was a splendid estate, at least half as large as Promontory Point. And it was as well the poor amiable fellow had detected no "whisper of height'' in Sir Mark's manner; he'd likely be horrified did he know that the baronet was apt to refer to him as "our *nouveau riche* neighbour.'' Rossiter's main concentration was on more pressing matters, however, and he asked anxiously, "Did you sustain a heavy loss?''

"Nothing I cannot absorb, and in truth that is the least of my worries, so let us hear no more of it. I wish I had been available to you when first you came home, but now you must tell me how I may be of service. If 'tis a matter of funding, only name the—''

"No!'' Rossiter sprang to his feet, revolted. "Damn your eyes! Do you think I would come begging, when—''

Standing also, Bracksby said contritely, " 'Pon my word, but I am a clumsy fellow. I should have realized you would turn to people of your own station, rather—''

Rossiter whirled and caught him by the shoulders. "Rudi,'' he said through his teeth, "if you weren't the most well-meaning of fellows, by God I'd deck you for that!''

Since Bracksby was sturdily built and vibrant with health, while Rossiter for all his extra inches was thin and pale and very obviously not at the top of his form, this point was debatable. But Bracksby lowered his eyes and stood in silence, looking humiliated.

Releasing him, Rossiter stalked to the mantel and, gripping it, glared down at the empty hearth. "Since I came home, I've struggled to come at the root of all this. I've interviewed everyone willing to talk with me, who might know something of it.''

"Be dashed if I follow you, Gideon. Something of—what?''

"Of a conspiracy to effect the deliberate, calculated ruination of my father!''

119

His jaw falling, Bracksby sat down abruptly. "Good God! No, dear boy—you cannot be serious! I mean, what you imply surely would indicate a large-scale plot. A dangerous business, Gideon. With all due respect, I cannot think—"

"You cannot think the Rossiter interests sufficiently compelling to inspire such a plot? No more can I.'Tis what makes this so confoundedly baffling."

"Good Lord! Does poor—Er, I mean, does your sire believe this?"

"He does. I'll own I did not, but I am coming to think it not so unlikely after all."

"I suppose . . . vengeance, perhaps?"

"My father admits to having enemies, but none he insists who would feel so ill-used as to resort to such a scheme. The men from the shipyard suspect arson. Why? So far as I am able to determine, there have been no workers dismissed this past year who might have cause to harbour a grudge. Why arson?"

Watching him uneasily, Bracksby said, "Well now, if it *was*—er, arson, might there perhaps have been a party who wanted the land? Has Sir Mark rejected an offer to buy?"

"There have been no offers. Besides, there is ample open land in the area that I am very sure the present owners would be happy to part with."

Bracksby pursed his lips. "A competitor?"

"That occurred to me. But the shipyard that was originally to have built the frigates was in Scotland, and destroyed during the Rebellion."

"Was it! Now, there you might have a motive, old fellow."

"I might, had any of the owners survived. The father was shot by drunken troopers. Both sons died at Culloden. And 'twould have to be a sadly disordered mind to lay all that tragedy in my father's dish. Besides, where would they obtain funds for such vengeance? Any family remaining must be pauperized."

"Hmmn." After a moment, Bracksby said cautiously, "So what it all comes to in the long run, is that you think Sir Mark's troubles were deliberately contrived. But he had no real enemies, nor is there any apparent motive for a—er, plot 'gainst him."

Gideon smiled, then wandered closer. "In other words, hopelessly illogical. Rudi, you know him quite well, and I've been gone so damned long. Have you ever heard anyone speak with bitterness or malice against my father? Can you think of anything—any occurrence, any quarrel, any smallest incident—that might relate to the matter?''

"No. 'Pon my soul, I cannot."

"Your country estate marches with ours. Have you ever seen anything unusual in the way of guests at the Point?''

"Never. Er, . . . forgive me, but you were severely wounded in Europe. Is it not possible, dear boy, that—that you are—er, not quite yourself? That the strain of all this falling on your shoulders when you should by rights have come home to rest and recuperate, might have—"

"Set loose a flock of bats in my attic?" Rossiter sat down again. "Very likely. But, humour me a moment longer, I beg. Derrydene is a friend of yours. Where might I find him?''

"Moscow."

"Moscow?" gasped Rossiter, incredulous. "What the devil . . . ? D'you mean—in *Russia*?''

"Yes. That one. Is there another? I'd not realized . . ." Bracksby lapsed into thought, saw Rossiter's expression, and went on hurriedly. " 'Tis the bell, you know. No, never start snorting fire and smoke, dear boy. I am perfectly serious. Derrydene is fascinated by bells. All shapes and sizes. Collects 'em. His house is a veritable museum of the things. It seems the biggest bell in the world is in Muscovy—er, Moscow. 'Twas hung in a belfry near—what's it called?—Uspenski Cathedral, or something of the sort. The bell weighs two hundred tons. Or it did. They'd a fire there a few years back, and it fell down and a bit broke off. Eleven tons of it. Well, Derrydene has been absolutely mad to see it. That is why he withdrew his funds, and—Egad! You never thought . . . ? *Derrydene?* Oh, no—really, Gideon!''

Rossiter walked slowly down the stairs, paying no heed to the repulsive looks that came his way, his ears closed to the contemptuous remarks, his thoughts turning wearily on what Bracksby had said. Derrydene's departure now seemed reasonable enough, in view of his fixation with bells. Certainly, to follow him to Russia could not be considered. Another nail in the coffin of hope. That left only one last unexplored channel: Lord Norberly, a man who travelled somewhere in Scotland. Or perhaps Wales.

Sighing, he went in search of Viscount Glendenning. There was no need to linger in this house, where his presence was an insult to most of the guests and an embarrassment to his hostess.

But Tio had tried, and he must not leave without expressing his thanks.

There was no sign of the viscount in the large music room that had been made over to those who wished to dance. The five-piece orchestra was playing a lively air, but there was no dance presently in progress. People stood about in little groups, the gentlemen impressively gallant in their full-skirted coats, gems flashing from lace cravats and white hands; the ladies delightfully feminine in their colourful gowns, plying their fans with the graceful coquetry that was not as easy as it appeared, since movement of their arms was restricted by the great panniers of their skirts. Watching the charming scene rather wistfully, Rossiter suddenly became aware that the merry chatter had ceased, and that everyone was staring at him. For the first time, the extent of his rejection by the society of which he had been a part came home to him. How many of these people had been dealt crippling losses by the failure of Rossiter Bank? How many had been ruined when the investment company had failed? Or had held shares in Rossiter Shipping? He could scarce blame them for the disgust with which they regarded him. But his father was wrongfully judged. And he was *not*, nor ever would be ashamed of his name! His chin came up slightly, his shoulders squared, and he faced them unflinchingly.

Far to the side of that hushed room, Sir Gilbert Fowles said with a curl of the lip, "Someone really should remove that blot from our landscape."

Marguerite Templeby, Viscount Glendenning's shy young step-sister, murmured softly, "Oh, but he is magnificent!"

Sir Gilbert scowled and opened his mouth for another sally that was cut off as a burst of excitement sounded from the hall.

Not sorry for the interruption, Rossiter turned to discover the cause. A clamorous group of gentlemen was assembling at the foot of the stairs. A lady wearing a gown of white satin and having a remarkably tiny waist, stood halfway up the stairs, her back to those who waited below. Rossiter wandered closer, trying to see what was happening. Without warning, the lady tossed a posy over her shoulder. The flowers were in a tiny vase mounted in a filigreed container, and it flew high over the heads of the crowd. Rossiter saw something whizzing at his face. He threw up a hand to protect his eyes, felt something strike him, and clutched it instinctively.

An excited roar went up. "Who won? Who caught it? What lucky fellow will escort our goddess to the ball tomorrow?"

The excitement faded. Through a stupefied hush, Rossiter saw every face turned to him, saw the aghast expressions; heard a man exclaim, "Good God, no! Not him!"

On the stairs, my lady whirled about, her wide skirts swirling to reveal her glittering jewelled slippers. Her laughter died abruptly. Gideon Rossiter's lean features seemed to leap at her and all the colour left her face.

He glanced down at the flowers he held. "I seem to have intruded on a private lottery," he drawled coolly. "You would doubtless prefer to throw again, ma'am."

A young exquisite lisped, "Thath right! Throw again, lovely one."

Over the immediate chorus of agreement, my lord Kadenworthy snapped, "Don't be such a clunch. Fair's fair."

Naomi heard both comments. She drew a steadying breath. What a perfectly frightful thing! But to turn back was unthinkable. She said frigidly, "You have won, sir. Unless you do not choose to be my escort?"

All eyes turned to him; some hopeful, most condemning. He longed to be able to toss the flowers back into her proud, beautiful face; to free her from this contretemps and show his indifference to her—to them all. But to do so would be to insult her.

He lied stiffly, " 'Twould be my very great pleasure to escort you, my lady."

❧ *Chapter 9* ❧

"Surely you are not leaving, Naomi?"

Not only was my lady Lutonville leaving this wretched soirée, but she could scarce wait to make her escape. Fate, with cruel whimsy, had played a very unkind trick on her. She was seething with rage, but because that rage must not be shown to a cynical world that would be all too ready to misconstrue it, she affected a bored amusement. It was not easy to refrain from gnashing her teeth at the gentle ladies who gushed over her "unhappy predicament," while glee sparkled in their eyes; or to keep from giving a sharp set-down to the gentlemen who either moaned that she was placed in a ridiculous situation, or vowed bloody reprisals 'gainst Captain Rossiter.

Recognizing the voice of an old friend, however, it was with genuine pleasure that she turned to embrace a tall young woman with a lovely and intelligent face and smiling hazel eyes. "Mitten! How wonderful to find you here! How are you, my dear? And how is little Joanna?"

Lady Anthony Farrar patted the hand she held and leaned closer to say confidingly, "Five months old, delectable, and doted upon by far too many willing slaves. 'Tis as well that by Christmas time she will have either a small Gilbert or Helen competing for the attentions of her father and her uncles, who already are in a fair way to spoiling her!"

Naomi's laugh held a note of wistfulness. "You look so happy, and so well. It must be wonderful to be cherished and protected by such a fine man as your Anthony. Truly, I envy you."

"Thank you, love. You may be sure I know I am very blessed." And watching her friend narrowly, Lady Farrar said, "I wish I could think you happy, also."

At once brightening, Naomi demanded, "No, but why ever should you judge me otherwise? Did I look provoked just now?" She saw a flickering smile, and admitted very softly, "I was not, Mitten. Provoked is too mild a word by half! If one more person commiserates with me over this fiasco—I vow I'll bite them! So you see, I must leave before I—further—disgrace myself!"

"You have never disgraced yourself. Although you tried hard enough."

The flush on Naomi's cheeks deepened a little, but Lady Farrar went on quickly, "I've heard tell that one of the penalties of being an accredited Toast, is the enemies they make among London's ladies. An you leave now, 'twill not be a disgrace, my love, but a retreat. Before you are halfway to Falcon House the gabblemongers will be claiming you left shedding tears of mortification. Only think of the lovely time they will have, grieving for your embarrassment."

"Aye. And giggling behind their fans, the cats," stormed Naomi. "While they wallow in all the details of Rossiter's libertine propensities and my—"

Lady Farrar blinked. "His—what? I'd not heard such things of Gideon."

"Only gossip about me, eh? Lud, where have you been, Mitten?"

"Fiddle-de-dee!" exclaimed Lady Farrar, whose friends seldom addressed her by anything but her nickname. "Pray do not turn around, but that little tabby Melissa Coombs watches us as though you were about to suffer a seizure. Naomi, you *must* stay, and have a jolly time however much you loathe it. If only to deny them the satisfaction of seeing you leave in a huff."

She was perfectly right, of course. Her wisdom was confirmed a few minutes later when Naomi returned to the music room and glimpsed the faint disappointment in the eyes of several ladies who yearned for but had never achieved the status of a Toast. And so she stayed, and her gaiety was so unfaltering that only a few guessed that beneath her merry lightheartedness dwelt an impatience and vexation that increased with every moment.

It was almost a quarter past one o'clock before she slipped away to search for Katrina and beg that she be driven back to Falcon House. There was no sign of her friend on the ground floor. Tired and cross and with a persistent headache, she was determined to escape more sympathy, so made her way to the first-floor saloons by way of the servants' stairs. Turning into the main hall she hurried past two rooms where heated political discussions waged, but Katrina was not among the ladies present. The door to the next ante room was wide open. Inside, several gentlemen sat at cards. There was a burst of laughter and mocking voices accused someone of "surrendering too easily." As she passed, chairs were being pushed back. Dismayed by the sound of a high-pitched and all too familiar giggle, she thought, 'Reggie Smythe! Oh, no!' She could scarce endure the dandy's malicious tongue at the best of times and knew all too well how he would delight in slanting his vicious barbs at her. One swift glance confirmed that it was indeed Smythe, together with his bosom bow, Sir Gilbert Fowles. Shuddering, Naomi whipped past and sought about for a refuge.

A merry group stood chatting a little distance along the hall. Nearer at hand was a recessed alcove with French doors, now closed, which gave onto the balcony at the rear of the house. She darted into the alcove. The balcony doors were stiff and resisted her efforts, but she succeeded in pushing them open, whirled into the cool darkness, and quickly shut them again, then leaned her cheek against the doors, listening. She heard men's voices and the despised giggle, but no outcry. With a sigh of relief, she turned, started to take a step and recoiled in horror. There was *no balcony*! Or at best, only a suggestion of one. She was perched on what was no more than a decorative window ledge about fifteen inches deep! But of course! She had come up the servants' stairs rather than the main staircase, and was not at the rear but on the west side of the mansion! How could she have been so idiotically confused? It was little short of a miracle she'd not fallen to her death when she ran outside! She felt quite faint with fright and shrank back against the doors, suddenly reminded of the only fear Gideon had ever shown her—his intense fear of heights.

Trembling, she told herself sternly that there was no need to be such a weakling. Her situation was easily resolved. All she had to do was open the door (very carefully), and go back inside. She reached for the handle and gave a sob of terror. There was a handle, but it was decorative only and did not turn. The doors could not be opened from the outside!

Panicking now, trying not to give way to tears, she beat against the glass. She could hear the buzz of talk and a woman's shrill laughter. Were they all deaf? Why did they not come to help her? Probably, because they were making so much noise that her own rattling at the doors was drowned. Well then, she would break the window. If she could contrive to get her slipper off. She clung with one hand to the door handle. She dared not bend down, nor even look down, and she discovered that to raise her foot constituted quite a challenge. When she groped for her shoe, her wide skirts not only impeded her, but she almost lost her balance. With a gasp, she pressed back against the house, her knees beginning to feel like blancmange. She must try again. Perhaps, if she could ease the high-heeled Spanish slipper down to her toe, it would be more easily grasped. She wriggled her left toe against the back of her right shoe. It took a few minutes, but at last the slipper was off her heel. Holding her breath she pushed her skirts aside. She had to hold her foot out as well as up, for her panniers forbade her reaching it otherwise. Balancing carefully, she made a wild snatch for the shoe, and it flew off and sailed from sight. "Oh, you nasty thing," she wailed. But there was, thank heaven, another shoe. Reaching for it once more, she paused.

With hideous clarity she could picture the scene that would result when she broke the window and was (hopefully) rescued. What a delicious tidbit she would provide the guests, and how they would delight in spreading it about a city that throve on gossip. "Did you hear about poor Naomi Lutonville? Gideon Rossiter made her look a proper fool at the Dowling Soiree, whereby she is gone demented, and was found wandering along the window ledges!" Or, worse—"Poor Lady Lutonville was so distraught at the prospect of suffering Rossiter's escort that she attempted suicide and was rescued at the last minute!" The next thought was worst of all. Lud! They might even say she had tried to kill herself for unrequited love!

All thought of breaking the window was abandoned. At least for the moment. Her eyes had become accustomed to the darkness now, and she looked about for some other means of escape. To the left was the corner of the building. On the right, however, and just below her ledge, the roof of the conservatory extended from the house, and beyond that was another ledge like this one, with French doors that stood slightly open. She could even see tobacco smoke drifting from the room. If she could but cross the conservatory roof and reach that ledge, she could bide her time until the occupants left, then slip back inside and no one would be the wiser.

With the renewal of hope her nerves seemed less shredded, and keeping her back tight against the wall she began to edge along cautiously. Her great skirts impeded her progress, and she was soon obliged to relinquish her grip on the door handle. Her only hold now was supplied by the grooves between bricks but—thank heavens!—the conservatory roof was only a deep step down. She peered at it anxiously. For the most part the roof was glass, but there was a wide band of masonry abutting the house that looked sturdy enough.

Gritting her teeth, she inched as close to the edge as possible, then dug the fingertips of her right hand around the edge of a brick, and, crushing her panniers ruthlessly, managed to turn so that she faced the gap. She gathered her nerves, hoist her skirts, and stepped down. She was so relieved when her toes touched the roof, that she almost fell, and pressed close against the wall of the house for support.

Once again, the width of her skirts left her no alternative but to keep her back to the wall, and she inched along until she came at last to the far ledge. She could hear male voices, in what sounded to be a heated discussion. Braver now, she raised her panniers and stepped up. She had done it! She looked back across the gap to the balcony from which she had escaped, and felt a thrill of pride. It really had been quite a feat, but her finery had paid a price. Her gown was covered with dust, cobwebs, and a few leaves. She gave a little moan. Much chance she had of escaping attention now! Unless she could get inside and tidy herself after these silly men finished their squabble and took themselves off.

She crept to where she could see around the half-closed draperies. A potted palm restricted her view but she could glimpse the back of a red velvet coat. A dark blue sleeve came into view; and a graceful hand encompassed by ruffles of Mechlin lace. The long fingers held something, but she could not see what it was. If they were playing cards, she thought miserably, they might be here half the night!

The hand moved and set a small object on the table. It was not a card. To her astonishment she saw a chess piece, very similar to the one she had lost during the hold-up, only fashioned from green jade and set with emeralds. Staring at it, she thought, 'Papa is still here, then?'

How quiet they were; their argument intense, but almost whispered. One voice rose then, harsh with anger. ". . . perfectly sure! Do you think I'd not have tried? Everyone is different."

The other man swore, then said something softly, ending,

". . . a menace to us. On both counts! He must be silenced. When the others learn—"

"They will not learn until a meeting is called. And we cannot call a meeting until six is recovered."

"Six may not be recovered. How then? We will have no choice but to make a substitution."

"Chancy, at best. Perhaps impossible. And who to trust with such a secret?"

"And all our lives! But we dare not delay too long."

The first voice said dryly, "In here, especially. Make up your mind. One more try, and then—my plan?"

A brief hesitation, then a reluctant, "Oh, very well."

The gentleman in the red coat stood. Opposite him, the hand took up the green chess piece.

'Thank heaven!' thought Naomi.

Seconds later, the draperies billowed outward and she could hear music and distant voices from the hall. She peeped inside. The ante room was empty.

"That there friend o'yourn," repeated Tummet, settling the breakfast tray across his employer's lap and thrusting a napkin into his unready hand.

Yawning, Rossiter protested, "What—th' devil you doing? Y'know I don't like taking m'breakfast in bed."

"You want lunch instead?" asked Tummet with a villainous leer, and swung the window curtains wide to admit a glaring flood of daylight.

Rossiter groaned and threw up one hand to shield his eyes. "What o'clock is it?"

"Eleven and five minutes. Jug bit, you is. Proper. Well? You wanta see the swell, or not?"

Rossiter peered with revulsion at the egg sprawled on a slice of toast, and retreating to the coffee cup, asked, "Do you refer with your customary savoir faire to Lord Glendenning?"

"No, I don't. That there lieutenant bloke."

Holding his head on with his free hand, Gideon said, "Morris? Yes, by Jove! Of course I want to see him!"

Two minutes later, in the act of taking a mouthful of coffee, he stared, and choked. "What . . . the deuce . . . ?"

Lieutenant James Morris strolled over to occupy the chair Tummet drew up for him. "Awful, ain't it?" he said lugubriously, and reached for a slice of toast. "Thieves."

Rossiter said, "Did they drive a waggon across your face? Jupiter! 'Tis an epidemic."

" 'E means as I got me daylight darkened," explained Tummet. "You want 'is egg, guv? The Cap'n ain't feeling strong enough to slice it."

Rossiter passed his plate to Morris and sent Tummet off for some more toast and another cup of coffee. "When did this happen, Jamie?"

"Week ago to the day. Didn't set much store by it at first. But when I heard what happened to your man, I thought I'd toddle up to the Village and see how you went on. Had the fiend's own time finding you. An I'd known you lived on the side of a mountain, I'd not have come. I say, are you all right, old lad? Look a trifle green."

"Tummet says I'm jug-bit, and I fear he's in the right of it." Rossiter grinned wryly. "I stayed up 'til the wee hours trying to solve my problems with a bottle of cognac. Did the thieves break into your home?"

"Regrettably. I chanced to wander into my bedchamber and caught one of the bounders ransacking my chest of drawers. We had a lively turn-up 'til his cohort joined the fray. Did you ever hear the like of it? Inside the house!"

"Bastards! What did they take?"

Morris waved his toast. "That's the one good thing, Ross. Didn't take much at all. Turned everything onto the floor, and filched my purse. I think there was about three guineas in it. There were some pretty fair stick pins and two fine rings lying atop my highboy. Must've missed 'em."

Rossiter frowned and asked thoughtfully, "You said you heard what happened to my man. Did you mean Tummet?"

"No, you gudgeon! Your groom. The fella you sent to collect the things we left at the Red Pheasant last week."

"What about him? Did he not deliver your belongings? I gave him strict instructions to come to Sevenoaks on his way back here."

Surprised, Morris said, "D'you mean you didn't know? Fella was set upon. Our village grocer made a delivery to the house and found him lying by the road."

"Jupiter! Was he killed?"

"No, fortunately. Struck down by a cudgel. But the odd thing is that he had your belongings in the coach, as well as mine. You'd a dress sword and a really pretty bracelet in there, yet they were left."

"Oh, good. I bought that bracelet for my sister. I was afraid 'twas in my saddlebags."

"Afraid . . . ?"

"They were stolen also, Jamie. Only in that instance everything went, of course. I fancy the Town thief couldn't very well stand about on the flagway, sorting out his spoils."

Morris shook his head wonderingly. "See what you meant about an epidemic. I've brought your things with me, by the way."

Tummet returned, carrying a laden tray, and Morris smiled his approval.

Rossiter demanded, "Why was I not informed that our groom was attacked at Sevenoaks?"

" 'Cause I was told to keep me mouth in me pocket, mate." Tummet winked. "Guv, I mean. Yer brush-and-lather said—"

"Brush and lather—father!" inserted Morris, triumphant.

"Right, mate," confirmed Tummet with a broad grin. "Sir Mark, 'e says as if the Cap'n knowed about the groom, 'ed be orf arter the thieves 'stead of tending to more important business, so none of us wasn't to say nothing."

Applying strawberry jam to toast, Lieutenant Morris licked his thumb and asked, "What more important business?"

Rossiter hesitated only briefly. Then, he told him about the conspiracy.

After luncheon Gwendolyn took a basket and secaturs into the garden. The sun was bright, but not very warm, and a chilly breeze stirred the weeds and set the tree branches tossing. She limped along the cracked brick pathway to the flowerbeds. Despite the neglect some quite nice roses had managed to grow, and the bright faces of daisies danced to the tune of the breeze. The slight girl put down her basket and hummed softly as she began to gather the best of the blooms.

The early afternoon was quiet, but she could hear a dog barking somewhere; a deep bark. She stopped humming, and sighed. It was the first time there was no dog in her life, and she kept to herself how much she longed for another puppy. She would only have had to hint at it and Newby would have bought her one. But this was not the time. For all she knew, they might wind up in some horrid little garret somewhere. She shivered, then scolded herself. At church on Sunday the vicar had said one should put one's troubles into the hands of the Lord, and she had done that. In fact, the Lord must be getting rather tired

131

of all the troubles this one small family had asked Him to solve. Still, having done so, it showed poor faith to continue to worry.

She inspected the bouquet she had gathered. The daisies made a nice contrast to the brilliance of the roses. She cut some fronds of fern, then carried her basket back to the house.

She was clever at arranging flowers and was quite proud when she carried the vase upstairs and scratched at Gideon's door. There was no response, and she crept inside.

At once she heard male voices. He was out on the balcony with someone. She decided to leave her small gift on his table. He would be pleased when he came in and found them. Dear Gideon was always so grateful for the least little thing that—

"Oh, but that's beastly unfair, Ross! You know very well I have first claim on Falcon! You've no right to meet him before I do!"

Gwendolyn put the vase on the table and stood very still, her breath held in check as the two young men strolled in from the balcony.

Laughing, Gideon said, "*You* shot him by accident, my good dolt. Whereas *I* throttled him quite deliberately."

"I hope you chose pistols. You're not much good with—" Morris saw Gwendolyn then. "Oh—the deuce!" he exclaimed, turning very red.

Rossiter looked up, froze, then made a fast recover. "What a charming bouquet. For me, cheerful sparrow? I thank you."

Gwendolyn remained silent and motionless, her eyes accusing him.

"Er—allow me to present my comrade in arms," he went on hurriedly. "This bruised gentleman is Lieutenant James Morris. Jamie, at last you meet my dear sister, Miss Gwendolyn Rossiter."

Morris bowed, his embarrassment heightened when his outflung hand toppled the vase of flowers. Instinctively, Gwendolyn hurried to right it. Gideon had spoken of his sister in such glowing terms that Morris had expected to meet a great beauty. Unprepared for this small crippled girl with the bright but unremarkable face, he hid his surprise gallantly, and murmured an apology.

Gwendolyn was very pale, but she managed to respond politely, then excused herself and left them.

The two men looked at each other.

Rossiter said, "Damn!"

Limping along the hall, Gwendolyn's mind was beginning to

132

function again. The man Gideon was to meet was named Falcon. That must mean August Falcon. She felt cold with fear, but in another instant was raging. How unutterably silly gentlemen were! Here was Gideon, come home from the very jaws of death, and certainly aware of how much he was loved and needed. And instead of being grateful and behaving with some vestige of common sense, what must he do but at once challenge one of the most deadly duellists in all England! What a fool, that she had lovingly collected flowers, when she might better have cracked the vase over his idiotic head!

There was no use appealing to him, of course. Or to Papa, or Newby. They were all afflicted by the same diseases: Masculinity, and that impregnable fortress against which tears, pleading, or common sense could not hope to prevail—the Code of Honour.

" 'Elp! Murder!'' Mr. Tummet dodged behind a gilded chair in the gracious entry hall of Falcon House, and flailed his tricorne at the snarling muzzle of the big black dog that strove to come at him.

Two footmen ran up. One called, "Here, Apollo! Nice doggie!''

The monster turned, showing an impressive expanse of bared teeth, and the footman jumped back.

His companion said, "I'll fetch Mr. Falcon. Just try not to upset him, mate.''

"Upset 'im?'' cried Tummet. "I'd like to—Get away you 'ound of 'ell!''

Apparently annoyed by this appellation, Apollo charged in, barking so that the prisms rattled in the great central chandelier.

Tummet resorted to his tricorne.

So did Apollo.

"Leggo, 'orrid 'ound,'' demanded Tummet, hanging on and heaving. "Look what yer doing to me titfer-tat!''

"What the devil . . . ? Apollo! Back, sir! Back!''

Mr. August Falcon stalked across the hall, and the dog gamboled to meet him, shaking Mr. Tummet's tricorne, and growling with the air of a puppy who was only playing.

Falcon appropriated the hat, and when the dog jumped up after it, he struck the animal lightly on the nose with the palm of his hand. "My apologies,'' he said crisply, restoring the tricorne to its owner. "My dog is not allowed in this part of the house.''

Tummet eyed the wreckage sadly. "Pity 'e don't know it. I 'spect you think I should be grateful 'e only et me 'at, and not me leg bone, what 'e tried to digest last time I come 'ere."

Falcon shrugged. "One might think you would learn by experience and keep away."

"Brung a lady, I did, mate."

"I did—*what*?" rasped Falcon.

" 'Ow do I know what you did?"

Falcon's black brows met over the bridge of his nose. "Impudent dolt! You may call me—'sir.' Not—'mate'!"

"Ar," said Tummet with his villainous grin. " 'E don't like it neither. Me employer. Cap'n Gideon Rossiter. I'm 'is valet. Sir. You going to buy me a new titfer-tat?"

The dark blue eyes widened and irascibility gave way to wonderment. "Valet . . . ? I do not believe—Yes, I do, by Jove. Is typical of Rossiter, be damned if it—What the devil is a titfertat?"

"A 'at, mate. A dicer. Cor! You Quality coves don't know yer own language! And what abaht the lady?"

Falcon's eyes had become somewhat glassy. Making a recover, he said, "My butler will pay for your—er, dicer. However, you have wasted your time, and shall have to take the lady home again. Miss Falcon was out late last night, and will not receive callers today."

"She ain't come to see Miss Falcon. Come to see you, ma—er, sir. Which you'd know if you 'ad servants what was trained proper."

A footman approached, eyeing Apollo warily. "A lady has called to see you, sir." He proffered a salver with a calling card on it, then jumped back as the dog looked at him.

Still enthralled by Tummet, Falcon said, "Fool. You know the dog won't hurt you." He glanced at the card and his brows lifted. "A single lady?"

"Miss Rossiter 'as got something of great import to discuss," said Tummet. "I knows what it is, but it ain't no use offering me bribes and rewards. I ain't gonna say nothing 'bout it. 'Twixt you and 'er, it is."

This speech left the footman's jaw dangling and his eyes wide with shock.

His own eyes holding a rare twinkle, Falcon started off, the great dog at his heels. "Where have you put her?" he called over his shoulder.

The footman gulped, "In—in the book room, sir."

Entering that well-appointed chamber, and sternly relegating Apollo to the desolation of the hall, Falcon expected to find Miss Rossiter perched nervously on the edge of a chair. Although she must be aware that it was most decidedly improper for a lady to call on a bachelor, this particular lady, however, was not perched on a chair, nor did she appear nervous. Small and with a look of fine-boned fragility, she stood before a bookcase, examining a volume which she replaced, turning to face him as he closed the door.

He eyed her disinterestedly. There was nothing to distinguish her, aside from the fact that her frank and unmaidenly stare was disconcerting. Her unpowdered hair was a very light brown, drawn back from a rather thin face to fall in curls behind her head. She had Rossiter's well-shaped sensitive mouth, and high forehead, but her eyes, which he thought fairly good, were blue rather than grey. 'Dull,' he thought, 'and with neither looks nor charm.' He drawled, "You wished to see me, ma'am?"

Aware that she had been judged and found wanting, Gwendolyn smiled. "If we are to dispense with introductions, may I sit down?"

He had been dealt a scold. Falcon's mouth tightened. He said with cold hauteur, "My apologies. I am August Falcon."

"Oh, yes. I was in no doubt, you know. 'Tis just that one is supposed to be polite."

At this, he gave her a sharp look, but her expression was so innocent that he decided she was naive rather than sarcastic. He bowed her to a large armchair. "Pray be seated, ma'am."

Her limp surprised him. He looked away at once, but she had seen the startled glance, and asked easily, "Did you not know I am lame?"

"No." Again, she had put him offstride. Irritated, he said, "You apparently know more about me than I know about you, Miss Rossiter."

"Well, you're famous, aren't you. I mean, everyone talks about you. I was quite looking forward to making your acquaintance."

He thought, 'Good God! She's candid enough!' and said with an unpleasant sneer, "I trust you are not disappointed, madam."

Gwendolyn scanned him thoughtfully.

She should have shown him shyly lowered lashes, and a faint blush, and have wallowed in a tangle of apology and confusion. Her obviously judicial scrutiny was the outside of enough! After a good twenty seconds had dragged by, he enquired, "Would you wish that I turn my head?"

Outside, Apollo gave vent to a long and ear-splitting howl. Waiting until it ceased, "Yes, if you please," said Gwendolyn sunnily. "To the right."

Dumbfounded, he gawked at her guileless smile. "Now—'pon my soul, madam! You must have some presumably *sensible* reason for calling?"

"Oh, dear. Have I been rude? I suppose I should have said I am not at all disappointed, and that you are just as handsome as I was told." She blinked as his frown diminished. "Only I am not very good at making insincere remarks," she added. "Any more than are you."

He looked at her as from a great height and murmured, "Indeed? Perhaps you will be so good as to explain my offense."

"There is none. The fact that you refrain from uttering foolish platitudes is not offensive to me." Seldom at a loss for words, this left him looking so nonplussed that she appended kindly, "Usually, when people notice I am lame, they say they are sorry. You did not."

Apollo was howling again. Irritated on two counts, Falcon snapped, "Why should I be sorry? I do not know you, and you do not seem thrown into the dismals by your affliction."

"Very honest. And, however well meant, spurious sympathy is so provoking and usually spoken more to impress one with the good nature of the speaker, than with a genuine interest and concern. As for my feelings—I should like not to be lame, of course. But I always have been so, and am accustomed to it. After all, 'twould be very much worse an I was suffering, as so many poor souls do. Only . . ."—briefly, her eyes were very sad—"I should like to have had children." Looking up, smiling, she said, "Ah, I am boring you."

Straightening the ruffles at his wrist he answered crushingly, "I expect you will eventually tell me why you came."

Uncrushed, she said, " 'Tis simply that I would be very grateful if you would please not fight my brother with pistols. Oh, I apprehend that ladies are not supposed to know about such things as duels. But I do know. And I do not want Gideon to be killed. He has only just come home."

"Jupiter, madam! This is most improper! And at all events," Falcon raised his voice so as to be heard over the grieving hound, "Rossiter had choice of weapons. Not me."

"That should be 'not I,' " she corrected kindly. "But if Gideon chose pistols, he is very silly, for they are horrid, deadly things, whereas—"

Bored, he stood. "Be at ease, ma'am. Your brother chose swords." His eyes glinted maliciously. "Which will avail him nothing."

"Oh dear! Are you very good?"

He bowed. "Now, if that is all—"

"Is not all! I don't want him killed with a sword, either!"

"Would you suggest we fight with feather dusters, Miss Rossiter?"

"I would suggest you do not fight with anything! 'Tis a very silly custom to have prevailed into modern times, and typifies the male predilection for dramatic displays that solve nothing! You never see ladies behaving in such nonsensical fashion."

She was really incensed. Amused in spite of himself, he argued, "In point of fact, women *have* gone out! Only—"

"Oh, fiddle! You split hairs, Mr. Falcon. And 'tis most difficult for me to talk to you with your dog howling like that. Can you not keep him quiet?"

"Alas, I am a perpetual disappointment. Apollo wishes to come in. And since you are leaving—"

"Then let him in," she said, opening her eyes at him.

He hesitated. He really shouldn't, but this ill-mannered, opinionated chit deserved a lesson, and it would certainly get rid of her. "As you wish," he murmured suavely, and went over to open the door.

A black tornado raced into the room, pounced around his master twice causing the floors to shake, then saw Gwendolyn. The hair stood up across his shoulders. Growling menacingly, he crouched.

"Behave," said Gwendolyn sternly.

Apollo did not intend to bite her badly. But she must be made to leave his house. With all his teeth in full view, he started for her.

Falcon, who had watched with covert amusement, sprang, but missed, and Apollo lunged at the slender girl.

Gwendolyn had kept her cane as inconspicuous as possible, but now she raised it and said one magical word. "Fetch!"

Apollo's ears went up and his hair went down. Tail wagging, he panted with eager expectation.

"Hey!" cried Falcon.

Gwendolyn was already tossing the cane. Apollo plunged after it, sending his advancing master reeling. A table crashed into

137

the chair Falcon clutched at, and he sat on the floor hard and without elegance amid the wreckage of the Chinese vase that had gone down with the table.

The cane retrieved, Apollo rushed back to offer it again, his tongue lolling happily.

Gwendolyn looked at the momentarily speechless Falcon, and smiled. "He *does* love a game, doesn't he?" she said.

⚜ Chapter 10 ⚜

Gideon stood very erect in the centre of the withdrawing room and waited out the storm. Sir Mark had cut him off each time he attempted to speak, and now stamped up and down, raging, and flinging his arms about. Elegant in shades of gold, Newby leaned against a credenza, a faint smile on his lips as he toyed with a lady's jewelled high-heeled slipper. Gideon tried to concentrate on the intriguing slipper, which looked vaguely familiar, but his father's strident tones could not be shut out.

". . . a sad disappointment to a man when his son and heir is so insolent as to disregard his wishes! I warned you, and you cared not, but have in your sublime arrogance shamed me by agreeing to escort that baggage to the Glendenning Ball! Well—"

"Your pardon, sir. I escort the Lady Naomi Lutonville who, whatever else, is not a baggage!"

Gideon's eyes were grey ice, and in his voice a note never before heard by Sir Mark, who stared, briefly taken aback.

"Hoity-toity," murmured Newby.

"And I tell *you*, sir," thundered Sir Mark, his face purpling, "that Naomi Lutonville *is* a baggage! With the instincts of a baggage, and a traitorous ingrate for a father! And I'll not have you seen with her! You hear me?"

It was probable that all the residents of Snow Hill could hear him this morning. It took every ounce of Gideon's willpower to suppress his rising temper, but Sir Mark's eyes had a hunted look, and the high colour of his drawn features attested to the state of his nerves. Therefore, he tightened his lips and evaded. "Pray tell me what it is you wish me to do, sir."

Newby gave an amused snort. "You know blasted well what

139

my father wishes you to do. Go elsewhere tonight. And go alone."

Gideon eyed him coldly. "Very gentlemanly, 'pon my word."

"You should have returned her damned flowers at once," snarled Sir Mark.

"I attempted to do so."

Newby said with a flourish of the shoe, "But the great lady, out of her passion for you—and despite your shabby treatment of her—implored you to be her escort!" He gave his mocking laugh. "And so buzzes the bee!"

"Had my lady taken back her flowers," replied Gideon, "all London would have said she was justified in rejecting a Rossiter. She knew that, and was sufficiently gracious to spare me humiliation, and hold to her given word."

Sir Mark scowled. "You give the chit more credit than do I. Even so, 'twill not serve. You will send around a note before lunch, claiming that you are ill."

"My regrets, sir. I cannot."

"Hell and damnation! Do you dare defy me in mine own—"

"I have been warned not to escort her, sir."

The steely words cut through Sir Mark's rage, and he echoed, staring, "*Warned*, you say?"

"By whom?" asked Newby, with a bored look. "The Mandarin? I heard he is ill, so you've no immediate cause to fear being challenged by him, brother."

"Especially since we are already engaged to meet."

"You—*what*?" roared Sir Mark. "More notoriety? Why a'God's name did he call you out?"

"I chanced to half-strangle him because of certain remarks he made."

For once shaken from his affectation, Newby gasped, "*You* attacked—Falcon? You must have been properly wits to let! Or foxed!"

Gideon shrugged. "I'll own to having been a little provoked."

A gleam had crept into Sir Mark's eyes. "When you first came home, you said you'd not known of my troubles until you disembarked. Who told you? Falcon?"

"With neither tact nor diplomacy."

"*Vraiment*. He lacks either attribute. Then, he was the one warned you not to escort Lady Naomi?"

Gideon hesitated, then drew a crumpled paper from his

pocket. "This was delivered by a street urchin this morning, sir."

Sir Mark took it, and read aloud, "These to Captain Gideon Rossiter: London has not forgot how to deal with men of dishonour. If you wish to live to dwell with your father in Newgate, you will not force Lady Lutonville to endure the shame of your escort. You will instead return what you stole. Be warned. Keep away from the Glendenning Ball."

There was a moment of silence. Then Newby clicked his tongue. "Stealing? A harsh word, twin. Do tell us what you have purloined."

"I've not the remotest notion. I can only think that either something I bought in the Low Countries was of greater value than I believed, or that someone mistakes me for another."

Sir Mark said heavily, "Pah! 'Tis so much fustian, designed to cloud the real issue. But in the face of such threats a gentleman has no choice. Tell Wilson at what time you wish the carriage to be brought round, Gideon."

"Thank you, sir. But since you now keep just the one coach I'll not deprive you of it. My man will hire a carriage."

Sir Mark nodded, and walked out. At the door, he turned back, a weariness in his eyes. "Have a care, boy. Likely some enemy seeks to avenge himself on me by striking at you."

Touched, Gideon said with a grin, "Never worry, sir. I survived the war. I fancy I'll live through the peace."

Newby straightened as Sir Mark walked into the hall and out of earshot. "Clever of you," he murmured, "to *chance* to stand in exactly the right place to catch the fair lady's bouquet. Or was it contrived, perhaps? A way for you and she to—ah, frolic in some secluded ante room and outwit my poor dense dolt of a sire?"

He recoiled abruptly, his sneer fading into consternation as Gideon turned his dark head. The eyes were narrowed, the mouth a thin line and there was a set to the jaw that Newby had for a time forgotten.

"I strive to hold my temper with you," said Gideon very softly, "because despite your spite and sniping, my father is fond of you. And because you are kind to Gwen." His hand shot out and clamped about Newby's wrist. "But I warn you, spread any more of your slander about me, or about Lady Lutonville, and I shall indulge my natural instincts and give you the thrashing you warrant."

"You do not know 'twas me." Newby's eyes were frightened.

141

"Curse you, you are tearing my laces!" He swung up the slipper menacingly. "Stay back!"

Gideon laughed. "A fine weapon for a man! But not quite your size, is it?"

"Oh, very witty. But you'd give a deal to know where I got it, wouldn't you?"

"Would I?" Gideon relaxed his grip, and knowing his brother, shrugged, and said uninterestedly, "We have little in common, twin. I have no taste for gossip."

Newby was massaging his wrist tenderly, but a crafty expression replaced the resentment in his face and he said, "I was in the vicinity of the Dowling house last evening, and I wandered around to the back so I might look into the ballroom. I thought 'twould be such fun to see our gallant fighting man draw some of the treatment I've had to endure these past months."

"You must have enjoyed yourself," said Gideon with disgust.

"Prodigiously. And even more so when this interesting article"—he waved the slipper—"came sailing through the air and barely missed me."

Gideon's brows went up. "Do you say a lady hurled her slipper at you? Who was this resourceful female?"

His thoughts on the event, Newby did not heed his brother's sarcasm. "Unhappily 'twas too dark for me to see. I waited for someone to reclaim it, for certainly it has a value. But since it very likely fell from a bedchamber . . ." He grinned suggestively. "The lady must have been—otherwise engaged . . ."

"A hot-blooded wench, evidently. I've the fancy you mean to benefit from your little adventure. How? Even were you to advertise that you have found her lost property, she would scarce dare claim it. And if you sell that pretty thing for the gems in the heel I doubt 'twould bring very much at the pawnbroker. I've heard they only use second-rate jewels in—"

"Give me credit for more ingenuity," said Newby smugly. "The lady who lost this left her reputation behind. Only think how grateful she must be an 'tis discreetly returned. All I've to do is discover which fair creature owns such a shoe, and I may win far more than any pawnbroker would pay me."

Contemptuous, Gideon drawled, "As ever, you are all gallantry." He walked out of the room, leaving Newby hot with rage but also reminded that one could push his twin only so far, and that despite his injuries those slim hands were still incredibly strong.

Morris was dozing in the window seat when Gideon returned

142

to his small parlour. There was no sign of his valet, and he was obliged to summon Bernard, their solitary footman, who reported that Mr. Tummet was gone out in the carriage with Miss Gwendolyn.

Gideon stared at the bland face, wondering why the deuce Gwen would have commandeered his unconventional valet.

The question was still at the back of his mind when he accompanied Morris down the front steps to where a sweating boy held their horses. He pulled on his gauntlets, glancing without admiration at the antics of Morris' highly strung thoroughbred. "Can you control that nervous nag or shall you have to carry him?"

"I'll have you know," panted the lieutenant, "that Windsong is a real goer and cost me a pretty penny! Wait 'til you see him run. He all but flies!"

"I do not doubt it. I've yet to see him rest more than two hooves on the ground at the same time. He should have been named Whirligig not Windsong!" Stifling a smile at his friend's indignation, he said, "At least, the rain has blown over. Whereabouts is this flat of yours?"

"Off Clarges Street. But I ain't going there just now, dear boy. Thought I'd drop in on Falcon."

Frowning, Gideon swung into the saddle. "Not very good form, is it? Surely you can arrange your meeting after he and I have fought."

"Yes, but the delectable Miss Katrina might be about. Damn, but I forgot about this deuced mountain!"

With an attempt at nonchalance, Gideon said, "Close your eyes, my Tulip. Let the nags worry about it."

Five minutes later, he stifled a sigh of relief as his frightened mare trod on level ground once more.

"Be damned if I can fathom why you fellas choose such ghastly residences," grumbled Morris. "Falcon must live at the very farthest-flung reaches of civilization, and you choose to perch on some blasted eagle's nest!"

"Then let us dispense with your call at Falcon House. No, really, Jamie, one does not attach the heart of a lady by challenging her brother."

Morris pursed his lips. "Under normal circumstances, I agree. In Falcon's case, however, I'd think Miss Katrina would be dashed glad to have the clod chastised."

"Best think again. Miss Falcon dotes on him."

"You must be mistaken, dear boy. An angel like that could

not possibly be blockheaded. Which reminds me, what of the poor block who was attacked whilst returning my belongings? Have you seen him?''

"Yes. Byrd was properly mauled, but he is going along well now. He said the louts who attacked him were masked and vicious in the extreme. And that they seemed to be looking for something.''

"Egad! One might think we had stole some highly secret plans and smuggled 'em home.'' Morris paused, frowning. "You know, Gideon, we all had you marked for a downy bird. Might you be—'' His eyes began to glow, and he exclaimed, beaming, "You are! You work for Intelligence, by Jove!''

With difficulty, Rossiter subdued a shout of laughter. He glanced up and down bustling High Holborn, and leaning closer to his friend, hissed, "Weeds and winkles!''

Morris' jaw dropped. "W-weeds and—*winkles* . . . ?''

"Quiet, you dolt! There are ears everywhere! That is the password.''

Flushed with excitement, Morris exclaimed softly, "Stap me! I *knew* there was something smoky afoot! All this business about conspiracies and chessmen and rank riders, and thieves who go in terror of 'the Squire!' All of a piece, is't, dear boy? Well, I've rumbled you, so you've no choice but to own up. What's to do?''

"Insurrection,'' whispered Rossiter.

"Good God! But—we just had one! Those curst Jacobites, what?''

"They only wanted to seize the throne. This lot plan a bloody rebellion. And death to all cows,'' added Rossiter, inspired.

Morris blinked at him, stunned. "All—er, what?''

"Cows. Fiendishly clever, no? Only think on it, Jamie. Without cows there would be no milk, no cheese, no beef. England without roast beef?'' He shuddered. "We would be lost! At the mercy of any aggressor who—''

Despite himself a twitch had appeared beside his lips, and with a cry of mortification Morris tore the tricorne from his head and began to belabour his companion furiously. "Of all the—cheating—lying—devious . . . !''

Ducking frantically, and racked with laughter, Rossiter pleaded, "*Par pitie! Par pitie!* I could not resist it! No, really, Jamie, spare me! Everyone stares.''

Indeed, many amused faces were turned their way, and a lady wearing a great deal of paint and far too many jewels leaned from her sedan chair, shaking her fan at them in laughing reproof.

Morris flushed scarlet. "Well, I trust you enjoyed your fun," he said huffily. "I am very sure that as usual, gullible Morris provides a perfect foil for his clever friends. And you, sir, would be the better for a companion as quick witted as yourself. Good day to you!"

He drove home his spurs and was away. Rossiter was after him like a flash. A glance over his shoulder and Morris' ready grin dawned. He bent lower in the saddle and it was a race, the two young men galloping at reckless speed through the heavy traffic, leaving behind a trail of cursing coachmen, profane riders, and hooting boys.

At the corner of Gray's Inn Road Rossiter caught up, leaned from the saddle and seized Morris' rein. "Wait up, Jamie!" he panted. "I've but now realized what you said."

"What did I say? And I want no more of weeds and winkles, damn your eyes!"

"Thieves who go in terror of 'the Squire.' 'Tis exactly what Tummet said! That the louts who attacked him were desperate to find something for—'the Squire.' "

Morris looked dubious. "Don't see anything remarkable in that, dear boy. Lots of servants refer to their employer as the Squire."

"Perhaps. But surely, some would tend to say, 'the master,' or 'the governor' or something of the sort? Does it not seem odd that in both these instances the same phrase was used, the same sense of desperation conveyed?"

"You say that the robberies were not coincidences, eh?"

"Consider, Jamie. The ransacking of Promontory Point, your thieves, the attack on Byrd—By heavens! Perhaps my stolen saddlebags as well! There *must* be some connection!"

Deep in thought, they rode on slowly, turning at length onto Great Ormond Street, where the distant roofs of the Foundling Hospital could be seen, with open countryside beyond.

"But a'God's name, why?" said Morris, baffled. "It makes no sense unless somebody wants something we brought back from Holland. I brought nothing to inspire such frenzy. No more did—Oh, what luck!"

Glancing up, Rossiter's reaction was slightly different.

Three ladies strolled towards them, followed by a footman. Two were startlingly lovely and clad in the height of fashion.

The third had a fine-boned face and a mischievous look, and walked with the aid of a cane.

The two men dismounted at once. Very aware of the aloof hauteur in Lady Naomi's eyes, and the frown on Miss Falcon's beautiful face, Rossiter bowed and paid his respects.

Miss Falcon, a vision in a walking dress of light rose, nodded to him with cool disapproval. Lady Naomi wore a pale green toilette and a cream damask cape richly embroidered in the same green as her gown. A broad-brimmed hat of cream straw with green ribands hanging down the back was set *à la bergère* atop the belaced cap perched on her lightly powdered curls. She bowed politely but there was a sparkle of vexation in her green eyes.

"I am so glad we fell in with you, Gideon," said Gwendolyn merrily. "Are you come to fetch me?"

Rossiter started and wrenched his gaze from the lady who had been for so long the embodiment of his every dream. "Er, no. I thought you had gone out for a drive, under Tummet's escort." An elbow was in his ribs. He ignored it, but the succeeding jab almost made him stagger.

It was quite apparent that two of the ladies wanted nothing so much as to terminate this encounter. Gritting his teeth, Rossiter introduced the persistent lieutenant, and Miss Falcon's chilly demeanor was replaced by an expression of horrified accusation. "You are the man shot my brother!" she exclaimed, drawing back.

"Pray do not take me in deep aversion," pleaded Morris earnestly. "I'd not have done so had I not thought he was a rank rider. 'Twas a perfectly natural mistake."

" 'Twas nothing of the kind . . . ," she began indignantly.

Morris attempted a gabbling and involved explanation, during which Rossiter turned aside and said quietly, "I'd not realized you and my sister were still—ah, acquainted, ma'am."

Lady Naomi turned her cool gaze to him. "You object, Captain Rossiter?"

"Of course he does not," said Gwendolyn. "We have had such a lovely cose, Gideon. Mr. Falcon has the finest dog, and let me throw a stick for him, only he took a little tumble. Mr. Falcon did, I mean, and was in such a humour we decided to leave him alone with it, didn't we, Naomi?"

My lady smiled at her. "He was rather cross, but you must not regard it."

"Just so," agreed Rossiter. "August Falcon is renowned for several traits, but a conciliating manner is not among them."

"True. It has in fact become a rare quality in a gentleman," sighed Naomi regretfully.

Rossiter gritted his teeth. "Am I obliged to offer him an apology, Gwen?"

"No, no," said Naomi. "You must not trouble yourself with the niceties."

"Still, Apollo *did* break a vase when I was playing with him," admitted Gwendolyn with a sparkling look.

"Then I shall most certainly replace it."

"Thank you, dearest. That would be nice."

"If a trifle difficult," murmured Naomi, watching a sparrow hop along the iron railings beside them.

"How so, ma'am?" asked Rossiter. "Do you infer this vase to have been the only one of its kind in the entire world?"

"Not at all. I imagine there must be others. In China. His grandmama brought it with her, I believe."

Gwendolyn halted with a distressed cry. "Oh, how dreadful! I could see he was terribly angry, but I thought 'twas because— Oh—Gideon!"

"Never worry so, Gwen," said Naomi, relenting. "I doubt Mr. Falcon ever looked at the silly thing."

"Of course he did. Clearly, he worships his grandmother's memory."

Naomi patted her hand kindly. "Then we shall find another vase. My father is quite expert on antiquities. I'll ask him to—" Glancing up, she stepped aside hastily.

They were blocking the flagway, and the two large matrons now approaching did not propose to share the right of way. Rossiter guided Gwendolyn away from their aggressive advance. Still striving to win a kindlier attitude from his goddess, Morris was lost to all else and became the recipient of a sharp prod from a parasol. He uttered an involuntary yelp. The matron who had folded her weapon so as to attack him, now snapped it open again. It was of brightly hued purple and white silk with a scarlet fringe, and it turned Morris' Windsong into the whirligig Rossiter had named him. Neighing his terror, the big horse reared and spun. Morris tried to pull him down, but was sent reeling. He collided with Katrina and knocked the dainty reticule from her hand. Gwendolyn was well clear of the debacle, and Rossiter sprang forward, swept Naomi into his arms, and whirled her around.

"Oh! Put me down at once!" cried Naomi angrily.

An iron-shod hoof flailed down about four feet from her cheek. Katrina gave a cry of alarm.

"Oh, Gad! I am so very sorry," groaned Morris, belatedly succeeding in controlling his rambunctious animal.

Katrina's footman, who had been engaged in conversation with a shabby individual, now came running up, and he and Morris bent simultaneously to retrieve Katrina's reticule. Gideon heard the thump as their heads collided. The footman gave a shocked cry and his wig and tricorne fell off. Gasping, Morris snatched determinedly for the reticule. Unhappily, he retrieved it upside down. Coins rolled in all directions; a pencil, notepad, card case, chain purse, handkerchief, a brush, an advertisement for cucumber lotion, a small pair of scissors, a brooch, two letters, a pot of rouge, a scone wrapped in paper, a flea comb, and a carrot were scattered about the flagway. A hand mirror shattered as did a vial of scent, the latter splashing Miss Falcon with cloying fragrance that was customarily applied by the drop. She uttered a wail of embarrassment. The footman knelt and started to retrieve the numerous casualties, and Morris groaned dismally.

Passers-by had found the incident highly amusing, and a big man accompanied by a very fat and hilarious lady shouted that it was "as good as any farce."

Naomi pulled away from Rossiter's arms and fixed him with a stern frown.

He enquired blandly, "Are you all right, ma'am?"

"I was *perfectly* all right, and nowhere near—"

He made a gesture of dismissal. "There is not the need for thanks," he said, with somewhat questionable magnanimity. "A gentleman must always stand ready to protect a helpless damsel."

"Hmm," said Naomi. "Katrina, you are not harmed?"

Miss Falcon might be unharmed but she was close to tears of mortification. In a shaken voice she urged that they return home at once, for they must have a nap this afternoon.

The three ladies embraced and said hurried farewells. Rossiter engaged to call for Lady Naomi at half past nine o'clock, and poor Morris, hanging his head in shame, wished the earth might open and swallow him.

Turning back towards Falcon House, Katrina all but sobbed, "I reek! Oh, I shall smell of Camellia Caprice forever! I have *never* been so humiliated! Whatever must they have thought?"

"That you carry a vast amount in your reticule, love." Her eyes alight with mischief, Naomi said, "Never fret. Your laundress will get the scent out, I am persuaded. But in truth, you carry some unexpected articles when you go out for a stroll."

"I took the scone to feed the ducks in the park yesterday, and quite forgot! And the carrot was for my mare. But—the *flea* comb, Naomi! 'Twas for Apollo, but—What if—Oh, how awful!"

Naomi chuckled. "No, really. Even those two would never think 'twas for your own lovely head, dearest."

"I do hope not," sniffed Katrina. "Faith, but I marvel Lieutenant Morris survived the war. He is a perpetual disaster!"

"And so terribly smitten, poor fellow. He could scarce have played his cards worse! He must first shoot August, then come nigh to trampling you with his half-broke horse, next engage in the fiasco with your footman, and compound his offenses by emptying your reticule. Truly, I could not but feel sorry for him. He looked ready to sink!"

"And I was of a mind to sink him! Bad enough he must make me a figure of fun, but had it not been for Captain Rossiter—Naomi, I was sure that wild animal's hoof was going to strike your face!"

Naomi said tartly, "He would certainly have done so—had he the legs of a camelopard, or whatever 'tis they call them now."

"Giraffe, I believe. No, was the horse that far from you? Then I wonder why Captain Rossiter must snatch you up like that?"

Naomi gave her a level look. "Do you, indeed."

Momentarily forgetting her own humiliation, Katrina said with saintly innocence, "I suppose it must have been very dreadful to be crushed and swept up in his arms like that. In view of—er, everything."

Infuriatingly, Naomi felt her cheeks burn. She said, "I vow I purely *dread* this evening! Whatever has become of your footman?"

The footman in question, having collected all the contents of the reticule and restored his own dignity, was presenting Rossiter with a folded paper. "A h'individual h'asked me to put this in your 'and, sir," he said. "Jest before"—he flashed an aggrieved glance at the glum Morris—"the h'incident with the 'orse."

Rossiter thanked him and soothed his ruffled feelings by sending him after his ladies with a florin in his palm.

"And now, Miss Gwendolyn." Rossiter turned to his sister.

"I'll have an explanation, if you please. What were you thinking of to drive out with Tummet? How came you to be in this part of town? And where the deuce *is* the dimwit?"

" 'Twas such a lovely day," she began airily.

"It was drizzling!"

"Well, yes it was—earlier. But I was sure it would clear up. As it did, for that very aggressive lady had need of her parasol, did you not notice?"

"Gad, but I did," sighed Morris.

"I longed to go out for a drive," explained Gwendolyn, "and since we are so short of servants just now, Mr. Tummet said he would be happy to serve as footman—"

"A fine footman! The slippery fellow abandoned you—or did you send him off?"

"I suppose it must have been a misunderstanding. I had thought he was to wait, but—Oh, how fortuitous! Here he comes now!"

The approaching carriage slowed and stopped. Tummet called, "Whatcher, Cap'n!"

Rossiter handed his reins to Morris and stalked to the window from which his valet's bewigged head protruded. "Where the devil have you been? And how *dare* you abandon Miss Rossiter?"

"Cor!" said Tummet, wounded. "As if I'd do such a 'orrid thing! Snug as a bug, yer sister was. Wiv the friends of 'er bosom!" He leaned farther from the window, and said in a hissing croak, "Lend us yer ear 'oles."

"I'm more like to lend you my boot," declared Gideon wrathfully. "What rascality have you been about now?"

"Comes a time, Guv, when a man's faced with one o' them there not-so-nice's." Tummet nodded lugubriously.

"I—am—in—no—mood—" began Gideon through his teeth.

Tummet had already noted the glint in his employer's eyes, however, and he translated hurriedly, "That is ter say—crisis, Cap'n. And *that's* what E. Tummet faced. Not fer 'imself, mind-ya. But fer the gent what took 'im on. Loyalty. That's me motter. So seein's 'ow a decision was gotta be made, I made it."

"Did you. Well, I am making one of my own. In fact—"

"I don't go about wiv me weepers shut, mate," interrupted the indomitable valet. "You remember when I was knocked abaht by them ugly coves and lost me sovereign nation? Well, I seen one of 'em. The back of 'im, that is."

Interested now, Gideon exclaimed, "Did you, by God! So you followed? Good man! You never lost him?"

"In a manner of speakin' I did. When 'e went inside. By the side door, a'course. Didn't see 'is face, mind, but I knew 'im by 'is perishing strut."

"Where did he go?"

"To a very tidy mansion. Very nice indeed. Luxoorus y'might say. On Soho Square." Tummet grinned as he saw Rossiter's eyes narrow, and nodding his head, he whispered, "That's right, mate. The 'ome of yer papa's dear old friend, what's s'posed to be orf in foreign parts. Sir Derrydene!"

"By . . . God!"

Within minutes Tummet was seated on the box, Gwendolyn had been installed in the carriage, and the coachman was guiding his team back towards Snow Hill.

Watching all this with mournful abstraction, Morris mounted up, and accompanying Rossiter along the street, said miserably, "Well, I properly made mice feet of the business, once again."

"Oh, I'd not say that, exactly," murmured Rossiter, a half-smile tugging at the corner of his mouth.

Morris sighed. "Good of you. But it's no use trying to ease the blow. She must take me for the king of clods. Even Lady Naomi looked at me as if I was wits to let. Which reminds me—what the deuce were you doing with her?"

"What d'you mean—what was I doing with her? I was gallantly risking my own life so as to save her from being trampled to death by your insane animal."

"Walker!" said Morris jeeringly. "Windsong's hooves came nowhere near her!"

"Perhaps, from where you were standing it appeared in that light. But where I stood, it was—" laughter danced in his grey eyes—"quite different."

"I'll warrant it was, you rogue! Some fellows have all the luck! What of your note? Anything to the purpose?"

"Begad, if I hadn't forgot it!" Rossiter fumbled in his coat pocket, found the note, and reined in so sharply that a following horseman almost caromed into him.

"What is it?" demanded Morris, ignoring the spleen of the annoyed rider. "You look like the sheep that ate the wolf!"

"And feel the same! Look at this." He handed over the crumpled note, and Morris read:

Mr. Rossiter.

I no what your trying to proov, and I no something. Not much. Im a pore man sir, but maybee we can help each other. I will wate at Number 18, Appleblosom Lane until four o'clock. Its orf Whitechapel Road.

Sined, Tom Brewer.

"Hum," said Morris, returning the note. "Terrible spelling. And it smells like a trap, you realize?"

"Yes. But I think I dare not ignore it."

"Jolly good. I've not been in Whitechapel for years, but it's as well I brought my pistol. Do you go armed, my Tulip?"

"Of course. But to say truth, I'd as lief you didn't come. This is my affair, and may take some time, and you have other matters to settle."

"I do not scruple to tell you that you are a scaly scrub," said Lieutenant Morris, indignant. "You want to hog this to yourself, yet would be the first to complain did you get your throat cut! Which you doubtless will do you go in alone, for if 'tis a trap the odds are bound to be heavy. You know very well I have had a bad day, and a good brawl would cheer me up. But, no! I am to be sent off with—"

Laughing, Gideon said, "You great gudgeon! I shall be exceeding glad of your help, as you know very well."

Morris grinned at him and turned his horse eastward. "If Appleblossom Lane lies in the rabbit warren I think it does, we shall be lucky do we find it in time to get to the ball this evening."

"We'll find it," said Gideon determinedly.

An hour later, he was a good deal less optimistic. They had reached Whitechapel Road without much difficulty, but had then plunged into a labyrinth of streets that had gradually deteriorated into narrow refuse-strewn lanes, and then into dark, gloomy alleys. Three times they'd stopped to ask the way, and their ragged and dirty informants had been willing enough to supply directions that were "clear as a bell" but which turned out to be murky as mud. Their most recent instructions, imparted by an insolent boy, had been so confusing that they'd disagreed as to whether to turn left or right at the second alley. As a result, Morris had gone left and Rossiter had reined his mare to the right, where he now found himself at the junction of Crabtree Lane and Elderberry Court.

It was a far cry from either elderberries or courts. A squalid, reeking alley, with the blackened timbers of sagging warehouses to the left, and row houses to the right which were posted as having been condemned. "And rightly so," Rossiter muttered, scanning woodwork that hung in rotted strips, boarded-up or cracked windows, and the occasional furtive scamper of rats. Yet some poor souls still dwelt in this nightmarish hole, for as he rode past he heard the thin wailing of an infant; a woman's shrill, drunken laughter; the bitter cursing of a man. 'Good God!' he thought, appalled that any Englishman should have to lodge his wife and children in such a ghastly slum, and realizing also that some of his own men had probably grown up in similar squalor.

And then, on a sagging post before him, were the barely decipherable words: Appleblossom Lane.

"Victory!" he muttered.

The mare tossed her head and whinnied as he rounded the corner. He could scarce blame her, for this area was even worse than Elderberry Court. Tall warehouses loomed on both sides to shut out the sunlight. There were only three houses to be seen, and they were at the far end of this perpetually shadowed "lane" that might almost have been a tunnel. Gideon rode on, pistol in hand now, ears straining and eyes alert.

He was almost to the end of the "tunnel" when it came to him that it was very quiet. Unnaturally quiet. The mare danced nervously, but the end of the lane was clear and a quick glance behind revealed no sign of lurking footpads.

He could not have said what made him look up. A dark shape was hurtling down at him, all arms and legs. Before he could aim the pistol, he was smashed from the saddle. Sprawling in the mud, dazed, he instinctively fought to get up. The mare neighed shrilly. A voice shouted, "Grab her! Quick!"

A boot flew at Rossiter's head. He jerked away, but another smashed into his ribs and he doubled up. Through the pain, he thought dully, 'Four of the bastards,' and was vaguely shocked when a woman screeched, "Search 'im! But take care you don't mark 'is face! The Squire don't want 'im marked!"

"The Squire!" Those words seared into Rossiter's reeling brain, and anger brought a resurgence of strength. A large shape bent over him. Rough hands tore at his pockets. He struck out with all his strength. A startled oath, and someone fell. It was too close quarters for swordplay, but struggling to his knees, he managed somehow to wrest his dagger from its sheath and strike

153

out blindly. The howl was deafening. "The perisher's got a knife!"

"Not fer long, 'e ain't," snarled a coarse, deep voice.

A boot drove hard at Rossiter's arm and the dagger fell from his numbed fingers. The boot kicked out again, but the instinct for survival was strong, and Rossiter's years of soldiering stood him in good stead. He jerked aside, clutched the boot and pulled. A man shot over him, colliding with another ruffian who was in the process of swinging a hefty cudgel. The cudgel found the wrong mark and the air resounded with howls of wrathful profanity. The cudgel fell. Rolling, Rossiter snatched it up and clawed his way to his feet. A hard-driven fist landed beside his right ear, sending him staggering, but his back slammed against a wall and he battled to stay upright. A beefy face was in front of him. He drove the cudgel at it and the face convulsed and sank from sight. A fist flew at his jaw, and he deflected it with the cudgel, then landed a right uppercut, sending the ruffian flying back. But a long club flailed from nowhere and landed squarely on his left shoulder. He knew dully that he was down, but for a horrible interval pain smothered everything else.

Someone growled echoingly, ". . . ain't got it, I tellyer."

A brutal hand was dragging him up. Beery breath, and a voice demanding, "Where is it, soldier boy?" A knife glittered before his dazed eyes. "Tell us afore we 'ave ter—"

"Troops, forward! At the double!"

'Jamie,' thought Rossiter numbly.

Shouts of rage and alarm. Hoofbeats. More than one horse.

The woman screeched, "Narks! Narks! Shab orf!"

Savage cursing. The hand with the knife vanished, but a boot rammed into Rossiter's stomach. Writhing, he heard the shrill female voice, "Keep stickin' yer nose where it don't belong, me 'andsome darlin', and next time, we'll scrag yer!"

A pistol roared. Running feet. Howls, and a fight somewhere close by.

Rossiter was very sick.

❧ *Chapter 11* ❧

"I am indeed grateful," declared Rossiter, cautiously lifting his arm as Tummet had requested. "But how you came to be there I cannot fathom. I had left you with strict instructions to take Miss Gwendolyn home."

"Popped 'er into the coach, safe as a sturgeon, Guv," said Tummet, leaning over the bed and easing off the torn wreckage of the coat. "Only I 'opped orf and 'ired meself a 'ack. Can you lift yer arm up a bit more?" Rossiter complying, he went on, "Now fer this 'ere what once called itself a shirt. I follered you, just in case you needed a 'and, like."

"And I had the devil's own work to come up with you," said Lieutenant Morris, carrying a tray with decanter and glasses into the bedchamber and closing the door softly behind him.

Flinching from Tummet's efforts, Rossiter swore, then said, "Well, I never was more in need of reinforcements. Had it not been for you two—"

"You'd a' cocked up yer toes," said Tummet. "Six to one ain't fair odds, Guv. But I gotta say that fer a chap what's nothing but skin and bone, you fights like a troop of cavalry! A 'ole perishing troop! Blind me if I ever see a gent laying about 'im wiv so much spirit! Makes me proud I took you on, which I can't say no better! Lean forrard a bit, if y'can."

Rossiter obliged. "In point of fact, they didn't mean to kill me. The woman kept screeching that my face was not to be marked."

"They may not have marked your face," said Morris, frowning. "But they were less charitable with the rest of you."

Glancing down at his lurid bruises, Rossiter told his valet to lock the door. "I'd not have Gwendolyn see this mess."

"No need for that," said Morris. "You may be *à l'aise*, my trampled Tulip. The lady is perfectly well, and at the moment engaged in applying a poultice to the jaw of your footman, who has the toothache. A remarkably kind little creature, an I dare remark it."

"She's one in a million," agreed Rossiter. "But I wish I knew what the deuce she was about at Falcon House this morning." He looked at Tummet steadily, and receiving only a smile of angelic innocence turned his attention to more immediate problems. "You're sure no one saw me come in?"

"Have no fears," said Morris handing him a glass of Madeira. "We were able to slip in the side door without causing any of the maids to faint. However, I think you shall have to disappoint Lady Naomi after all. Cannot go cavorting about tonight with your middle looking like—"

"Good God!" Sir Mark had entered the room unnoticed, and now stood pale and shocked as he scanned his battered son. For a moment he stared, saying nothing. Then he lifted his eyes to Gideon's face. "When you said you'd been wounded, I never dreamed— Zounds! I marvel you lived, boy!"

Morris said cheerfully, "He damn near didn't, sir."

Gideon hastened to point out that he was "in good point now."

"Ho yus you ain't," argued Tummet, and taking Sir Mark aside, said in a confidential manner, "I'll fetch some 'ot compresses, sir. To bring them bruises out. You jest keep 'im where 'e is, and don't let 'im go popping orf nowhere." He gave the baronet an encouraging nod and went out.

Sir Mark looked after him, shook his head as if to clear it, then pulled up a chair and sat down. "What happened?"

"Somebody objects to my enquiries, it seems." Gideon eased himself back against the pillows. "I was warned to keep my nose out of what doesn't concern me." He sampled the wine and began to feel slightly less fuzzy-headed. "Newby said that you both have been trying to come at the root of it all. Were you ever attacked, sir?"

"Never. But with you here, stirring things up again, mayhap my enemies are beginning to be alarmed."

"Hmm. Or they may think I have learned something."

Sir Mark demanded eagerly, "Have you?"

Gideon frowned, and said slowly, "Something—odd. This morning Tummet thinks he spotted one of the ruffians who ransacked Promontory Point."

156

"The devil!" exclaimed Morris.

Sir Mark said, "Did he, by God? Where?"

"Going into Derrydene's house in Soho."

They both stared at him, speechless. Then, Sir Mark said, "Why in the name of all that's holy should Louis Derrydene want to search Promontory Point? Besides, the man's out of the country. I'll tell you frankly, Gideon, I'd not place much credence in what that man of yours says. Wouldn't trust the fellow as far as I could throw him! Did he see the ruffian's face?"

"Only his back, sir. But he is quite sure 'twas the same man."

"Fustian! Likely giving himself airs to be interesting. Whoever broke into the Point did so because they knew a great house was standing empty. And whatever Louis Derrydene may be about, I give you my word it ain't the burglary business!"

Morris, who had retreated to stand looking out of the window, came back and leaned against the bedpost. "I caught some bounder trying to rob me, sir. Tackled the beastly fellow, but he had friends, unfortunately."

"Simple robbery," said Sir Mark, irritated.

"So simple they took very little, sir," argued Gideon.

"Understandable. Morris says he interrupted the thieves."

"Yes, that's so." Morris was considerably daunted by his friend's formidable sire, but he said bravely, "But no one interrupted the men who attacked your groom when he went to fetch our belongings from the Red Pheasant."

"Do you say," demanded Sir Mark with a fierce scowl, "that these petty thefts, in none of which anything of much value was taken, are connected to the collapse of my bank and my companies, the destruction of my shipyard, my son's having been viciously beaten today? If so, sir, I'd be much obliged would you explain the connection to me, for I'll own myself too dense to make head nor tail of it all."

Morris flushed, and stammered nervously, "Wish I c-could, sir. Never was much good at riddles."

Gideon said, "Father, in each of these instances the rogues have referred to 'the Squire,' and—"

"Well, what in thunder is so dashed unusual in that? I fancy my employees refer to me in the same fashion."

"Yes, but—"

"Now listen to me, my boy. I've seen more of life than have you and I know blasted well 'tis full of the strangest coincidences. You have your work cut out to discover who is behind the plot to destroy me. Do not be turned aside by this other

157

havey-cavey business. You were attacked this morning because you are coming close to the man who is behind it all.''

"I hope so, sir. But they *searched* me. Why? Unless it *is* part of the other affair and they think—''

Sir Mark gave a disgusted snort. "Of course they searched you. They were sent to frighten you off, but no common hireling is going to resist the chance of seizing a gentleman's rings, or purse, or whatever. You told me yourself that you're of the opinion someone mistakenly supposes you or Lieutenant Morris have brought home something of value.''

"Yes, but—''

"Then they have doubtless discovered their error, so don't maudle your mind with nonsense.'' He started to the door, then hesitated, and came back to stand by the bed. "Gideon,'' he said in a gruff voice, "I gather I am luckier than I realized in that you came back from Holland alive. I'd—er, I'd not see you killed, boy. You will take care?''

Touched, Morris said, "Never fear, sir. I'll keep an eye on the gudgeon.''

Sir Mark stared at him. "You cannot guess how that relieves my mind,'' he said dryly.

"You would not dare!'' Already wearing her ball gown, Katrina's eyes were wide, and she gazed at her friend in awe.

"Oh, yes she would, Miss Katrina,'' said Maggie, coaxing a strand of Naomi's hair into a glowing ringlet. "It don't matter to my lady if folks says as I doesn't know how to send her out. When my lady's in a taking like this—''

"Oh, hush, you silly girl,'' snapped Naomi, snatching the comb. "Go! Go! I shall manage my hair myself!''

Maggie threw her apron over her head and departed, wailing. Once in the hall, her wails ceased, and she smiled to herself. When my lady got over her pet and was full of remorse (as she always was, the sweet soul), there would be a gift offered in repentance for her harshness. It would be the lavender cap this time, thought Maggie happily. My lady never had much cared for it, but it would look lovely with her own new Sunday gown. And if a certain first footman, by the name of Mr. Robert Hinton, come creeping round with his saucy words and saucier hands, he'd discover that ladies with caps of lavender silk and lace could look so high as they wanted! She tripped along the hall, humming softly.

Naomi was also humming, turning the mirror this way and

that as she studied the back view of her coiffure. Maggie really had performed her usual magic, and the clustered curls looked rather nice. "I see no reason," she said loftily, "why everyone must be the same. There is no law says we all must wear powder, is there?"

"There is no law which says a gentleman must fight an he is insulted. But they all do."

"Precisely. Gentlemen are so many silly sheep, which is not to say I shall be the same."

Katrina said quietly, "Then, alas, you must judge me also a silly sheep."

At once contrite, Naomi flew to hug her. "Oh, but I am a horrid cat! I wonder you bear with me! Your hair looks divinely in that silver powder. But then *you* would look divinely were you to go bald in public!"

Laughing, Katrina said, "Do not even *think* such a thing! And your auburn hair is truly glorious, Naomi. I fancy you will be the rage of the ball, and poor Captain Rossiter scarce see you the entire evening."

"One can but hope," muttered Naomi, returning to the dressing table and fastening an emerald necklace about her white throat. Gideon had been used to say the nicest things about the colour of her hair . . . She caught herself in a sigh, and smothered it hurriedly. "I declare," she said, "between my wretched escort tonight, and this miserable business about my slipper, I am all a'twitter! Everyone is whispering and trying to guess *who* the wicked lady is, and *how* her slipper chanced to fall from an upstairs window . . . ! Oh, Trina! Why must people have such horrid minds?"

"Only some people, dearest. And after all, nobody knows 'tis your slipper. If you can but get another made before—"

"How can I? You may be sure all the gabblemongers are watching the shoemakers like hawks. I do not dare go myself to Mr. Painton's shop, and no matter whom I sent, or how much I paid, the news would leak out, and I should be judged again, when I did nothing more than—"

"Than come near to breaking your pretty neck, and in such foolish cause! Truly Naomi, if August knew—"

"Lud!" Whirling about Naomi gasped, "You'd not tell him?"

"Of course not. And if he did know, he would censure you privately, but never betray you. The one you've to outwit, my love, is Mrs. Golightly."

"Samantha? Heavens! Why?"

159

"Do you not recall? She was in Painton's when you gave him the order for the slippers. She may not have noticed, but—"

"Oh! *Oh*!" moaned Naomi, sinking her face into her hands. "I had quite forgot. That horrid girl has always loathed me! She was fairly mad for Gideon before I went to Italy, and I heard she made herself into a proper figure of fun, flirting with him at parties after I was gone." She glanced up with a tragic air, saw Katrina staring curiously, and added a hurried, "Not that I give a button for that, of course. But—oh, Trina! She is sure to be there tonight. An she asks me where my jewelled slippers are . . . !"

"She'd not be so pushing, surely? Oh, dear! She would! My poor Naomi! Whatever shall you do?"

"Bluff my way, I suppose. Somehow. But people will be eager to believe her, does she spread the word. And he— Everyone will say I am a . . . guttersnipe." For a moment she looked so crushed that Katrina was aghast, then the proud little head tossed up, the drooping mouth curved to a defiant smile. "A pox on the lot of 'em! I must prepare for the arrival of my knight-errant. And pray he'll not come wearing a coat five years behind the fashion!"

A footman came with several corsages. A darkly red rose set in a filigreed silver holder; a tiny bouquet of cornflowers and baby's breath; another of dainty pink roses; a delicate cluster of lily-of-the valley and maidenhair fern. "Oh, this one is perfect!" exclaimed Katrina, taking up the lily-of-the valley, and glancing at the card.

"Yes, indeed," said Naomi, pleased. "Who sent it?"

She saw her friend's face fall, and scowled. "Then I shall wear the red rose! 'Twill make a nice contrast."

Half an hour later, watching as she descended the staircase, Rossiter caught his breath. Her *robe à la Francaise* was a shimmering sweep of palest green and silver brocade, cut very low in the bust, the stomacher emphasizing her tiny waist. The hem of the green satin underdress was caught up into deep scallops. Her unpowdered head was held regally high, the candlelight awaking flashes of dark red fire from amongst the rich brown of the glistening curls. As she drew nearer, she studiously avoided looking at him, her averted and disdainful face giving him the chance to study the delicate curve of her cheek, the firm little chin, the vivid, shapely mouth. Surely, someone so lovely could not be faithless and immoral?

At the fourth step from the bottom, Naomi lifted her eyes to look without marked delight at her escort. Despite her rather unkind remark to Katrina, she knew Gideon well enough to be assured that his appearance would not disgrace her. She had not, however, been prepared for the sight of him in full regimental evening dress, and to see him standing there, tall and straight, his cloak flung back from one shoulder, his tricorne under his arm, his fine eyes fixed on her face, momentarily struck all power of movement from her.

They stood there, gazing at each other. Two people once ineffably beloved, now separated by an impregnable barrier of hurt and disillusion.

Naomi gave herself a mental shake and started down once more, lifting her panniers slightly.

Enchanted, Gideon saw the candlelight glint on the emerald buckles of her slippers. Just as the light had caught her slippers at the Dowling Soiree, when she'd turned on the stairs after tossing the bouquet! He had a clear picture of his brother, flourishing a jewelled slipper and sneering, "The lady who lost this at the Dowling Soiree left her reputation behind . . ." And the dear illusion shattered. He thought achingly, 'Naomi . . . Naomi . . .' and heard his own voice say coldly, "Good evening, ma'am. I fancy you relish this no more than do I."

My lady shrugged. "There will not be the need for us to do more than arrive and leave together."

A footman came up to offer her cloak. Rossiter took it, and disposed the garment about Naomi's shoulders. Handing her onto the terrace steps, knowing he was moving awkwardly, he glanced at the vivid rose pinned to her bodice. "How charming. A nice contrast."

"Is it not?" One slim finger touched the glowing bloom. "I received several posies, but alas, one cannot wear them all. La, but I am remiss! You were so kind as to send me a corsage, also. Such pretty cornflowers. I thank you, sir."

He thought, 'She knows perfectly well that I sent lily-of-the-valley, which she always loved,' but he said, "I am only grateful you noticed my poor offering, ma'am. So often the delicate is overwhelmed by"—he glanced again at the red rose—"the ostentatious."

"But I do not consider cornflowers in the slightest ostentatious," she said, opening her eyes at him.

"I am very sure that a lady with your experience of the world knows quite well which flowers compliment her—personality," he riposted.

161

"Oh, yes," she murmured, showing him all her teeth and longing to sink them into his neck.

He was assisting her into the carriage, then. A rented carriage, obviously, and with dreadfully hard and uncomfortable seats. Gritting her teeth, Naomi thought it was all of a piece, and that the evening would likely continue to deteriorate.

As it transpired, her worst fears paled before reality. By the time they reached Laindon House, she was convinced that Rossiter had drunk his dinner. He sat opposite her in the farthest corner of the coach, said not a word, and surreptitiously braced himself against the side each time the vehicle turned a corner, as though fearing he would tumble from the seat. 'Twill be famous,' she thought bitterly, 'an he falls down in a drunken stupor in the middle of the reception line!''

He descended from the coach in a stiff and ungraceful fashion, and having handed her down, walked across the carpeted flagway as though he could scarce manage to set one foot before the other, causing her to give an inward moan of apprehension.

Predictably, once inside the great house, they were the object of much attention. Heads turned their way, fluttering fans covered chattering lips, even as amused eyes left little doubt as to whom was being discussed. Naomi was embraced, smiled upon, and gushed over. How daring of her to disdain powder. And her hair was simply adorable, so she must not regard what people would say. But of course, ha, ha, ha, that had never weighed with The Lutonville! The eyes of the ladies slipped past her, to rest upon her escort with scorn or speculation, and not a few with surprised admiration. That was because of the uniform, of course, thought Naomi, for despite his infamy it became him. The stares of the gentlemen were less kind, but they were frustrated also, because however much they despised the Rossiters, they could not very well insult a fellow guest wearing their country's uniform.

The Earl of Bowers-Malden, impressive in black and gold, bowed over Naomi's hand and told her she looked ravishing. His large and outspoken countess smiled and murmured that she was "a brave gel," then turned to Rossiter. "And you also, Gideon," she said. "Are you fit to be here?"

'Most definitely—not!' thought Naomi.

"Good question," quipped someone audibly.

Over several barely subdued sniggers, Rossiter said, "Very fit, thank you, ma'am. And proud to accept your hospitality."

They were through the line then. He started to extend his arm,

162

but paused, noting the eager gallants who were already converging upon them. "You would doubtless prefer me to leave you to your—admirers, my lady."

Naomi managed a laugh, and rapped him lightly with her fan. "Do you imply you are not among 'em?" she said coquettishly. "Fie upon you, sir! Have you no chivalry?"

" 'Course he ain't, delightful damsel," simpered a tall young exquisite, shouldering Rossiter aside, then recoiling sharply. "The devil!" he exclaimed, indignant.

"Not in front of the lady," admonished Rossiter, with a reproving shake of the head. "And you should take care where you put your feet, sir."

"He is very right y'know, m'dear Farrington," smirked Reginald Smythe, contriving to seize and kiss Naomi's hand. "Did he step on your toe, poor fella? You shall have to wash your shoe. Or burn it," he added, *sotto voce*, drawing a laugh from the gentlemen closing in around Naomi.

"No, but you are naughty, Reggie," she trilled, giving his hand a playful pat.

He raised his quizzing glass and peered down at her feet. "And I suspect you also have been naughty, adored one," he responded.

Naomi's heart gave a jolt and she knew she had turned pale. She reached out to Mr. Harrier. "Alfred!" she said, her voice unwontedly shrill. "How well you look in that luscious plum."

"And you are simply divine, light of my life," lisped the dandy, saluting her fingertips.

From the corner of her eye she saw Rossiter being edged from her proximity. And they all managed so well to quite ignore him. He staggered slightly as Lord Sommers pushed past. She could only pray that if he did succumb to his potations 'twould be when she was on the other side of the ballroom.

Rossiter watched the crowd gathering about her. Gradually, deliberately, she was swept away from him. He smiled grimly, and glancing to the right encountered a battery of stony stares. Assured that the view to his left would be much the same, he sauntered towards the ballroom. The crowd broke away as he approached. He felt his face grow hot as backs were turned, and he was given a wide berth.

A dowager with a very elaborate wig put up her fan and from behind it asked audibly, "Am I acquaint with that most dashing young captain?"

163

The stocky gentleman beside her glanced at Rossiter and said something in a low-pitched, aghast tone.

"Oh, Lud!" exclaimed the lady. "I suppose young Horatio invited the creature! 'Pon my soul, but poor Bowers-Malden has his trials with that scatter-wit heir of his!"

There was some smothered laughter. A muscle rippled in Rossiter's jaw, and he walked on, his head held high and proud. It was, he thought, going to be a long evening.

The quadrille ended at half past eleven, and Naomi's cheeks were tired. She'd never dreamed how difficult it was to be obliged to smile constantly, and decided that the moment she left this wretched ball she would scowl for three days. Rudolph Bracksby was among the group of beaux who greeted her return from the dance floor. The quiet gentleman's pleasant face was a welcome sight, and she was glad to grant his request to take her down to supper. There were cries of outrage at this infamy, and her admirers begged her to reconsider. At last, however, Mr. Bracksby was able to lead his lady down the stairs and conduct her to a little table against the wall. Leaning back in the chair with a stifled sigh of relief, Naomi saw Mrs. Golightly seated with a group of her cronies, among whom Sir Gilbert Fowles, all teeth and guffaw, was holding forth. With an inward moan, Naomi put up her fan and tried to be invisible. A moment later, she knew she had failed.

"Here you are, my love! I declare I feared I'd never have a word with you!" Samantha Golightly surged into the vacant chair. A tall young woman, whose large white teeth and neighing voice inspired the uncharitable to designate her "horsy," she moved with a bouncy gait that did little to dispel the illusion. Her only claims to prettiness were manifested by a pair of snapping black eyes, and a splendid bosom. She wore an extremely décolleté pink satin gown, which concealed very little of her principal attribute, and several gentlemen watched hopefully as she leaned forward, regarding Naomi with a triumphant grin.

"Good evening, *dear* Samantha." Naomi put on her smile once more. "Is it not a delightful party? Bowers-Malden has outdone himself. As usual."

"Oh, indeed, indeed. Which is in despite Tio, of course. That rascal! How could he upset his papa's guests by inviting Gideon Rossiter? To say nothing of putting you in so unenviable a situation. Everyone feels so *sorry* for you, my poor sweet. 'Tis cruel, *cruel* that you should be obliged to endure the escort of such a notorious creature. And especially after your own unfortunate—ah, relationship with him was—"

"Good evening, Mrs. Golightly." Bracksby set a plate of delicacies and a glass of iced punch before Naomi. "How kind in you to entertain my lady whilst I was gathering these tidbits." He retrieved his own plate and glass from a hovering waiter, then stood looking rather helplessly at the small table. "Oh—pray do not get up, ma'am," he added in his gentle voice.

Mrs. Golightly, who had shown no sign of getting up, rose at once. "Dear Mr. Bracksby. You must keep this poor child entertained, for truly she has much to bear. Never fear, Naomi. We none of us believe the nonsense about your slippers. I fancy you are wearing them tonight, in fact. No?"

"Slippers . . . ?" echoed Naomi, staring at her with a commendably blank expression.

"Why, yes. You surely have heard that a lady's jewelled slipper fell from a bed—" She giggled, and fluttered her eyelashes with appalling coyness. "Well, from one of the *upper* rooms at the Dowling Soiree. And that everyone—but *everyone*—is casting bets on the identity of the naughty girl. Never fear, I have assured several people, dear Naomi, that although you wore jewelled slippers that evening, yours is not the one was lost."

"Good gracious," said Naomi. "An I had dreamed such petty gossip was abroad, I should have worn those same shoes, if only to disappoint the gabblemongers."

Mrs. Golightly blinked, but she was not one to shy from a shadow, and said in a confiding whisper, "A very wise notion, my love. Slip away and change them. That will teach everyone a lesson!"

"Such a friend you are, dearest," purred Naomi. "And what a pleasant selection you have made, Mr. Bracksby. I feel sure Mrs. Golightly will wish you to sit down. 'Twas lovely chatting with you, Samantha."

His lips twitching, Mr. Bracksby seated himself. Mrs. Golightly took herself off looking triumphant, and Naomi muttered, "Cat!"

"The lady was right in one sense, however," said Bracksby. She shot a startled glance at him.

He shrugged. "I fear it cannot add to your consequence that poor Rossiter is your escort tonight, ma'am."

"Oh," said Naomi, relieved. "I fancy most people know the circumstances. Besides, Captain Rossiter is not to be blamed

165

for his father's predicament.'' And she thought, 'Good gracious! Why should I defend the creature?'

"How like you to be so forgiving.'' Admiration lit Bracksby's dark eyes. "One can scarce wonder at Gideon's dogged determination to escort you. Although I feel sure he realized he would be cut.''

Naomi frowned a little and sipped her punch. She murmured, " 'Tis not a greatly successful evening for either of us.''

In a markedly deserted corner of the ballroom, which everywhere else rang with talk and laughter, Rossiter had much the same thought. He had expected to be shunned, but he had found it difficult to keep his face impassive when several old friends had looked straight at him with no sign of recognition. Tio Glendenning had rushed to his side whenever he was able, but Tio was bedevilled with the numerous obligations of a host, and had time for only a few words before he was rushed away again. Bowers-Malden had been so gracious as to go out of his way to come up and chat briefly, which was good of the earl, all things considered. And when she left the reception line the countess had paused to remark kindly that Gideon looked quite "wrung out'' and to urge that he sit down for a while. He yearned to follow her suggestion, but dare not. He would be less obvious were he seated, and he intended to give no one the opportunity to sneer that he was ashamed and trying to hide. Also, there was the fear that if he once sat down he might not be able to get up again, for his bruises seemed to become more stiff and painful by the minute.

One benefit of his ostracism was that it gave him time for thought, and his mind struggled to make sense of the events of this long and busy day. Someone had gone to the trouble to ambush him and then warn him off. And if someone had a reason to want him to stop his investigation, then there must be something to be concealed.

There was also the matter of Tummet's recognition of one of the bullies who had broken into and searched Promontory Point. That the thief had gone to Sir Louis Derrydene's house was both intriguing and baffling. Sir Louis was supposed to be in Russia. If he really had stayed in London, it was possible that he had some shady little business afoot and needed the services of a hired ruffian to accomplish it. Was it likely, though, that he had merely *chanced* to hire the same man who'd previously broken into the Point? 'Pushing coincidence altogether too far,' thought Rossiter. Yet if 'twas not coincidence, if there was a connection, what was it? How could a conspiracy, planned and carried out before his own return from the army, relate to this rash of thefts all apparently having to do with some object either he or Jamie Morris had picked up in Holland? It made no sense to—

". . . should not have been allowed to enter where there are decent people assembled! Are you gentlemen intimidated by a uniform?"

The nasal tones were all too familiar. Rossiter discovered that he was no longer alone. Mr. Reginald Smythe and several other gentlemen stood nearby. There were several heated declarations of a willingness to "take action." They were a motley crew, probably pot valiant, but some other gentlemen were wandering this way, looking grim. Rossiter tensed, wondering if they would dare eject him forcibly. The other guests would probably be willing enough to look the other way, in which case this situation could become dashed ugly. He turned to face them, meeting their hostile stares haughtily.

Coming into the room on Bracksby's arm, Naomi noticed the sudden hush, and saw heads turn. She glanced curiously in the same direction. There could be no doubt of what was happening. Rossiter looked proud and defiant, but he also looked terribly alone. Instinctively, she started forward.

Bracksby caught at her hand. " 'Twere best to stay clear, ma'am. They'll likely do no more than ask him to leave."

Agitated, she said, "Reggie Smythe has hated him forever. Where is Tio, or Gordie Chandler, or Bowers-Malden?"

"Likely maneuvered out of the way. Oh, Gad! Here's Crenshore! His father was ruined when the bank failed! Come, my lady. We must—"

But Naomi was already hurrying towards the ominous little group.

Cyril Crenshore, large, flushed, and aggressive, had stepped directly in front of Rossiter. "You've a choice, Captain," he grated. "Leave quietly, or—"

"La, Captain Rossiter," said Naomi, strolling up beside Bracksby. "Do you not claim your dance, I shall have no alternative but to allow Mr. Bracksby to take your place, as he begs to do." She stood there, plying her fan gracefully, and looking both enchanting and serenely unaware of the atmosphere of barely suppressed fury.

"Take Rudi, lovely one," said Mr. Crenshore, who adored her. "We've a matter of business to discuss with this fellow."

Rossiter bowed, wondering why the deuce Bracksby had brought Naomi into this mess. "I relinquish my claim, ma'am."

Naomi's eyes flashed with vexation.

Bracksby said, "Ah, but I do not care to win by default, Gideon. I feel sure that these gentlemen can chat with you at some more opportune time."

He spoke in his usual mild tones, but Crenshore was reminded of his manners. It would be exceedingly poor *ton* to create a fuss while in this house as a guest. Scowling, he stepped back. Several of the other gentlemen exchanged glances and retreated also.

Irritated, and aware he was losing support, Smythe blustered, "You surprise me, Rudi. 'Pon rep, but y'do! I'd have said you'd be first to see the need for decent people to—"

"To remember they are gentlemen and that ladies are present?" interposed Bracksby. "Then you would be perfectly right, my dear fellow."

Smythe flushed. "Perhaps you were not a victim of the alleged failure of Rossiter Bank, but I can assure you—"

"Perhaps," interpolated Rossiter icily, "you would wish a private meeting to discuss the matter, Smythe."

Naomi gritted her teeth.

Bracksby said in a low voice, "Gideon, for the love of God! Do you mean to challenge all London?"

"If need be," snapped Rossiter.

Smythe, however, had paled. It was well known that he fought with his tongue, and the thought of an actual duel evidently appalled him.

"Come, Captain," trilled Naomi. "You gentlemen can have your discussions whenever you please, but the orchestra will be striking up a country dance at any second, and you know how I adore the Roger de Coverly."

Perforce, Rossiter extended his arm, and she rested her hand on it, fluttering her fan at him, and smiling her most bewitching smile.

Reginald Smythe said with a titter, "Do you mean to change your slippers before—or after the dance, dear lady? I have it on excellent authority you have vowed to do so."

Rossiter felt the little hand tighten on his arm and from the corner of his eye saw that Naomi had lost all her colour. He said lightly, "Now there is a most excellent notion, ma'am." Green eyes, wide and shocked, flashed to him. He shrugged. " 'Tis the only kind thing to do, you will allow. The poor gabble mer-

168

chants have nought to sustain 'em but gossip. You must put them out of their misery. Come, my lady. I will gladly escort you to Falcon House.''

Accompanying him from the room, horribly conscious of the countless stares that followed them, Naomi was thinking numbly that this was how a gladiator must have felt who had rescued a Christian from the lions, only to be thrown into the arena in his stead!

❈ *Chapter 12* ❧

The night air was chill but dry, the sky a moonless blue-black but lit by great low-hanging stars. Naomi shivered, drew her cloak tighter about her, then woke up. "My heavens!" she exclaimed, turning to Rossiter who stood tall and silent beside her. "Whatever are we doing?"

"You came to my rescue," he said urbanely. "Now I return the favour."

"I am in no need of rescue," she lied. "So you had best tell the boy to cancel your carriage."

"But surely, ma'am, you do not mean to keep poor Smythe and his friends and Mrs. Golightly and *her* friends in such fearful suspense? 'Twill take but a few minutes at this hour to reach Falcon House. You can change your slippers and— Ah, here is my coach."

He took Naomi's arm, and even as she argued she was somehow swept up the steps, Rossiter gave swift instructions to the coachman and climbed inside, the door was slammed shut, and they were rolling away.

"For a man in his cups," she said bitterly, "you move fast, Captain Rossiter. I had thought to have offered you a dance."

"You should be glad, ma'am, that I escort you to change your slippers rather than subject you to embarrassment on the dance floor."

She gave a small sound of impatience and he smiled into the dimness. "You—ah, *do* have at least one of the famous slippers, I trust?"

"What?" With a surge of hope she asked eagerly, "Do you say you know where the other—" She heard his soft laugh then, and drew back. "Oh! Horrid! You tricked me!" Tears stung her eyes. "Well, you may gloat over your shabby victory, and in-struct your coachman to turn back. You do but waste our time."

His hand came up to grasp her averted chin and turn her face. "You really judge me base, don't you." He saw the glitter on her cheeks then, and said in a gentler voice, "Now, whatever our differences, be a good girl and answer me. Have you the one slipper?"

"Y-yes," she gulped. "But what good is—" His fingers covered her lips.

"When we reach Falcon House, run and get it. I will bring you the other, and—"

Tingling with excitement, she pulled his hand away. "No! An you know where the other one is, I go with you to find it. Then we will get mine."

He frowned. "Very well. But on one condition. You must tell me—truthfully—how and where you lost it."

"Hah! As if you need to be told! In a bedchamber, of course. Where I was dallying with—with August Falcon!"

He said contemptuously, "You cheapen yourself with such rubbish! Whatever else, Falcon is a gentleman. Besides, he was not there. And despite all I have heard of you, madam, I most certainly do not believe you were dallying in a bedchamber. With anyone! Now let us cry truce for this one night. Is it agreed?"

She fought a sudden and infuriating need to burst into tears, and to conceal this weakness, said tartly, "Agreed. You acquit me of dalliance in one of Lady Dowling's bedchambers. I acquit you of arriving to escort me when you were foxed."

Silence. Then he said, "As you have doubtless heard, my father is convinced his financial catastrophe was contrived. My efforts to prove it have evidently offended someone, because this morning I was, not very politely, requested to desist."

She gave a gasp. "How dreadful! And I imagined—"

"Oh, I am aware. Your imagination is well developed, my lady. Will it stretch, I wonder, to an interesting account of the loss of your slipper?"

"If that is your notion of a truce, Captain Rossiter—" she began stormily.

He reached for the checkstring, and when the coachman opened the trap told him to disregard the first destination and proceed at once to the second. Settling back against the squabs, he said, "You are very right, my lady. Pray accept my humble

171

apologies, and let us try again. How *did* you lose your pretty slipper?''

She shrugged. ''Very well, but I fear your sensibilities will be offended.''

Five minutes later, Rossiter confirmed her fear. ''By heaven!'' he exclaimed, horrified. ''I cannot believe that a well-bred lady would do so crazy a thing! You should have broke the window at once and cried for help! Did it not occur to you that the *ton* would be disgusted by such an escapade?''

''It occurred to me,'' she said, bristling, ''that many prosy and prim individuals might regard it as such.''

Swept by a searing wrath, he seized her shoulders and shook her. ''Prosy and prim, my eye! You are a lady of Quality! I cannot credit that despite your upbringing you would take such mad risks only to—Yes, devil take it! I can! You were ever a tomboy despite your lovely fragility.''

She closed her lips over the furious set-down she had been about to deal him. ''Lovely fragility'' was quite acceptable. ''Perhaps you will be so good as to remove your hands from me at once, sir! And instead of censuring me as though you had the right—which you do not—tell me where in the world we are going.''

Rossiter frowned at her for a minute, then released her.

''To Snow Hill. And you may count yourself fortunate that the gentlemen had left that room before you reached the ledge.''

''Which was not a bedchamber,'' she pointed out. ''And why Snow Hill? Oh, Lud! You live there now! Do you say 'twas *you* found my slipper and have kept it from me?''

''But of course,'' he sneered. ''I had intended to blackmail you with it, as you suspected! Which you richly deserve in return for your assistance in finding me so—unique a valet!''

He could all but see her mischievous little smile. Her voice was full of mirth as it came out of the darkness. ''The Guttersnipe Domestic Registry. At your service, Captain.''

A silence. Then he said, ''I wish you will have the charity to forget I said that. It was very bad. And you did me a great service, indeed. I could not wish a finer valet.''

''La, but I think you quiz me, sir! Besides denying me the satisfaction of hearing a litany of grievances.''

''Then *assurement* you shall have them. He threw my brother into a state of paralysis; left my father at a loss for words, for the first time in living memory; has, I suspect, done battle with our few male servants so that although they despise him they are frigidly polite to him, and—above all, he infuriated August Falcon by addressing him as 'mate.' Ah, what would I not give to have seen it!'' Smiling to hear her lilting laughter, he added quietly, ''He also risked his neck to extricate me from a rather sticky corner this morning. So you see he is truly—''

The carriage gave a lurch and he was flung back. Naomi squealed and reached out instinctively, and he grasped her hand and held it strongly.

''This confounded toboggan ride,'' he grumbled.

She asked uneasily, ''Can the horses climb to the top?''

''They manage, poor brutes. But I doubt they like it any more than do I!''

''I can readily apprehend you would not like it, for 'tis steep as any mountain!'' With a chuckle, she said, ''Do you recollect when we found the old tree house in the woods and you'd not admit you were afraid to climb up?''

She saw the white gleam of his smile through the darkness. He said, ''Yes. And having used the last of my courage to prove I was as bold as you, I was too scared to climb down! I thank you for reminding me of my intrepid boyhood!''

She laughed. ''Well, I thought it very gallant, for when my petticoats caught on that splintered branch, you overcame your fears and rescued me.''

''Hmm. And then all but fainted! A fine hero!''

''Far more heroic than had it been done by someone with no fear of heights.''

Surprised by the kindness in her voice, he turned to her. The flambeaux outside a house they passed shone into the carriage. Naomi was leaning back her head, smiling at him, looking almost ethereally lovely . . .

They were both startled when the door was flung open. The carriage had stopped, and the lackey had run from the house to assist them.

Rossiter came back to reality. ''I shall be but a moment, ma'am.'' He climbed down the steps and called to the coachman to drive along to where the street became a little wider. ''You can make your turn there.''

The coachman nodded and whipped up his team, grumbling about mountains he'd take care never to go to again.

Limping towards the house, Rossiter asked the lackey if Sir Mark was at home.

''No, sir. He and Mr. Newby took Miss Gwendolyn to—''

There came an odd sound like a tree branch splintering. A

startled shout rang out. Rossiter swung around. The horses were rearing, neighing their fright. He saw the coachman leap from the box and had a brief bewildered thought that the man had lost his wits. In that fragmentary second, he realized that the coach was jolting oddly. It started to lurch backwards. 'My God!' he thought. 'The pole has split!'

He was sprinting even as that terrifying realization dawned. He drew level with the coach and the door was flung open, but before Naomi could get out there was a sharper crack. The pole snapped off short, and the coach began to roll backwards down the hill leaving driver and team behind. Racing in frenzied pursuit, Rossiter saw the coach hit one of the many ruts in the road and slew sideways. One wheel bumped up onto the flagway and sent a link boy leaping for his life. The carriage rocked and spun. Rossiter was sure it would overturn, but the splintered pole crashed against an iron fence and scraped along the rails with an ear-splitting clanging. The wild plunge was slowed. A small respite, but it gave Rossiter the chance to draw alongside. Sobbing for breath, he gasped, "Jump!"

To do so was a physical impossibility. Clinging to the door frame, Naomi had all she could manage to prevent herself being flung back onto the seat again. The coach teetered crazily. Rossiter sprang at the door, grabbed Naomi's arm and wrenched with the strength of desperation. She was torn from the coach. He caught her, staggered, and fell backwards.

The carriage was rolling again, gathering speed. It thundered down the hill, barely missed a solitary horseman, crashed into a brick wall and overturned to lie upside down, one wheel flying off, and the remaining three spinning madly.

Rossiter dragged himself up. Naomi sat beside him, looking dazed. He gasped, "Are you all right?"

She said tremulously, "I think . . . 'tis not safe to be nigh you, sir," then threw herself into his arms. "Oh . . . Gideon . . . !"

He held her very tight, whispering, "Thank God! Thank God!"

The bootblack had been sent to the stables to hire another carriage; Tummet and the butler were down the hill with the driver of the wrecked vehicle; Naomi had been ushered upstairs to be ministered to by the cook; and the lackey was brushing Gideon's uniform coat. Having washed, put on a clean shirt, and tidied his disordered hair, Gideon donned his dressing gown and went slipper hunting.

Monsieur Delatouche was snoring by the fire in Newby's parlour while awaiting the return of his employer. When Gideon marched in without benefit of a knock, went straight into the bedchamber and appropriated the dainty slipper from atop the chest of drawers, the valet started up and launched into an anguished protest. Gideon instructed him to refer Monsieur Newby to Captain Gideon, and left the man wailing.

The lackey had worked wonders with his coat, and in no time he was downstairs again. He went into the withdrawing room, poured himself a glass of cognac, and stretched out in a chair, reliving the moments when two soft arms had clung about his neck and a warm and shapely little body had been pressed tight against him. Magical moments, made the more precious by the awareness that Naomi had escaped almost certain death. He closed his eyes for a second. Suppose he'd not been in time? Suppose she had been swept down that hill? How would he be feeling at this moment? And he knew, and trembled. What a fool to ever have thought he could forget her! How could he have been so stupid as to envision life without her? She was his, and always would be, no matter what had come between them, for without her there would be no life.

He heard the whisper of feminine draperies then, and came at once to his feet, turning to her eagerly.

She came into the room looking a little pale but otherwise none the worse for her ordeal. There seemed, in fact, to be a glow about her that enhanced her beauty, so that he was awed, and stared at her speechlessly.

Gazing at him in turn, she thought that he looked haggard and tired, with dark smudges under his eyes. But the tenderness in those eyes set her heart to pounding wildly, and she blushed and hurried to give him both her hands. "Well, sir," she said rather shakily. "On your first day home you rescued me from highwaymen, and tonight you have saved my life once again. I trust you do not mean to make a habit of such behaviour? Faith, but I doubt I could support any more of these exciting episodes!"

" 'Tis said things always happen in sequences of three," he answered, smiling, and bending to kiss her fingertips. He stepped closer, still holding her hands, enchanted by the sudden shyness in her eyes. "Naomi, are you really all right? My God, but I was scared!"

175

"And I," she confessed. "I thought I was doomed. Had it not been for you coming up so fast . . . For a man who could scarce walk, you fairly flew, Gideon."

He said whimsically, "For a moment I feared I would pass you by and be unable to stop! A fine figure I would have cut!"

She put a cool finger across his lips. "No. We must not make light of it. I have to thank you for—"

"For hiring that stupid coach?" he interrupted, frowning. "I should have made certain it was safe before I entrusted your precious self to it!"

They were still standing very close together and the old magic was at work, so that the lost years and all her bitter griefs melted away. Looking up at him, she half-whispered, "Am I really precious to you, Gideon?"

She was more than precious; she was his dear and delicate perfection. He murmured huskily, "You are my—"

"I fetched a cup of tea for my lady," said Cook, coming briskly into the room and directing a censuring frown at Gideon.

The two young people fairly sprang apart and turned guilty faces to the motherly woman.

Cook put the cup and saucer on a side table, looked from one to the other, and made no move to depart. The wife of Sir Mark's coachman, she had been assistant to the chef until the scandal had caused that highly excitable French gentleman to remove to a less notorious household, whereupon she had taken over as ruler of the kitchens. She had only known Gideon for two years prior to his departure for the army, but she considered him part of "her family" and thus subject to correction where needed. She folded brawny arms across a massive bosom and fixed him with a steady stare.

Naomi murmured that she was most kind, and Gideon, flushing to the roots of his hair, felt like a small boy caught in some prank, and stammered, "Oh. Er—yes. You are very good. Thank you."

"The young lady's had a awful experience, sir," said Cook. "Likely you'd want me to keep with her."

'Oh, God!' thought Gideon. "I—er—I was just—Just—er . . ." Inspired, he said, "Returning her slipper! Here—here 'tis, Lady Naomi." He whipped the slipper from the floor beside his chair, and offered it triumphantly.

"Oh!" cried Naomi, overjoyed. "You really did find it for me! Thank you so much!"

Beaming at Cook, Gideon said foolishly, "So you see, 'tis quite all right."

Naomi sat down, dimples peeping, and sipped her tea.

Cook relented. She would have a word with the captain later, on the impropriety of being alone with an unwed damsel in his father's withdrawing room. But recollecting that she must put a hot brick in Miss Gwendolyn's bed, she rustled her way to the door, said a reluctant, "Very well, then . . ." And having made a great show of opening the door as wide as it would go, gave Gideon a look that spoke volumes, and rustled off.

"Oh, Lord!" he gasped, sinking into a chair and taking out his handkerchief. "I am sunk far beneath reproach!"

Naomi gave a little ripple of laughter. "Rakeshame," she whispered.

"No—do not!" he pleaded, mopping his brow. "Truly, I had no thought to compromise you. What a ghastly thing!"

"Ruined for a slipper," she said, waving it merrily. "Gideon, if you *knew* how grateful I am that you were able to restore this to me!" And, drawing a bow at random, "I rather fancy Newby wanted to give it me himself."

Watching him obliquely, she saw the sudden steely look and knew she had guessed rightly. His brother had found her slipper and had cherished far different plans for its return.

Gideon smiled then. " 'Twas the least I could do, since I was unable to return the other object you—er, lost."

"The other . . . ?" she echoed, her attention on the whimsical smile she had missed so terribly. Remembering then, she started. "Oh! The chess piece! Which reminds me, Gideon. 'Tis the strangest thing."

Misunderstanding, he kept one wary eye on the doorway, and pointed out, "I never saw it, but your papa evidently valued it highly."

"Yes. But that is not what I meant, exactly. You see, I didn't quite finish telling you what happened at the Dowling Soiree. The chessman I lost is an antique piece, and Papa thinks he can never replace it because there is not another set like it. But, Gideon, there is! The gentlemen in that room had one!"

He frowned and sat straighter. "What gentlemen? I thought they were gone by the time you reached the other ledge."

"No. I had to wait outside until they went away. La, but I thought they would quarrel forever! And then I saw that there was a chessman on the table—almost identical to the one I lost,

177

save that it was green, not red, and looked to be set with emeralds."

Intrigued, he said, "It must indeed be valuable. Were you able to discover where 'twas purchased?"

"But of course," she teased, setting her cup aside. "I tripped through the open door in all my filth, and they fancied me an angel who'd flown down from heaven!"

He laughed. "*Touché!* You little wretch, I deserved that. I wish I might have seen their faces had you done so. Who were they, by the way?"

"I've no notion. I could only see the back of one gentleman, and the hand of another. They were behaving in so odd a way. Whispering almost, though they were alone in the room. And then they became angry, or at least, one did, and he said he was perfectly sure about something, and that everyone is different. Which seemed a foolish thing to remark."

"Hmm. Is that all?"

"No. 'Twas then I really became frightened, for the other man said that somebody was a menace. 'On both counts,' he said. And that this menace person must be silenced. Does not that sound grim? And there was something about a meeting that could not be held until six were recovered, and that all their lives were at risk."

"By Jove!" exclaimed Rossiter. "It sounds grim indeed, and as if you'd stumbled into a proper barrel of hornets. Thank heaven you were not detected! So they finished their game and left, did they?"

"They left, but they had not been playing chess, for there was just the one piece, and no board."

"And they said no more?"

"No. Only— Wait!" She frowned a little, trying to remember. "There was something . . . Oh, yes! The second man was grumbling about a delay. And the first man said something about 'One more try,' and that then it would be *his* plan."

Rossiter muttered, "There's a deal more here than meets the eye! I wonder if . . ." He sprang to his feet and paced to the window, his tired mind grappling with possibilities. " 'Twas not 'til you lost the chess piece that the robberies began," he muttered. "It never dawned on me there could be any connection, but—"

Naomi stiffened. "Robberies? What robberies?"

He limped back to her, his eyes alight with excitement. "Why, a whole string of 'em, Naomi. My saddlebags were taken the very first morning I arrived in Town. Then Promontory Point was broken into and ransacked—no, wait! That was *before* I reached Town, come to think on it! Just after you came, in fact! Then, the man we sent down to the Red Pheasant was attacked, and Jamie's home was broken into. And—yes, burn it!—the louts who ambushed me this morning—''

He stopped, because Naomi had come to her feet and was staring at him.

In a rather odd voice she said, ''But the men who attacked you were, you said, retaliating 'gainst your enquiries about the bank failure.''

''Yes. But they also were searching for something, and they used the very same expression as all the others! They called their employer 'the Squire'! Don't you see, Naomi? It may all be connected!''

She said slowly, ''I see. Then you believe this man called the Squire could be responsible for all your father's troubles.''

''There's a link somewhere! I'd swear to it! And your plotters in the Dowling ante room are in it up to their aristocratic eyebrows!''

''And it all started when I lost my father's chessman.'' Her voice was ice, her whole demeanor one of frigid hauteur.

''Well—yes, but—''

''Do you, by some chance, mean to imply that my *papa* is this evil and mysterious 'Squire' of yours?''

''Good . . . God!'' whispered Gideon. '' 'Twould make sense, except—''

''Except that it makes no sense at all!'' Anger sparked in her eyes. ''La, but I think your father's obsession has overcome your power of reason, sir!''

''I shall hope that my son retains sufficient of that commodity to offer me a *good* reason for your presence in my house, madam!''

The acid voice brought Gideon's head jerking around.

Sir Mark, a proud and commanding figure, stood in the doorway, with Newby smiling beside him, and a troubled Gwendolyn peeping between them.

''There was an accident, sir,'' said Gideon. ''Lady Lutonville is—''

''Is much beholden to you, Captain Rossiter,'' she intervened glacially. ''Despite your mental aberrations, I owe you my life.''

''Why you are here at all, ma'am,'' said Sir Mark with contempt, ''is more than I can fathom.''

"I will explain later, Father," said Gideon tersely. "Naomi, if you—"

His father's resonant tones overrode his effort. "We saw the wrecked coach, and I regret you were shaken up, ma'am. But if you are sufficiently recovered, I expect your noble father would not wish that you linger here."

"No more I shall, sir," she riposted, very pale, but with her little head high. "I bid you good even."

Sir Mark stood aside and she swept through the doorway with the poise and pride of a queen.

Gideon was after her in a flash. "Naomi! Wait! You've no carriage!"

Sir Mark caught his arm and snapped, "I ordered my coachman to wait. He will convey her ladyship to her destination."

"Not without my escort, sir," said Gideon, meeting his father's enraged glare with a flashing look of his own.

"You are worn to the bone. Newby will see the lady home."

Newby bowed low. "With the greatest delight."

"Thank you. No," said Naomi. The footman placed her cloak about her shoulders, and contriving to keep the slipper hidden in the folds of her gown she started away.

Gideon moved quickly to open the door. As Naomi swept past, she declared haughtily, "I will not occupy the same coach with you, Captain."

"Naomi—for the love of God!"

"Let be, dammit," cried Sir Mark, his face brick red with rage. "Newby!"

Fearing lest this ghastly quarrel should deteriorate into an exchange of blows, Gwendolyn cried in her clear little voice, "Perhaps you could take Newby's horse and ride escort, Gideon."

He threw her a grateful glance.

"Certainly not!" Newby stood firm until Gideon was level with him, then he shrugged nonchalantly and stepped back.

Tummet hurried to the foot of the steps. "I bin talking with the jervey, Guv. Proper aside of 'isself, 'e is!"

"So he should be! Does he know this lady was nigh killed in that disgraceful accident?"

"Likely not, Cap'n. Seein' as there wasn't one."

Halfway down the steps, Naomi paused, and stared at him. "Do you say I imagined this whole horrid business, Tummet?"

He touched his brow to her respectfully. "I says as it wasn't no accident, melady." With a sober glance at Gideon he said,

"That pole was near sawed through, Guv. If it 'adn't of been good English oak, it'd likely 'ave snapped orf afore you got out, and we'd be planning two funerals this very minute."

"The devil!" whispered Gideon.

"Dear me," murmured Newby.

"Another villainous act to credit to my father's account," said Naomi with a curl of the lip. "I am very sure he would plan his own daughter's murder!" The footman handed her into the carriage, and she sat back against the squabs, suddenly unutterably weary; unutterably sad.

Gideon limped to the groom who stood holding Newby's horse.

"No!" roared Sir Mark. "You damned young fool! You'll fall out of the saddle!"

"The devil I will," said Gideon under his breath, but he was dismayed by the effort required to mount up.

The jervey ran to his stirrup, wringing a greasy hat in his work-roughened hands, his eyes frantic. "Melor'—I gotta wife and five babbies. Me coach was all I 'ad, melor'! We'll starve, fer sure, melor'! *Please*, melor'!"

His face seemed to ripple. Gideon gripped the pommel with one hand, and knew he was very tired indeed. "I'm sorry about your coach," he said. "Tummet—arrange for repairs, and see what you can find out about all this."

The jervey mumbled incoherent thanks. Tummet nodded, and Gideon urged Newby's grey down the hill.

"I cannot think what you imply, ma'am," Katrina Falcon's cheeks were a trifle flushed, her eyes sparkling with rare anger as she faced Mrs. Golightly at the side of the dance floor.

"But not a thing, my dear." Mrs. Golightly's fan fluttered, and above it her black eyes glittered with triumph. "I *never* credited that even Naomi Lutonville could be so daring as to lose her shoe in such vulgar fashion. I have done *all* in my power to scotch the scandal, but—"

"I was unaware there *was* a scandal," said Katrina.

Reginald Smythe murmured with a small smile, "And i'faith, we all know how gentle and generous a heart is yours, dear lady."

A laugh went up, and Mrs. Golightly said, "How very true, and is there anything more touching than blind loyalty among friends?"

More people were joining the little group, and Mr. Harrier

181

lisped, "Is the divine Lutonville come, or has Rossiter kidnapped her away from us?"

"Ain't back yet, dash it all," said Mr. Crenshore, sighing. "Missed my dance, begad!"

"That naughty, naughty boy," gurgled Mrs. Golightly. "I wonder what he can be thinking of to keep her away so long."

"Perhaps the lovely lady has mislaid her other shoe," said Mr. Smythe with a titter.

"Well, I ain't mislaid mine, and will be only too glad to use 'em on any filthy-minded gabblemonger in need of a good kick!"

The cold words cut like a knife through the ripple of laughter, and heads turned.

August Falcon, striking in a habit of dark blue velvet, the pocket flaps and great cuffs of his coat sleeves rich with embroidery, sauntered up with Lady Naomi on his arm. My lady looked a little pale, but her smile was brilliant and she plied her fan with exquisite grace.

All eyes shot to her feet. Two dainty jewelled slippers sparkled in the light from countless candles.

"Oh—my . . ." whispered Samantha Golightly, her face falling.

Reginald Smythe raised his brows, thought 'Be damned!' and said admiringly, "But how clever of you, dear lady."

Falcon's dark gaze was fixed on the dandy. "What a pity about your mouth, dear Reginald."

Smythe lifted a questing hand. The halfmoon patch his man had applied still seemed in place. "How so?" he asked anxiously.

"It annoys me," purred Falcon.

Katrina took Naomi's hand. "I am so glad you are back, dearest. Oh, you *did* change your slippers!" She looked steadily at Mrs. Golightly. "I wonder you bothered."

Rudolph Bracksby wandered up. "Where is Captain Rossiter?"

"Falcon likely shot him," said Crenshore with a grin.

"Not yet," drawled Falcon. "I would purely dislike to deprive our dauntless Reginald of that pleasure."

A laugh went up, and people glanced about for the "dauntless" Reginald. Mr. Smythe's sense of self-preservation was strong, however, and he had already slipped quietly away.

Naomi's admirers closed in around her, pleading for the next dance.

Katrina took her brother's arm. "Why are you come?" she

asked softly. "I'd thought you already laid down upon your bed. You have not really come to cuffs with Gideon Rossiter?"

The words hissing through a set smile, Falcon answered, "Come to cuffs with him, Trina? Why ever should I be so restrained? 'Tis my firm intention to run him through. Sixty-nine times!"

❦ *Chapter 13* ❧

Katrina Falcon had never been one to lie abed in the mornings, and although she had retired very late the previous night, she was up and dressed by ten o'clock. She went straight to Naomi's bedchamber. Her friend was sitting at the dressing table wearing a most fetching wrapper of pale orange satin trimmed with ecru lace. She presented a charming picture, but she was scowling at her reflection, and meeting Katrina's eyes in the mirror, said gloomily, "He is ready for Bedlam, is what it is!"

Stifling a smile, Katrina sat on the bed. "Captain Rossiter? From what you told me last night, I would have to agree. I still can scarce believe you had such a narrow escape. You are so brave, dearest. It purely astounds me that you managed to come to the ball as if nought had happened, after that horrid man almost caused you to be killed!"

At once reversing her stand, Naomi said hotly, "He saved my life! He has always been absolutely terrified of heights. He fears that dreadful hill, but he found the courage to run down it so as to pull me from the coach, and—" Her impassioned words ceased. Blushing, she added hurriedly, "And he is treacherous and deceitful."

"And treated you roughly when first you met."

"He did." Naomi took the lily-of-the-valley corsage from the little vase on her dressing table, and stroked a leaf absently.

Troubled, Katrina said, "Worst of all, he behaved disgracefully to his poor *chère amie* in Holland."

"Yes," whispered Naomi, flinching a little. "I could never forgive him for that. Never!"

"No lady could. So 'tis of little moment that the man has

gone demented, as indeed he must have done, to make such awful accusations 'gainst Lord Collington.''

Naomi said nothing.

Standing, Katrina walked to the window and looked out at the misted garden. "How very fortunate, love," she said, "that you are no longer betrothed. Now that would *really* be a mare's nest.''

"Yes.''

"If you had cared for him, I mean.''

"Oh.''

Katrina turned and looked at her friend's rather wilting figure thoughtfully.

Naomi stared at the flowers in her hand for a long moment, then dropped them into the wastepaper basket beside the dressing table. "I think—'' she began, then stopped speaking, startled by a wild outburst of barking, some assorted shouts, and a crash.

"Oh, dear,'' muttered Katrina, hurrying to the door. "Apollo! If he wakens August . . . !''

She went quickly down the stairs and found Lieutenant James Morris pressed against the wall in the entrance hall while two lackeys strove to hold the ravening hound that leapt and strained to come at him. Katrina paused, frowning, and was about to retrace her steps when she saw that the lieutenant held a bloodied handkerchief to his wrist. Dismayed, she told the lackeys to put Apollo in the side garden.

"Did he bite you, sir?'' she asked. "Indeed, I am most sorry for it. He is an ill-tempered animal. Pray let me see.''

Morris' wrath melted away as he gazed on this beauteous creature. Her gentle hands were moving his handkerchief aside. He could catch the sweet scent of her, and trembling to her touch, he watched her, and hoarded the seconds.

"Oh, dear!'' sighed Katrina. "He did tear the skin a little, and 'twill bruise I fear.''

"Mmm . . .'' he murmured dreamily.

She glanced up. He was smiling at her with such patent adoration that she could not but be amused. She took his arm and led him firmly to the kitchen, where neat maids hastened to bring bowls of hot water and cloths for the relief of the wounded. Had Morris been aware of all the eyelashes fluttering at him, he would have retreated in horror, but he had eyes for only one lady. Katrina saw, however, and their admiration caused her to look at the lieutenant again. He really was quite a well-favoured young man. And, la, but he was bashful, his face reddening when his eyes met hers, and his glance falling away. She rather liked shyness in a gentleman. She washed the wound with strong soap, which made him gasp, then sprinkled it with basilicum powder and bound it up quite proficiently, asking if it felt a little better now.

"G-good as new," stammered Morris. "Your hands are so—" He saw the chef frowning at him, and floundered. "So—er— Not like a real nurse, ma'am. Oh, egad! Wh-what I mean is—"

Katrina hid a smile. "You have had much experience of nurses, I understand."

"No, no!" he declared desperately. "Scarce knew any. Do assure you! I— Oh! Well, that is to say, I *have* of course, but not in a—er— Only in a—a quite respectable—" She looked at him again, a laugh in those glorious eyes that slanted in so bewitching a way, and his knees turned to jelly. "Lord, what a clunch I am! Miss Falcon, will you pray believe I did not intend to shoot your brother? Er, not exactly. And—and I'd no least idea he would be indisposed for so long a time."

"Even if you shot August by mistake, your action was ill considered, sir. And I cannot like recklessness."

"No, of course not. Dreadful trait. *Truly*, I am very sorry, ma'am."

She walked with him into the hall. "My brother would be nigh recovered by this time, I must admit, save that he is a difficult patient, at best."

Morris brightened. "Heard he was hot at hand. Drives you to the ropes, does he? Ain't surprised, though the fella who would cause anxiety to a creature so gentle as yourself, ma'am, must be a proper slowtop, and—"

"Not such a slowtop as to permit you to call upon my sister, Morris!"

Wearing a red and purple satin dressing gown that made Morris blink, August Falcon was coming down the stairs. His black hair was rumpled and unpowdered, causing him to look even more menacing than usual, and the dark blue eyes fairly hurled anger.

Morris tore his shocked stare from that garish dressing gown, and made an effort to recover. "Ain't no law forbidding a man to pay a morning call."

Falcon paused on the last stair, his glance flashing to his sister. "Whatever is your aunt about? I trust she don't permit that

186

you receive every military rattle who abuses my father's door knocker!''

"I ain't a rattle!" protested Morris indignantly. "And Miss Katrina didn't receive me. Fact of the matter is, I come to call on *you*!"

A lackey opened the door to the book room, and Falcon waved Morris inside.

Following, Katrina said, "I was bandaging the lieutenant's hand, dear."

"For which I am eternally grateful," declared Morris fervently.

Falcon murmured, "Full of sound and bombast and doubtful of achievement."

Scarlet, Morris said, "If you care to know it, Falcon, that's a vicious dog you've got!"

"Well, well!" A grin replaced Falcon's sneer. "Apollo gave you a proper greeting, did he? The animal earns his keep."

"An you'd the least discrimination, you'd not give the brute house-room!"

"Nonsense. Apollo is a fine fellow."

"You'd not think him so fine had he ever bit you."

"*Au contraire.* He *has* bitten me."

"Gad! Why the deuce would any rational person keep a dog who bites the hand that feeds him?"

Falcon gave him a scornful look. "Because he bites, of course. What did you want to see me about?"

"Oh." Morris glanced uneasily at Katrina, who stood with her hands demurely folded, enjoying this foolish conversation.

"Er—it's to do with Gideon Rossiter," Morris explained.

"Rossiter!" Falcon's lean countenance flushed. "If there's one thing I don't choose to talk about before I have my breakfast, 'tis that son of a—"

"August . . . ," murmured Katrina reproachfully.

Fuming, he said, "You'd best leave us, ma'am. If we're to discuss Rossiter I'll not be responsible for my language!"

She shook her head at him, but went out.

"About the duel," began Morris, as the door closed.

"To hell with the duel," snarled Falcon. "Any discussion of that can be handled by my seconds. Burn it, I thought you'd come to take him!"

Staring, Morris said feebly, "Take him? Take him—where?"

"What the devil do I care? Just get the beastly fellow out of my house! And for the love of God, stop gaping at me like a landed trout!''

Closing his sagging jaw with an effort, but still severely shocked, Morris gasped, ''Do you say that Gideon Rossiter *stays* with you? Why, if ever I heard of such a thing! You're engaged to *fight* him day after tomorrow!''

''I know that, you looby!''

''Well,'' said Morris, taking on a judicial air. ''It's dashed improper, is what it is! I cannot expect *you* to mind the conventions, but—''

''Why?'' jeered Falcon. ''Because I'm a half-breed?''

''Because you're a hot-at-hand knock-in-the-cradle,'' Morris answered equably. ''With not the least notion of how to go on.''

Falcon uttered a sound somewhere between a howl and a snort and sprang at him.

Coming into the room Rossiter was in time to see Morris reel back, and steady himself against a reference table.

Feeling his jaw apprehensively, the lieutenant muttered, ''You'll meet me for that, Falcon.''

''Try if your feeble wits can recall that I already challenged you.''

''Besides which,'' said Rossiter, closing the door, ''you must wait your turn, Jamie. What are you doing here?''

''More to the point, dear boy,'' said Morris, straightening, ''what are *you* doing here? Ain't at all proper, y'know.''

Falcon said sneeringly, ''We have offended his sense of propriety.''

''I'm not surprised,'' said Rossiter. ''And I don't really know what I'm doing here, to say truth. I remember riding in last evening, but—''

''But having damned near caused Lady Lutonville to be killed, you had the confounded gall to fall asleep in the saddle.'' Falcon gave an irate snort. ''When we tried to pry you loose, you simply fell off and since we couldn't wake you, I was damned well obliged to let you rack up here for the night. A fine laughing-stock I shall be an the word gets out!''

''Lord, yes,'' agreed Rossiter, embarrassed. ''I do beg your pardon. And thank you for your hospitality. What Naomi must think of me, I dare not guess. I was to have taken her back to the ball.''

Falcon scowled at him. ''I took her. And if there is one thing I abominate, 'tis being obliged to get up and put on ball dress after I am settled into my bed!'' He turned on Morris, who had

188

uttered a shout of laughter. "How typical that you would find that amusing."

"Well, I do," admitted Morris gleefully. "Does my heart good to see you put out. Blest if ever I saw such a quarrelsome fellow. I vow were you alone on a desert island, Falcon, you'd fight *yourself*!"

"How fortunate that in the meantime I've Rossiter to fight. And then"—Falcon's smile was unpleasant—"you. To which end, Morris, the sooner we sort out these inchoate matters—"

"In—what?" echoed Morris, curious.

Falcon groaned. "In-choate, you clod! Would you wish that I spell it?"

"No I would not! Never use such jawbreakers. Damn, Falcon, I don't hold nothing 'gainst you because of your face, but you might make an effort at least to speak the language! 'Inchoate,' indeed! If ever I heard such a cockaleery word! And speaking of cockaleery, that dressing gown . . ."

Grinning, Rossiter slipped into the hall. He noted absently that it was truly a splendid house, beautifully appointed, but he was more aware that his time was very limited.

A lackey eyed him woodenly. Rossiter said he had a message for Lady Lutonville, and asked for her whereabouts. The lackey conducted him to a large dining room with doors opening to the terrace.

Naomi was busied with her sketchbook in a little summer house at the far side of the garden. Her great skirts billowed about her, and sunbeams slanted through the trellised roof to paint a sheen on her powdered curls. It was a charming picture, and having crossed the lawn Rossiter paused with one foot on the step, to commit it to memory.

Still slightly breathless from her scramble to set this scene, Naomi glanced up, convincingly surprised, only to become even more breathless. Why must his dark hair curl so charmingly? Why must that wistful look in the deeply lashed grey eyes wreak such havoc with her pulses? Why was it so difficult to summon the anger and resentment she should feel for him?

He moved nearer and stood looking down at her.

"I hope you are recovered," she said coolly. "I should have realized last night that you were close to exhaustion, and—"

"Stop it," he interrupted, his voice stern. "We've more important things to say to each other."

Naomi stood. "We have nothing to say to each other, unless 'tis—"

189

She was seized in hands of steel and wrenched to him. With a gasp, she tried to break free, but he jerked her closer and bent his head. His lips found hers, hard and bruisingly. Long years of yearning went into that kiss. Fighting him, struggling, furious, Naomi was unable to break free. He was too strong, and her silly heart was thundering so madly that her mind spun. A wave of ecstasy drowned indignation, propriety, caution, and brought a dizzying need to respond. She seemed to melt against him. Her hands crept up to his shoulders, then slid around his neck, and she was kissing him back with a passion that left her breathless, so that when he at last released her she lay limp and spent in his embrace and hid her heated face against his cravat.

"Oh, Lud!" she gasped feebly. "I fancy everyone in the house saw that."

He smiled. "Good. Beloved," he lifted one of her clutching little hands to his lips, "do you not see that we cannot fight the inevitable? You always were meant to be mine. And I always will adore—"

"You forget," she whispered, striving to be sensible, while her every nerve quivered with love and desire for this ruthless man whose arm held her so wonderfully tight.

"My Holland family?" He sighed. "I should have told you—"

"No. No—pray do not." She found the strength somehow to pull back and stand erect. "It is no use, Gideon."

"I know," he said softly. "I am a rake and a libertine. You are a wanton. But I love you, and you love me. No, never deny it. Just now—"

"That was a moment of weakness." She bit her lip. "We are farther apart than ever, for now, to add to all else, you suspect my father of heaven knows what infamy. And he has already forbidden me to see you."

"As has mine," he said quietly, and nodded as her startled gaze shot to his face. "Sir Mark feels that your sire turned his back when most he was needed."

Her eyes fell. She said sadly, "So what hope is there for us? We must say goodbye and—"

"When I die, perhaps," he interposed, seizing her hand again. "What we must do now, my dearest girl, is come at the root of this business. Likely we will find your papa had nought to do with any of it, and—"

"You are too generous," she said, angry again. "What of

190

your papa and the charges brought 'gainst him, not by vague and unfounded suspicions, but by the government and the—"

"So here you are, Gideon." Majestic in a fine coat of brown velvet embellished with gold braid, Sir Mark had come up unnoticed, and his strident voice cut off Naomi's words.

She jumped and turned very red.

Gideon swung around to meet his father's irate glare. "Good morning, sir. You are early abroad."

"Aye! Searching for you! While you allowed yourself to be captivated into remaining here, did it never occur to you that your brother, your sister, and I might be anxious for your sake?"

"Your pardon, Sir Mark, but I did not captivate Gideon into remaining here," said Naomi, irked. "He was completely exhausted by the time we arrived last night, and quite unable to—"

"Well, that is a relief, at least," declared another voice. The Earl of Collington paced gracefully across the damp grass, the picture of aristocratic elegance in a claret-coloured habit, a jewelled quizzing glass swinging from one white hand, and disdain clearly written on his handsome features. "I think you must have forgot, my lady, but I gave you quite explicit instructions with regard to your future—ah, associations."

Before Naomi could respond, Sir Mark snarled, "An your instructions had to do with my son, Collington, they were redundant. I have long since ordered Gideon to keep away from your daughter."

The earl's quizzing glass was raised. Through it, he surveyed first a rebellious beauty, then an icy-eyed young soldier. He smiled faintly. "The captain does not appear to take orders very well. Come, my lady. Your visit here is at an end."

Gideon said sharply, "My lord, 'tis only fair to warn you—"

"No!" cried Naomi, afraid of what he might say.

Falcon marched across the lawn. He looked dashing, although his dark face was murderous. "My lord . . . Sir Mark . . ." His bow was extravagant. "My father will be shattered to have been absent on so *momentous* an occasion. I collect you were unaware he is presently in Sussex."

Sir Mark had the grace to flush before that cynicism.

"How unfortunate," murmured the earl.

"Most unfortunate." Falcon added nastily, "Unless 'twas Rossiter you came to find? Connected with . . . a meeting, perchance?"

"A damned good notion," growled Sir Mark, scowling at Collington.

Gideon murmured, "Or a missing chess piece?"

Naomi gave a gasp. Falcon looked puzzled. Sir Mark swore under his breath.

Collington drawled, "Fascinating as is this conversation, alas, I cannot linger. Your servant, messieurs. If you please, Naomi . . . ?"

Keeping her eyes downcast, she put her hand on his arm and he led her away.

"I tell you," said Gideon earnestly, "that blasted chess piece is bound up in it somehow! I wish to God I knew how!" Clinging to the strap as the coach raced through the late morning, he waited for a response and, receiving none, turned to his friend.

Morris leaned back against the squabs, smiling vacantly at the postilion's back.

"Hey!" said Gideon.

Sighing, Morris murmured, "M'father will adore her. So will the family."

"Did you hear one word I said, you star-crossed dolt?"

"Ain't star-crossed! I've found the most wonderful girl ever created, and I intend to wed her. What has star-crossed to do with that?"

"Oh, nothing at all. Save perhaps that her brother swears to blow a hole through you, and if you instead blow another hole through him there is some slight possibility he would object to your marrying his sister. In either case you haven't exactly won his esteem, Jamie."

Blinking, Morris returned to reality. "Who are you to talk of winning esteem? If ever I heard of people living in glass houses and flinging stones! To judge from that scorching scold he dealt you, your honoured sire ain't delighted with you, my Tulip."

"No," acknowledged Gideon rather grimly. "My apologies that you were present through it all. He's really not such a bad old fellow. At least, I got you away."

"So you did." Morris looked around, frowning. "Away to where, might I ask? And what am I doing in this coach? I was reduced to blancmange after hearing Sir Mark comb you out, and you took advantage of it to kidnap me, damn if you didn't!"

Gideon laughed. "You agreed to come, and I thought it very

192

good of you. But an you wish to be put down . . ." He reached for the window.

"In this wilderness? What are you about, you villain? I'll have no more of your minor wars, and so I tell you!"

"We're coming into Canterbury, as you'd know did your eyes see aught but Miss Falcon. As to what I'm about—Jamie, I am in a fair way to being convinced that the chess piece Naomi lost is in some way connected with my sire's troubles."

Morris stared at him. "My idea exactly! The ringleader is that curst chessman. I felt when he was in my pocket that actually, *I* was in *his*, and—" He threw up one arm to protect himself, and having begged for mercy, settled back, laughing. "No, really, dear boy. You must allow 'tis far-fetched. But you'd Collington facing you an hour ago. Why didn't you ask him? An he knew something, he'd likely tell you. Good man, the earl." Gideon's speculative gaze turned to him, and Morris added reinforcingly, "M'father says so."

"And how if your sire is mistaken, and Collington is the man behind my father's downfall? A fine figure I should cut asking him for information!"

"Collington?" Morris groaned and drew a hand across his eyes. "Poor lad, you've a proper rat's nest 'twixt your ears! Why do you not accuse the Archbishop of Canterbury? Or the Lord Mayor of London? We might have as much fun with them."

Gideon said quietly, "I'll hire another coach in Canterbury, and you can go on to Sevenoaks. I shouldn't involve you, at all events."

"No, you shouldn't. Mind you, I'd be glad of a brawl did you point me the villain, and say 'There he stands! Tally ho!' But you're tilting your lance 'gainst every windmill in sight, and each more unlikely than the last! I wonder why I had it fixed in my foolish head 'twas Derrydene you suspected?"

"I do suspect him." Gideon frowned. "And perhaps I am tilting 'gainst windmills. The devil's in it that I don't know who I'm fighting, Jamie. Dammitall! 'Tis like trying to grapple a shadow."

"And what shadows do we grapple in Canterbury?"

With a faint grateful smile, Gideon said, " 'Tis my hope that the jeweller who repaired that confounded chessman may be able to tell me something."

"If he ain't connected with the murky business, he'll know nothing. And if he *is* connected with it, we'll likely wind up with our throats cut! Besides, how d'you know which jeweller? There are likely a dozen or so in Canterbury.''

''When Lady Naomi came to Promontory Point that first day, she mentioned a jeweller's shop in Stour Street. It shouldn't be hard to find, surely?''

His optimism proved well founded, and an hour later, the two young men stood on the flagway, gazing at Shumaker's Jeweller's Shoppe.

Morris sighed. ''Well, you were right, dear boy. 'Twasn't hard to find.''

A tug at his boot roused Gideon. He glanced down. A tiny monkey with a red shako strapped to his head blinked up at him and waved a tin cup. Mechanically, Gideon took out his purse and dropped a groat into the cup, and the monkey scampered, chattering, to the organ-grinder. That large individual, wearing an ill-fitting scratch wig, and with a purple kerchief knotted around his throat, beamed, and turned the wheel, and the piercing notes of some unidentifiable melody shattered the quiet. Gideon raised one hand, and the organ-grinder stopped, his soulful dark eyes scanning the customer questioningly. ''You no like-a da music, signor?''

Stepping into the kennel, Gideon lied, ''Very much. But I'd liefer have information. Can you tell me what happened here?''

The big man gave him a pitying look. ''It burn-a down.''

''So I see. Do you know when?''

A crafty expression dawned. Twirling his fine moustachios the organ-grinder said, ''Might.''

Gideon extracted a florin from his purse, and held it up. ''Try. And you need not trouble with the accent.''

The man grinned. ''I knowed you was a downy file, Guv'nor. Right y'are, then. The shop catched fire Tuesday night. Poor old Doc was workin' late. The constable says as he fell asleep while he was meltin' dahn some gold, or summat and woke up makin' his excuses to Saint Peter. Funny.''

Much shocked, Morris said, ''You've a dashed strange notion of what's amusing! If you want to know, it ain't in the least funny to be burned. I've never burned to death, mind you, but I burned my hand once, and—''

''No disrespeck intended, sir,'' interposed the organ-grinder hurriedly.

Gideon asked, ''Did you mean that there was something odd about the fire, perhaps?''

''Ar. You got it right, sir! We called Mr. Shumaker 'Doc,''

'cause he were school eddicated. And—clever? Cor! You shoulda seen the way he could put broke things back tergether. Funny, though, that with a name like Shumaker he were a clockmaker!''

Morris gave a shout of laughter in which the organ-grinder joined heartily. "Now that *is* funny, begad," Morris agreed. "Blister me, but the fella should better have been called Mr. Time, eh?" The two men howled anew and the monkey jumped up and down chattering excitedly.

When the uproar quieted, Rossiter said, "Is that all you have to tell me, Mr. Organ-grinder?"

The big man wiped his eyes with an end of the purple kerchief, and said breathlessly that Doc had been a very tidy worker. "You'd never a thunk he'd cause no fire. He'd a good trade, poor chap. The gentry useter come wi' their timepieces from miles around, they did. Workin' on summat o'yourn, was he, Guv?"

"I'd heard of his work. I pity his widow. Does she live nearby?"

"Useter. Gone now, poor creeter."

Morris inserted, "I say! Was she killed too?"

"No, sir. Moved away, she did. Yestiday. Her brother come and helped her pack up. Poor old mort. I 'spect she couldn't stand bein' all alone. So she upped and went to live wi' her brother. Not that he was no bargain, by the look of him."

"Had she no friends hereabouts who would have stood by her?"

The organ-grinder fingered his chins, pondering the matter. "Yus and no. Doc had. But his missus—a queer sorta woman, she was, if ever I see one. 'Course, they all is, ain't they? Women I mean. All touched in the upper works, one way or t'other. But that Mrs. Shumaker— Cor! I dunno how Doc coulda stood her! Nervous as two cats in a thunderstorm, she were. I come up behind her once. Bright as terday it was, and bein' a kind-hearted soul and meanin' no harm, I says, 'Mornin', ma'am.' That's all. Jest—'Mornin', ma'am.' And she goes straight up in the air and gives a screech like a ungreased wheel, then gallops orf dahn the road so that everyone's a-starin' at me and wonderin' if I give her a pinch where I shouldn't oughter. Me face was that red it pretty nigh catched light all by itself it did! No tellin' what a woman like that'll do next, is there?"

"No, by Jove," said Morris with ready sympathy. "Dreadful thing! I recollect once—"

Gideon interrupted quickly. "Do you know where this brother of hers lives, by any chance?"

"No, I don't, Guv. It come as a surprise ter me, matter o'fact. Never knowed as she had a brother. I wish her well of him. A big'un, and 'andsome as a bearded cockroach. The kind you wouldn't wanta meet in a alley of a dark night!"

Gideon thanked him, handed over the florin, and watched him stroll away, the little monkey clambering up his shoulder to sit there chattering, and the strident music ringing through the warm air.

The two men walked on, side by side, Morris humming along with the melody, and Gideon deep in thought. When the organ-grinder's efforts were diminished by distance, Morris asked, "What now?"

"Emerald Farm," said Gideon. "I really must look in on the old place, just to be sure all's well. May have to move my family down there, and I've not had a chance to see it since I come home."

Morris glanced at him obliquely. He took setbacks well, did Ross, but this must have been a blow to his hopes, as far-fetched as they were. He said carefully, "Look, m'dear fella, if there's anything I can do . . . ? I mean, I know you've suffered a great disappointment, and with the duel fixed for Saturday, I—"

"Disappointment!" Gideon's eyes were ablaze with excitement. "To the contrary, this confirms everything I'd suspected! The jeweller was silenced, do you not see? And his wife, heaven help the poor lady, has been borne away, heaven knows where, lest she say something untoward! I am on the right track, my James! By Jove, but I am!"

"Lord help the Archbishop of Canterbury!" groaned Morris.

❧ *Chapter 14* ❧

Because they'd had a late start and Rossiter must return to London before nightfall, he had been most particular in his selection of a coach and four. The light vehicle he'd chosen had not taxed the team unduly, the postilions had set a spanking pace, and with two brief halts they came in less than three hours to the Sussex border and the chain of hills known as the Weald.

The road swung in an easterly loop to bring them around to the south and the access road, and from their high vantage point they caught several glimpses of Emerald Farm. During his grandmother's lifetime, Rossiter had visited it in winter and summer and never failed to find it a delight. The house itself faced south and was built on a low rise, with higher hills lifting emerald shoulders behind it. A long, low, half-timbered structure, the roof deeply thatched, it stood serenely amidst its lush pastures and fields as it had stood for over a century, the many windows twinkling in the sunlight that painted a golden glow on the whitewashed walls. No smoke rose from the chimneys, and the silence was broken only by the distant lowing of cows, the twittering of birds and the occasional bustling stir of the breeze.

They were still some way off, but Morris thought it looked deserted. As they rumbled over a wooden bridge, he said, "Jolly nice. How much land?"

"Roughly two square miles. This stream is the eastern boundary, and the hills mark the northern line."

"Tidy little parcel. Who manages it for you?"

"I've a couple living here who used to work for my grandmama. They keep four farmhands, I understand." Gideon's glance raked over the meadows. "Though you'd not guess it at the moment," he muttered, looking rather grim.

197

They drove on along the well-kept road edged with rioting wildflowers, through fields where young corn waved softly, or the feathery heads of carrots marched in neat rows. Distantly, cows stood hock deep in the lush meadow grasses. A curving drive led to the house, and the postilions stopped the team in front. Gideon climbed from the coach. His hail brought no response nor sign of life. Touched by apprehension, he strode up the steps between flowerbeds where daffodils bobbed golden heads to the tune of the breeze and tulips splashed their bright colours against the stems of lofty hollyhocks. The front door was not locked, and he hurried inside only to halt, shocked into immobility.

Following, Morris gasped, "Lord save us all!"

The wide hall was littered, drawers pulled from the sideboard and tossed heedlessly. The tall case clock had been wrenched open, the pendulum torn off, the glass door cracked from top to bottom.

They walked, stunned, into the spacious withdrawing room that Gideon remembered as being so warm and welcoming, and was now a shambles of overturned chairs and tables, broken vases, torn cushions, even the pictures having been pulled down and thrown haphazardly about the floor.

"They were thorough," remarked Morris. "You've got to give 'em credit for that."

"I'd like to give 'em a sight more than credit," said Rossiter grittily. "Damme, but they want that accursed chessman!"

He went back onto the steps and called to the postilions to take the carriage to the barn and bait the horses. Returning, he and Morris made a rapid and painful inspection of the house. Room after room had been ransacked and wrecked. It was a violation; a painfully wrenching invasion of this personal place, which was inexpressibly dear to him. Coming slowly down the stairs, he tried not to show the extent of his rageful grief, and muttered, "I hope to God none of my people were hurt in this debacle!"

"Oh, my *goodness*! Gideon!"

Wearing a beige travelling gown and with a beige lace-trimmed cap perched atop her high-piled curls, my lady Lutonville stood in the entry hall, her maid peering curiously over her shoulder.

The sight of her was balm for Rossiter's bruised spirit and he went quickly to take her outstretched hand. "If it needs this to bring you to me," he said with his wry grin, " 'tis worth it!"

"I came for quite another reason," she answered. "La, but how dreadful this is! What senseless destruction. I am so sorry. I know how you always have loved this old place. Did you catch sight of the vandals?"

"No. We arrived but ten minutes ago."

Morris growled, "I wish we *had* seen the filthy louts!"

In her distress, Naomi had been aware only of Gideon. Belatedly, she said, "Lieutenant, I ask your pardon! Whatever must you think of me? I had not meant to ignore you."

He bowed with unfailing courtesy, and assured her he quite understood her reaction. "Nasty shock for you, ma'am. You didn't expect to walk into this."

"No, indeed." Naomi looked sadly about the wreckage. " 'Tis frightful! Frightful! What of your servants, Gideon?"

"Would that I knew." He righted an overturned chair. "I had hoped to show you the farm under different circumstances. My apologies that you must see it in such a state."

Morris picked up a heavy silver candelabra. "They do not appear to have robbed you, at all events." He glanced at Maggie, who looked pale and frightened. "C'mon, m'dear," he said bracingly. "Let us start to set things to rights."

They all began to pick up those articles not hopelessly smashed. Retrieving a little clock, Naomi listened anxiously for the tick, then handed it to Gideon. " 'Tis still running, thank goodness. Oh, how silly we are! We can accomplish so little. You will need help to tidy this poor house." She saw that he was watching her rather quizzically, and went on, "I fancy you must be wondering why I am here."

"I scarce dare ask."

"I came to tell you that you owe my papa a most humble apology, sir. He has found the chess piece!"

"Be dashed," exclaimed Morris, hurrying over to them.

"How?" asked Rossiter.

"In the strangest fashion. Papa received a package through the Post yesterday. 'Twas from the jeweller in Canterbury, explaining that he had given me another gentleman's property by mistake. He enclosed the chess piece belonging to Papa, and desired that the other be returned to him. Which will," she acknowledged thoughtfully, "be rather awkward."

"More so than you might think," said Morris.

Rossiter asked tersely, "Did the jeweller name this other gentleman?"

"No. But it's simple to discover, surely?"

The two men looked at each other.

Rossiter said, "You are quite sure, Naomi? You *saw* the other chessman?"

She frowned. "I might have guessed you'd not believe me! Or is it that your burgeoning imagination now sees my father as having lied! Well, I can assure you that is not so, for one of the reasons he came to Falcon House this morning was to show me the piece."

Puzzled, Rossiter muttered, "Then—why the need for all this, I wonder?"

"I would think that should be perfectly clear. You were mistaken in believing it has aught to do with the lost chessman. At least, with the one belonging my papa!"

He was silent, staring fixedly at a broken china bowl.

Morris picked it up and said rather helplessly, "Might be stuck back together, I suppose, dear boy."

Rossiter sighed. "We shall be obliged to buy gallons of glue."

Her heart touched by his twisted attempt at a smile, Naomi's resentment fled. "Oh, never say the whole house is like this."

"As bad, or worse," answered Morris disconsolately.

"Whoever they are, whatever they want," said Rossiter, "they're devilish determined." His own words sounded defeated, and impatient with himself, he pulled back his shoulders and looking into Naomi's lovely and concerned face, said in a more cheerful voice, "You are very good to have driven all this way to bring me the news. But I think you are here without your father's permission, eh, ma'am?"

The tenderness was in his eyes again, a silent caress that enthralled her. She said in a faraway voice, "I am of an age to go about as I choose."

"Quite the lady of independence," he teased.

"Not so independent I would willingly distress him. Any more than you would wish to offend Sir Mark."

They both knew that they were not discussing her having called at the farm, and they gazed at each other, lost to their surroundings and their companions until Morris coughed, and suggested for the second time that they should go and find the constable.

Rossiter said with a start, "What? Oh—er, well I rather suspect that is where my people must be, Jamie."

Also startled, Naomi felt her cheeks redden. Flustered, she turned to Morris and asked, "Pray what did you mean, Lieutenant, when you said 'twould be more awkward than I knew to return the other chess piece to the jeweller?''

"Burned up," said Morris succinctly.

"Good heavens! Mr. Shumaker was b-burned?"

Morris nodded. "With his shop."

She gave a gasp, and sat down in the chair. "Oh, poor man! How dreadful! And he was such a kind little person!"

"Naomi," said Rossiter thoughtfully. "While you were at the Dowling Soiree you saw a chess piece similar to the one your father had lost. Did you mention that to anyone?"

"No. And in point of fact, it was not at all similar."

"But, I thought you said—"

"I said 'twas the same, or almost the same, as the piece I had lost. But, you see the piece I lost was—"

"Was not your papa's. Of course. My apologies for being so dense."

"I was dense also," she said, smiling at him. "I should have realized 'twas not a chessman at all."

"Castle?" enquired Morris.

"No. I meant 'twas something else. Not part of my father's chess set."

Puzzled, Rossiter said, "But you had seen his set before, surely?"

"No. Never."

"Does he play often?"

"I've never known him to do so." She hesitated, then admitted with a rather bitter smile, "An he did, I might not be aware. Unhappily, we share few interests. He had told me that the piece I was to collect from the jeweller was of great antiquity. That is why I did not question the fact that it was so—strange. Quite different from any chess piece I ever saw."

Among the debris on the floor was a torn sheet of paper. Rossiter picked it up, found a pencil, and handed both to Naomi. "I know how clever you are with your sketchbook. Could you draw the article you lost?"

Using a book for backing, she began to sketch. " 'Twas smaller than this, actually. About three inches tall," she murmured. "And surprisingly heavy. It was of pink jade, I think. Rounded at the top . . . so. Like a gravestone. And with what looked for all the world to be rubies inset here . . . here . . . and here . . ."

Watching her intently, Rossiter said, "Jove, but it does indeed

201

look like a miniature gravestone. Was there any other design at all?''

"Yes," she said, her pencil busy. "A carven face, similar to some of the drawings that have been found where the ancient people dwelt, so that it appears like a tiny man, with—''

Morris wandered up to peer over her shoulder, and exclaimed, "Blister it! That is my toy!"

Two pairs of surprised eyes shot to him, and Maggie, still tidying industriously, paused to stare at him, and say under her breath, "At *his* age!"

"Your—*what*?" gasped Rossiter.

Tearing at his hair in remorseful humiliation, Morris cried, "Oh, Jupiter, what a dolt I am! I thought 'twas a *toy*!"

Rossiter demanded wrathfully, "Do you say *you* have it? And have said nothing, all this blasted time?"

"Mea culpa," groaned his friend. "I trod on the silly thing just after I shot that clod Falcon. When you started raving about a chess piece it did not occur to me— Well, I would *never* have thought of it as such!"

"What the devil did you do with it?"

"Popped it in my pocket. When I reached home, m'sister was there to greet me, with all the family, don'tcha know, and I presented it to my little niece." He turned to Naomi and explained sheepishly, "Didn't have nothing else, you see. Left the rest of my gifts at the Red Pheasant!"

"Then you know where it is," said Gideon. "You can get it back!"

"I'll—er, try. Have to post out to Guildford. Gad!" Morris looked daunted. "Have you ever tried to wrest a toy from a little girl?"

Naomi suggested with a smile, "You must make her an exchange, Lieutenant. A pretty doll would likely be more welcome than that small ruby man, or—whatever it is."

"Take the carriage," said Rossiter urgently. "I can use one of the hacks we keep here. Be a good fellow and bring the ruby figure to Snow Hill tomorrow, will you?"

With a good-humoured wink at Naomi, Morris grumbled, "I collect I must be grateful to be allowed to overnight with my sister."

They walked outside. Both vehicles had been taken to the barn, and Naomi asked that Morris give her coachman instructions to prepare to return to Town. Watching the lieutenant's swinging stride as he left them, Rossiter murmured, "Poor Jamie. He pays a price for his friendship with me."

"As do we all," teased Naomi.

He glanced at her, smiling. He was less gaunt than when he had first come home, and looked calm, but she knew him, and was aware that behind his poise he was grieved and raging because of the savagery perpetrated on his home. It was so typical that he would put aside his own concerns, and worry for his friend at such a moment. Sympathy brought a tightness to her throat. She said impulsively, "*Mon pauvre*, what a horrid time you have had. You must wish you had not come home."

He lifted her hand to his lips. "No, how could I wish that, when I had lost everything that gave my life meaning? My headstrong pride robbed me of my family, my home, my heart. . . . " One long finger touched the delicate curve of her upturned cheek. "I deserved what I brought upon myself. The worst aspect of it all was that my foolishness wounded others. Had I stayed in England, I might have persuaded my father to—different practices, so that all this worry and heartbreak could have been avoided. My sister need not have known such anxieties. I would not have lost my love. . . . "

Fighting to be sensible, when she longed to throw herself into his arms, she said, "You seem very sure of that last, sir."

"I am very sure I mean to win her back to me."

'No man should have such speaking eyes,' she thought, and was relieved when the carriage came rumbling up, Morris waving from the window and calling cheerily that he would "climb that confounded hill" again in the morning.

Rossiter waved, and shouted, "Be sure 'tis *morning*! I know you, slugabed! And have a care!"

The carriage was past then, and Naomi said, "I shall say farewell also, Gideon."

"But you have not yet told me why you came."

"You know very well." She turned away, but he did not relinquish his grip on her hand.

"An honest answer, an you please, my lady."

"I was coming this way, at all events. I go to Ashleigh to—er, to visit Mr. Neville Falcon."

"I wonder Miss Katrina did not accompany you. She is said to be most fond of her papa." Naomi disdaining to respond to this provocation, he suggested, "It might be as well to tell your coachman you have changed your mind again." She frowned at him, and he pointed out, "You just gave orders that he was to take you back to Town."

"Oh. A—er, slip of the tongue, is all."

"My grandmama used to say one should not tell fibs, else one's mouth will become crooked." His fingertip drifted across her lips.

Determined not to shiver, she twisted her mouth grotesquely.

With a low laugh he said, "If you make your lips so kissable, dear heart, they will surely be kissed."

At this, she trembled, and ducked her head.

He murmured, "Naomi . . . Beloved—look at me."

She raised her eyes, met his own, and was lost. "I am . . . so afraid," she whispered.

Disregarding the possibility that the coachman would see them, or that Maggie might very well be watching from the window, Gideon pulled her into his arms. She clung to him, her cheek pressed against his cravat.

"Afraid for *us*, my lovely sprite?"

"Yes. No. I do not know, but— Oh, Gideon, I have such a dreadful fear that—that something terrible lies ahead! I think I could not bear it if—"

His hand was under her chin again, tilting up her face. His eyes adoring her, he asked, "If—what?"

Tears gemmed her lashes. She said threadily, "You have suffered so much. If aught were to happen to you . . ."

Exultant, he cried, "Then you do still care for me! Praise heaven! I have not lost you! How I dreamed of bringing you here to Tranquillity Terrace and—"

An arrow seemed to pierce her. Unutterably shocked, her eyes opened very wide. She pushed against him trying to wrench free, a sob of mingled pain and rage escaping her. "Oh, but you are vile! Vile! And I am a stupid, trusting fool! How *dare* you use that name in front of me, when you and your horrid light-skirt—"

His hands gripped her arms like steel bands. Without the faintest sign of remorse, he said, "My, how the gossips have gabbled! Sweet, foolish little one—do you not yet know?"

"I know I will not love you again," she sobbed, scattering tears, and with her lips trembling pathetically. "I *will* not let you hurt me again! You are . . . are without conscience or decency! Womanizing all over Europe . . . and w-with children in . . . in every port!"

"Oh, egad," he groaned. "I had forgot about my children."

204

"Forgot!" Appalled, she gulped, "Infamous *brute*! I only hope—"

"Be quiet," he said very softly.

Really, the command was redundant, for she could not utter a word with his lips crushing her own. For three whole seconds she tried to fight him, but once again, her resistance was overborne and she drifted with abandoned delight through a time that might have been a second or an hour, until Rossiter sighed and drew back.

Dazed, she opened her eyes. His cheek was against her hair. His arms, so strong, so dear, still cradled her. She uttered a whimper of frustration. She had weakened again! Despising herself, she pounded one small fist against his chest, and moaned feebly, "I hate you, Gideon Rossiter!"

He chuckled. "If that was a demonstration of your hatred, you may hate me forever. And indeed, were I as base as you believe, I'd scarce blame you."

Pulling back her head, she looked up at him searchingly.

He wiped away a tear very gently. "Have you *no* notion of how much I love you? Can you really suppose that with your precious image always in my heart, I could really care for any other lady?"

"But—" she began, uncertain but yearning to be convinced.

He had not wanted to talk about this, but it was very evident that his reticence had deepened her doubts. He said reluctantly, "Beloved one, when I was in the hospital for so long, there were times when— Well, when hope seemed rather useless, and reality was so—unpleasant that I fashioned myself a retreat: a lovely country house just like this one. I put you in it, and as the months went by, I pictured you growing from the girl I had left behind, into a gentle and beautiful lady."

Incredulous, she whispered, *"Me?"*

He said tenderly, "You were the lady I fled to so very often, and this was our refuge—my Tranquillity Terrace."

"Oh, my dear! My dear," she said, joy mingling with pity for his ordeal. "I feel so ashamed. But—but everyone said . . . I mean—you spoke so often of your lady."

"I was delirious at times, and they tell me I raved so that the other fellows thought—" He shrugged, and admitted with a boyish grin, "They were all so envious. I decided not to spoil my newly acquired reputation. Besides . . . 'twas a very personal thing, and not to be shared with others."

205

Radiant, she said happily, "Then—then you really *did* still love me?"

"Every single minute. Perhaps you should know that— Oh, blast!" He put her from him hurriedly.

A horseman came at the gallop to draw rein before them. The rider, a well-preserved but weathered-looking man on the far side of fifty, touched his cap respectfully. "So you seen it, sir," he panted. "Sorry I am you should come home to—to this wickedness! I took me wife into Tunbridge Wells. She were that put about. I'd say welcome, but—'tis a sad sight to greet ye."

Rossiter shook hands with the sturdy farmer. "You were not hurt, either of you?"

"Not her nor me, no sir. They come whilst we was takin' my grandson to the dentist 'smorning. My men see 'em, and come up to the house, not liking the look o' things. They got theirselves beaten, and tied up, poor chaps, so I took 'em to the 'pothecary in the Wells. The constable be on his way here." From the corner of his eye he had already taken in Naomi. Now, he glanced at her shyly.

Rossiter said, "My lady, this is my farm manager, Zebediah Upton."

The farmer flushed and snatched off his broad-brimmed hat.

Naomi nodded to him pleasantly, too happy to care that once again she was compromised, since she was ostensibly alone here with Gideon.

"Lady Lutonville is my betrothed, as you know, Zeb," said Rossiter smoothly. "I'd brought her down to see her future home."

The farmer shook his head. "What a pity. I be that sorry, ma'am!"

"So am I," said Rossiter. "But I'd as lief not have her ladyship mixed up in this business." He turned to Naomi, his eyes softening. "You must go, my love. If your coachman takes the back road through the hills, you'll avoid our intrepid constable." He led her towards the coach that had come up, and murmured, "I'm glad you did not object to being named my betrothed. You'd as well become accustomed to it, for I do believe we are close to solving this puzzle. And then, my little lovely thing, you shall have to find another excuse for rejecting me."

She looked at him lovingly. "I collect 'tis time wasted to pretend I mean to try very hard."

"We have wasted too much time already!" Feeling eyes boring into his back he kissed her hand lingeringly. "Your coach-

206

man watches us, you know, and will doubtless report this to your father. Or had you advised him you meant to come here?''

"I was not so daring. But never worry. I am of age, and Papa can do no more than rage at me."

His hand tightened. "You're sure? An I thought he'd dare to—"

"Beat me?" She smiled. "I should tell Samantha Golightly and 'twould be all over Town within seconds, which he would not at all like! I think I see a rider coming, dearest."

He glanced around. "So you do. Go now. I want you out of this."

Leaning to him, she asked in sudden anxiety, "What do you mean to do?"

"Nothing tonight. I'll likely be delayed here while the constable asks endless useless questions, and writes endless useless conclusions in his notebook." He handed her up into the coach. Maggie came running in answer to Naomi's call, and was assisted inside also.

Gideon asked, "When shall I see you again, my lady?"

Her mouth drooped and she said sadly, "Oh, how I loathe to deceive him. I feel so sly."

"Would you wish I keep away, love? I will, sooner than distress you."

" 'Twould distress me more not to see you. But, I fear it shall have to be the park, for the time at least. I ride most mornings at seven, Gideon."

"Not alone," he promised with a smile, and slammed the door.

Naomi leaned from the window. "You will take care?"

"I have every reason to guard my future—now," he answered, then waved the coachman on.

Gideon had no sooner returned home that evening than Gwendolyn was scratching at the door of his tiny private parlour. She told him worriedly that Sir Mark had been in a passion when he'd come home from Falcon House that morning, and that this afternoon his man of the law had called, "looking ponderous." Gideon did his best to soothe her apprehension, and refrained from imparting his own unhappy news. When she left him so that he might change his clothes, Tummet warned him, with a marked twinkle in his eye, that Mr. Newby had been "fair aside of 'isself over a certain me-and-you (shoe)." Gideon gave a grim smile, and went downstairs prepared for battle.

Newby was waiting for him in the lower hall and launched into a fierce denunciation of the "theft" from his room, and of his brother's top-lofty arrogance in having interfered with his plans.

"I fail to see what difference 'twould have made," said Gideon with a shrug. "The lady who mislaid it—"

"Naomi Lutonville," snarled Newby.

"You cannot prove that. And should you set such a rumour abroad, people will realize that you were the one who found the slipper and failed to return it. Scarce the act of a gentleman, twin."

He started to move past, but his brother caught at his arm. "Much use 'twill be to behave like a gentleman when we are starving in a foul Westminster hovel, or clapped up in Newgate! I could have employed some rascal and wangled a pretty penny for the slipper. What—does that offend you? Then turn up your sanctimonious nose, and be damned! *You've* your oafish farm, and clod that you are would likely be willing to rusticate among the yokels. What have *I*? Where am *I* to turn?"

Newby's voice had grown shrill, and his handsome face was white and strained. Realizing that his twin was actually terrified, Gideon said quietly, "You will live with us at Emerald Farm, of course. But—"

"Keep your confounded charity! Sooner would I rot in the Gatehouse!"

Gideon shrugged. "A doubtful piece of rodomontade. And your fears are premature. Can I but gather a few more facts, I'll be ready to lay my case before the Lord Chancellor's committee, and belike my father will be absolved of blame."

"To what end? The old fool has bungled away our wealth, our houses and lands! Collington is full of juice and would not miss a few hundred to avoid a scandal. And a few hundred would help in the New World!"

"Help yourself only, my brave fellow? Or did your plans perhaps include a thought at least for Gwen?"

Despite his selfish panic, Newby was genuinely fond of his sister. He bit his lip and muttered, "She'd never leave my father."

"But *you* would. Knowing you are his favourite, still you would carelessly abandon him! You'll strive to better purpose, twin, do you forget these megrims and help me. I'd be glad of your assistance, for there are—"

"Assistance in what? Gathering your so-called *facts*? Gathering rubbish, more like! The committee will laugh at you. But you'd best gather fast, my poor simpleton. Papa's lawyer brought word the committee is to meet again on Tuesday. The creditors will present their claims, and my father will surely be adjudged guilty of fraud—where will your famed pride be then?''

Stunned, Gideon pushed past and hurried to Sir Mark's study, Newby's angry titter following him.

His knock went unanswered, and he opened the door. Sir Mark was leaning back in his chair, staring at the pile of papers on the desk before him. He looked for the first time an old man, crushed and defeated. Longing to be able to tell him that all was well, that disaster had been averted, Gideon walked in. "My apologies that I was delayed, sir. But I fancy you will—''

Sir Mark looked up. His face was haggard and twitching, his eyes full of tears. "I am to appear . . . before the committee . . . on Tuesday," he said brokenly. "I tried so hard to right the wrong, Gideon. I—I *did* repay many men. But I have failed you all . . . My lawyer says there is no hope. I shall be found . . . guilty of—of fraud and criminal neglect. They will take everything that is left. I sold the Conduit Street house and the shooting box in Leicestershire. You knew that, of course. Promontory Point will go too . . . The estate where Rossiters have been born for centuries . . . I shall be clapped up or deported. A despised and dishonoured . . . bankrupt!''

His own eyes blurring, Gideon hurried forward. "No, no, sir. Never say so! I've gathered much information to substantiate your theory that you were the victim of—''

"Of—whom?'' The older man's eyes searched his face. He pleaded, "Have you discovered why 'twas done? Have you learned the name of my enemy?''

"Not definitely. But—''

With a flash of temper Sir Mark interrupted, "You might have done, had you tended to your investigations instead of frippering about chasing nonsensical chess pieces that have nothing to say to *anything*! I wonder you bothered to come home at all! All you achieve is to quarrel with Newby, who has always been devoted to me!''

Gideon said quietly, "I think you do not mean that, sir. You know I have tried.''

The blaze died from Sir Mark's eyes. "Aye. You have.'' He sighed heavily. "I'm sorry, boy. Pay me no heed. Newby was right, I suppose. We should have taken what was left and . . . and run.''

"No, no! Indeed you must not despair, sir."

Sir Mark bowed forward and sank his face into his hands. "Do you know—what it *means*?" His voice was a groan, the words muffled. "It means I cannot ever be elected to the House of Commons. I can no longer be a justice of the peace. I could never be a mayor or—or an alderman. I cannot serve the poor, or be a member of a county council, or a parish council . . . God knows what else. I am thoroughly disgraced. God knows how I shall ever hold up my head again! Oh! Lord help me! I am truly beyond the pale!"

With a sobbing cry Gwendolyn limped past Gideon and gathered her father into cherishing arms. "Do not! Oh, do not grieve so, dearest Papa. Gideon is here now. He will help us. He will not—not let them . . ." Lifting an anguished face, she blinked away tears, and gulped, "Will you . . . Gideon?"

He threw aside his reserve and hastened to put his arms around them both. "No indeed," he said huskily. "We will win yet, Papa! I promise you!"

❧ *Chapter 15* ❧

In the century and more since King Charles I had graciously opened Hyde Park to the common people, it had become a popular place. In addition to the innocent pleasures of walking, picnics, and games, many duels had been fought here. The mile-long Rotten Row was a parade ground for the elite. Rossiter had not expected it to be crowded at seven o'clock on a cloudy morning, however, and he was more than a little exasperated to see some half dozen riders escorting three ladies, one of whom was Naomi. She was wearing a creamy beige habit with big gold buttons. Her hat was a jaunty, high-crowned creation, and as he approached he could see that she was all light-hearted coquetry, her merry little laugh trilling out in response to some remark, the orange ribands of her hat fluttering in the rather chill wind as she swayed to the cavorting of her high-spirited bay mare.

Rossiter rode to join them as Viscount Glendenning was complaining that Lady Naomi was cruel to refuse his offer to drive her down to Richmond.

"But I attended your ball, Tio," she answered mischievously, "and I must not be too particular, you know."

"Besides which," put in Lord Sommers, "Lady Naomi goes with me to the military review at St. James'. Now do not break my heart by refusing, sweet enchantress. You said you would, you know you did."

"I said I *might*, my lord," Naomi qualified, tapping his arm gently with her riding whip, her green eyes smiling at him.

Trying to edge his black between Sommers and Naomi, Mr. Harrier lisped, "And she might *not*, Sommers! Especially since I can offer a boat party—"

"Which will be rained on, *assurement*," laughed a clean-cut

211

young major who was unknown to Rossiter. "You will be far better advised to go with me to my mama's musicale, lovely one."

"You are all so good to me," said Naomi. "And did I intend to accept any of these delightful invitations, Hilary, I would certainly consider—"

"Gideon!"

Rossiter had been so intent upon his beloved that he'd scarcely noticed the other two ladies. Now, he was amazed to hear Gwendolyn's voice call his name, and to discover her mounted on a quiet chestnut gelding, and watching him fondly. Gordon Chandler rode beside her, and beyond Chandler were Miss Falcon and Cyril Crenshore. Quite aware that the cheery banter had ceased, and that several frigid glances came his way, Rossiter guided his mount close to his sister.

"What on earth are you doing here, cheerful sparrow? I'd fancied you snug in your bed at home."

"Luckily, you are mistaken," said Chandler, ever gallant. "Are you well, Ross? Miss Gwendolyn tells me you'd a pair of narrow escapes on Wednesday."

"Which is surprising to none," observed Mr. Crenshore, sardonically.

Ignoring him, Gideon said, "I'll own time has not hung heavy on my hands since I came home. Now tell me, Gwen, how came you here? And what are you about letting this hedgebird escort you?"

Chandler laughed, and Gwendolyn said blithely that no lady could wish a more pleasant escort. "You know I love to ride in the early morning, and Miss Falcon was so kind as to invite me to join their party today. Tummet brought me. I thought you must have known, for he said he left you a note."

It had taken Rossiter some minutes to decipher that note. Several words were quite incomprehensible, but the gist of it appeared to be that Tummet had gone to the port with a hen to hide her bosom in a box. At that point, amused but mystified, he'd abandoned the effort. Glancing back now, he saw that Tummet was indeed plodding along behind.

The valet doffed his hat and enquired with a leer, "Get me note, Guv?"

"I did," called Gideon. "What did it say?"

Tummet looked at a sympathetic cloud. "Cor!" he told it. And to his employer added with offended dignity, "I writ plain as to what anyone could see that I'd gorn to escort Miss Gwen to ride with her bosom bow—which is a word, or words, meaning friend what is closest to her 'eart.''

"Perfectly correct," said Gwendolyn, and added softly, "what did you think he said?"

Gideon chuckled. "Never mind. What the deuce is he riding?"

"King Arthur's charger, by the look of it," said Chandler. "I'll allow you to chat with your pretty sister, Ross. Only provided you are polite to the lady." He drove home his spurs, and joined the forward party.

Crenshore clearly wished to ride ahead also, but Katrina would not be manoeuvred into abandoning the Rossiters and said with her kind smile, "Do you go on, sir, for there is a matter I must discuss with Miss Rossiter."

Scowling, Crenshore left them.

Katrina lowered her voice. "Lady Naomi is anxious to speak with you, Captain Rossiter. She asks that you meet her in the large clump of willows by the Serpentine."

"Thank you, ma'am" he said gratefully. "You are very good. Especially, since you must have formed a very poor first opinion of me."

She looked at him with anxiety in her fascinating eyes. "My brother and I are not accepted, as you must know, and—"

"Stuff," interrupted Gwendolyn, ever loyal. "I saw how the gentlemen fought to be beside you, and would still be doing so had you not been so kind as to stay by me."

Katrina smiled. "They enjoy to flirt with me, perhaps. And we've a few friends, like Lord Horatio, who acknowledge us. But I know how most people feel about us. That is why—having been judged myself and found beyond the pale, I hesitate to judge others."

"But you do judge me, I think," said Gideon quietly.

She hesitated, then said, "I fear you, rather. Naomi is my dearest friend. I'd not see her hurt again."

This implied criticism caused Gwendolyn to frown a little, but she kept silent.

Gideon prompted, "And you think I will hurt her?"

"Sir," said Katrina, "I wish I did not. But—I will speak plainly. Although Naomi and the earl have not enjoyed a close relationship, he *is* her father, and she was much too well bred-up to now run counter to his wishes. With both your parents so bitterly opposed to the match"—she gave a regretful little gesture—"I see only heartbreak ahead—for both of you."

213

Ten minutes later Gideon was pondering those words as he waited in the small grove of willows by the lake. Perhaps in other eyes their prospects for happiness did not seem too bright just at the moment, but he was quite sure now that his lady still loved him, and nothing could dim that wondrous knowledge. Failure was not to be thought of; Fate could not be so cruel as to reunite them only to part them forever. Besides, they had located the ruby chess piece, and when Morris brought it to Town another part of the puzzle would fall into place. Morris would likely not arrive until this afternoon, however, which should allow plenty of time for the small matter he meant to attend to. He reached down to his saddle holster and transferred the pistol into the right-hand pocket of his coat. Just in case.

A slight drizzle began to add to the air's dampness. Logically the riding party would soon break up. He had given Tummet strict instructions not to desert Gwendolyn this time, and Horatio Glendenning had been trying to persuade the girl to take luncheon at Laindon House, where his step-sister was staying. The prospect of seeing an old friend had brought stars of happiness into Gwen's blue eyes, and it was more than likely that she would accept the invitation.

He heard an approaching rider then, and Naomi cantered to join him. Her eyes radiant, her cheeks a little flushed, she reached out to him and he took her hand and kissed it, murmuring, "I wish I dare kiss you properly."

"So sure as you did, Reggie Smythe would chance to pass by. Besides, I have had a horrid time trying to elude Camber."

He knit his brows. "Camber?"

"Of course, you've not seen him. He worked for us in Italy, and now Papa has decreed he is to be my groom. I fancy he has orders to protect me from gentlemen with the kind of gleam in their eyes that I perceive in yours, sir!"

He grinned and led her under the leafy umbrella of the willows. "He won't see any gleams under here. And now I can claim my proper kiss."

He leaned to her, his arm slipping around her shoulders, and she lifted her face. After a rapturous moment her mare began to dance about nervously, and they were torn apart.

Naomi said dreamily. "I am not sure that kiss was entirely 'proper,' Captain Rossiter."

"True." He sighed. "And it might have lasted a little longer had—"

"Sshh!" she hissed. "Camber!"

The rider on the tall piebald horse was indeed a big fellow. His stock was immaculate, his livery sat well on his broad shoulders, and his modest wig was neatly curled. But not all the efforts of tailor or wig maker could ameliorate the heavy overhanging brow, the truculent look in the extremely deep set eyes, the lantern jaw. He was coming straight for the trees, but a woman's laughter sounded from beyond some massed rhododendron bushes, and he at once touched home his spurs and rode in that direction.

"Phew!" said Rossiter. "I think I'd as well not have to deal with that one! He's a rough-looking customer."

"I'll own I've never cared for him. His hand was crushed in an accident a few years ago, and Papa feels he would never find work elsewhere, so he keeps him on. I think . . . he is very loyal."

"Then I cannot fault him for his looks, can I? He may yet find us, however, and I've little time, so you'd best tell me your news."

She found herself reluctant to do so, and evaded, "First—what happened with the constable? And what did your father say?"

He possessed himself of her hand again. "The constable was dignified and surprisingly intelligent, but could do little more than promise to post descriptions of the culprits. More to the point, none of my people was badly hurt. I found my father . . ." He paused, his expression becoming sombre. "Well, I thought it best not to tell him about the farm."

"He is not ill, I trust?"

"Sick at heart, poor old fellow. He is to appear before the committee again on Tuesday."

Her hand flew to caress his cheek. "Oh, Gideon! I am so sorry."

"And I, love." He kissed her palm gratefully. "Which is why I must make my move today."

At once alarmed, she exclaimed, "Move? What move? Oh, Lud! You are at your scheming again!"

"Be calm, little sprite. Now tell me quickly. You are troubled, I think. I have worried lest your father might have been angered when you returned. You were late, I am assured."

"Yes, but he was not as provoked as I'd feared." She hesitated. "Mr. Bracksby was to dine with us, and he is so entertaining a gentleman."

215

"He is. A splendid fellow. I'd not realized he was acquainted with Collington."

"I was rather surprised also, but they must be good friends, I think, because . . . Mr. Bracksby asked for my hand."

"The *devil* he did!" His grey eyes flashing, Gideon exclaimed hotly, "Of all the unmitigated gall! I judge him my friend, and he slithers into an offer behind my back! By God, I've a mind to call him out!"

Naomi chuckled. "And this from the man who complains that August Falcon is hot-at-hand! My dearest, how was Bracksby to know we are still—er, I mean—"

"You mean that you still love me," he prompted.

"A little bit, perhaps," she said, with a bewitching dimple and a saucy flirt of her shoulders.

This time, there was no approaching groom to terminate their embrace, and after a while, Gideon said huskily, "Only a 'little bit,' my lady?"

Breathless, she straightened her hair. "Sufficiently that I refused poor Mr. Bracksby."

"So I should hope. Did you give him a reason?"

"I told him I shall never marry, and—Gideon—no! Wicked one!"

"Then tell the truth, my beautiful imp."

She gave her little rippling laugh. "I told him that our betrothal should never have been broken, and was to be reinstated."

'Collington will be in a flame,' he thought, and asked, "Was your papa very displeased?"

"He was lived, but Mr. Bracksby interceded for me. With great firmness. He turned the conversation to the lost chess piece and its strange return, and Papa became calmer. I retired before Mr. Bracksby left, and I was sure Papa would come to my room and scold me. Thank heaven he did not."

"Have you seen him today?"

"No. I left before he came downstairs."

"My dear brave lady. All the more reason for me to get to work."

"Do you mean by inspecting the little ruby chessman?"

"No. I suspect the indomitable Jamie still lies snoring. I mean to get into Derrydene's house and have a look about."

Naomi gave a cry of alarm. "How? What do you hope to find?"

"I've no least idea, but he was one of my father's major stockholders, and saw the crash coming in time to withdraw all his funds. I have been unable to talk to him, but I'd give a deal to know from whence came his advance knowledge. I hope to find some correspondence, or a ledger, or *any* least evidence of wrongdoing.''

"But—but if there *is* such evidence he will surely have it well hid! It would take you too long! Oh, my love! You will be discovered!''

"Not an I am careful. Derrydene is in Russia, and his nervous lady is at their country seat.''

"No! She is not! I saw her but yesterday when I was driving out of Town.''

"Do you know her well?''

"Not at all well, for my papa despises her husband and will have nothing to do with them. But I've met her at social functions, of course. That horrid Reggie Smythe was out riding and he stopped to chat with a lady in a carriage. I glanced to see who was suffering from his attentions, and caught a glimpse of the captivating Lady Ada.''

"Are you quite sure, dear girl? That will make things a trifle more chancy.''

"I am very sure. I think she did not wish to be seen, for she drew back at once, but I saw that way she has of fluttering her hands. 'Twas Ada Derrydene, past doubting.''

"Hmm. I thank you for the warning.''

"But you mean to proceed nonetheless. You are prodigious exasperating, sir! Pray tell what I am to do when you have got yourself shot for a robber?''

He grinned. "I'll have you know, Lady Cheerful, that I am a skilled miller of kens, as Tummet would say, and have in fact considered taking up the trade so as to restore my fortune. You cannot object, ma'am, since I'm well aware that your great-grandsire was a successful pirate.''

"I shall ignore that wicked libel,'' said Naomi, and added thoughtfully, "what you need, dearest, is a diversion.'' She brightened. "And I do believe the pirate's great-granddaughter knows the very thing!''

"See here, lovely one,'' he said uneasily. "I'll not have—''

Naomi's eyes grew round with excitement. "La, but 'twill be famous! I must first change my dress, and then . . .''

"The thing is, dear ma'am,'' cooed Naomi, handing the butler her umbrella as she walked into the entrance hall with Lady

217

Derrydene, "I have for so long been fairly yearning to look at your husband's collection of bells, and knowing you must be lonely whilst he is away, I thought I would pay a call, and perhaps persuade you to let me see some of them."

"Ye-es." Lady Louis Derrydene had been a great beauty in her youth, and was still a very handsome woman. On the far side of forty, she had a voluptuous figure, a girlishly coy manner, and long graceful hands of which she was most proud. Her doelike brown eyes surveyed her beautiful caller uncertainly, and she said in a high-pitched fluttery voice, "I was just going out. You see, most of the servants are in Bedfordshire during Sir Louis' absence."

"Ah, then I have called at an inopportune time?"

"Oh, no. I am sure my husband would not wish— Pray do come in, Lady Lutonville. I am not definitely—That is to say . . . I will be glad to show you some of the bells."

"You are too kind. I must instruct my groom—"

"Quinn will do that." Allowing the footman to take their bonnets and cloaks, Lady Derrydene turned to the butler. "Quinn, bring tea to the green saloon, and pray tell Camber to drive the team around to the stables."

Naomi was divested of her cloak, and followed her reluctant hostess along a chilly hall where occasional tables and wall recesses held bells of all shapes and sizes. Gideon should be at the rear by now, surely . . . "Oh, ma'am," she trilled excitedly, seizing a large hanging bell, "I cannot resist! May I try this one?"

Even as she spoke she was swinging the bell vigorously.

The resultant clamour was gratifying. Lady Derrydene gave a shriek and clapped her hands over her ears; two cats raced up the stairs in search of sanctuary, and Gideon had ample time to open a rear window and climb into the book room.

During his loitering about the alley he had made sure that there was no one in the back garden, and that most of the curtains were drawn over the tall, narrow windows. There was still the possibility, however, that his unconventional entrance might have been witnessed from the upper windows, or that a neighbour's servant might have chanced to see him stroll across the lawn. He waited, listening intently, ready to make a run for it in case of a hullabaloo. A second deafening peal of bells almost shocked him out of his boots. Instinctively swinging around, he sent a fine old carven globe tottering, grabbed for it, and swore softly as it crashed to the floor and split in half, the twin sides

218

spinning off in different directions. Fortunately, Naomi's vigorous effort drowned the sounds of his clumsiness, and he gave a sigh of relief when there was no sound of a following investigation.

He ran a keen glance around the room. The crowded untidy bookcases spoke of usage; there were a few comfortable chairs, and a long reference table with three drawers. He went swiftly to the latter. The drawers held the accumulation of years: torn book covers awaiting repair; reference sheets; several magazine articles on great country houses; yellowing pages from *The Spectator* with encircled political articles having to do with the recent tragic Uprising; some childish sketches; broken quill pens; crayons; pencils; rulers. He rifled through the drawers hurriedly, finding nothing to lend any substance to his suspicions. Convinced he was in the wrong room, he moved softly to the door and eased it open.

Distantly, he could hear Naomi talking at full pitch and with scarce a stop for air. He grinned. Lady Derrydene must think she'd taken leave of her senses. The long hall stretched off gloomy and deserted. Most of the doors were closed. To the left was the entrance hall. Probably, the dining rooms were at the same end of the house. Derrydene's study was most likely to be in this area. He turned to his right, and moved quickly and quietly along, wishing he'd had the foresight to remove his spurs, and trying to keep them from jingling. The next door loomed up and he raised the latch carefully, opened the door a crack and peeped into a shuttered morning room. To his horror, it was occupied. A footman and a housemaid were wrapped in a passionate embrace. Stifling a gasp, Rossiter pulled the door to and gingerly lowered the latch. Another bell was chiming merrily, and he called down blessings on the head of his industrious co-spy as the faint click of the latch was drowned in the uproar. The door across the hall was the last, and if this did not turn out to be the study, that chamber must be on the first floor. If he was to attempt it, he must move fast. He crossed the hall, listened at the door, and went inside.

"Aha!" he whispered.

The study had the tidy look that spoke of an absent owner. It was a pleasant room, with rugs of warm colours, red velvet hangings, and deep chairs. Rossiter fairly sprang for the large desk. Disdaining the many papers and unopened letters on the top, he attacked the drawers. One after another yielded only untidiness and clutter. There were old, apparently unpaid bills;

reports from Derrydene's tenants in Bedfordshire; indecipherable letters from the Dowager Lady Derrydene; reports from a Tutor at Eton (seeming to indicate despair).

Abandoning the drawers, Rossiter skimmed through the papers on the top of the desk. More reports; more letters; more bills. And then, a single sheet, the direction, in block letters: TO—SIR LOUIS DERRYDENE. And the letter itself consisting of just four printed words. "Six absent. No meeting." Staring at that message blankly, Rossiter could all but hear Naomi telling him of the two gentlemen at the Dowling Soiree and that they had said "something about a meeting that could not be held until six were recovered." One of those same gentlemen had held a green chessman that Naomi said was similar to the one she had lost. The chessman again! Each time he sought to discover what was behind his father's trouble, he seemed to run headlong against those confounded little figures. " 'Tis too much," he muttered. "It *cannot* be pure coincidence!" He folded the letter and slipped it into his pocket, then went on searching.

There was nothing in the pile of newspapers and correspondence, but an engagement book lay open on the desk. He turned back to the beginning of the year, and turned the pages swiftly. Most of the scrawled notes referred to meetings and appointments. Impatient, he riffled the pages hurriedly, then checked. The date was Tuesday, thirteenth of February, 1748. The notation read: "Do not forget Five!" His pulses beginning to race, Gideon flipped more pages. On February twenty-seventh, his hand checked once more. 7:00 P.M. Davies.

He gasped out, *"Davies!"* The same Davies who had embezzled over a hundred thousand pounds from Rossiter Bank? It was a fairly common name—it could be another man, but intuition told him it was not. A week before the crash, Sir Louis Derrydene had seen Davies privately. Why?

Taut with excitement, he flipped the pages. Thursday, March seventh. "Withdraw." His fist crashed onto the desk. He snarled, *"Withdraw!* Yes, you withdrew—you filthy, treacherous hound!"

Footsteps sounded in the hall. The engagement book still in his hand, he made a dive for the door and pressed back against the wall beside it. He held his breath as the latch was raised. Thrusting the book into one pocket, he reached into the other for his pistol.

A hand gripped the edge of the door and held it open. A man's

London voice said reassuringly, "There y'are, me little duck. Did I not tell yer? Empty as a bishop's purse."

A girl sounded scared. "I tell you I heered *summat*, Alfred. A man what was very cross, and bein's the master's back, I thought— If he should catch us . . . !"

"He's got more important things ter think on than you and me, never you fear. Come on, now. We'd best not get Cook into a uproar, wondering where you is. Be a good little gal, and we'll go fer a row on the river Sunday."

The door closed on an ecstatic, "Oooo!"

Rossiter slipped the pistol back into his pocket.

". . . the master's back . . ." Was that simply Derrydene? Or was Derrydene also the mysterious Squire to whom the bullies had referred? Either way, thought Rossiter, there was some proof now. He had the engagement book, and the succinct letter. Surely the Lord Chancellor's committee must pay some attention when he explained it all? But if Sir Louis had indeed returned from Russia (if he ever *went!*) every minute's delay here increased the danger of discovery. He eased the door open. The amorous footman and his lass had vanished and the hall was hushed and empty.

Moving swiftly, Rossiter returned to the book room. He started for the window. His boot sent something scuttling across the floor and he glanced down to discover one half of the globe he'd knocked over earlier. The drizzle had stopped and a weak sun sent an enquiring beam slanting across the rug. It awoke a blue sparkle from inside the globe. Curious, Rossiter bent lower. His breath was snatched away. He took up the half globe and removed an object that had lain concealed inside. A small figure carven from what he thought to be lapis lazuli, the beautiful blue stone so much admired by Marco Polo. There could be no doubt but that this little fellow was related to the figure Naomi had sketched. It was of the same size and shape, but the "face" had an oddly humorous expression. It was surprisingly heavy for its size, and was set with no fewer than six fine sapphires.

"By God . . . !" breathed Rossiter.

"Put it down," said a cold voice.

He froze, then jerked around.

He had never much cared for Sir Louis Derrydene. During the six years since last he had seen the baronet, the pasty cheeks seemed to have become even more inclined to sag, the small mouth looked paler and tighter, the tendency to corpulence was more pronounced. But the hand holding the horse pistol was

221

steady as a rock, and there was no doubting that death shone from the hard dark eyes.

"Well, well," drawled Rossiter. "So my father's trusted friend has crept from his hole."

A faint flush lit the flabby cheeks, but Derrydene repeated softly, "Put . . . it . . . down."

"Why? It will look so nice with"—he ventured a wild guess—"with six."

And he had struck home! He saw Derrydene's white hand jerk, saw the small mouth fall open, the little eyes widen with shock, and knew it was now or never.

The half globe was still in his left hand and it was quite heavy. He hurled it straight at Derrydene's face and in the same instant flung himself to one side. His conviction that the baronet would not hesitate to shoot was verified. The pistol bloomed smoke and flame. The retort was deafening, but Rossiter had moved very fast, and the ball hummed past him. Teeth bared with rage, Derrydene sprang, flailing the pistol at his head. Rossiter ducked, evading the blow. Derrydene snatched for the jewelled figure. He was bigger and heavier than Rossiter, and surprisingly strong. Reluctant to hit an older man, Rossiter panted, "Let go! I don't want to—hurt you."

Derrydene's response was to again smash the pistol at his face. He jerked his head aside, and the weapon grazed his temple. Locked in a desperate struggle, they reeled about the room, sending chairs and small tables flying. Rossiter knew that time was running out; the shot had certainly been heard. At any instant Derrydene's people would be in here. He tore free and retreated. The baronet charged him. He swayed aside and gave a helping hand. At speed, Derrydene encountered the wall, and went down heavily.

Feet were pounding along the hall. Rossiter scooped up the little blue figure, and raced for the window.

"You're . . . dead," choked Derrydene, gobbling with frustrated fury. "You damnable . . . interfering fool. You're a . . . dead man!"

Rossiter called, "Can't stop to chat. Sorry," and was over the sill and sprinting across the back lawn.

Someone howled, "Stop, or I'll shoot!"

"Not today," muttered Rossiter, and zigzagged. Two shots thundered out. He felt a tug at his right elbow, then the wall was before him. He cleared it with astonishing ease and not so much as a pang from his many bruises.

The clock on the dingy wall of this dingy room emitted a staccato rattling sound, then chimed once, a second chime being added after several intervening seconds, as if in afterthought. Glaring at it, Gideon stamped back to the bench where Naomi waited.

"Two o'clock!" he growled. "We have been here nigh on two hours! Derrydene has likely already been in touch with his solicitor and fabricated some cock-and-bull story to conflummerate the authorities. Such as they are!"

"If he is not on his way back to Moscow," said Naomi.

He swore under his breath. "I vow that clerk was very well to live. He reeked of ale! I wonder if he even sought the magistrate, or is fallen asleep t'other side of that door."

He began to pace up and down again. Naomi watched him lovingly. When she'd heard the first shot she had thought for one ghastly moment that he must have been slain. Lady Derrydene had run, screaming, down the hall, and she had followed, dreading what they might find. As they'd passed the dining room, two more shots had rung out, and she'd caught a glimpse of Gideon soaring over the wall with an easy grace that had set her fears at rest. She had stayed long enough to determine that although he was practically apoplectic with rage, Derrydane was relatively unharmed. Then, she had quietly slipped away, sending a lackey to call up her carriage. Gideon had joined them at the next corner, and rode beside the carriage to Bow Street.

A watchman had guided them to this unfortunate chamber. He had listened, goggle eyed, to Gideon's terse demands that constables be at once sent to apprehend Sir Louis Derrydene. Muttering that he must "fetch someone in authority" he had gone away, to reappear with a clerk. The clerk had explained that the magistrate was busied with another case, and that it would be necessary to first take down "the particulars." Not all Gideon's rageful insistence on the necessity for speedy action had moved this stolid minion of the law, and he had laboriously written out his report, then gone in search of the magistrate.

Disregarding the constable who sat by the outer door, Gideon strode to the inner door and pounded on it angrily. "Hey!" he shouted. "Have you all expired in there?"

"Now then, sir," protested the constable, running over, much shocked. "You cannot be a'doing of that in here! I speck as his honour's at his luncheon and you'll just have to wait."

"I *have* been waiting! Two confounded hours! And the

lady—" Gideon returned to sit on the bench beside Naomi and take her hand. "My poor love," he exclaimed contritely. "You must be starving hungry! I'll call up your carriage and have you taken home. This idiotic magistrate will probably—"

"Do you refer to me, Captain Rossiter?"

The dry voice came from a stringy little man with a grey face and a grey and greasy wig, who had taken a seat behind a battered desk against the rear wall, and was surveying them through a dirty quizzing glass.

Gideon sprang to his feet and hurried to the desk. "Sir, I presume that you have read my statement and seen the evidence I handed your clerk. There has already been much time lost, and you must make haste, else this scheming rascal will—"

"I have here," interrupted the magistrate, turning his quizzing glass on the various items before him and peering at them near-sightedly, "one letter; exceeding brief and of little significance. One engagement book containing entries of no interest. And what appears to be a child's toy. I find it little short of incredible that on the strength—or perhaps I should say the weakness—of these objects, you expect me to take seriously the allegations you have made 'gainst a respectable and titled gentleman."

"Good God, man!" burst out Rossiter. "Did you not read my statement? It took that block of a clerk the better part of half an hour to—"

"Now then, sir," intervened the constable, again coming forward and looking shocked. "You mustn't talk to the magistrate like that there. You must call him 'your honour' and you must be respeckful when—"

"Respectful! Why you dimwit, don't you know that while we fripper about and do nothing, Derrydene is doubtless making haste out of the country?"

"Sir Louis Derrydene," said the magistrate in his sour voice, "is a gentleman whose only misstep in an otherwise exemplary life appears to have been to become associated with Rossiter Bank."

"*Associated*, do you say, sir," roared Gideon. "That scoundrel damn near ruined my father with his trickery and—"

"And I will not allow slanderous statements of no foundation to be made in this court," interrupted the magistrate shrilly. Jabbing his quizzing glass at Gideon, he leaned forward. "I have heard some cock-and-bull fustian in my time, Captain Rossiter. But this—this mishmash you have brought me is downright ri-

224

diculous! You have wasted my time, sir; you have treated this court with contempt; you have used unseemly language before not only the appointed representative of law and order, but"—the quizzing glass slid to the side, the little eyes glittered, and the wizened face contorted into a grimace that might have been a smile—"before this lovely lady." He returned his gaze to the fuming Rossiter, and his smile became a scowl. "Disgraceful," he said, and rapped his quizzing glass on the desk. "Fifty guineas."

"Fifty guineas!" exclaimed Rossiter. "What the deuce for? You have done nothing!"

"We will make it—*sixty* guineas," snapped the magistrate. "And one more outburst will provoke me into indeed doing something, sir, for I shall have you clapped up, sir!"

Naomi hurried to Gideon's side and bent her most winning smile on the representative of law and order. "I do apologize for my affianced, your honour," she murmured softly. "He is but now returned from the Low Countries, where he was seriously wounded and came near to dying. He is not quite himself as yet. In fact, I do suspect . . ." Ignoring Gideon's impatient growl, she leaned nearer and lowered her voice to a confidential whisper.

The nostrils of the representative of law and order caught the essence of *eau de jasmin*; the quizzing glass was brought to bear on the rich soft swell of my lady's snowy bosom, and the little beady eyes softened. "Poor fellow," he murmured. "Poor fellow. I quite understand, my dear. You are to be commended for your loyalty. Take him away. As for you, sir," the quizzing glass swung to Gideon's angry face. "You are greatly blessed, and do not deserve it. I shall lower your fine to twenty guineas, and warn you not to waste the time of this court in future!"

Seeing Gideon's expression, Naomi rested her hand on his arm. "Please pay his honour, my love. 'Tis time for you to go home and have your nap."

Seething with frustrated fury, Gideon exchanged his evidence for twenty guineas, and retreated in disorder.

❧ Chapter 16 ❧

"Never saw anything like it." Viscount Horatio Glendenning sat at the table of the cheerful breakfast room in his father's house, and gazed curiously at the miniature in the palm of his hand. "It's a murky brew to be sure." He looked up. "What d'you mean to do with the silly thing, Ross?"

Much restored by the delicious luncheon Lord Bowers-Malden's chef had prepared for them, Rossiter said, "Try to find some expert who can tell me something of the figures. I've a mind to take them to Oxford and see if anyone at the Bodleian knows aught of their history. What do you say, my lady?"

Naomi put down her coffee cup and admitted that she could not understand what the tiny figures had to do with Sir Mark Rossiter's troubles. "More to the point, dear Tio, is what will happen now. If Sir Louis Derrydene has Gideon arrested—"

Rossiter bent forward to place his long fingers over her hand and say with a reassuring grin that there was no cause to worry on that score. " 'Twould draw attention to his crafty schemes, which is the last thing he wants." He glanced at his friend. "I'm far more concerned with the probability that the bas—the rogue will slither out of the country."

Naomi said soothingly, "Well, you have sent Tummet to watch his house, dear. He will let you know at once if there is any sign of that."

"And if he does," said Glendenning, "what shall you do?"

Rossiter scowled. "Everything in my power to prevent the treacherous cur escaping before he can be brought to book."

"You may count on my help, dear boy. London's been downright boring of late. I'd enjoy a lively scrap for a change."

"That's dashed good of you, Tio. I wonder, though—might

226

your father help us, do you think? The backing of a man of influence would be invaluable, and he seems to have kept an open mind about the Rossiters. To an extent, at least.''

Glendenning gave him a rueful look. ''Beastly luck, Ross, but Bowers-Malden is in Ireland. Went to have a look at a mare he's been particularly interested in. He left yesterday morning, and I don't expect him to return for at least three weeks.''

''Hell!'' muttered Rossiter under his breath, and racking his brains, said, ''Perhaps—Boudreaux . . . ?''

Naomi said uneasily, ''Surely Lord Boudreaux is out of favour, since his nephew was discovered to be a Jacobite sympathizer?''

Startled, Rossiter's gaze shot to Glendenning. ''Not Trevelyan de Villars? Good Lord! Did they execute him?''

''Tried to, dear boy. But he managed to get to France and I hear is now most happily married and soon to blessed by *un petit pacquet*. Still, your lady is quite correct, his uncle's help, even were it given, might prove more an embarrassment than a blessing.''

Rossiter's heart sank. Gordon Chandler's sire would stand by them, he knew, but Sir Brian Chandler's health was not good, and he seldom stirred far from his great estate near Dover. 'Whatever is to be done,' he thought, 'I must do it.' And he must do it fast, because Jamie had likely arrived by this time. He glanced at the clock uneasily. ''I wish Gwendolyn and your sister would come home. How long have they been out shopping?''

''Oh, hours,'' said Glendenning breezily. ''When they have chattered their way through the bazaars and milliners, I believe they mean to visit every bookshop on London Bridge, and will likely not leave until the last one is closed. Matter of fact, Marguerite has invited Gwen to stay for a few days. Have we your permission, Ross, to keep your pretty sister with us?''

''Lord, yes!'' Relieved for several reasons, Gideon said, ''Gwen will be in alt! Thank you, Tio. You're—er, sure Lady Bowers-Malden will not object?''

His lordship declared that his mama was exceeding fond of Gwendolyn, and would be delighted. Then, with a conspiratorial wink he excused himself to go and call up the carriage.

Thus left most improperly alone with his lady, Rossiter lost no time in taking her into his arms. Naomi was worried, and clung to him, anxious to know when and where they would meet again. He told her that he'd promised to ride with his father the following morning, and would be unable to meet her in the park. She accepted this falsehood without question, and they then devised a plan whereby either Tummet or Maggie would relay messages. Such hole-and-corner tactics were abhorrent to them both, but Gideon promised that the need for secrecy would soon be over. Despite the total inefficiency of the authorities, he was convinced his evidence would influence the Lord Chancellor's committee. Once his father's good name was restored, it should, he said cheerfully, be a simple matter to clear the way so that he could marry the lady he loved so deeply.

"One thing," he warned, kissing the end of her dainty little nose. "Do not run off with Bracksby before I've the chance to formally offer for you again. He's a jolly good man and I'd hate like the deuce to have to put a period to him."

Trying to match his insouciance, Naomi said pertly that she was far more inclined to run off with Reggie Smythe. The price she had to pay for that piece of flippancy left her deliciously breathless, and she was able to leave Gideon with hope in her heart, and a smile on her lips.

The skies had darkened, and thunder was rolling down the sky by the time Gideon returned to Snow Hill. Lieutenant Morris had already arrived and was closeted in the book room with Sir Mark and Newby. They looked up from inspecting the ruby figure, and Morris said aggrievedly, "You send me off with instructions to make haste. Having risen at the crack of dawn and fought my way through numerous desperate encounters for your sake, I arrive to find you are gallivanting about somewhere!"

With a grin, Gideon wrung his outstretched hand. "An I know you, Jamie, your dawn cracked at ten o'clock, and your desperate encounters involved no more than fighting your way from the breakfast table! Still, you deserve a medal for bringing me this article!" He took up the ruby figure and looked at it curiously. "If only you could speak, little man . . ."

Sir Mark said, "I'd sooner hear from you, boy. What have you been about?"

"Quite a deal, sir. Has anyone come—er, looking for me?"

Newby drawled, "A messenger brought a letter for you."

"I have it here." Sir Mark handed Gideon a sealed paper. "And a Bow Street Runner came to enquire about the accident with the coach on Wednesday night. Very ponderous and pains-taking. All wind and no worth.''

Gideon broke the seal, and read aloud:

Dear Captain Rossiter:
   I understand that you are in possession of one of the pieces of the Jewelled Men collection. I also am a most ardent ad-mirer of these works of art, and 'tis my hope to eventually own the entire set. In view of the antiquity of the figures, I will not insult your intelligence by offering a lesser sum than One Thousand Pounds for the piece you hold.

''God bless my soul!'' gasped Sir Mark.

Newby whistled softly. ''How can so small and unattractive an object be so valuable?''

Gideon exchanged a glance with Morris, and read on:

   We have not met, but I stay at the Inn of The Blue Heron in Kensington Village, and should you be in the least interested in my proposition, you will be most eagerly welcomed by—
                                         Your fellow collector,
                                         Thomas Kendall-Parker

''One thousand pounds,'' muttered Lieutenant Morris. ''Jove, 'tis a vast sum!''

''He'll have to double it, at least,'' said Gideon, and setting aside the letter, took the blue figure from his coat pocket and laid it on the table.

''Stap me!'' Newby leapt to his feet and snatched it up. ''You've more sense than I credited you with, twin. These two together will command a princely sum! If this Kendall-Parker fellow offers a thousand, you may be sure they're worth two or three times that much!''

Sir Mark said, ''To judge from the graze on your forehead, I think you did not come by that easily, my boy.''

''Not exactly, sir.'' Gideon related the day's events as suc-cinctly as possible, his story often interrupted by exclamations of excitement or anger. When he finished, Sir Mark was on his feet, his face flushed and eyes sparking wrath. ''That treacher-ous hound! Not content with the betrayal of his trust, Derrydene has the bare-faced gall to threaten my son!''

''And I fancy is well on his way to France by this time,'' muttered Newby.

229

"I doubt that," said Gideon. "I've Tummet keeping watch on his house, and Glendenning has promised to send word at once should Derrydene attempt to run." He added, "Do you see now, Papa, how these strange little figures are in some way bound up with the conspiracy 'gainst you?"

Sir Mark said triumphantly, "Then you own 'tis indeed a conspiracy?"

"I think we must all see that now, sir," said Morris. "The thing is, we've to convince the Courts."

"Those blockheads at Bow Street should have acted at once on what Gideon told them," said Sir Mark angrily. "But my word carries some weight yet, I think. I shall go to the Horse Guards. I've an introduction to General Underhill, and with luck I'll persuade him to—" He paused as an ear-splitting clap of thunder shook the windows.

The door opened, and Wilson announced, "A messenger from Lord Horatio Glendenning."

A liveried lackey was shown in, raindrops gleaming on his cloak and tricorne. After a swift scan of the room, he went straight to Gideon. "His lordship's compliments, sir, and I am to say that your man has been relieved for a few hours, but will go back on guard at ten tonight. His lordship don't think there's much danger of flight, because in accord with your instructions, two Watchmen has also been set outside the house."

"Good!" exclaimed Gideon. "Then that rascal is laid by the heels for tonight, at least!"

"*You* suggested the Watch keep an eye on Derrydene's house?" said Sir Mark. "I wonder they heeded you."

"They would not have, if the suggestion had come from me, sir. I asked Tio to request it—in his father's name."

"Jolly good notion," said Morris, laughing. "I fancy Sir Louis is biting his teeth with frustration."

Gideon tipped the lackey and sent him off with a note of thanks to Lord Horatio. Glancing at the window, he said, "It looks to be a bad night, Father. Perhaps you should postpone your call at the Horse Guards."

Sir Mark did not enjoy negotiating the hill in wet weather, and he agreed to this, adding, "We'll all go over there first thing in the morning."

Gideon said apologetically, "I'm afraid 'twill have to be just you and my brother, sir."

"Why, damn?" demanded Sir Mark, at once firing up. "I should like both my sons at my side, for once!"

Morris precipitated another uproar. "Gideon has a prior appointment in the morning, sir. With August Falcon."

The skies were low-hanging and leaden, the air was chill, and in the jolting carriage Morris, not at his best before breakfast, grumbled. "Perry Cranford's a good enough fellow, I give you that. But—Kadenworthy? Gad! Of course, one has to consider that Falcon's not exactly surrounded by admiring cronies, but I hope he don't have Kadenworthy for a second when I fight him. Cannot abide the man."

Rossiter pulled his cloak tighter and said thoughtfully, "I think I don't know the gentleman. Didn't he go out with de Villars once?"

"Yes, and Treve almost told his tale for him! They're friends now, I hear. Lord knows why. Kadenworthy's tongue is every bit as acid as Falcon's."

"Your future brother-in-law," said Gideon slyly.

Morris groaned. "One has to take the bitter with the better."

Amused, Gideon asked, "Have you made any progress, Jamie?"

"She smiled on me"—a dreamy expression replaced Morris' gloom—"and told me I was brave. And she bandaged my hand. Her touch was light as any feather."

Rossiter peered at the bandage. "You should change that, y'know."

"Never!" Morris touched the grey linen very gently. "Her little hand placed it there, and there it shall stay."

"Gad, but you're properly smitten! Lord knows, I wish you well, but—if the lady ever should accept you, would your father—er, be displeased?"

"What the deuce d'you mean by that? Miss Katrina is the loveliest creature in all England, and if you insinuate that my papa might object because some stupid bigoted fools say she's a half-caste—"

"You think he would not, then?"

"Most definitely not! And—and if he did . . . Well, I'd win him over, be damned if I'd not." He sighed and said ruefully, "You and I tread thorny paths to win our ladies, eh?"

Gideon's slow smile dawned. "True. Speaking of paths, Jamie, do you go with me to see this collector fellow when my silly duel is out of the way?"

Morris said staunchly that he certainly meant to "trot along." Inwardly, he was apprehensive as to the outcome of this meeting. Not quite two weeks ago the military surgeon had told Gideon to enjoy a good long rest and he would soon be as fit as ever. Far from resting, his life had since been one long riot. Oddly enough, he did look better; probably because he was so deep in love with the Lady Naomi. Still, the bruises on his side were more lurid than ever, and although he made light of it, he tended to move rather stiffly. If only Falcon wasn't such a damned fine swordsman . . . Of course, if the ground was marshy that might even the odds a trifle. He peered out of the window hopefully.

The skies were a little brighter when they reached the site, which was located in the fields some half-mile beyond the end of the park. Viscount Glendenning and Falcon's seconds, Peregrine Cranford and Lord Kadenworthy, were already looking over the ground. Gideon was acquainted with Cranford, a slim and handsome young man with intensely blue eyes, a ready smile, and a quick temper. Shaking hands, Gideon said, "How d'ye do, Perry? I see you've had a spot of trouble. Accident?"

"Prestonpans," answered Cranford with a grin. "We'd a small war of our own whilst you was away, you know. My silly foot disputed the right of way with a gun carriage." He saw Rossiter's instinctive sympathetic wince and said cheerily, "But don't be thinking this peg-leg a hindrance. I can hop about pretty well, as you'll soon discover."

Gideon clapped him on the back and turned to Kadenworthy. That tall and elegant gentleman gave him a nod and a cool stare and was apparently quite unable to see his outstretched hand. "I trust your man has webbed feet, Morris," he drawled. "He has a fine bog to fight on."

Morris stared at him in icy silence.

With so many matters preying on his mind, Rossiter had momentarily forgotten his disgrace, and he flushed a little as he turned to ask Glendenning whether Falcon had arrived.

"He's in his carriage, playing cards with the doctor," said the viscount, throwing an irked look at Kadenworthy.

The seconds conferred briefly. Since this was a matter in which blows had been struck and apologies were neither offered nor expected, there had been small effort to achieve a reconciliation between the principals. The swords, both hollow and well balanced, were compared for length, and approved. The seconds had agreed to obtain the services of only one surgeon, and that gentleman now left the carriage, bag in one hand and an apple in the other. Minutes later, Rossiter and Falcon, having removed

232

their coats and rolled back their ruffles, stood face-to-face with swords raised in the salute.

Falcon opened the offensive. He had an odd way of fighting, crouching slightly, his left arm held palm up but out to the side rather than extended behind him in the customary fashion. His thrust in *carte* followed the barest of exchanges after the initial salute, as though he had quickly taken the measure of his opponent. Rossiter, no mean swordsman, instantly parried with the heel of his blade, returned the thrust within the sword and returned to his guard. He was astonished to hear Falcon's half-whispered "Good," and saw the thin lips curve into a smile. No opening was allowed, however, and a second later Falcon's sword darted for his chest in a powerful *tierce* thrust. Again, Rossiter parried successfully, and returned in *tierce*. Falcon shifted into *sexte* and increased the pace of his attack, and the swords rang together like rapidly erratic bell chimes, the duellists moving gracefully despite the fact that the condition of the ground had forbidden they remove their shoes.

From the outset Rossiter had known not only that he faced a magnificent swordsman but that as he'd suspected his bruises and the old wound in his leg were going to hinder him. He had not the slightest doubt but that although Falcon meant to enjoy himself, this would not be a killing matter. On the other hand, they had agreed on "first blood," and to be disabled at this particular time did not at all suit his plans. His lips tightened determinedly, his eyes narrowed to an intent stare, and he bent every ounce of his concentration on the struggle.

Falcon, very fast, and obviously in his element, not only set a fierce pace, but covered a lot of ground, so that the seconds, each with sword drawn and ready, were obliged to be constantly on the move. Following a flurry of attacks, lightning swift, Falcon thrust in *seconde*. Rossiter parried with a prime parade and returned the thrust in prime, recovering in the nick of time as Falcon essayed a brilliant counter disengage.

"Hey!" yelled Cranford, a note in his voice that caused Glendenning to at once run in to strike up the blades of the duellists.

They all turned to discover the cause of the objection. Besides being very red-faced, Cranford was standing at a decidedly odd angle, gripping his right knee.

Glendenning said, "Oh, I say! Are you stuck, Perry?" and hurried to him.

Cranford was indeed stuck, his peg-leg having sunk deep into the mud.

There was a good deal of hilarity and horseplay involved in the rescue effort, and Morris and Glendenning cheered lustily as Cranford was freed. Falcon's brow was black, however, noting which Morris said innocently, "Cheer up, Falcon. The duel is quite *inchoate*, you know."

This deliberate provocation caused Rossiter to chuckle, but did little to improve Falcon's fast-deteriorating mood. Ignoring Morris, he demanded, "Why the deuce didn't you wear your false foot, Cranford?"

"Blasted thing's always falling off," said Cranford apologetically. "Sorry, August. I hadn't counted on that confounded storm last night, else I'd have brought it up to Town with me."

Kadenworthy asked, "All right, Perry?"

Cranford said he was perfectly all right, but he eyed the muddy ground apprehensively.

Morris suggested to Falcon that he postpone. "You look ripe for a seizure, old boy, and likely should lie down and rest awhile."

"Of course I shall not postpone," snarled Falcon, and meeting Kadenworthy's ironic glance, added in an undervoice, "fellow's got the nous of a newt!"

Intrigued, Morris asked, "Who has?" and peered at Kadenworthy. "Jove, but you're right. His nose *does* look rather like—"

"I said *nous*, you silly block!" roared Falcon. "And I referred to *you!*"

"Did you, by Jove!" Morris turned to Kadenworthy, whose brown eyes suddenly were glinting with amusement. "My apologies, my lord. I thought he meant—"

"Damn you, you thought nothing of the kind," said Kadenworthy. "And if you must know, Morris, my nose is often admired as being truly Roman."

Falcon snapped, "You have my unqualified permission to stand here and admire it, Morris, so that the rest of us can get on with this."

There was a concerted laugh, and with an amused eye on Falcon's choleric countenance, Rossiter requested that they move to less cut-up ground. This was soon accomplished, and the *affaire d'honneur* resumed.

The interruption had provided Rossiter with a much-needed respite, but Falcon was angry now, and fought with an intensity that kept Rossiter constantly on the defensive. Time and again his sword turned Falcon's thrusts at the last instant, but turn them it did, so that a grudging admiration dawned in Falcon's night-blue eyes, and Morris began to hope his friend might yet win this fight. Hard-driven, Rossiter risked a feint, appearing to give Falcon a wide opening. Falcon thrust savagely and for an instant Rossiter thought he'd allowed his point to stray too far to the right. His sword flashed into a lunge, but to his surprise the blade went over his opponent's head. Falcon's foot had slipped. He uttered a shocked cry, and impelled by the force of his attack, he shot past Rossiter, sprawled face down, and slid for several yards.

Morris' shriek of laughter brought howls from the others. Breathing hard, and grinning widely, Rossiter tucked his sword under his arm, and went to extend a helping hand.

Falcon sat up and glared at him in muddy and impotent fury. His chin, his immaculate shirt and breeches, were a disaster, and his sword was plunged hilt deep in the grasses.

Morris ran up, and grasping the weapon wrenched it forth and waved it on high, shouting irrepressibly, "*Excalibur!* Long live . . . the king!"

The air rang with their laughter, the surgeon's hilarity reducing him to tears.

It was a mirth Falcon did not share. "You . . . damned silly *dolt*!" he spluttered, springing to his feet and tearing the sword from Morris' hand. "Think it funny, do you? By God, I'll show you—"

Rossiter stepped in front of the enraged man and said sharply, "Control that ugly temper, Falcon, and try for a little sportsmanship. Morris meant no offence."

"Yes, I did, Ross," sighed Morris, wiping his eyes. "I meant to show him how *nous* he is!"

Falcon made a gobbling sound and sprang for him.

Weak with mirth, Glendenning pulled Falcon back. "Morris, *will* you behave? No really, August, you're supposed to be fighting *Rossiter*. At all events, we must terminate this fiasco. You're in no condition to—"

"Devil I'm not," snarled Falcon, livid. "We'll finish. Here and now! Unless Rossiter's looking for the coward's way out."

All amusement faded. Breaking the sudden hush, Rossiter said coolly, "I'll allow your man a moment to clean his hands, Perry."

"Good of you," said Cranford, frowning.

Falcon used his handkerchief to wipe the mud from his hands, then took up his sword, and the unconventional duel went on.

235

If Falcon had been dangerous before, he was deadly now, fighting with a grim savagery that left little doubt of his intent to take revenge for his humiliation. Rossiter occasionally managed to attack, but without fail his blade was parried and the answering thrusts taxed his skill to the utmost. His left shoulder throbbed fiercely, and his breath came hard from lungs that burned. Every movement of the sword seemed to tear at his bruised side, and his footwork was markedly less agile than at the start. Falcon's sword was a brightly shining living thing that attacked with never-ending speed and vigour, darting at him from all angles. Rossiter fought on doggedly, but no one was more surprised than he when a desperate glizade sent the weapon spinning from his opponent's hand.

A shout of excitement went up from the seconds, and the doctor, who had dropped his apple and gazed, riveted, at the ferocious fight, gave a whoop.

Nobody moved to pick up the weapon, and Falcon stood mute, staring in obvious amazement at his adversary.

Pantingly incapable of speech, Rossiter wiped his sweating sword hand on his breeches, and waited.

Through that startled moment came a shriek. "Gideon! Gideon!"

"Oh, my *God*!" groaned Falcon.

Rossiter stared in disbelief. "Gwen . . . ?"

"*Stop!* Stop at once!" Holding up the skirts of her riding habit, and leading her horse, Gwendolyn limped to them.

"I say," muttered Morris, aghast. "This ain't proper, Ross! Get her away!"

"The first sensible remark you were ever heard to utter," said Falcon, walking over to reclaim his sword.

A flurry of draperies, a whiff of roses, and a very small boot stamped down on the weapon. "You must *stop*!" she panted. "Listen to me!"

"Here—get off," growled Falcon, gripping the hilt and tugging tentatively.

"I will not! Oh, you horrid man, *will* you desist?"

Much embarrassed, Rossiter panted, "I don't know how—you discovered where we were, Gwen, but you really—must not interfere in a—"

Falcon, who had dropped to one knee, drew back. "She's going to bend my sword," he protested fumingly. "Get her off!"

236

In response, Gwendolyn dealt him a telling blow with her riding crop. "Wretched creature! Have done!"

He gave a yelp, and threw up one hand to protect his head while holding the grip of the sword with the other.

Titillated, seconds and surgeon retreated to a safe distance, while watching avidly.

Gwendolyn saw Rossiter advancing, stern-faced, and jumped up and down twice.

"Stop that at once!" cried Rossiter. "You'll cut yourself!"

"Cut herself, my eye!" said Falcon bitterly. "Now look what she's done!" He held up a sword that curved rather pathetically. "You've bent my Colichemarde, you silly chit!"

Morris wheezed. "Try it for a scythe, old boy."

Ignoring the barely suppressed laughter, Falcon raged, "I *told* you I wouldn't kill your stupid clod of a brother!"

"You—*what*?" demanded Rossiter.

"She came and begged me to spare your life," said Falcon.

A horrified gasp went up.

Momentarily diverted, Gwendolyn said sternly, "Gentlemen do not tell tales!"

Rossiter flushed scarlet. "Gwen! You *never* did so awful a thing?"

"Oh! What am I *thinking* of," cried Gwendolyn, recovering herself. "*Listen* to me! Something—"

"Besides, I *ain't* a gentleman," jeered Falcon. "And you may think you've spoiled our duel, my girl, but—"

"Damn you! Don't call her 'my girl,' " interrupted Rossiter fiercely.

"*Will—you—stop?*" shrieked Gwendolyn at the top of her lungs.

Cranford muttered nervously, "We'll have the Watch here in a—" He shrank into silence as Gwendolyn's wide eyes flashed to him.

"Naomi . . ." she said, turning to her brother. *"Naomi . . ."*

Falcon pushed between them. "What about Naomi?"

She looked up at him, her eyes suddenly brimming. "She has been—*stolen*!" she wailed, and throwing herself on his chest, burst into tears.

Three carriages raced across London on that cool Saturday morning, scattering traffic and avoiding disaster by a hair's breadth. Rossiter, his sister, and Lieutenant Morris occupied the first coach. Falcon and Lord Kadenworthy followed close behind; and bringing up the rear, Horatio Glendenning and Peregrine Cranford were accompanied by Dr. Lockhart.

With his arm tight around his sister, his face pale and strained, and a sick terror gnawing at him, Rossiter asked, "Did you recognize any of them, Gwen? Did you see anything at all that might help us find them?"

Gwendolyn shook her head miserably. "We were riding, you see. There weren't many people in the park because it was rather chilly. We heard some horses coming up behind us, and before I realized what was happening, they'd pushed in between us, and Naomi was—was sort of . . . swept away at the gallop! It happened so fast! At first, I thought it a mistake . . . I couldn't believe . . ." Her voice scratched into a sob.

Scowling, Morris said, "And Lady Naomi did not cry out? She made no effort to get away?"

"No. I think she would have had no chance. She was quite surrounded. There were five men, and all wearing cloaks with the collars turned up, and hats pulled low. I—I didn't even see one face! Oh, poor Naomi! She was so kind to invite me to ride. And—now . . ." Gwendolyn looked up into her brother's drawn face frantically. "They won't hurt her? You don't think they would hurt her?"

That fear was tearing Gideon's nerves to shreds. Naomi was spirited and courageous, but she was a lady of gentle upbringing, suddenly helpless and alone in the hands of a set of vicious criminals. She must be terrified—praying for him to come to her. And by God, he *would* come! Somehow, he'd find her!

Full of sympathy for the anguish in his friend's eyes, Morris said bracingly, "Oh, I wouldn't be imagining such villainy as that, ma'am. You said they shouted that Lady Naomi would not be harmed if you kept away from the Watch. You've done that."

Rossiter pulled himself together. "Yes. You've been splendid, Gwen. Tell me, was Camber with you? You surely did not ride alone?"

"He was with us at the start, but Naomi wanted to go for a gallop, since there were so few riders in the Row. She said Camber would not approve, so we—er—"

"So you gave him the slip." Morris shook his head. "My sister was used to do hare-brained things like that."

Rossiter asked, "How did you find us?"

"I knew about the duel," she replied in a small, shaken voice. "And I know duels are often fought in the park, but I didn't know where to look until Tummet came up and—"

"Tummet!" interrupted Rossiter harshly. "Was he with them?"

"No, no. I think he was following them. I was so frightened, and so glad to see him! I explained what had happened, and he said I must find you, and told me where to come."

The eyes of the two men met. Morris said softly, "You never think—Derrydene?"

"By God, but I do! I left Tummet watching that house. He must have seen the bullies come and decided to follow them. I only pray he keeps after the filthy swine!"

"And you believe they will be in touch with the earl?"

Gideon nodded. "Unless I'm very much mistaken, Jamie, Naomi is being held for ransom. And the ransom price is those two damnable little jewelled men!"

❧ *Chapter 17* ❧

Simon Lutonville, the Earl of Collington, ran in most undignified fashion to the open front door of his London mansion as the three lathered teams came at the gallop around the corner from the Strand and lurched to a halt at the kennel.

His face set and grim, Rossiter sprang from the leading coach without waiting for the steps to be let down, and was first to reach the earl.

"You've heard what happened, sir?"

"Aye, and unable to move a muscle 'til you saw fit to come here, blast you!"

The earl looked wild and distraught as he took in the small crowd assembling on his doorstep. "Who the devil are all these people? Oh, it's you, Glendenning. Well, come in. I collect you're all aware of this damnable business!"

They followed him inside, the doctor still clutching his bag. Leading the way to his study, Collington said in a voice harsh with strain, "I demand to know why my daughter should be held to ransom because of some havey-cavey affair involving *you*, Rossiter! I told her to keep clear of you! God knows, I warned her that your entire family is an unmitigated disaster! Had she but—"

Rossiter broke into the hysterical tirade with a sharp, "My lord, we have time only to find a way to free Naomi. I beg that you will tell us what you know of it."

Collington stared at him in shocked fashion for an instant, then drew a hand across his mouth. His eyes closed, and he swayed a little. Morris jumped to steady him, and Dr. Lockhart ran forward and helped guide him to a chair. Rossiter went to a credenza where was a tray with decanter and glasses. He poured a generous amount of brandy and hurried to thrust the glass at the doctor.

"Oh, very good," said the little man. "Take some of this, my lord."

Collington sipped, sighed, and appeared to recover somewhat. He blinked up at them, and muttered in bewilderment, "The deuce! You're all mud, Falcon!"

"Sir," said Rossiter, seething with impatience. "Naomi . . ."

The earl's hand jolted. "Lord! What am I thinking of? There—on my desk!"

Falcon was closest, and snatched up a grubby sheet of paper. He read aloud:

Collington:
    Lady Lutonville will be released when Gideon Rossiter returns the two icons he stole. Alone, and at the earliest possible moment, he must bring the icons to the Duck and Mermaid Inn, which lies one mile south of Gravesend, on the Maidstone Road. When he arrives, he will go to the room which has been reserved in his name, and there await instructions.
    If you fail to persuade him to this, or if anyone follows, or accompanies him to the inn, you must accept full responsibility for the result.
    It has been necessary to confine your daughter in an old house which is in exceeding poor condition. 'Tis remarkable that it has not yet burned down. It could catch fire at any minute.
    How sad if such a rare beauty should meet so tragic an end.
    I trust it is unnecessary to warn you that any attempt to contact the authorities will be fatal. For the lady.
    There will be no further communication.
    You have until midnight, Sunday.

Through a moment of total silence Rossiter stood perfectly still, his face a white enigmatic mask.

Collington rasped, "Well, sir? Well? I hope you know what 'tis all about, for by the Lord Harry—I do not! Where are these icons you stole? And what d'you mean to do about it?"

As one in a dream, Rossiter reached out. Falcon handed him the sheet of paper and Rossiter scanned it, noting the crude printing, the lack of any direction or signature. He folded it neatly and deliberately, but they all saw his hand tremble.

"I mean to find her, sir," he said.

Collington snatched the letter and brandished it wildly. "Damn, sir! I demand to be told—"

Already striding from the room, Rossiter flung over his shoulder, "The moment I learn anything, you will be informed, sir."

Following him, Morris asked quietly, "Derrydene's, Ross?"

"No," said Rossiter. "Snow Hill."

Twenty minutes later Wilson opened the front door in his stately fashion, then sprang aside as seven gentlemen rushed past him.

Running to the stairs, Gideon shouted, "Is Sir Mark at home, Wilson?"

"He is gone, sir. To the—er, Horse Guards, I believe."

"Has Tummet returned?"

"No, sir."

Gideon raced on, Morris close behind him.

Falcon threw a disgusted glance around the hall and demanded, "Where is the dining room?"

Wilson gestured. "There, sir. Would you wish to—"

"Bring a luncheon. For all of us."

"But—sir," Wilson's chin sagged. "I doubt the chef can cook—"

"I don't mean a hot luncheon, you fool! Anything you can get here within five minutes. And wine."

"B-but, sir! I must—"

"At—once!" said Falcon in a tone that brooked no argument. Wilson fled.

Flinging open the door to his bedchamber, Gideon strode to the desk.

Morris said, "Then you mean to hand them over? You ain't going to search for her first?"

Gideon wrenched at the drawer and took out the box in which he'd placed the two jewelled men. "If 'twas Katrina Falcon, what would you do?"

Morris shuddered. "Lord! It don't bear think—"

A choking exclamation cut off his words.

His face ashen, Rossiter was staring down at the large pebble he had unwrapped. "Dear God!" he whispered, and tore open the second small wrapping. Another pebble fell into his hand.

Bewildered, Morris gasped, "But—I *saw* you wrap 'em up! You must have the wrong box, dear boy."

Not answering, Gideon continued to gaze blindly at the pebbles in his hand. Then, "That mercenary little *hound*!" he whispered between his teeth, and sprinted for the door, his expression so savage that Morris stared after him, aghast.

Comprehension came then, and with it, dismay. "Lord help us," muttered the lieutenant, and ran into the hall.

Newby's room was a shambles, with clothes strewn about, drawers left open, the presses half empty. Gideon tugged at the bell pull, then rummaged through the piled articles atop the chest of drawers while Morris watched in silence.

A maid ran in. Her eyes reflecting astonishment at the condition of the room, she dropped a curtsy and asked shyly, "Your wish, sir?"

Gideon turned, breathing hard, his eyes narrowed slits of rage. "Mr. Newby. Did he leave with my father?"

"No, sir." Retreating a step, she stammered, "Mr., er, Newby woke up feeling unwell, and—and Sir Mark drove out alone."

"I see. But my brother's health improved later, correct?"

"Yes, sir. Mr. Delatouche said Mr. Newby thought the waters at Bath might help him. And so Mr. Newby went there. And he took Mr. Delatouche along of him."

Morris saw Gideon's knuckles gleam white as he clung to the top of the chest of drawers, but his voice was calm when he asked, "And you have not heard from Sir Mark since early this morning?"

"Oh, yes, sir. We have. Come to think of it, it was just afore Mr. Newby left. Sir Mark sent round for a change of clothes. The lackey what come says as Sir Mark and General Underhill found out they's related in a distant way, and Sir Mark is invited to overnight with the general."

Gideon stared at her blankly.

"Dash it all," said Morris, "but you're a good little gal. Tell me now, did Mr. Newby not leave any word for his father that he was going away?"

The maid blushed. "I can't say, sir. But I did see a letter on Sir Mark's bed, like it might've—" She broke off with a startled squeal and ran aside as Gideon plunged for the door.

" 'Pon my word," she exclaimed. "The captain seems a mite upset, sir, I do hope as nothing's wrong?"

Morris sighed. " 'Fraid Captain Rossiter's been storing milk in a sieve," he said ruefully, and hastened after his friend.

The maid stared after him, wishing she might see the day that Captain Rossiter spent one second messing about with milk—in anything!

Morris entered Sir Mark's bedchamber, and halted, his apprehension justified. Gideon knelt beside the bed, head bowed onto his arms and a crumpled sheet of paper in one clenched hand.

"My poor fellow," said Morris gently, bending over him.

Gideon did not move. "He's . . . taken them . . ." His voice was muffled and shaking. "He says . . . he's off to the New World. My God!" His voice broke on what sounded suspiciously like a sob.

Horrified by such an unnerving display of emotion, Morris sat on the bed and patted Rossiter's bowed shoulder awkwardly. "Do you think he's gone to that collector fellow? Kendall-thingummy, wasn't it?"

A silence. Then Rossiter said dully, "I have loved her—all my life . . . But I went off, like a perfect fool, and—and left her. I threw away six . . . precious years. I keep remembering her at Emerald Farm . . . just the day before yesterday. The way she looked at me, with her pretty mouth trying so hard not to—not to weep . . . and how her voice trembled when she—she said she would not love me again. 'I will not let you hurt me,' she said. And—" His voice rose to a cry of agony. "God help me, but I've hurt her! I'd better have died than—than hurt her again!" His clenched fists beat at the bed. Racked, he bowed lower.

"What a disgusting display," drawled a contemptuous voice from the door.

Scowling, Morris jerked around. "Leave him be, Falcon. He's suffered a great shock, is all."

"Shock, my Aunt Maria! He suffers from lack of spine, more like!"

Rossiter raised his head and put shaking hands over his face. "Yes," he whispered. "I never knew, you see . . . what 'twas like to be . . . so afraid. If—if they harm her . . ."

"Well, much you are doing to prevent it! I came up to wash and find a clean shirt. An you can command some trace of gumption, I'd also like to see these famous icons."

Rossiter dragged himself to his feet, and turned around.

Morris stared, shocked. This strong man with the splendid battle record, who had so bravely endured his long and painful hospital sojourn, had in just a few minutes been shattered not by a physical thing, but by the terrible hand of grief. He was shaking visibly, his face was haggard and deathly pale, a dazed look of pain in his eyes made it hard to meet them, and there were deep lines between his brows and beside his mouth.

"They're—gone." Rossiter held out his brother's note.

"What?" Falcon snatched it, read, and swore furiously. "That slithering little bastard! Where has he run to?"

Rossiter put an unsteady hand to his temple. "I—cannot seem to—to think."

Seizing him by the cravat, Falcon snarled, "Wake up, damn you!" Infuriated, he drew back his hand. It was caught in an iron grip, and Morris said angrily, "You'll just make it worse. Did you never love anything, Falcon? Any *lady*?"

"Yes, I did, damn you!" Wrenching free, Falcon said, "If my sister had been made off with by some stinking swine, I'd not be sitting here whimpering, I can tell you! And considering he loves her so blasted much, 'tis a pity he didn't remember it whilst he was cavorting about with his lightskirts in Holland!"

"Is no good to water last year's cabbages."

Taken offstride, Falcon stared at him. "Why the *devil* are you babbling about cabbages?"

Morris' lip curled in disgust. "One cannot expect a man with all your *nous* to understand a simple simile!" He flung up one hand. "No," he said with rare dignity, "I'll not come to cuffs with you now. Only try not to be such a fool! Go and get your shirt. Gideon's room is the end door on the right. I'll take him downstairs. After he's put some food and brandy inside him, he'll likely come to himself."

For a moment Falcon looked more inclined to do bloody murder than to follow this sensible suggestion, but he ground his teeth, muttered darkly about a "day of reckoning," and took himself off.

Morris put his arm across Gideon's shoulders. "Come along, my poor fellow. Lord, but you're shaking like a leaf."

His teeth chattering, Gideon said, "I'm so—cold . . . Jamie."

"Yes, dear boy, and small wonder. You came home torn to rags, and in no case for what has been levelled at you here. I vow you'd have had a better chance at recovery had you gone back to the Regiment! Come—we'll find something to warm your innards, and you'll feel more the thing in no time. I only wish Tummet was here. He'd know—"

"*Tummet!*" Gideon's head jerked up. His eyes brightened, and a faint flush showed on his drawn cheeks. Gripping Morris by the shoulders, he said vehemently, "Of course! Tummet! That rascal's hot after them, I'll wager! If all else fails, he'll be able to tell us where they've taken her!"

It was then five minutes past twelve o'clock, Saturday afternoon.

"Lookit all this 'ere muck! A man might think as 'is 'igh and mightiness would've kept it clean!"

"Aye. A daft mon might think that, Billy lad! Can ye no juist picture the grrreat mon hissel', squatting on his noble haunches tae gather up old sacks and rubbish? And for why should he? He didnae invite the bonnie lassie tae drink a dish o'tea wi' him!"

A laugh went up, and the first voice grumbled, "Orl right, Mac. Orl right. Laugh. But you'd best 'ave a care wi' the candles. One spark and this ruin'll be a perishin' bonfire afore we're ready!"

A constant creaking and thumping from somewhere outside made it difficult to hear what was said downstairs, but that ominous snatch of conversation penetrated the veil of sleep. Naomi opened her eyes very wide and began to remember.

When these ruffians had ridden between her and Gwendolyn she'd thought for an instant that they were either very rude individuals, or some friends playing a trick on her. That momentary bewilderment ended when a strong arm had swept about her shoulders, a hand had clamped over her mouth, and a harsh voice had warned that if she made a fuss her friend would be killed. Unable to see whether Gwendolyn was also held captive, she'd had no choice but to submit, scarcely able to believe that this was happening in broad daylight.

A carriage had waited at the edge of the park. As once before, she'd been tossed unceremoniously inside, but this time two hooded men had seized her in brutal hands, to quiet her struggles and gag and tie her. A foul-smelling hood had been dragged over her head, and, blinded, torn between rage and terror, she had been driven away. The ropes hurt her wrists; bounced about on the seats, listening to the coarse jests of her captors, she was scarcely able to breathe, and her mouth had felt dry as sand by the time they stopped somewhere. The hood was taken off and the gag removed. A big man sat opposite, and there were others on each side of her, all wearing those terrifying hoods. Curtains were drawn across the carriage windows, but she'd heard bird songs and thought they were somewhere in amongst trees.

The man opposite had said, "Don't you scream now, milady. No one wouldn't hear you. 'Sides, we don't mean you no harm, long as you behave." Her immediate attempt to speak had been foiled by her dry throat. The man on her right thrust a flask at her, saying in a growl of a voice that it was "only lemonade, but we thought you'd like it better'n gin." She had drunk thirstily and found it sweet and wonderfully cool. But it had been more than lemonade evidently, for she remembered nothing from that moment until she had awoken to find herself being carried up a narrow stair and laid on a cot, her head aching so miserably that she'd been glad to fall asleep again.

Her head was easier now, and she began to look about. She was in a room about nine feet square that smelled of dust and something else she could not quite identify. The walls were of crumbling stone and looked as if they'd never seen paint. Far above was a half-loft, evidently blessed with a window, for the only light came from that area. There was no ladder, however, and without one it might as well have been on the moon for all the hope she had of reaching it. The cot she lay on was positioned against one wall, and the blankets and pillows were clean and sweet smelling. Driven by curiosity, she sat up, and received another surprise. Opposite was a small table on which were a standing mirror, a hairbrush and comb, some copies of *The Spectator*, a Bible, and a book of poetry. Adjacent to the table was a washstand with soap, towels, a bowl and pitcher, and on a nearby chair, a warm dressing gown.

She heard footsteps, and sprang up hurriedly as the door opened. A man entered, wearing a loose face mask that reached down to his mouth, and carrying a laden tray. One plate was piled with thick slices of buttered bread, cold ham, and a large portion of cheese; a smaller plate held a piece of rhubarb pie, and there was also a glass of ale.

"I'm waeful sorry we had tae scare ye, ma'am," he said, putting the tray on the table. " 'It goes agin the grrrain wi' me tae mishandle a wench. But ye'll nae come tae grrrief lest ye gie us trrrouble. Ye can see we've made provision fer ye yonder, and there's a, er—" He broke off, and ended with a shy gesture, "Under the wee bed."

The small part of his face that was visible below the mask had reddened. He retained a vestige of decency, evidently. Encouraged, Naomi said, "You're the one they call Mac. A Scot, I think."

"I am that. And dinna be readying tae make me a brrribe, milady. My life's nae worrrth much, but such as 'tis I'm partial tae it, y'ken."

She had been preparing for just such an offer, and hoping she

247

sounded unafraid, she said scornfully, "You will surely hang when my father finds me. If you're a rebel trying to gather funds to buy you safe passage to France, I could arrange for you to get twice that much."

He grinned. "Ye're a cool one, and ye've come tae the right of't, sure enough, but dinna fash yesel, lassie. Your pa's not aboot tae find ye in this Godforsaken spot. And was I tae go against the Squire, I'd ne'er see the bonnie heather this side o' judgment." He turned to the door. "I'll be—"

Naomi ran to touch his sleeve, then shrank back as he whirled on her, crouching, his lips drawing back from his teeth in a soundless snarl, a long knife appearing as if by magic in his hand.

"Go on, then," she cried fiercely. "Kill me! Much good will I be to you then!"

Taking a long whistling breath, he straightened. "Dinna e'er do that agin, woman! I nigh slit yer pretty gizzard!" He stared at her proud but pale face. "Och, but 'tis a lovely wee thing ye are! And I like a lassie wi' spirit."

Her hopes rising, she stretched out an imploring hand. "Then—help me! I'll see you are not charged. I swear it!"

As if moved to pity, he said very softly, "I'll tell ye this only— we mean ye nae harrrm, if yer pa does as he's told. Likely he will, and ye'll be safe home wi' him this time t'morrer." He went out, and pulled the door shut.

The sound of a bar slamming down on the other side was echoed by a sharper crack. Naomi heard alarmed shouts and flew to press her ear against the heavy oak door.

She heard the Scot call, "What's aboot?"

Another voice answered, "Bill saw a cove skulking around."

"Losh, mon! 'Twas likely juist a poacher. He didnae shoot him, I hope? We'll hae the Runners doon here like flies if—"

Bill's dour tones then, holding a note of triumph. "There'll be no Runners, Mac. I caught the perisher square and 'e went into the river." He chuckled. "Very accommodating, I must say."

"And very needless," said a high-pitched voice angrily. "You got us inter a Capital Act is what you done!"

"Kidnappin' of a person o' Quality is a Capital Act, Paddy, so if they catches us we're fer Tyburn Tree anyway. As I sees it, 'tis best ter take no chances. If that there creepin' cove was a poacher, nobody's goin' ter miss 'im. And if 'e was 'ired ter keep a eye on the tasty piece we got upstairs, 'e ain't goin' ter run back ter fill up Captain Perishin' Rossiter's ear'oles, is 'e? A stitch in time, me dears. A stitch in time.''

These sentiments provoked a heated argument, but Naomi closed her ears to their angry voices and sank down against the door, her heart heavy. She said a little prayer for poor Camber, or whoever had fallen victim to this gang of ruffians. After a while, her inherent optimism began to assert itself, and she got to her feet again. If there was only some way to get up to the loft. Even if the window was too small to climb through, she might be able to throw out a note or do something to attract attention to her plight. She looked around the room again, searching for inspiration. Her gaze lingered on the bed, and she said a thoughtful, ''Hmm . . .''

Then, she went to the table. It was prosaic and unromantic behaviour, but she was hungry.

Because of their hope that Tummet would arrive here, or that Newby would come back, the little band made the Snow Hill house their headquarters. The need for secrecy forbade enlisting the aid of the household staff, but Dr. Lockhart, who had insisted upon being part of the search, agreed to remain at the house to receive progress reports, and explain the situation to any returning family member. At half-past twelve o'clock, the determined seekers set out.

Peregrine Cranford and Falcon went straight to the Derrydene house, and were dismayed to find it closed up and apparently unoccupied, the knocker off the door, and all the window curtains drawn. Repairing at once to Bow Street, they were advised by the irritated magistrate that the two Watchmen had been withdrawn when Sir Louis and Lady Derrydene had left the premises shortly before noon, escorted by several gentlemen. Responding to their indignant protests, he said that had any charges been brought they would have been against Captain Rossiter's man, who had very obviously followed the Derrydene party. Restraining Falcon, who was clearly ready to commit bloody murder on this obstructive minion of the law, Cranford exercised considerable tact and eventually was begrudgingly advised of the route taken by the Derrydene party.

At once, the two men set off at speed for the southwest, and were elated when they received confirmation of the Derrydene group's having passed the third toll gate only half an hour before them. They lost the trail at Woking, and wasted an hour searching. But coming into Guildford at six o'clock, they found such a group had taken rooms at a posting house, using the name Atkinson. Further investigation took them to the dining room, where they located their quarry, only to find a middle-aged lady of questionable respectability, escorted by five rowdy men. Whether by accident or design they had followed a false trail. Disheartened and weary, they commenced the long journey back to Snow Hill.

Glendenning and Kadenworthy, meanwhile, acted on Gideon's belief that his twin would not go to the interested collector, Mr. Kendall-Parker, until he had tried to ascertain the real worth of the miniatures. They spent several fruitless hours visiting London's finest jewellers; more hours visiting lesser known jewellers; and finally resorted to antique dealers, many of whom closed their shops early on Saturdays. About to give up, however, they had been rewarded by the information that an elderly authority on jade art had been lecturing at a Tottenham Court Road gallery that day. They rushed to the gallery and were told that several gentlemen, including one who roughly fitted Newby's description, had brought objects for appraisal. Unfortunately, the antiquarian had left an hour earlier, bound for his Windsor home.

A cold wind had come up, but to Windsor they rode, arriving at quarter past seven, just as the antiquarian was going out again, to have his dinner. He was of modest means, and was delighted to accept an invitation to be the dinner guest of ''Mr. Laindon'' and ''Mr. King.'' He guided them to a far more expensive tavern than he usually frequented, and during the course of a most excellent dinner, admitted that he knew of the collection of Jewelled Men. He'd not been aware of its existence, however, until this morning, when a young gentleman had brought him two of the pieces and asked for an estimate of their worth. *Very* interesting articles, to be sure, and the entire set might be of considerable value, depending upon the number of pieces and the quality of the inset gems. He knew of a collector who might be prepared to offer as much as two hundred pounds for each piece, but—one *thousand*? Good gracious me—no! So disappointed the gentleman had been, and had flown into a rage, and stamped off in a huff. No, he did not know in which direction the gentleman had gone, but he had been accompanied by a rather obsequious individual who could very well have been his manservant.

Half an hour later, the viscount and Lord Kadenworthy turned their horses back towards Town, not entirely disgusted with the results of their efforts.

Rossiter and Morris had gone first to the Inn of the Blue Heron, in Kensington Village, arriving shortly before one o'clock. The host was obliging but knew nothing of Mr. Kendall-Parker save that he had booked two rooms on Thursday evening and paid through Sunday. He had instead left late this morning, with word to none, taking his luggage and his manservant with him, so that he apparently did not intend to return. Morris interviewed the grooms, ostlers, and stable boys regarding anyone who had come to see Mr. Kendall-Parker, while Rossiter questioned the indoor servants. A housemaid thought to have seen Kendall-Parker talking with a gentleman in the back garden; a groom vaguely remembered a young swell asking for the guest; but neither could recall what the visitor looked like, and their descriptions of Mr. Kendall-Parker would fit a thousand small, middle-aged gentlemen.

Disappointed, Gideon arranged to meet Morris at Don Saltero's Coffee House in Cheyne Walk at six o'clock, and they separated. Morris journeyed first to Snow Hill in the desperate and vain hope that Tummet or Newby might have returned. He next went to the livery stable which had supplied Newby's carriage, only to learn that the postilion had already returned, and been hired again, but was expected back momentarily from taking a dowager to Hampstead Village. The "momentarily" became five and forty minutes, through which Morris fretted and fumed. However, when the postilion drove in, he was able to relate that his "early morning gent" had paid him off at The Bedford, in The Piazza, and Morris was off again.

Gideon had embarked on a tour of Newby's haunts: his club, his friends, the various taverns, coffee houses and ordinaries he frequented. Where he was not given the cut direct, Gideon was answered with varying degrees of hauteur or contempt, all responses being negative. His hopes soared when one bored young dandy said he had seen "Ol' Newby" at the famous Fleet Street ordinary, The Cock, but then he yawned and recollected that had been the day before yesterday. Frustrated, and constantly fighting panic because of the inexorable passage of time, Gideon went prayerfully to meet Morris, as had been arranged, and was given the unhappy news that neither his twin nor his valet had been heard from, and that Morris' journey to The Bedford having been fruitless, he had enquired also at the Blue Boar, the Black Bull, the Old Bell, and several other less famous hostelries without success. Longing to continue the search at once, Gideon knew he must exercise common sense; it had been a long and

251

nerve-racking day, and if he was to keep alert he dare not overtax himself. He forced himself to swallow some of the food they ordered, and had to struggle against strangling his friend, who ate heartily.

Shortly after seven o'clock, they separated again, this time to pursue their enquiries at the various coaching stations. Gideon found it difficult to believe that a man who placed a high value on his personal comfort and privacy would willingly endure the delays and discomforts of a stagecoach. Still, it was possible that Newby would resort to such a mode of transportation if he thought it would grant him concealment. But again, he drew a blank. As far as the harassed ticket agents could remember, no gentleman of Newby's description had purchased a ticket today.

It was dark by the time he completed his section of the most likely stations. They had agreed to return to Snow Hill at this point, and he had been up since dawn and was very tired, but he could not give up. He rode along the Dover Road for ten miles, stopping at each toll gate to make enquiries. One gate keeper told him in amusement that he'd seen "a round dozen Newbys" today; another growled irritably that he'd no time to stick his blasted nose into every blasted coach what blasted well passed through his blasted gate. Whether friendly or irate, the result was always the same—Newby had either not been seen or was not remembered. The night had now become so dark that to ride on was to court disaster, and the rising wind made progress an exhausting battle. Hunched over in the saddle, Gideon turned his weary mount back towards London. Most hotels and inns remained open throughout the night; he would keep trying.

By ten minutes to three o'clock a full gale was roaring around the house on Snow Hill, rattling the shutters, howling in the chimneys, sending curtains billowing on their rails. Gideon came into the house slowly, and re-lit some candles in the withdrawing room. He was achingly tired, but there were things to be done before he sought his bed. Perhaps he could allow himself to rest, just for a minute. He sprawled in a deep chair, stretched out his long legs, and with a sigh of relief put back his head. At once he saw two great green eyes, full of love and tenderness; a vivid, full-lipped mouth; the perfect curve of a petal-soft cheek; the dainty nose that was always ready to tilt proudly upward when he exasperated her; all the bewitchingly feminine curves and roundnesses of her warm young body. Where a'God's name did they hide her? Was she safe and well and out of the wind?

252

Was she huddled in some damp and miserable shack, alone, terrified, starving perhaps; or—worse, in the hands of lusting brutes who might maul and abuse and— He cut off that nightmare line of thought desperately, and started to read the notes Dr. Lockhart and the others had left for him.

Derrydene had evidently made good his escape, but it was very obvious that some progress had been made. Failing to obtain a higher price from the Windsor antiquarian, Newby had probably given up and sold the jewelled men to Kendall-Parker. He would not dare show his nose here, and was probably hiding somewhere until he could obtain passage to the New World. He wouldn't be able to do that on a Sunday, and might in fact have days or weeks to wait for a ship. Tomorrow, he *must* be found. He might still have the miniatures, or if he had sold them, he might be able to supply some information about where Kendall-Parker could be reached. There were a thousand places where he could hide. To visit them all would take weeks, so they would have to start at first light with the most likely of those they . . . had not already . . .

He jolted back to awareness. The notes had fallen from his hand, and he'd almost slept—a luxury he must not yet indulge. He carried a branch of candles into the book room. Sitting at the reference table, he began to compile a list of possible locations. Twice, he almost dozed off, but he battled sleep until he had completed his task. Then, he took his candles and went slowly up the stairs.

A couple of hours to rest. Then he could try again. He *must* find Newby in time! But if he failed, he would keep the rendezvous and pray he could negotiate, that he could offer something—anything—to win Naomi's release. If the worst came to pass and they would not listen, if they killed him, surely—*surely* they could not be so inhuman as to carry out the ghastly threat against his beautiful lady?

He found that he had halted and was staring blindly at the stairs. He would *not* fail her! And he was not alone, thank God! The others had stood by him. Even Dr. Lockhart had waited here until midnight. They had tried so hard, and between them, covered so much ground. Morris had stayed here and was already asleep, but the others had dispersed, promising to return early in the morning.

They had until Sunday midnight . . .

And—it was *already* twenty minutes past three o'clock Sunday morning!

❧ *Chapter 18* ❧

Naomi's hopes to work on her plan of escape were thwarted when the drug she'd been given in the carriage combined with the terrors of her day to overpower her, and she slept the afternoon away. She awoke when her dinner was carried up. The food was of surprisingly good quality, and although the hooded individual who brought it was surly and uncommunicative, he evinced no interest in her, for which she could only be grateful. It was already too dim in the room for her to forward her scheme tonight, and there was nothing to do but go to bed. Later, she heard the men quarrelling, and at some time in the wee hours there was a drunken brawl, apparently over dice. Terrified lest their thoughts should turn to her, she whispered prayers into the pitchy darkness. The shouting stopped at last, but the wind howled all night, shaking the old house so violently that at times she was sure it would collapse.

The blankets she'd been given were coarsely woven but warm, so that in spite of the chilly night and the perils besetting her, she dozed off again. Her slumbers were fitful, however, and she woke at first light to find the wind still howling, and the air full of dust, which made her sneeze. She got up at once, and listening intently could hear no sound of movement, so put her plan into action.

Her abductors were evidently being well paid, or else had been instructed to leave her alone, because they had made no attempt to steal the diamond pin she wore in the blouse of her habit. It was a sharp pin, and unclasping it, she tiptoed to the door, dragging one of the blankets with her. She sat huddled against the door, her ears straining, and used the pin to work at the wool strands until she had loosened several. It took much longer than she had hoped, but at last she had unravelled some long strands. She tugged until the other ends came free. The next few strands were easier. Taking care not to get them into a tangle, she began to plait them together. It was surprising then, how quickly it went. Within an hour she had quite a respectable length of makeshift rope.

She glanced at the loft. It extended only halfway across the room, and the floorboards were ragged and uneven, with several sticking out several inches past the others. If she could make a ladder, and cast it over one of the protruding planks, she might be able to climb up there. She might also break her neck if either the plank or her "ladder" would not support her weight, but there was no way of knowing what fate those crude beasts downstairs had in mind for her, and if there was a chance to escape them, the risk would be justified.

Her heart jumped into her throat when she heard a step on the stairs. She had already wound the first length of rope around her waist under her habit. She flew back to the cot, thrust her violated blanket underneath the other one, then climbed in herself. The cot creaked, but the uproar outside would probably conceal the sound. She closed her eyes and tried to look as if she were fast asleep.

She heard the bar lift, and from under her lashes saw a big sturdily built man, wearing the inevitable face mask, carry in a tray, and a panikin of hot water.

"Hey! Stir your stumps, woman!" he called roughly.

Naomi opened her eyes and blinked at him.

"Breakfast," he said. Below the mask, his thick lips twisted into a leer. "Best enjoy it, 'fore it gets cold. If that soldier boy of yours don't do what he's bin told, it might be the last breakfast you ever get!"

An icy hand gripped at Naomi's heart, but she refused to let him see how much he'd frightened her. Sitting up, she said scornfully, "Do not be so silly. You wouldn't kill me! A helpless lady of Quality? All England would hunt you down!"

He gave her a thoughtful look, and nodded. "Belike you're right, and I'll own as it'd be a pity. You're a pretty one, and you've give us no screechin' and cryin' and high-stericks. Thing is, we'll get paid handsome fer this job. But if we don't do what the Squire says, we'll get a coffin, quick. The cove what has to tell *him* things didn't go jest right— Cor! That cove is a dead cove! 'Sides, how's the Watch or the Runners goin' ter find us? After this old place burns down *you* won't be able ter say nothing. Nobody knows who we is, so who's goin' ter blame us fer bein' unkind, eh?''

Chilled, she said desperately, "Your employer knows. And do you think he would let you live, to blackmail him?''

"What—does you take him fer a flat?'' He laughed harshly. "Lor' love yer, missus, we can't blackmail him as we never seen! No one never sees the Squire. Never.''

"But—surely *whoever* he is, he knows that I have done nothing to threaten him. How would it serve him to take my life away? What does he hope to gain from all this savagery?''

"Ah—now there I'll be blowed if I can answer proper. All I knows is that it ain't a matter o' money.'' He shrugged in mystification. "But what would be worth all this rigamarole 'cepting money?''

Stunned, she thought, 'Those wretched jewelled men! Gideon was right, they must be very important indeed!' She said, "I do not know. But it goes against the laws of God that I be murdered! You do your master's bidding, but it is *your* immortal soul that would be fouled by so terrible a sin. Can you live with that on your conscience?''

She wrung her hands in her intensity, and she looked fragile and appealing, her fresh young beauty like a bright flower in that stark and ugly room. Staring at her, even the hardened criminal was moved for an instant to compassion. Then he said curtly, "You're all alike, you gentry lot. Talk innercent folks round in circles with yer eddicated tongues. It don't pay ter be civil to yer.'' And with a snort and a sense of ill usage he took himself off, slamming the bar down behind him.

Naomi gazed at the door, her eyes wide with fear. Did they *really* mean to set fire to this place? Was she really to die so horribly, so alone, far from her love and her friends? She closed her eyes and pressed her hands to her mouth, feeling sobs well up in her throat. She could see Gideon's lean face, the smile in the long-lashed grey eyes, the look of tenderness that made her heart ache with longing. How terrible this must be for him. How frantic he must be, poor darling. He had the miniatures, and she knew that without question he would trade them for her life. But he judged them very important and must not be made to give them up if it could possibly be avoided. He was very likely trying to find her. The chances of him doing so seemed very remote. But he was so brave, so dauntless, if any man could find her, he would. It came to her then that they might *want* him to find her; that this might be a trap, with herself as bait, to

256

capture and destroy him. The very thought sent wrath blazing through her. How *dare* they use her in so evil a cause? Did they suppose that because she was a woman she would sit helplessly and wait for her love to sacrifice himself for her sake?

"Much they know of women!" she said, scowling at her tray. She looked at it more closely. Eggs—cooked much too much, a thick slice of ham, a crumpet, a mug of steaming coffee. Turning to the washstand, she poured some water into the bowl and began to wash her face. Before she sat down to breakfast she would first make herself clean and tidy. And after she ate she would get to work so as to teach those villains downstairs that a lady of Quality did not give up without a fight!

His army training stood Gideon in good stead and he opened his eyes as planned at six o'clock. At once fully awake, he paused only for a brief but impassioned prayer, then tugged on the bell pull. He had left instructions last night that an early breakfast was to be prepared for eight at least, and the footman came almost at once with a ewer of hot water and word that Cook was already at work in the kitchen, but that he could not seem to waken Lieutenant Morris.

Gideon went to the guest room and excavated the untidy mound of blankets until he unearthed his friend and shook him into a dulled wakefulness. Usually only semi-conscious until after his first cup of coffee, Morris moved fast this morning, and was shaved and dressed in time to accompany Gideon down the stairs.

True to their word, the other searchers arrived soon after half-past six, and with them, Gwendolyn and Katrina, neither of whom could bear to be out of touch with whatever happened. They all gathered in the dining room and did justice to the meal Cook had prepared.

Gwendolyn's loving eyes at once noted her brother's haggard appearance, and her sympathetic heart ached for him. She urged that he let her go to General Underhill's house and notify Sir Mark of their latest disaster. He did not voice his fear that she also might stand in danger, and asked instead that she and Miss Falcon remain here, so as to receive and relay whatever information was gathered.

Katrina said, "Does it not seem strange to you that the earl should not have come? Surely, he must be frantic with worry."

"I think Naomi and her father had not enjoyed a very warm

relationship," said Gwendolyn bluntly. "He is a most intimidating creature."

Falcon gave her a stern look. "Even were that outspoken remark true, she is his daughter. Besides, Naomi told me that his lordship has appeared more fond of late. Perchance the old boy mellows with age."

Morris pursed his lips and observed solemnly, "Summer rains will not bring new growth to a withered tree."

After a brief, stunned pause, Falcon exploded. "What the *devil* have rains and trees to do with the Earl of Collington? I vow, Rossiter, why you keep this block with us is more than I can fathom! His head's a ballroom for maggots to caper in!"

Laughter relieved their anxieties briefly, then they were forming plans for the day. There was considerable disagreement among them, Falcon and Kadenworthy declaring that the time had come when the authorities should be called in and a full-scale search launched, and the rest of them vehemently opposed to taking such a risk. Gideon put a stop to their wrangling by saying that since he intended to make the lady his wife, he must be allowed the final decision, which was that they would continue their efforts until four o'clock, and then return here. If by that time they had not located Newby, he would ride at once for the Duck and Mermaid Inn at Gravesend, and the others could pursue whatever plan they might then formulate. There was an exchange of sombre looks, but no more arguments.

By seven o'clock they were clattering down the steps and starting off on their several errands. The first task for Gideon and Morris was to find Sir Mark. The rest were to split up and enquire at toll gates on all the main port roads. If these yielded nothing, they would then resort to their sections of the list of most likely hotels, posting inns, taverns, and hostelries, which Gideon had divided among them all.

General Underhill lived at a pleasant house in York Street. Despite the early hour he was not at home, having been called back to the Horse Guards on some urgent matter, and Sir Mark Rossiter had not yet risen. The general's buxom housekeeper was highly indignant that anyone would pay a call at such a time of day, and was further incensed when Gideon demanded to be at once conducted to Sir Mark's room. One glance at the lady's flushed and outraged countenance caused Morris to quail and offer to wait with the horses.

Sir Mark's initial annoyance at being awoken before eight o'clock on a Sunday morning gave way to horror when he

258

learned of the kidnapping. That emotion was banished by soaring fury when Newby's part in the disaster was revealed. Newby might, roared Sir Mark, be concerned for their future, but he would never have taken "those repulsive little objects" and tried to sell them. "As for jeopardizing the Lutonville girl's life— Poppycock! The boy's an honourable gentleman and would *never* do so dreadful a thing!"

It was in vain that Gideon declared he realized Newby hadn't known about the kidnapping when he took the icons. Sir Mark would not listen, and embarked on a blistering denunciation of Gideon's "lifelong jealousy" and total lack of filial affection for his twin.

In spite of their differences, Gideon was deeply fond of his father, and had only once allowed temper to overmaster him, his breeding demanding that a son ever treat his parents with the utmost respect. Today, his patience was strained to the limit, but briefly he endured. Abruptly then, his voice cut like a steel sabre through the bitter tirade. "Be so good as to stop, sir!"

His jaw dropping in astonishment, Sir Mark stopped.

"My feelings for Newby," said Gideon, "or his for me, are of no import at this moment. What matters is Naomi's life. You had as well know that I love her with all my heart, and mean to make her my wife. Nothing—*nothing*—will stay me from doing everything in my power to save her. And I will allow *no one* to stand in my way! Newby *has* taken the jewelled men, and he *did* leave you a note to that effect. I should have brought it, but I did not expect you would question my word." Sir Mark attempted to interrupt, but Gideon swept on ruthlessly. "If he still has them, he must give them back. If he has sold them, he must tell me to whom, and where I may find the purchaser. There is very little time left, and I do not ask, sir—I *demand* that you tell me if he has been here—or where I may find him!"

Scarcely recognizing this awe-inspiring stranger for his own son, it occurred to Sir Mark for the first time that he would like to have seen the boy go into action. He said without heat, "I don't know. I've not had speech with him since I came here."

"Have you any notion where he would go an he was troubled? Particularly, if he desired not to be found?"

Again, Sir Mark bristled, but the pale grim face silenced his indignation. "No. None. Unless . . . to Smythe's, mayhap."

Incredulous, Gideon echoed, "*Smythe's? Reggie* Smythe?"

"I said—*perhaps*! They are friends and sometimes have got into—er, scrapes together, I believe."

"Good God!" whispered Gideon, and turned on his heel.

"Wait!" cried Sir Mark. "Underhill should return at any moment. I'll ask him to help. He's a good enough—"

"*No!* Nobody must know! They threaten her instant death if word leaks out! For the love of God—promise you'll tell no one, sir! And if Newby comes here, promise you will bring him at once to Snow Hill!"

Touched by his intensity, Sir Mark could only acquiesce and watch, amazed, as his tall son stalked out.

Mr. Reginald Smythe had rooms in Pall Mall, and was at early Church service. Gideon and Morris split up and used the time to make enquiries at nearby hotels. Their efforts proving vain, they then rode to Westminster Abbey, where Mr. Smythe was in the habit of attending services. The fact that Morris and Rossiter wore riding dress offended several churchgoers, and Morris blushed painfully when a formidable dowager pronounced to a friend in stentorian tones that today's young people had been sadly taught if they felt it proper to undertake a journey on the Sabbath.

Fortunately, Smythe was soon found, strolling with several cronies and laughing over the "boredom" of the sermon. Gideon accosted him with little ceremony. Smythe was unobliging as ever and chose to take exception to Gideon's behaviour, which he termed "crude and offensive." Fearing that a bout of fisticuffs was imminent and shuddering to think of such a scene on the very steps of the Abbey, Morris intervened with a disjointed plea for cooperation. Smythe imitated him scathingly. Seizing Smythe by his ornate cravat Gideon snarled a demand for immediate information. One of Mr. Smythe's friends ventured to tap Gideon on the shoulder and suggest that he remember his manners. Gideon's response, delivered with murderous succinctness, resulted in several of the little group suddenly recalling pressing engagements elsewhere, while the remainder, catching sight of long-lost friends, wandered off. Deserted, Mr. Smythe said sulkily that Rossiter was a damnably ill-bred fellow, and that he had not seen Newby for two days, at the very least.

Another door was closed.

Gideon tore out his pocket watch. It was five and twenty minutes past ten o'clock.

Gwendolyn ran to the door, searching her brother's face as he walked inside. He was pale and there was a whiteness about his mouth that alarmed her, but his smile was calm and his eyes

260

were resolute. Stifling a sob, she reached out to him. "Oh, my dear. I am so very sorry."

He pressed a kiss on her forehead. "Has anyone come back yet?"

She nodded miserably. "Yes, at noon. I fear they learned nothing."

Walking in, Morris sighed, "I think we have been to every inn, tavern, and hotel in London! 'Tis as if the beastly—I mean, 'tis as if he'd been swallowed into thin air."

"London is not a small town," Gideon pointed out wryly. "Who is here, Gwen?"

"Papa came home, and is in the withdrawing room with Katrina. Your friends all left again. They are determined to go on searching, until—"

She paused, and they all tried not to hear the case clock chime three times. Gwendolyn asked in a stifled voice, "Gideon—whatever shall you do?"

He knew what he would do. And he dreaded that even his own life would not satisfy the man, or men, who wanted those icons so desperately.

He said, "Whatever I must, to save her." She looked terrified, and he added, "Gwen dear, we've not stopped all day. Poor Jamie must be ravenous. Would you . . . ?"

"Of course." She limped off towards the kitchen.

Morris said, "One would think you had no servants, Ross."

"I know. But she wants so to help."

They walked toward the stairs together. Watching his friend's face, Morris muttered helplessly, "You mean to go and try to reason with those dirty bastards."

Gideon shrugged. "An you have a better suggestion . . ."

"You'd as well put a pistol to your head! The kind of animal who would threaten a helpless girl would not think twice about killing you if you arrive empty-handed. You know that."

"I only pray they may not make good their threat against her!"

The lackey hurried to answer a thunderous assault on the front door. With his hand on the post at the foot of the stairs, Gideon turned, still daring to hope that one of the searchers had returned with good news. It was, however, the Earl of Collington who rushed in, hatless, his hair windblown, his manner wildly distraught.

"Villain!" raged the earl, running to seize Gideon by the shoulders and shake him violently. "Where is my daughter?

261

What have you done to bring this disaster down upon us? Why is she not restored to me by this time?''

Pitying the man's distress, Gideon said, ''Sir, I sent a lackey around last night and again this morning, to explain what—''

''To explain that you have done *nothing*! That you are letting all these hours pass while you make no attempt to save her!'' His voice rose to an hysterical shrillness. ''Why do you not take them their idiotic icons?''

Detaching Collington's grip from his shoulders, Gideon said, ''My lord, you are overwrought. If you will but—''

''You don't mean to part with 'em,'' shouted the earl. ''They're too *valuable*, eh? By God, but you're just another thief like your worthless sire!'' He tore a small pistol from his coat pocket. ''Well, I'll not stand by and let you—''

Gideon grabbed Collington's wrist, forcing it upward. The pistol exploded, the retort ear-splitting in the narrow hall. Trying not to hurt the half-crazed man, Gideon took a blow across the face and reeled back. Morris ran to his aid, and Naomi's large groom pushed past the lackey to hold his employer back, but the earl fought them like a mad thing so that it was as much as they could do to restrain him.

The hall was suddenly crowded as Sir Mark and Katrina rushed from the withdrawing room, and Gwendolyn, Wilson, and two maids ran from the kitchen.

Sir Mark thundered, ''How *dare* you, sir! Stop this nonsense at once!''

Panting, Collington stopped struggling and glared at him. ''An 'twas *your* daughter, you might have some pity!''

Heavy wheels rumbled in the street. From the front door, Wilson called, ''There's a waggon stopped outside, sir. They're . . . Good heavens! They're carrying someone here!''

Gideon reached the door as it swung wide. A laden waggon with blocks behind the wheels stood at the kennel, and two countrymen in gaiters and smocks were carrying someone up the steps on a hurdle.

As he was borne inside, the injured man turned his head weakly.

''Tummet!'' exclaimed Gideon.

''Go!'' muttered Enoch Tummet. '' 'Fore they . . .'' His eyes moved to the side and he stopped speaking.

Gideon sent a lackey running for Dr. Lockhart. Gwendolyn, who had hurried to the side of the hurdle and bent low over Tummet, said in a rather scratchy voice, ''He has been—been

262

shot . . . I fear.'' She went off with Katrina to assemble linen and medical supplies.

Gideon turned a narrowed stare on the waggoners. "You are very good to have brought him. You must let us repay you for your trouble. Where did you find him?"

One of the waggoners said shyly, " 'E wuz crawling by the road, sir. We reckoned at first as 'e be over the oar, as they say. But then my mate seed as 'e wuz hurt. All as 'e could do wuz ask us to bring him here. Which we done, hoping as it bean't wrong, sir.''

Sir Mark said, "You did exactly right. Now, if you'd just—"

Tummet tugged at Gideon's sleeve and croaked urgently, "You must go, Guv. Quick. Yer lady—"

"Lady Naomi?" Gideon bent over him. "What about her? Do you know where she is? Is she all right?"

There was a vivid bloodstain on Tummet's shirt, and he was obviously weak and in pain. His eyes darted to the side. He mumbled, "It's—it's—"

"Yes, my poor fellow," said Gideon gently. "What can you tell me?"

The earl, who had watched this dramatic scene in bewilderment, peered at the injured man and said, "You will be well rewarded if you bring word of Lady Lutonville, my good man. Try to tell us."

Tummet sank back. His gaze fixed on Gideon, he muttered, "Me daughter's . . . pill, Guv. Daughter . . . . pill . . ." And, sighing, he closed his eyes.

"Mind's wandering, poor fellow," said Sir Mark, and instructed Wilson to show the waggoners to Tummet's room.

Watching them climb the stairs, Morris said a puzzled, "But, he—"

Gideon gripped his arm, as if himself in need of support. "I had so hoped he might bring news for us. I know his daughter has an inflammation of the lungs, but I thought someone was caring for her." He shook his head despondently. "Natural enough that she is all the poor fellow can think of." His grip on Morris' shoulder became crushing. "Jamie, I mean to have another try. Newby may have overnighted at my cousin's house in St. Alban's. Is a sorry hope, but our last one. Will you come with me?"

Morris stared at him. "But, of course, dear boy."

Collington said anxiously, "And then you will give them their accursed icons? You'll not leave it too late?"

"We'll be back in time. I promise you, sir."

They hurried out to where a boy was walking their horses. Gideon tossed the boy a shilling, and they mounted up and made their perilous way down the hill.

Morris said, " 'Tis my thought you should have told Collington the truth, Ross. He's a right to know you do not have those jewelled thingummys. And what in the name of creation was all that about Tummet's daughter?"

"My intrepid valet." Gideon's eyes blazed with excitement. "God love the man, he was trying to tell me something!"

"Trying to tell you something? Then why the deuce didn't he spit it out? Your ear was not a yard from his lips, and—"

"And there were other ears as close. No, do not ask me who put Tummet into a quake, but someone did. If ever a man tried to speak with his eyes! He was at his rhyming slang again!"

"But he didn't *say* anything! Only that you must go—quick. And something about—"

"About his *daughter*, Jamie! Tummet *has* no wife, and no daughter!"

"Yes, he has! You said yourself the poor girl has an inflammation of—"

"You great gudgeon! I said that only to stop you from remarking that you didn't know he *had* a daughter. Tummet recognized someone in that hall, I tell you, and I've a damned good notion—" He checked, frowning. "Well, it must wait. For now, what we've to do is discover what rhymes with 'daughter.' "

Shaking his head in perplexity, Morris tried to be of help. "Slaughter. Bought her. Shorter—"

" 'Shorter!' Jove ! Then if 'pill' were to become 'hill' . . ."

"Shorter Hill! I *say*! That's jolly clever! Out near Wimbledon Village, as I recall. And ain't there an old abbey on that same hill?"

"There is indeed! And 'tis nigh half-past three! Ride, Jamie! Ride!"

Ride they did, racing down the rest of the hill in the teeth of the wind; eastward into the city, past St. Paul's with a thunder of hooves and cloaks flying out behind them, on at the gallop until they reached the mighty River Thames and were threading their way through the traffic on London Bridge. They had of necessity to slow then, and Morris asked breathlessly, "What d'you mean to do, Ross? 'Tis pretty open country, save for the abbey."

"Aye, and that's where they must have her, Jamie! Hopefully, they won't be expecting us. We can keep in the trees until we come to the base of the hill, and perhaps we will catch some sight of the bastards. Once we're sure, you can ride for the Watch, whilst I—"

"Devil I will! Think you're to have all the fun? Come on!"

They were off the bridge then, and again the wild gallop, the angry shouts of affronted fellow travellers, the endless pound of hooves, the blustering wind that was so irksome, but Gideon was as a man reborn now, his eyes alight with eagerness and hope burgeoning in his heart.

South and west they rode now, the traffic easing when they left the crowded city streets and came into open country. They were near the village of Wimbledon when they came within sight of Shorter Hill and by mutual accord reined to a halt. The ancient abbey no longer rose in bleak dignity against the sky. It had ceased to be, and all that remained was a scattered pile of rubble. Staring at that forlorn relic of a once great building, Morris whispered, "Oh—deuce take it!"

Rossiter said nothing and scarcely daring to glance at him, Morris saw that the white line was about his mouth again, and the little pulse had reappeared beside his jaw. 'Poor old fellow,' he thought. And he called to three boys who were playing among the stone blocks.

They ran over, their hair wind tossed, their cheeks rosy, bright eyes full of awed expectation as they took in the two dashing young men with swords at their sides and pistols in the saddle holsters.

Rossiter asked, "What happened here, lads? Did it burn?"

"Nay, sir," said the taller of the boys. " 'Twere the big gale a year ago last fortnight. Wuss'n this one, it were."

The second boy contributed eagerly, "Me dad says as the abbey were too old to stand up under the gusts any longer. Hunders o' years it been pounded at."

Not to be outdone, the smallest boy piped, "It all come down in a rush, it did, sir. Bang! Thump! Crash! Just like that!"

Morris thanked them, and tossed some coins and they scrambled joyously for the prize.

In silence the two men dismounted to rest the horses. Rossiter's shoulders slumped for a moment, and he drew a hand across his eyes. What a fool, to have been so sure, to have counted the victory almost won. And how shattering the disappointment.

265

He took out his watch. They had ridden hard, but it was already twelve minutes past the four o'clock limit he had set.

"Well," he said slowly. "We made a mistake, Jamie. It must not have meant Shorter Hill, after all."

"Perhaps," said Morris, deeply troubled, "poor old Tummet really has got a daughter. We must get back, Ross."

"Yes. But, while we wait for the horses, we can rack our brains. Does 'slaughter' join with anything to make a vestige of sense? Slaughter—Bill . . . ? Still? Drill? I can think of no Slaughter Hill, can you?"

Despite the bright tone, he looked so drawn, and longing to spare him, Morris said, "A drink might help my brain. Don't know about you, but I'm as starved as I am thirsty. Begad, I'd even welcome a glass of—"

"*Water!*" cried Rossiter. "*Water*, Jamie! Not Shorter!"

"Water—Hill?" said Morris, doubtful. "Never heard of it, but—" He gasped as Rossiter's hand closed crushingly over his wrist.

"Water . . . *mill!*" Gideon's eyes narrowed to glinting slits. "My God! They have her at the old mill!" He was in the saddle again and wheeling his horse.

Leaping to catch the bridle, Morris demanded, "What mill? Where? Oh, Gad! You never mean *yours*? I mean—Promontory Point?"

Gideon nodded grimly. "Is a jolly jest, no? To hold my lady on the lands we have lost! And that damned mill is rotted and unsafe, Jamie. I only pray it did not blow down last night!"

He wrenched at the reins, but Morris hung on. " 'Tis all of sixty miles!"

"Yes. I should reach there by eight o'clock. Half-past eight at the latest."

"You're mad! Your horse is tired now, and you're not—"

"I'll hire another. Let go."

"You don't know what you go into, you dolt! Wait 'til we can get help, at least."

"Very well. You ride back to Town and bring Tio and whoever will come. I'm going on."

"But suppose you're wrong again?"

"Then I shall ride straight to Gravesend. Let go!"

"But, Ross! You cannot hope to—"

"Dammit! You waste time! Go and get Tio—but don't tell him where Naomi is 'til you're on the road. Stand clear!" Rossiter drove home his spurs. The horse plunged, and Morris jumped back. Crouching low in the saddle, Rossiter was away, galloping eastward in a desperate race against time.

❧ *Chapter 19* ❧

Plaiting with intense concentration, Naomi was making good progress. Her improvised ladder looked crude and ungainly, but seemed strong, and she could only pray it would support her weight. Twice, she had come horribly close to being caught at her task, and only the mighty voice of the wind had saved her from being discovered as she'd made a wild dive for the cot to thrust her ladder under the blanket.

As the hours had passed the mood of her captors had deteriorated. She now knew that there were five of them, and at intervals three others came and went. They seemed to have small liking for one another, and became ever more contentious. There was another serious quarrel in mid-afternoon between Bill and the man with the high-pitched voice, who she thought was called Paddy. The Scot had cursed them furiously, and warned that they'd "have the lamp over," the very thought making her heart stand still. They'd quieted at length, but they were surly with one another, and it was clear the wait was telling on their nerves.

The Scot brought her lunch, and she said in desperation, "Mac—you won't let them kill me? You're not that kind of man, I know it."

He stared at her for a long moment. "In your worrrld, lassie, folks are gentle, belike. In mine, folks canna afford tae be." Turning to leave, he said over his shoulder, "But dinna be despairrring, forbye. 'Tis only two o'clock, and ye've till midnight for your mon tae do as he's bid."

He went clumping downstairs. With her ear pressed to the door, she heard him say heavily, " 'Tis a bonnie wee lass. I dinna bargain for murrrder, y'ken!"

"None of us did," growled Bill. "But I don't mean to go agin the Squire."

Their voices were drowned by the clamour of the wind. Naomi huddled against the door. If it was humanly possible, Gideon would not let her die. Beyond all doubting he would give up the jewelled men in exchange for her life. There was no reason to be so afraid. He would come. Or he would arrange for her release. And if, for some terrible reason, he could *not* rescue her, she had her ladder. She did but need to strengthen the top loop, and she could try it out. The best time, probably, would be after they brought her dinner at about six o'clock.

She gave a start as the wind thundered against the house, and the floor shook. Dust filtered down from the loft until the air was full of it, and she sneezed violently. Retrieving her ladder and the much depleted blanket, she went to work again, trying not to think of what she would do if the window in the loft was too small for her to get out, or if the ladder did not hold her.

By about half past five o'clock her task was finished. She tugged and wrenched at the rungs, but they did not break, and she hid the ladder in the bedding, not daring to test it until after her dinner had been brought up. The wind seemed to be rising, the gusts battering the old house so that she sometimes thought that if she was to die here, it would be from the building's collapse rather than by any evil scheme of her captors. There was no use trying to read, for it was quite impossible to keep her mind on the words. She washed, and tidied her hair, then sat on the bed and waited.

At last boots were clumping up the stairs. A different tread, she thought. The man who brought in her tray was a young giant. She'd identified all their voices by this time, and knew this must be the one they called Jolly. She thought he looked as jolly as a great big spider. From behind the slits in his hood his eyes gleamed at her. He put down her tray gently enough. She tried to get him to tell her when she would be released, or if anything had happened, but he just stared, then walked out.

She did not even look at the food, but set the tray aside, knowing they would probably not come for it until morning. If at all . . . Unwinding her rope ladder, she again inspected it anxiously. She had made six long thin braids, then plaited three together for each side, crossing and tieing them to form the rungs, and at the top she had fashioned a larger loop. Please God it would prove strong enough!

The wind roared, the men downstairs squabbled and bick-

269

ered, and Naomi climbed onto the chair and made her first attempt to cast the rope over the plank. It fell short. Her following efforts sailed to left or right. Not once did the loop come near the protruding end of the plank. She tried until her arm was tired and she was so frustrated that she could have bitten the silly ladder. The room began to grow dim as the sun sank lower. It occurred to her then that she needed a weight, but there was the danger of it falling and alerting her gaolers. Still, the wind was making so much clamour, they'd likely think it just a branch hitting the house, or a loose board, mayhap. She searched about for something to use, and decided on the tin mug they had brought for her ale. She pulled a strand from the remnant of the blanket and used it to tie the mug to the top loop. "There," she said proudly.

Back on the chair again, she gazed up at the plank, took careful aim, and threw. The ladder sailed far past the plank, fell back, then swung there. She gave a sob of chagrin, and pulled, but it was caught somehow. And with a numbing surge of terror, she heard footsteps on the stairs. Someone was coming up to get the tray! Frozen, she crouched on the chair, staring at the door.

A great crash shook the room. The feet paused. Bill's voice shouted, "What in hell was that?" and the steps retreated. Naomi gave a sob of relief, and not caring what had caused the crash, tugged desperately. Her ladder came free at last. She threw up a hand to protect her face as the mug plunged at her. It sounded as though they were murdering one another downstairs. She dare not go to the door to listen, but made another throw. Again she missed, and the ladder came swooping down. She caught it, but then dropped it entirely, clasping a hand to her thundering heart as a shot deafened her.

By the time Gideon reached the lane leading to Promontory Point it was ten minutes past eight o'clock. He had been in the saddle almost continuously for over twelve hours, constantly buffeted by a relentless gale, and had last eaten at seven o'clock this morning. By rights, he should have been exhausted; instead, he felt exhilarated. He was close to Naomi now, he was sure of it, and well before time. He had failed to find those accursed icons, but somehow or other he would win his lady to freedom.

Leaving the lane, he guided the tired horse into an apparently dense clump of formidable holly bushes and followed a narrow path invisible from a distance of six feet, which led through the holly and in amongst the trees, bypassing the lodge. Proceeding with every nerve alert along this escape route of his boyhood, his caution was rewarded. Some half-mile beyond the lodge gates he caught a whiff of tobacco smoke and drew his mount to a halt. Seconds later, he could catch snatches of talk, sometimes clear, sometimes half drowned by the fury of the wind.

". . . wonder the Squire left her in the hands of such . . . not leave a cur with Bill Forbes, and Paddy's not . . ."

"Worse, if you was t'ask . . . Squire 'spected 'twould end long afore now."

"Aye. You'd'a thought . . . would've paid up right away."

He was very close now, and heard a sniggering laugh. "If he'd knowed where she is . . ."

"Good thing he don't know, mate. Nobody . . . stuck out here in the wind, when we might be snug . . . more'n I can understand. Ain't no one'll never guess she's here. Waste of our perishin' time, was you to ask me."

The other man sniggered again, and their voices faded as Gideon circled wide around them.

So his love *was* here! Thank God that this time he had not guessed wrongly.

The sun was going down when the great house came into view. It was painful to see it looking so sad and abandoned, with no ray of light showing from the many windows, no smoke curling up from the kitchen chimneys. The old mill loomed against the darkening sky, starkly picturesque. But here, where there should have been no light, were thin yellow gleams, widening when the wind disturbed the sacking or whatever had been used to cover the lower windows.

Dismounting, Gideon tethered the horse, stuck one pistol in his belt, and holding the other cocked and ready, crept nearer.

Smoke rose briefly from the chimney, to be at once whipped away by the wind, and the smell of cooking drifted on the evening air. There was no guard posted outside. He smiled grimly. Had they been his men, they'd have paid dearly for such overconfidence, but it stood him in good stead, for he had to leave the cover of the bushes and make a dash across the moat. He reached the other side, having heard no sudden alarms, and took refuge in a clump of hollyhocks. Scanning the old mill, he wondered where they kept Naomi. In their shoes, he'd have put her in the upper room and taken away the ladder to the loft where was the window, but they might have chosen to keep their captive where they could watch her.

A man's voice rang out in anger, the words unintelligible, but followed by a crash and shouts of rage. Listening intently, he could detect no feminine voice. She could be gagged, of course, but he felt that was unlikely. Even men of their type would not handle a helpless female roughly. They were obviously a quarrelsome lot, however, and would probably become more so if they indulged in ale or gin after their evening meal.

He still had several hours to spare, and logically he should wait. Morris might bring help. If Tummet had been able to tell the others where to come, they might already be on their way. But to leave Naomi captive for one second longer than necessary was abhorrent to him.

He scanned the old building carefully, his eyes lingering on the chimney. If he was to climb up there somehow, and block the opening, the smoke would likely drive them out and he might be able to surprise them. It might imperil Naomi, however, especially if she *was* gagged. Besides, the only conceivable way to reach the chimney was to climb up the crumbling old waterwheel, which reached almost to the roof. He shuddered, and then was staggered by a mighty gust. A splintering sound, and he leapt for his life as a big branch crashed down, missing him by scant inches. He eyed it thoughtfully.

Minutes later, he again risked being seen as he dragged the branch to the west side of the building, struggled and strained to stand it on end, then gave a strong push, and raced around to the rear.

The branch fell against the window with a crash that was followed by startled shouts from inside. Screened by the branches of a vine Gideon heard the door open, then saw two hefty louts slouch around the corner.

"This damned wind," snarled one, a north countryman to judge by his accent. "That perishin' glass went all over me puddin'!" He started to drag the branch clear. "Coom an' lend a hand, Paddy, it's gorn and stuck itself in here!"

The second man joined him, grumbling that he'd be "bloody glad" when this night was done. Together they tugged at the branch.

Like a flash, Gideon was around the corner. His pistol butt crashed hard against Paddy's head, and the man went down without a sound. His companion whipped around, one hand darting for the knife in his belt, but Gideon's left fist was already whizzing into an uppercut that levelled him before he could raise the alarm.

272

From inside came a protesting voice. "Wotcher fiddlin' at, Jem? There's dust blowin' inter everythink!"

Bending low under the window, Gideon made a mad dash to the front, positioned himself to the east of the door and cupping his hands about his mouth, turned away, and shouted, "Hey! Bill! Come an' . . . ," he mumbled indistinctly. "We can't . . ."

A mumble of cursing and heavy footsteps. The door swung wide and a tall man stamped out, still cursing. Gideon was after him in a lithe spring, his pistol flailing. Bill went down, but Gideon heard a movement behind him. Jerking around, he was in time to see someone jump back inside the mill. He hurled himself at the closing door, smashing it open, sending the retreating man sprawling. A pistol barked deafeningly and pain burned across Gideon's head as he launched himself over the fallen kidnapper, to crash into the young giant who had fired. A howl, and they were down in a threshing struggle. A mighty fist whizzed past Gideon's jaw. With all his strength he rammed home a right that connected squarely beside the ear, and the kidnapper became limp. From the doorway a cultured voice demanded angrily, "What in Hades is going on here? I told you—"

Springing to his feet, Gideon whirled to meet this new threat, and then stood very still.

"Be damned . . . !" whispered the Earl of Collington.

Momentarily deprived of breath, Gideon recovered himself. "Very likely," he said contemptuously.

Rough hands seized him, and his arms were wrenched back. A deep voice rumbled, "Sorry, melor. We was—"

"You were too busy guzzling gin to keep your wits about you," snapped the earl. "Let him go, but keep a pistol trained on him."

"What a consummate achievement," drawled Gideon, straightening his ruffles. "To hold your own daughter to ransom."

The earl spread his handkerchief on a deal table, then leaned against it, all graceful elegance. "You are not astonished, I perceive. Was I too lavish with my grief, perchance?"

"A little. But I was far from sure that you were involved."

"Still, you suspected. Why? My lost—ah, chess piece?"

"Partly. But one of the ruffians who invaded Promontory Point had lost a finger. Naomi's groom, Camber, has a hand mutilated by an accident. He wore gloves each time I saw him, but he fitted my man's description, and later was seen going into the Derrydene house.''

"Yes." Collington shook his head and said regretfully, "Poor Derrydene will pay for that bungle, I fancy. Still, I don't see how that led you to connect me with this particular business. And be dashed if I can think how you guessed we had Naomi here.''

"Tummet told me, although he had to resort to rhyming slang. At the time I was not sure whom he feared, but now I recall that you held a pistol, and that Camber stood by me, also with a pistol in his hand.''

The earl nodded. "Astute. I'll own I judged your man delirious. He babbled something about . . . his daughter's medicine, as I recall.''

"He said 'daughter—pill.' Which rhymes with 'water mill.' Information he has by now undoubtedly relayed to others.''

One of the ruffians yelped, "Hi! Do that mean as there'll be Bow Street Runners comin'? If it do, I'm slopin'!''

"You will leave when I tell you and not before," said the earl in a voice of ice.

The big fellow they called Bill came in, holding his head painfully. His small eyes alighted on Gideon and narrowed. He sprang forward, whipping back his fist.

The earl snapped, "No! We'll have none of that. This is a matter between gentlemen.''

Bill hesitated, glaring in frustrated fury. "I ain't no gent, and I gotta right! Knocked me dahn, 'e did!''

"I do not pay you to be knocked down.''

"You don't pay me 'tall. We're paid by the—''

The earl fixed him with a deadly glare and interposed in a low, rasping voice, "Do not *dare* take that tone to me, animal, else you'll not live long enough to be paid by anyone!''

Bill's eyes dropped. He muttered an apology and snatched at the gin bottle. The man Gideon had knocked down when he first entered had climbed to his feet and also decided to fortify himself with the gin. There was a small tussle, the bottle was sent spinning, and fell, the pale liquor splashing onto the dusty boards to the accompaniment of outraged howls.

"That could as easily have been the lamp," Gideon pointed out. "A fine set of rogues to entrust with your daughter's life!''

The earl smiled mirthlessly. "As a father, I fear I leave much to be desired. However, although Naomi is a tiresome chit, I do admire her spirit, and I assure you nothing will happen to her.

I'd not have resorted to this nonsense save that she was my best hope of inducing you to return the icons."

"If, for some peculiar reason, your main objective was to destroy my father, I fail to—"

"For some peculiar reason?" The earl's handsome face twisted into a mask of hatred. "You are your father's heir, Rossiter, and as such have no conception of what 'tis like to be a younger son! That was *my* miserable fate!"

"I really fail to see what your frustration has to do with my—"

"It has to do with your father because *he* caused it!"

Gideon stared at him, baffled. "My *father* caused you to be born a younger son?"

"No, fool! He was my friend, all through our school years. *Such* a good friend! We both were fourteen and my elder brother was escorting us home for the Christmas holidays when our coach was hit by flood waters. Ah, I see you are unaware of the incident. Allow me to enlighten you. My arm was broke and I was barely able to crawl to safety. Vincent was trapped in the coach. And who dived into the flood repeatedly, to save my so dear brother? Who kept his head above water 'til help came? My friend! My damnably courageous, interfering busybody of a friend! Mark *knew* my hopes! He *knew* what Vincent was. It would have been so *easy* for him to stop searching. But—no! Mark Rossiter had to show everyone how brave he was! And so he saved the snivelling cur. And condemned me to a life of purgatory! Living on the niggardly allowance Vincent made me, while *he* gambled away thousands at the tables. Scraping and scrimping to make ends meet for my family. Fighting to keep the estate from going to rack and ruin, while Vincent gave not a button for the old place. When I was sufficiently desperate and appealed to your noble father for help, he was all generosity. So gentle, so patronizing! Damn him! God, how I hated him!"

Appalled, Gideon said softly, "You've an odd sense of values, sir. I can scare believe that because you held so twisted a grudge you would wipe out the hopes and fortunes of countless innocent—"

"They deserved it, stupid fools." Collington shrugged. "But there is more to it, of course. Much more." He smiled a craftily secretive smile. "My particular business happened to fit in nicely. And I must say it went off surprisingly well."

Gideon thought of his father's haggard, worn face, and had to fight the need to wipe the leer from the earl's lips. He drawled,

"But there were more than just your brains behind it, I think. The—Squire's for instance."

There was an outburst of alarm from the other men. The earl seemed transfixed, and stood motionless, gawking at Gideon in almost comical consternation. " 'Sblood," he half-whispered. "I think I will find out how you learned that, you curst young puppy! And for a start, I'll take the two jewelled men you stole." He thrust out his hand. "Now."

Gideon smiled thinly. "Not now."

The earl glanced at Bill, and jerked his head.

Bill grinned. "My turn at the gent now, is it—sir?"

"Just search him," said the earl coldly.

Gideon said, "I did not bring them with me."

"We'll see that," jeered Bill. "Hold him, you two." His search was unnecessarily brutal, but thorough. He grunted, "He ain't got 'em."

Collington asked gently, "Where are they? You'll do better to tell me now, Rossiter. I dislike violence."

"Never you fear, sir, I'll be glad to help him remember," offered Bill.

The north countryman, half-drunk, said thickly, "So will I. And I know how t'make the perisher tell anythin'—damned quick." He snatched up a ragged newspaper and held it over the lamp so that it burst into flame. "If I was t'drop this," he jeered, lurching unsteadily towards Gideon, "y' pretty lady'd—"

Gideon sprang for him, but the vindictive Bill backhanded him hard across the mouth, sending him tumbling through a wheeling blur of light and shadow. Dimly, he heard a flurry of frenzied shouting. "Get some water! . . . Throw this on it! . . . Not the *gin* you idiot!"

There was a great deal of confusion, but the voices faded and faded until they were quite gone . . .

The colonel's guess that this would be a major engagement had evidently been correct. The smoke was thick on the battlefield. Odd that he could hear no musketry or cannon . . . Someone was damning the men furiously, demanding that they "get up there!" Boots stamped past, making the smoke swirl. His eyes stung, and he coughed feebly. He'd been hit again apparently, but he must get to his feet. The men needed him. It was very hot. Unusual for spring in the Low Countries . . . He could hear the voices again, becoming clearer now.

". . . can't get up *them* stairs, no matter what he says! . . . Be murder! . . . *Listen!* Them was shots! . . . Get out! Get out! . . . He's gorn ain't' he? . . . Hell with Rossiter! He nigh got the lot of us! Let him burn with her!''

Her . . . ? *Naomi!*

Gideon's mind cleared in a flash. The smoke was a pulsing orange. He could hear the crackling of flames. That drunken lout must have dropped his makeshift torch and this rotted old building was ripe for fire. And Naomi was upstairs. Perhaps tied! ''My God!'' he gasped, and lurched to his feet.

The scene tilted. Coughing, he staggered to the side, putting out a hand to steady himself against the wall. It was hot. He was alone. The men were running away, and Collington, the cowardly swine, had abandoned his helpless daughter to the flames! Rage seared through him. Tearing out his handkerchief, he covered his nose and mouth and groped his way to the stairs. Lord, but it was hot! There were flames on every side, and when he reached the stairs he met a solid wall of fire. A glowing tongue licked at his arm and the lace at his wrist began to smoulder. Retreating, he beat the sparks out. It was hopeless, all right. He could scarcely breathe, and his eyes were streaming. Turning, he plunged blindly for the door.

He was outside, choking, dizzied, the wind buffeting him again. Distant shouts and another gunshot registered on his mind dimly. He gulped in air. Flames and smoke gushed from the lower windows. The place was going up like a bonfire. He *must* get to her.

The wheel! He raced around to the side and stepped down into the sluggish stream. The old wheel loomed above him, up and up, seemingly to the clouds. His foot broke through the first blade, and it was no use. His knees grew weak at the very sight of that soaring wheel. But he *must!* He snatched at a spoke and climbed onto the next blade. It held and he went up, his right hand gripping the rim, his left clinging to one spoke until he could reach the next, since the spokes were sturdier than the rim or the thinner blades of the wheel. He kept his eyes on the small window in the loft, gritting his teeth, refusing to yield to the familiar and debilitating panic that was hammering at him, causing his heart to jolt, his legs to shake under him. His hands were wet with sweat; he could feel it trickling down his forehead and between his shoulder blades, and knew it came not from the heat, but from his lifelong terror of heights. Each movement was a battle against fear so intense that he was nauseated, but he forced his cringing body to climb higher. His love was trapped in that furnace beside him!

He was halfway up when a howling gust sent the wheel slamming against the wall of the mill. The blade splintered beneath his feet and only his hold on the spoke saved him. The impact tore his grip from the rim, and for a hideous few seconds he swung by his left hand alone, the old wound in his shoulder sending agonizing jabs through him. Consciousness reeled, but he sank his teeth into his lip and thought of Naomi's sweet face as he grabbed frantically for the rim. His questing foot found another spoke and he was able to steady himself and seize the rim with his right hand again. Gasping for breath, fighting weakness and fear, his streaming eyes barely able to see, he fought his way doggedly upward through ever thickening clouds of smoke.

Naomi clambered from the chair when she heard the shot, and ran to the door, pressing her ear against the wood. There could be no doubt now. There was a battle royal going on downstairs. She could hear shouts and cursing and crashes as they blundered about.

It was quieter suddenly. A temporary hush giving way to a clamour that held the unmistakable ring of panic. Nightmarishly, she caught a whiff of something burning. She felt faint. They had set fire to this horrid place and she would be burned to death up here!

Beating her fists on the door, she screamed, "Let me out! Help me! Please—don't leave—" But horror choked off her words. Smoke came curling under the door. She could hear a frightful sound—a crackling that grew louder by the second. Someone howled "Murder!" And another voice, fading, "Let him burn with her!"

She thought briefly that there must indeed have been a fight, and that one of them had been slain. She moaned distractedly, and tottered back to climb up on the chair. Her hands were shaking as she grasped her ladder. Taking careful aim, she threw. The loop slipped over the plank, and she held her breath, but when she tugged, down it came again. The air in the room was already growing blue with smoke, the smell of it strong and acrid, and her eyes began to smart. She knew with a sob of terror that she would have time for only one or two more tries and then she might not even be able to see the plank.

"Please dear God," she whispered. "Help me!" She tossed, blinking her tears away as she gazed upward. The mug swung down at her, but then stopped, and dangled far above. The loop

278

had gone over the plank! With a little cry of joy and gratitude, she tugged gently, then less gently. It did not come down. She hoist the skirts of her habit, gripped the sides of the ladder—oh, how frail and fragile they felt!—and put her foot in the first rung. If it broke, or if the plank was loose and came down, she was surely doomed. But although the ladder twisted and became very narrow, it didn't break. In her ears was a low and terrible roaring, and the air was getting warm. Praying frantically, she had to struggle to force her boot into the next twisting rung. The ladder swayed, the plank creaked. Her heart seemed to stop. Peering, it seemed to her that the plank was slanting downward. Was it going to break? Dear God in heaven—was she going to fall back?

"Naomi! Naomi! Are you in there?"

Gideon's voice!

She was so overjoyed she almost fainted. Her throat seemed to swell shut so that her answer was a barely audible croak.

Incredibly, wonderfully, she saw his face, dirty, bloodied, and beloved, peering down at her.

"Praise God!" he shouted. "Hold on tight, brave girl, and I'll pull you up."

Weak with relief her courage faltered, but she must not give way. Gideon had come and found her. She would not fail now.

He was heaving at the ladder. It twisted, and she clung desperately as he looped a rung over the plank, then heaved again.

An ear-splitting roar. A great surge of heat. The section of the floor by the stairs had given way. Naomi cried out in terror.

Looking down at her, it seemed to Gideon that she swung over a sea of smoke shot with fire. She looked so small, so terrified. If she didn't faint from the heat and smoke it would of itself be a miracle. The boards he lay on were cracked and half-rotted and creaked ominously with his slightest movement. If they gave way, he would die with her, at least. Coughing, blinded by the smoke, he pulled mightily.

Naomi did not see the blazing ember that floated up and set fire to the trailing end of her ladder, but Gideon did. One more rung and then he leaned until he could reach her wrists. She felt the iron grip of his strong hands and she was wrenched upward. His arm was tight about her and she was lying on the crude loft flooring, wheezing and sobbing for breath. Sparks and blazing pieces of debris were flying upward; she screamed as the lace on her petticoat began to burn. Gideon tore at the garment and

279

she wriggled out of it. The planks seemed to move, to slant down towards the inferno below.

Gideon was dragging her, shouting something lost in the uproar. With one hand clamped bruisingly about her wrist, he climbed through a tiny square window and guided her after him. She had a momentary and bemused thought that she was glad she wasn't wearing hoops.

Clinging to the waterwheel with one hand, and to her with the other, Gideon shouted, "Come to me!"

The waterwheel seemed a mile away, but she reached out bravely. His arm clamped around her, and she threw her arms around his neck. Other shouts rang out. Through the billowing smoke below came the anxious face of Lieutenant Morris, suddenly breaking into a beaming grin. "Here they are," he bellowed, waving frantically. "This way!"

Glendenning and Hector Kadenworthy raced up, carrying a long ladder. It was propped against the side of the wheel. Gideon guided Naomi to it, and Morris climbed up and helped her down. She was on solid ground, but between the dense smoke and the fact that her eyes smarted so, she could scarcely see.

A battered and dishevelled Falcon ran to join her. "Well, don't hang about, you silly chit," he said with oddly reassuring irritability. "The whole lot will come down at any second!"

Frantic, Naomi cried, "Where is he? Is he safe?"

Gideon was beside her, his face a mask of soot and blood, but his eyes worshipping her.

She sobbed, "Oh . . . Gideon . . . !" and was swept into his arms.

"Good *God*!" howled Falcon. "Not *now*, you fool!"

Gideon laughed shakily, and carried Naomi through the smoke.

They were halfway across the moat when the flames roared through the loft window. They all turned to watch.

A moment later the roof crashed down, and with a great gout of fire the old mill collapsed in upon itself.

❧ *Chapter 20* ❧

By two o'clock the excitement had died down and the house on Snow Hill was quiet again. The men from Bow Street had departed; Lord Kadenworthy and Peregrine Cranford had taken Katrina and a fast-asleep Lady Naomi back to Falcon House, with Horatio Glendenning and Falcon riding escort. Sir Mark Rossiter and Gwendolyn had long since retired, and all the windows were dark save for one. In the book room a branch of candles still flickered to the intrusive fingers of the wind, and smoke from the small fire occasionally puffed into the room.

Comfortably settled on the sofa to the right of the fireplace, James Morris stirred, yawned, and blinked sleepily. Opposite him, sprawled low in his chair, chin propped on bandaged hands, long legs stretched toward the hearth, Gideon gazed blindly into the flames.

Morris peered at the clock on the mantel. Stifling another yawn, he muttered, "Must you make a decision tonight, dear boy? Appears to me you'd do better to get a bit of rest. D'you hear someone—?" He glanced to the hall. "Oh, it's you, Falcon. Come back, did you?"

"No," said Falcon pithily. "You behold my shade, Morris." He waved a reassuring hand at Gideon, who had started up anxiously "Be *à l'aise*. She is perfectly safe, and fast asleep in bed at my father's house. Am I to be offered a glass of brandy?"

Morris shrugged. "Ross is all fingers and thumbs, and I ain't inclined to wait on you. Serve yourself, Lord Haughty-Snort. You can see the decanter."

Falcon considered him grimly, but containing his instincts, went over to the credenza. Returning, glass in hand, he said casually, "I dropped in at Collington's."

Both men sprang to their feet.

"The devil you did!" exclaimed Gideon.

"I wonder he did not put a hole in you," said Morris.

"Likely he would have done, had he been at home." Sitting on the edge of the reference table, one foot swinging, Falcon said ironically, "The butler informed me that his lordship had been called back to Italy on a matter of great urgency. Can you believe that the heartless villain did not even wait to learn whether his daughter had been rescued?" He sipped his brandy and snorted. "Faugh!"

Morris was shocked. "It's jolly good cognac, and it ain't polite to criticize—"

Falcon groaned. "I was referring to his lordship, my blithering dolt."

"He need not have fled the country had I perished," Gideon pointed out. "He must know I survived, and likely knows Naomi did also."

"No thanks to him, the merciless hound," growled Morris.

Gideon sat down again. " 'Tis very good of you, Falcon, to come all the way back here to tell me. You—er, did not mention Collington's part in it to the others?"

"I said nothing, as you desired."

"Well, if you ask me," said Morris, "the bastard should have been reported to the authorities at once! Why on earth—"

"That is your considered opinion, is it?" sneered Falcon. "And with what does Rossiter charge our noble peer?"

"You know blasted well! Kidnapping for a start, and—"

"Kidnapping his own child?"

"Oh, do try to use your famous nous! Lady Naomi is of age. She was imprisoned 'gainst her will and damn near slain! And Collington tried to force Ross to hand over the jewelled men as ransom."

"Did he really? Pray where is your evidence? Who witnessed Rossiter's confrontation with the earl in that damnable mill? No one. Who even *saw* Collington in the vicinity? Only those rogues we apprehended, and they are obviously too terrified to speak. One gathers transportation is less to be feared than the wrath of their legendary Squire. Where are these allegedly so valuable jewelled figures? No one knows."

"The ransom note!" exclaimed Morris triumphantly. "You can give 'em that, Ross!"

"I might, had I not stupidly allowed the earl to take it back when we were at his house."

"Very stupidly," murmured Falcon.

Irritated, Morris snapped, "At such a moment, only an insensate block of ice—"

"Or a Mandarin?" put in Falcon sweetly.

"Or a Mandarin—would be capable of rational thought!"

"And being *such* a notable judge of rational thought, Lieutenant, do pray favour us with your next edifying suggestion."

"Well, I will! You read that blasted letter, and I saw the jewelled men. We could testify under oath that—"

"Rubbish," exclaimed Falcon impatiently. "Even did they not judge you a silly fribble—and I ain't saying they wouldn't!—*you* served with Rossiter in the Low Countries and are known to be his good friend, and thus prejudiced. *I* am scarcely acknowledged to exist at all, and was I graciously permitted to speak, my testimony would be disregarded. And at the moment, *Rossiter* is even worse *ton* than I am. Without some tangible evidence the authorities would either laugh at us, or clap us up in the Gatehouse on a charge of slander and malicious mischief 'gainst a peer of the realm."

Persisting stubbornly, Morris argued, "We all know Naomi was kidnapped. She herself will—"

"She does not know her father is involved," interposed Rossiter quietly.

"And you don't mean to tell her, do you?" said Falcon.

"I hope she will never learn of his part in it." Rossiter looked at him steadily. "She has been hurt enough."

Falcon smiled his mocking smile. "What you mean is, you're afraid of losing her. She'd never wed you an she knew *her* father was instrumental in the ruin of yours."

"Blister it!" exclaimed Morris. "I hadn't thought of that."

"Never mind," said Falcon. "We are aware of your limitations."

Ignoring this barbed condescension, Morris asked, "Do you really mean to let him go unpunished, Ross? It don't seem right. The truth should be told."

"The truth!" Falcon gave a derisive snort. "I doubt we've come near to it."

Morris said, "Near enough to know that Collington held some peculiar grudge against Sir Mark and tried to ruin him. And that Derrydene was a party to it."

"Well, well. Our sage *can* think! If only for a short distance. Mayhap you can take us the rest of the way, Rossiter."

Gideon stood and went over to pick up the decanter. "In confidence, a little way, perhaps."

"Make an earnest effort to follow this, dear dolt," said Falcon.

"I'd like to follow *him*," said Morris, *sotto voce*, as Rossiter crossed the room to rather clumsily refill his glass. "Closely. With a lance in my hand!" Falcon glanced over at him suspiciously, and he added, "Tell us first, Ross. Which of them is this all-powerful Squire? Derrydene, or Collington?"

"I think neither. Those louts at the mill *knew* Collington, and one of them told Naomi no one has ever seen the Squire. Also, Camber, Naomi's groom, was with the ruffians who searched Promontory Point and beat Tummet; and we know that Camber called at Derrydene's house. For which piece of bungling Collington appeared to think Derrydene would be punished; presumably by the Squire."

Morris groaned. "You mean there are more of the swine lurking about?"

"Two or three at the least," put in Falcon. "You agree, Rossiter?"

Gideon nodded. "When Naomi overheard the pair who plotted in the Dowling ante room, they spoke of everyone being different. She thought they referred to the differences in people. To my mind, they spoke of the icons, and meant not *everyone*, but that *every one* of *those* objects is different."

"Aye. And if you recollect," Falcon put in, "they also said they couldn't have a meeting because 'six' was lost. So the figures are very likely numbered."

"Very likely," agreed Gideon. "And each member of their little club, or whatever it is, has a number of his own and an icon for—identification, mayhap."

"Stap me!" exclaimed Morris. "Six of the villains? All that planning and organization to ruin your father?"

"As a first step," said Gideon thoughtfully.

Falcon and Morris exchanged startled glances. Falcon echoed, "*First* step? You think they plan more mischief?"

"I think 'twas indeed a conspiracy 'gainst my father. But when Collington had me trapped in the mill and thought I was as good as dead and could not repeat what I knew, he told me there was more to it. Besides, if you remember, the soiree plotters said that all their lives were at stake." Gideon put down the decanter, and stood staring at it. "I know of only two crimes by which the life of a nobleman could be placed at risk."

284

Morris said in awe, "Murder. Or—*treason*! Oh egad!"

Leaning forward, Falcon asked intently, "Do you say you suspect a plot 'gainst England?"

"What sort of plot?" demanded Morris. "How is it connected with all this rascality?"

Gideon hesitated. "Would that I knew."

"But you *do* suspect," said Falcon shrewdly. "Zounds! That would be a merry frolic! I wish I may see you try to convince the Horse Guards!"

After a brief pause, Morris said solemnly, "You'll surely lose her if you do, Ross."

"And fail his country if he don't," Falcon snapped, scowling at him.

"You cannot know that," argued Morris.

Listening intently, Gideon said, "I think we've another caller."

"The Earl of Collington, no doubt," said Falcon. "Come to throw himself on your mercy."

A yawning lackey, looking astonished and clutching a dressing gown about him, threw the door wide.

Two tattered, muddy, and shoeless scarecrows staggered into the room.

"Well, well," drawled Falcon, surveying them through his glass. "A masquerade! How jolly."

"Good God!" exclaimed Morris.

"Newby!" said Gideon.

It was noon before Naomi awoke, and she lay still for a little while, piecing together the events of the last two chaotic days climaxed by their triumphal return to the house on Snow Hill. Worn out, she had slept in Gideon's arms for much of the journey. When they arrived, there had been so many welcoming faces: Katrina, hugging her and weeping unashamedly; little Gwendolyn, teasing her about being "such a sooty lady" even as tears trembled on her lashes; August, snorting with disgust at the emotional proceedings then scowling at Gideon, who was murmuring something in his ear. Sir Mark, beaming with joy and pride because his son had rescued her. Morris, Kadenworthy, Cranford, and Tio, all trying to explain at once exactly how everything had happened. And, above all, Gideon, filthy and scorched, even as she was, but his eyes radiant with love.

Not much else was very clear. She remembered Sir Mark calling for silence while he offered a humble prayer of gratitude for her safe return; briefly, she had wondered why her father was not there, but Sir Mark had explained that Lord Collington had gone off with his men, convinced she'd been taken to the south coast and determined to search there. For a while she'd been in a carriage again, before being delivered into the hands of a distraught and weeping Maggie. Very soon after that, the sheets had closed around her, she'd sunk into the soft feather mattress, and in the middle of her own grateful prayers, had fallen asleep.

She stretched luxuriously, looking around at the familiar room, hearing the familiar city sounds, wondering why she was here instead of at her father's house. Maggie came tip-toeing in, then rushed to embrace her again, as though she must touch her to be sure she was really safe.

Breakfast was brought in, and a letter arrived by messenger from her father expressing his great joy over her safe deliverance, and his regret that a most vital matter demanded his immediate departure for Italy. She was finishing the letter when Katrina came in, to fuss over her and ask many questions. August, she complained, would only shrug and say he had arrived too late to do much more than help apprehend some of the kidnappers, and watch Rossiter pretend to be a hero.

"He *was* a hero, Trina," declared Naomi, her eyes glowing. "When I saw his dear face looking down at me through all the smoke . . . Oh, I really thought I was going to die, and I longed so to see him, but never dreamed he had found me. And to think he climbed up that wheel, when he is so terribly afraid of heights! Truly, he must be the very bravest of men, and I would never have escaped had he not—" She broke off, blushing, because her friend was looking at her with such a fond smile.

"The 'very bravest of men' is waiting downstairs in great impatience," said Katrina, laughing. "Indeed, I wonder he has not forced his way up here, he is so frantic to see you!"

Naomi squeaked with excitement. The breakfast tray was abandoned in a rush. Maggie was summoned, and the new white taffety gown with the bluebird embroidery across the bodice and on the underskirt was selected. Half an hour later, Naomi's graceful descent of the stairs ended in a most unladylike run across the hall to the tall young man who had sprung up at her coming, and who now reached out eagerly to clasp her outstretched hands, and press each to his lips.

"Oh, your poor hands," she said, resting a feather-light finger on the bandages. "Did you burn them when you tore off my petticoats?"

He saw a lackey stiffen, and murmured, "For the love of heaven, take me to a private room, else I must outrage all Falcon's servants by kissing you here and now!"

She offered no objection to this most improper suggestion, and when the morning room door had closed behind them did not protest his even more improper behaviour. Some time later, sighing contentedly as she sat on the sofa clasped in his arms, she murmured, "This is very naughty, you know. 'Tis fortunate my father is gone away, else he would be most shocked, and likely name me a—guttersnipe . . ."

Gideon kissed her ear. "Gone away, is he?"

"I fancy your papa must have sent him word, because he writ me a very kind letter. I think I will not let you read all the things he says about your heroism! But something very urgent has called him back to Italy."

"Oh," said Gideon expressionlessly. "I hope he plans to return soon, for I mean to make you my wife, and must ask—"

"Do you, indeed?" she said, sitting up straighter. "Of all the presumption! Not so much as a declaration of affection, or a request to pay your addresses! I collect you think that because you make it a habit to save my life, and restore my stolen slippers, sirrah—"

"Fiddle," he said. "A man is not to be commended for saving what belongs to him." He put a finger across her parting lips. "And speaking of your slippers, lovely one, Newby has come home."

She had learned of Newby's treachery while they were driving from Promontory Point last night, and exclaimed excitedly, "Good heavens! With the jewelled men?"

"No. But with a most intriguing tale. As we guessed, he had tried to discover the value of the two jewelled men, and when he learned they were of far less worth than this Kendall-Parker fellow had offered, he rushed to Kensington to sell them to the worthy collector. He had his man, Delatouche, with him, and it seems that well-acquainted fellow recognized Kendall-Parker as a man of questionable repute, and relayed that fact to Newby. To render my brother's story as short as possible, Kendall-Parker was all affability, and pressed refreshments upon him. Being fore-warned, Newby contrived to switch glasses, just in case. Kendall-Parker took about two sips of wine and collapsed."

"Lud! What a villain! Was he dead?"

"No, but Newby thought he was. Kendall-Parker had sent his servant off—to order luncheon he said, but Delatouche was sure the fellow had gone for reinforcements. My brother had no wish to be mixed up in a murder case, so he snatched up the miniatures, and he and Delatouche fled. They were soon hotly pursued by a clutch of ruffians, and were unable to get back to Town. They racked up at some hedge tavern on Saturday night, intending to leave at dawn. Unfortunately, they both overslept, and didn't take their departure until noon, by which time Kendall-Parker's ruffians had found them.''

''How very silly of them,'' said Naomi scornfully. ''I suppose they were caught?''

''Yes, and properly mauled and robbed, then tied up and left miles from anywhere, *sans* purses, coats, or boots. They had a fine time freeing themselves and making their way back to Town.''

''Then this Kendall-Parker person has the two jewelled men, do you suppose? Or was he perchance an agent of the mysterious Squire?''

''The latter, I suspect. I wish him well of the accursed objects. At all events, my most precious sprite, you may dismiss them from your mind.''

''With the greatest of pleasure,'' she said, smiling. ''Faith, but I wonder Newby dared face your father! Whatever did Sir Mark say to him?''

Gideon's lips tightened, and a frown crept into his eyes. ''He was far more lenient and forgiving than I could be.''

'Of course he was, foolish creature,' thought Naomi. 'Newby was ever his favourite.' She said, ''I have failed to ask about poor Tummet. How does he go on?''

''Very well, I'm glad to say. The old rogue is tough as whip leather, and 'twould take more than a broken rib to kill him! We are greatly beholden to him, beloved. Had he not let me know—''

He broke off as a scratch at the door was followed, after a discreet pause, by the appearance of the butler. One all-encompassing glance informed that elegant personage of the propriety of my lady's position on the sofa, the calm poise of the gentleman who stood leaning one shoulder against the mantelpiece; and of the dainty enamelled earring which adorned the laces in the gentleman's cravat.

''Your pardon, my lady,'' said the butler with commendable gravity. ''A sergeant is come from the Horse Guards. Captain Rossiter is requested to wait upon General Underhill. At once.''

* * *

Gideon leaned back in the chair in the small office, and watched General Underhill narrowly. Had he met the man on the street and in civilian dress, he'd have taken him for a haberdasher, or an apothecary perhaps. Certainly he'd never have suspected him to be a general, a man who had seen extensive active service, and who was reputed to be a splendid tactician. Of medium height, slight stature and quiet voice, he was almost timid in his manner, quite cast into the shade, thought Gideon, by Sir Mark, who was seated nearby.

It had been a peremptory summons, and the general began by apologizing for bringing them to Whitehall at such a scrambling rate. "It was necessary, gentlemen," he said, smiling. "In view of the shocking kidnapping of Lady Lutonville, and because of a most unexpected event that will, I feel sure, greatly influence the Lord Chancellor's committee meeting tomorrow."

"Eh?" said Sir Mark, hopefully. "Have you been able to learn something, Sam? Jove, but you're a good fellow!"

The general raised his hands. "No, no. Really, you must not give me credit. Your son is responsible, I believe. It has to do with Sir Louis Derrydene. I must tell you that the poor fellow has shot himself!"

"The deuce he has!" cried Sir Mark, leaping to his feet.

Gideon could see Collington's handsome face and hear him saying, "Poor Derrydene will pay for that bungle." He felt chilled, and asked, "When?"

The general looked at him sharply. "Well, you're a cool customer, I must say. We believe 'twas early Saturday morning."

"Do you say," said Sir Mark, incredulous, "that Lady Derrydene drove away from that house, well knowing her husband lay dead inside? No, no! I cannot credit she would be so heartless."

Gideon said thoughtfully, "We were given to understand he had gone with her. They wanted us to think that, of course."

"I'll wager he was alive when she left," persisted Sir Mark. "Likely, he said he would follow her later."

"Very probable," said the general. "At all events, he left a letter. A full confession, my dear Rossiter! Admitting—in fact, boasting—that he planned and contrived the collapse of your financial empire; that he engineered the run on the bank, the loans that were not made good, the embezzlement. The fire at your shipyard was by his order, also!"

"Stap and split me!" gasped Sir Mark, sinking into his chair again. "How the man must have hated me!"

Thinking a great deal, Gideon frowned and was silent.

"The important thing is that you are exonerated," said the general. "The committee will have no choice but to find you blameless!"

Overcome, Sir Mark put a hand over his eyes, and could not speak.

Underhill said, "Well? Well, Captain Rossiter? You say nothing!"

"I am delighted, of course, sir. But the complexity of it all baffles me. Is the general aware that I found one of the jewelled men at Derrydene's home? Are we to infer that he himself was the wealthy collector? And that he engineered Lady Lutonville's kidnapping? An odd coincidence if the two affairs are not connected."

"An odd coincidence indeed, were it such a thing." Underhill explained, "Your father was correct in believing this to have been a most fiendish plot, Captain Rossiter. Derrydene's confession indicates a violent resentment of Sir Mark's successes, and rage that he was not acknowledged as being the true genius behind the scenes."

"Of course he was not," inserted Sir Mark, recovering himself. "Since that was not the case!"

"He did hint a possibly more—er, compelling motive. He appears to have believed you were—ah, engaged in an *affaire de coeur* with his wife."

Glancing at his father, astonished, Gideon saw the fine face redden.

Underhill grinned. "At all events, I fancy brooding and imagination did the rest, and bred a seething hatred; a desire for revenge that built until Derrydene could no longer control it. He had evidently thought his triumph complete until Captain Rossiter began to stir things up again. He likely realized that with the passage of time heads were cooler, and another investigation could spell disaster. He tried to frighten you off, Captain, with the attack on you. When that didn't work, your coach was tampered with."

Gideon said grimly, "Had that pole snapped a minute or two earlier, I would have been out of his way. And Lady Lutonville, also!"

Puzzling at it, Sir Mark muttered, "I fail to understand. Newby and I did our possible to come at the root of the business. We hired investigators, we brought in Bow Street and the Watch, and Derrydene was not disturbed. What did Gideon manage that we did not?''

'A home question,' thought Gideon, and waited to see what the general would offer in reply.

Underhill linked his hands on the desk and said thoughtfully, "I think, firstly, he captured the public interest. Much as your family was held in abhorrence, Sir Mark, here is a fine young officer come home from the war having been badly wounded. That he had to face such shocking news, and was at once attacked and villified, caused a stirring of sympathy—the British tendency to side with the underdog. From there 'twas a short step for people to wonder if there might be something to what you had claimed, after all.''

Gideon stared at him. "No, really sir, you cannot think that was sufficient to cause him to—''

The general raised a hand. "He likely did not realize you actually suspected him until you broke into his house. The papers you stole may or may not have proven sufficiently damning to warrant another investigation. However, by a quirk of fate that must have infuriated him, you had no sooner set foot in England than you came into possession of a key article. An item he had to retrieve at all costs.''

"The jewelled man," exclaimed Gideon. "That is what forced their—his hand!''

"Exactly so. In his confession, which is lengthy, Derrydene admits that he employed many men in his schemes to destroy your father, but the risk of blackmail was great, so he sent his instructions out by way of a trusted accomplice—a servant of a friend apparently, although he does not name the man. The accomplice had in turn to protect himself, so the instructions were delivered after dark, and the accomplice went masked, and always carried one of the jewelled men to prove his identity. You can imagine Derrydene's consternation when a figure was lost. If it fell into the wrong hands no end of mischief could result.''

"Blister it!" exclaimed Sir Mark. "Then you were right all the time, Gideon! That confounded chess piece really *was* connected with my troubles!''

The general said kindly, "And your troubles are over, Rossiter. I make no doubt the Lord Chancellor's committee will exonerate you of all blame!''

General Underhill's predictions about the meeting of the Lord Chancellor's committee proved entirely accurate. The meeting became chaotic when Derrydene's suicide was made known and his confession was read aloud. Sir Mark Rossiter was acquitted, and commended for his desperate efforts to rectify matters. He stood up, impressive as always, even in a sober habit of brown and gold. With the help of the Horse Guards, he announced, Samuel Davies, the embezzler, had been traced to an island off the coast of Spain and there was every hope that a large part of the funds would be recovered. There were cheers at this, and more cheers when he declared his intention of using the money to repay his investors at seventeen shillings to the guinea, and that the remainder would go towards reopening the shipyard.

At the impromptu celebration that followed the meeting, Newby, somewhat subdued but still trying, had several suggestions by which his father might better use the funds, if they were indeed recovered. Rossiter Court on Conduit Street must be reclaimed. Promontory Point must be renovated and improved and the ornamental water—

Sir Mark interrupted brusquely, "I have sold Promontory Point."

As stunned as his brother, Gideon stammered, "But—but, sir, it has been in our family for centuries!"

"Aye. And as my heir, you doubtless feel I should have consulted you." Sir Mark clapped him on the back. "My boy, you've done well, and I'll not again make the mistake of supposing you've no head for business. However, Bracksby has made a most generous offer for the Point, and with the funds we can restore the shipyard and put our people back to work. I believe Bracksby only makes the purchase to oblige me, and the good-hearted fellow promises to sell back the estate should I feel able to take it on again—which I certainly shall do. With the help of you two young rascals."

He smiled kindly at his younger son. "You are agreeable, I presume?"

"Oh—as you say, sir," said Newby, hollowly.

"Meanwhile," Sir Mark added with a twinkle, "I am not such a dunce as to be unaware of your hopes, Gideon. You mean to wed your beautiful lady and spend as much time as possible down at Emerald Farm. Shall she object, do you fancy?"

"I sincerely hope not, sir."

"Well," said Sir Mark expansively, "you have my blessing. I doubt Collington can object, in view of all you've done for him, but you shall wish to seek him out and get his approval, of course."

292

Plagued by the guilty awareness of how differently his father would react if he knew the whole story, Gideon mumbled, "Yes—er, of course, sir."

"Only look at him," laughed Sir Mark. "Blushing like a schoolboy!"

General Underhill looked up from the small pile of papers on his desk, then passed them to the stocky major who was his aide. The major began to leaf through the documents. Underhill scruntinized the young officer who stood at rigid attention before his desk, shoulders pulled back, head high and proud, eyes steady but unreadable.

" 'Twas my thought," murmured the general, "that you planned to wed Lady Lutonville."

Gideon answered, "Such is my intention, sir."

"And is she aware of this report you have handed me?"

"It is my hope, General, that she may never be aware of the matter in its entirety."

The general put up his brows, but made no comment, turning his attention to the three young men who stood just behind Captain Rossiter. Dispensing with the first two, he said, "Glendenning, I have been acquainted with your father any time these thirty years. Is Bowers-Malden party to your—suspicions?"

Lord Horatio shook his head. "Captain Rossiter has asked that we keep it as close as possible, sir."

"He has reason, belike." The general's eyes flickered over Falcon and settled on Morris. "You served with distinction, Lieutenant. Are you by chance of the Cornwall Morrises?"

"My father's cousin, sir."

Underhill nodded, left his chair, and took a turn about the room. Three of the men exchanged grim glances; Falcon merely looked bored.

"You will permit that I make quite sure I've a correct understanding of Captain Rossiter's report," said Underhill, hands loosely clasped behind him. " 'Tis your—ah, *shared* belief that a group of conspirators, led by some nebulous person called the Squire, threatens England. Unhappily, you do not know the precise nature of this alleged threat, nor when or where it is to be realised. Nor do you know the identity of this—ah, Squire person. Am I correct thus far?"

Gideon said, "Quite correct, General."

"Thank you. You base your suspicions upon two jewelled miniature figures, now vanished; some references to—ah, the letter *S*; and the number—six. We *know* that the late Sir Louis Derrydene used such miniatures for identification purposes while engaging in his intrigues. But you tell me this sinister individual called the Squire also uses these miniatures for some—ah, unknown, but presumably diabolical purpose. Derrydene, you say, is not the Squire.'' He paused with an apologetic smile. "Pray interrupt me an I make a mis-step while trying to find a way through all these—ah, tangled threads?''

Gideon's jaw tightened. "Yes, sir.''

The general nodded. "To continue then: As if all this were not sufficient, you charge that Lord Collington, an exceeding wealthy man, was so ruthless as to kidnap his own daughter and demand the miniature figures in exchange for her safety. Truly, a most reprehensible act! Am I then to infer that Lord Collington is this dastardly Squire?''

"If he is not the ringleader, he is most assuredly deeply involved, sir. And his Christian name is Simon.''

"Ah. The *S* figure.'' Smiling faintly, Underhill said, "Do you know, I rather hesitate to mention it, but—er, *my* first name is Samuel.''

Gideon flushed, and one hand clenched. "I certainly do not imply—''

"And mine,'' put in the major, "is Stephen.''

The general said genially, "I trust you do not look upon us with disfavour by reason of that circumstance, Rossiter?''

"We might,'' snapped Falcon, "an we considered this a joking matter.''

Underhill's mild gaze turned to meet a scorching glare from eyes of midnight blue. There was a brief but excruciating silence, while four men held their collective breath. The general disdained a direct response, however, and returned his attention to Rossiter. "In the event we do not consider this a joking matter, Captain, what *are* we to consider it? Attempted murder? A treasonable plot? I trust you *do* realize what you imply? And what the possible results of such implications could be?''

"Unfortunately—I do, sir.''

Underhill nodded and went back to his chair. He snapped his fingers and held out one hand. His aide rose immediately and gave him the papers, and for some minutes Underhill scanned them frowningly. When he looked up, Falcon was making no great effort to stifle a yawn. A glint came into the general's mild eyes, but if he was irritated, he concealed it. Leaning back, he looked at them thoughtfully, one after the other.

A slow smile dawned. "Gentlemen," he said, "my congratulations. You have done exceeding well. Not only have you exposed a treacherous scheme, but you have rescued a lady of birth and breeding from a horrible fate. Now, you place before me a warning that well may stand our England in good stead. The nature of your suspicions, however, renders it vital that we proceed with great caution. To accuse a gentleman of rank and fortune of kidnapping his own daughter might plunge us all into very hot water indeed. I fancy you realize that we have nothing tangible with which to prosecute the Earl of Collington. Captain Rossiter was the sole witness to his—depravity. 'Tis very obvious that the ruffians you apprehended fear their 'Squire' more than they fear deportation or the gallows. Whoever hired them likely holds a threat over their families. We shall get nothing from them, and even if we did, the statements of such commoners would scarce influence any jury sitting in judgment on a peer of the realm."

He leaned forward, linking his hands and looking at Gideon earnestly. "We must have proof not only of Collingston's part in the kidnapping, but of the further plot you believe he hatches. And in order to obtain such proof he must be given plenty of rope and watched day and night. I do not mean to charge you with such a task, Captain. Not only would it place you in a most unenviable position because of your personal involvement with his family, but you have done your share—and done it magnificently. Rest assured that I shall put my very best men on the case. Meanwhile, I must have your word, gentlemen, that you will discuss this matter with no one. It is to remain a closely guarded secret that goes no farther than this room. You will oblige me?"

They all swore to keep silent, whereupon the general stood once more, and came around the desk. "Captain Rossiter, you are a fine gentleman and a credit to your family and to your country. Will you do me the honour to shake my hand?"

Very red in the face, Gideon shared a firm handclasp.

General Underhill proceeded to shake the hands of Lord Horatio, Lieutenant Morris, and Mr. Falcon. He hesitated for the fraction of a second prior to that final handclasp, and Falcon's lip curled as he permitted his fingers barely to brush the general's outstretched hand.

Sufficiently embarrassed, Gideon refused the offer of a glass of sherry before departing, and with smiles and more words of praise, the colonel ushered them from the building.

In silence, they began to stroll along Whitehall.

After a minute or two, Morris said, "Well, that's done, thank the Lord!"

Rossiter muttered, "I wish I did not feel such a treacherous cur."

"Why should you?" drawled Falcon. "The old dodderer believed not a word you said."

"What the devil d'you mean by that?" demanded Gideon.

"He don't know what he means," said Morris. "Pay him no heed."

Falcon shrugged. "As you wish." He started to cross the street.

Glendenning caught his arm and hauled him back. "Oh, no you don't! Why did Underhill praise us, an he thinks we lied? And for that matter, why should he think so?"

Morris threw out his arms, bringing their stroll to an abrupt halt. "Every man at attention to hear the genius among us," he commanded.

Falcon tapped his chin with his quizzing glass and said thoughtfully, "Is time you owned it. Very well. I judge our general to be convinced Rossiter has pigeons in his loft. Morris, I fancy he justifiably deems a dense clod blinded by loyalty to a friend. You, my poor Tio, he undoubtedly believes to be supporting this drama only so as to throw smoke in the eyes of those looking into your evil past. And as for me," he finished, smiling his cynical twisted smile as they all broke into laughter, "my reasons were not even considered, since I am beneath contempt and of no consequence."

"An you were right," said Gideon, grinning broadly, "a man such as Underhill would scarce have let us off so easy. More likely I would be transferred to Bedlam, Tio would rusticate in the Tower, and Morris could revel in a promotion to corporal!"

Chuckling, Glendenning asked, "You did not really believe any of that stuff, did you, August?"

A rare twinkle lit Falcon's dark eyes. He said with a grin, "Does your sense of self-preservation nag you, perchance? Pay it heed whilst you can! As for the rest, my assessment served to banish the self-satisfaction in which you all wallowed. Besides, who can explain so devious a mind as that of a general?"

"You certainly cannot," said Morris, all righteous indignation. "If ever I met a fellow so eager to slip a cockroach into the pudding bag!" The others laughed, but Morris went on,

"Deuce take you, Lord Haughty-Snort, I wish you'd not come with us."

"Not so do I," said Gideon. "The general petrifies me and I was in sore need of you all. Truly, I thank you for standing by me today."

"I should think so," said Falcon.

"If you thought, you wouldn't," grunted Morris.

Falcon groaned. "Another profundity? Lord save us all, I wonder what this one may mean! And speaking of saving us, *do* you mean to flee the country, Glendenning?"

"I do not," declared Lord Horatio. "But I *am* resolved to henceforth associate only with people who are above reproach and will not further endanger my—ah, reputation."

"Very wise," said Gideon. "And I've to thank you, Tio, for allowing my sister to stay with you these past few days."

Glendenning bowed. "Miss Gwendolyn is always a delight."

"And the antithesis," drawled Falcon, "of your new resolution."

Gideon stiffened. "I think you must explain that, sir. Do you say my sister is *not* above reproach?"

"Were she *my* sister she would be reproached, I promise you," said Falcon, impervious to the steely glint in Gideon's eyes. "I'll remind you that she came to call on me, ostensibly to beseech me not to run you through. I put it to you that a single lady does not in propriety call upon a bachelor, and that I did not invite her! Not content with this breach of etiquette, in presenting what should have been a humble request, she contrived to knock me down, break my grandmama's vase, and ruin my dog! And to add insult to injury," he went on, warming to his theme, "she danced on my best Colichemarde and bent the damn foible!"

Weak with laughter, Morris collapsed onto Glendenning's shoulder.

Rossiter made a great effort to keep his mouth stern and said he would at once go home and beat Gwendolyn within an inch of her life.

"I will lend you my spiked cudgel," offered Glendenning, greatly amused.

"No, but seriously," said Gideon, "I do apologize, Falcon. We have treated you shabbily from start to finish. I shall certainly replace your vase, and—" He paused, knitting his brows. "Ruined your dog, you say? How the deuce did she manage that?"

"She threw her cane for the brute," said Falcon gloomily. "He used to be a fair watchdog. Now he offers a stick to everyone who calls. I vow an army of stick-wielding burglars could invade my home in perfect safety since she reformed him! And if you do not cease howling, Lieutenant Block . . . !"

Glendenning intervened, "Well, you have done your possible, Ross. Restored your father's good name, and won the thanks and praise of the King's General. What d'you mean to do now?"

Gideon took a deep breath. "Now, by heaven, I am going to get on with my own life!"

"Speaking of getting on with things," drawled Falcon. "Morris owes me a duel."

Morris wiped tears from his eyes. "So I do, by Jove! Will you second me, Ross?"

"After my honeymoon," said Gideon.

"But that is so . . . inchoate, my dear fellow," complained Morris.

Inside the quiet office, General Underhill stood at the window, and watched the merry group out of sight. He said quietly, "Well, Stephen? What do you make of it?"

The major pursed his lips. "A terrible thing, sir."

"Terrible, indeed." Underhill turned back into the room, and sighed. "A fine young officer like that. Splendid background, and a magnificent battle record. What a pity."

His aide asked, "What do you suppose caused it, sir? A mental collapse as a result of his wounds?"

"Something of the sort."

"You—er, do not think he should be—er—"

"Placed under restraint? No. And God help me do I err!"

"I wonder why the others support him?"

"Belike they have their reasons. Friendship. A love of notoriety, mayhap. Young Glendenning I fancy would be pleased to turn our attention from his questionable loyalties. And as for that devil, Falcon! Stap me—what insolence! One might think someone of his background—" He made an impatient gesture and did not finish the sentence.

After a while, the major asked, "Do you mean to warn Lord Collington, sir?"

"I fancy I should. But 'twould surely ruin young Rossiter's chance for happiness. And the boy has been put through sufficient hell."

"True. But . . . that lovely lady, sir . . . !"

They looked at each other, both faces troubled.

General Underhill said heavily, "Damn, but war can be a wretched business, Steve."

"It can indeed, sir!"

❧ *Chapter 21* ❧

Raindrops pattered softly against the windows of the luxurious carriage that splashed along the Dover road. Kissing the top of the curly head which nestled just below his chin, Gideon murmured, "Are you disappointed, love, that it must rain on our bridal day?"

Naomi leaned her head back against his shoulder and smiled up at him. "Nothing could disappoint me this afternoon. I am, at long last, Mrs. Gideon Rossiter."

He bent to kiss her rosy lips. "My father judged it a proper scramblement of a ceremony."

She chuckled. "Rushed into by special licence and with only two weeks' notice. Dreadful!"

"Two weeks, indeed! I have waited and yearned for you these past six years at the least, Mrs. Rossiter, and feared this day would never dawn! For which I have no one to blame but myself. And I do not ask that you give up your title, dearest girl."

"I know," she said tenderly. "But 'tis what I wish. That chapter of my existence is closed. The best part of my life begins now—as your wife."

She was kissed again, of course, and then they were quiet for a long while; the comfortable quiet of belonging. Holding her, loving her with all his heart, he yet was conscious of the shadow that lay over them. How would she feel if she knew what he had told General Underhill? How would she feel if she knew that the earl was responsible for all his father's misery? Would she be enraged if she guessed how, in striving to protect her from more grief, her new husband also deceived her?

"It was so kind of Uncle Bertram to act for my father," murmured Naomi. "Is a nice old gentleman, do you not think?"

"He gave the bride to me. How could I not think him a prince of uncles?"

"I wonder," she said, with a small sigh, "whether I will ever again see Papa."

Gideon started. "Why should you doubt it?"

She sat up straighter, pulled away, then turned to face him, her lovely face grave. She had dreaded this moment and now that it was here, her heart was thundering. "My darling husband, there is—is something I should have told you. But . . . I was so afraid, you see." She looked down, and when she lifted her head, her lips trembled a little.

He tried to speak, but she put her fingers over his mouth, and said unsteadily, "No, beloved. You must hear my confession, now that I—I have begun it. You think you know your wanton, but—you have no notion of how very devious and sly I am. I waited, my Gideon, until we were safely wed, and—and I can only pray you will not demand an annulment."

"Of all the idiotic—" he managed, frowning and pulling her hand away.

"Wait! Oh, wait! You *must* hear me! I shall never find the courage again!"

She looked so frightened, so shaken, and perhaps it was best that she tell him just how much she knew, so he waited.

"I have come to suspect," she said in a scratchy little voice, "that . . . that my father schemed and plotted with Louis Derrydene to . . . to ruin Sir Mark." Her eyes filled with tears as the terrible words were spoken. She cried, "Oh, Gideon! Can you forgive me for keeping silent? Do not hate me! Please! Do not—"

He swept her to him then, holding her close and dear against his heart, and murmuring between kisses, "Dear, silly, foolish little meadow sprite. How can I hate the lady I have loved all my life?"

Naomi sat up straight and blinked at him. "You *knew*! Oh, Gideon! Why did you not tell me? How I have agonized over the shameful business!"

"And I also. I did not dare mention it for fear that ferocious pride of yours might again come between us." He stroked her cheek, his eyes searching her face. "How did you know?"

"I think I began to wonder about it when you became so convinced that the little jewelled man was connected to Sir Mark's troubles. I remembered how angry my father had been when I lost the silly thing. But I did not really believe it was

301

true until we went to the Derrydene house so that you could search Sir Louis' study. Something Lady Derrydene said that morning troubled me, but I could not for a while think what it was. And then I remembered. She said to her butler, 'Tell Camber to drive the team around to the stables.' Papa had told me he scarce knew Sir Louis and had never been to his house. If that was truth, how could Lady Derrydene know my groom's name?'' She sighed, her eyes very sad. ''So many things came to mind, then. Little things Papa said to slight you, or your family. The way he kept teasing me about your—your reputation with women. How insistent he was that we terminate the betrothal. I realized that he hated Sir Mark, and had set out deliberately to ruin him. And I have been so—so wicked as to let you wed me, knowing that your father—an he knew it all—would straitly, and very justifiably, forbid our marriage! Truly . . . I am shameless!''

''Thank heaven,'' said Gideon huskily, and kissed her again. So she did not know the worst of it—that Collington had subjected her to so terrible an ordeal, and that he might be involved in even more serious plotting. God willing, he would shield her from that knowledge for as long as he lived.

He said gently, '' 'Tis too late for my father to stop us now. But although I honour him, I would have allowed nothing to come between us, at all events.''

Naomi gave a great sigh of relief. ''My poor conscience is easy at last! I can truly start afresh and forget it all.''

He wondered if she really could forget, and said carefully, ''An Lord Collington should stay abroad, shall you mind terribly, my love?''

She smiled happily and nestled closer. ''I have you,'' she murmured.

It was raining when they pulled into the yard of the Ship Inn at Dover. Ostlers with sacking held over their heads ran to lead in the horses. Beaming, the host threw open the door and ushered the bride and groom into a parlour warmed by lamplight and fragrant with the smells of wood smoke and dinner.

As they walked inside, laughing, and shaking the rain from their garments, a shout went up.

''Here they are!''

''Thought they could slither away and escape us!''

''You're fairly caught, you two slyboots!''

And they were surrounded by a merry crowd of well-wishers. Morris and Horatio, and Perry Cranford; Katrina, Gordon

Chandler, Gwendolyn, Rudolph Bracksby, and even Tummet, looking thinner but cheerful. All throwing rice and teasing them fondly; and Falcon grumbling that he would not be within ten miles of this place save that he'd been bamboozled by his sister, but demanding a kiss from the bride nonetheless.

"Oh, I feel sure Jamie would have been glad to drive Miss Katrina down," said Gideon with a twinkle.

"Any where, at any time," declared Morris fervently.

"Sooner than allow such a horrid contretemps—" began Falcon.

The commotion had attracted attention. A slender dark lady with a small girl beside her turned from the desk to glance their way.

A shrill scream rent the air. "Papa Ross! Papa Ross!"

Naomi whirled around, and turned chalk white as the curly-haired dark child ran across the suddenly hushed parlour, arms outstretched.

"Mignon! My babe!" Gideon bent, scooped her up and kissed her heartily, then turned to gather the lady into his embrace. "And my lovely Lilla!"

She clung to him, her voice breaking as she said in rapid French, "Ah, Gideon! At last we find you! My dear! My very dear! I feared you must be dead!"

Katrina whispered faintly, "Dear God!"

"I should have killed the bastard," said Falcon through his teeth.

Gideon turned to Naomi. "Here's a fine coil," he said guiltily. "Of all times to have to make you known to my family! This is Madame Jean Favre and the very young lady is Mignon, my—"

"You unprincipled 'ound!" The voice came from the door, and a tall man with his left sleeve pinned up came in, water dripping from his tricorne. "Do you seek my loved ones to steal away ze very moment we 'ave land in your country?"

He threw his arm wide and caught Gideon into a hug. "This it is well met, *mon ami*! *Mon cher ami* to whom I owe so much! Ah, and 'ere is Lieutenant Morris! We shake ze 'and, all so!"

Setting down the child, Gideon said, "Mrs. Rossiter, allow me to present Capitaine Favre, whose family became my own when—"

"When my dear 'usband 'e is left for dead on ze battlefield, and taken prisoner," interposed the lady. "We would 'ave starve, madame, save that my Jean and Gideon, although they fight on different sides, they 'ave the fine friendship from school days, and Gideon take us under 'is—'ow you say this, James?''

"Under his protection," said Morris, grinning.

"Stumblewit!" muttered Falcon.

"Oh, Gad!" gasped Morris, turning very red as many shocked eyes turned his way. "Only I—er, should not say that, of course! Assure you, Naomi, old Ross merely looked after 'em! N-nothing more, do promise you! Didn't do a curst thing, actually!"

" 'E do a very great deal," protested Madame Favre, bewildered. "Without my Gideon's always 'elp I 'ave not know what it would become of us!"

Naomi said feebly, "Then—then, *this* is your *family*, Gideon? But—but you said there were *three* children, and—"

"Ah!" cried madame. "Then, you 'ave know, *mon cher?* Nurse, she take my twins up ze stairs!"

"Twins!" gasped Gideon. "Jupiter! I thought I was making it up!"

"Wicked, wicked man!" said Naomi happily, her last shadow vanishing.

Madame Favre exclaimed in French, "So this beautiful creature, she must be your lady of the garden, and you are married to her! Ah, it is good, my dear, dear, Gideon!"

Much later that evening, when the festivities had finally ceased and the celebrants had all gone their separate ways, Naomi reminded her husband of madame's remarks. "There were," she called to him sternly, "altogether too many 'dears!' 'Tis quite obvious to me, Captain Rossiter, that you and Madame enjoyed a very agreeable relationship."

Sitting up in bed, his eyes glued to the door of the dressing room, Gideon agreed provocatively, "Exceeding agreeable. With regard to Mignon, especially. I am very fond of children. Speaking of which . . . are you ever coming in?"

"Oh! How naughty you are," she said, dimpling as she dabbed Mysterious Moonlight here and there. "I wonder that you dare say such things when you deliberately allowed me to think that all those horrid rumours were true! Why, sirrah?"

"Because you were so willing to believe the worst of me, of course."

"Your pride was hurt, was it?" she said indignantly, standing and blowing out the dressing room candle. "I think you are far more full of pride than ever I was, Captain Rossiter!"

"I grant you, 'tis a dreadful vice," he admitted with a grin.

"I promise never to indulge it a—" And he stopped, because Naomi had come in at last.

Her very décolleté nightgown was a drift of salmon-pink lace and net that allowed a tantalizing glimpse of the loveliness it veiled. Her glorious hair rippled in a glowing mass about her creamy shoulders, and as she stood there, her eyes were tender but very shy.

"Oh . . . egad," he whispered. "And I am telling another lie! 'Fore heaven, I must be the proudest man alive!" He reached out to her. "Come to me, my love—my life."

"Do you truly welcome a—a guttersnipe to your bed?" she asked, walking slowly and demurely across the room.

"I told you once," he said breathlessly, "that I must be time's greatest fool."

Naomi looked into his adoring face and ran to him. "The dearest, bravest, most gallant fool who ever . . ."

Captain Gideon Rossiter pinched out the candle.

❧ *Epilogue* ❧

It was very quiet in the darkened room, and although the air was wreathed with tobacco smoke, it held the clammy chill of a place where sunlight never shines. The single candlestick, set on a very old credenza against one wall, threw a dim light on the table and the five men seated there. They were as so many statues: silent, waiting, all clad in dark cloak and hood, and each face, although barely visible, covered by a mask.

At last, one of them muttered irritably, "The Squire is late."

The man to his right shrugged. "And likely vexed."

Across the table, a man drawled, " 'Tis all made right, and we achieved what was planned."

The smoke stirred, giving the only sign that the door had opened.

A sixth man entered. Tall, and clad exactly as the others, he moved soundlessly to the table, and at once the rest came to their feet.

"To the contrary, Two," he argued in a thin, colourless voice. "We achieved only part of what was planned, and suffered a considerable setback." His head turned, the eyes glittering through the slots in the mask as they rested upon one after another of those present. "I do not care for setbacks, and each of us is allowed but one mistake."

A silence.

Then, the man he had addressed as Two said, "We are six again, Squire."

"Happily so. And must proceed." The Squire raised one gloved hand in which was a small figure glittering with diamonds. "Despite our failure, we have achieved much, and all done with the authorities suspecting nought."

"As yet," muttered a tall, bulky figure.

The Squire chuckled. "Just so, Four. By the time they suspect, 'twill be too late. I am told young Rossiter tried to warn one of our splendid generals, and was writ off as a likely candidate for Bedlam."

A huskily built man asked in a growl of a voice, "Will it serve?"

"For the time," said the Squire. "But those interfering fools must, and will be punished, which is annoying, as it will disrupt our schedule. Meanwhile, however, to business. Will our new member identify himself by displaying his emblem?"

A man to his left held up the tiny figure of lapis lazuli and sapphires that Rossiter had found in the home of Sir Louis Derrydene.

The Squire raised his diamond-studded miniature. In turn, the others lifted their figures, the emerald, then the ruby, followed by a topaz, and finally, an opal.

"You know, new bearer of the sapphire, to what we are committed?" asked the Squire.

"To a new England," replied the novice, bowing. "Purged of the yokes of royalty and religion. A republic wherein the common men may share equally and none rise above the level of his neighbour."

"You know," intoned the bearer of the emerald figure, "who shall rule?"

The new member bowed again. "The land and all within shall be ruled by a committee of gentlemen qualified not merely by birth but by intelligence, an ability for leadership, and a willingness to act without regard for the conventions and restrictions of the past."

"And you know," said the man holding the ruby figure, "who selected you? And who is known to each of us?"

"I was selected by letter," answered the newcomer with yet another bow. "I do not know who sent it. None of us is known to any other. Save only the Squire."

The Squire bowed to him, and each in turn, the others bowed.

"Are you prepared," enquired the man with the emerald figure, "to submit to the initiation?"

"I am prepared."

The Squire turned and led the way to the rear of the room. The holder of the opal emblem carried over the single candlestick. It could be seen then that the walls were fashioned of stone blocks, shiny with moisture and green with lichen. An archway stood out from the solid rock of the rear wall, enclosing what appeared to have been at some time in the distant past, a small marble trough or water bowl. Set at waist level, it was dry now, but around the edge of the top ran a most elegant carving wherein deeply etched flowers and leaves intertwined.

The Squire stepped back and as the others moved closer to the bowl, he levelled a deadly duelling pistol. "You may proceed," he said. "In the appointed order. And then we shall begin our meeting."

They gathered closer about the bowl and one by one stepped back. At the end, the Squire relinquished the pistol to the man who had held the emerald figure. The pistol was trained steadily on the Squire and he stepped forward.

There was a whisper of sound.

A moment later, the room was empty, and the darkness and chill of the centuries once more held sway.

About the Author

Patricia Veryan was born in London and moved to the United States after World War II. She now lives in Kirkland, Washington. The author of eighteen previous novels, Patricia Veryan has been acclaimed "a worthy successor to Georgette Heyer at her very best" by *The Chattanooga Times*.